WERE THE
ANGELS WRONG?

WERE THE ANGELS WRONG?

SAUL GOLUBCOW

A Frank Wolf Mystery

WILDSIDE PRESS

For Those I Lost
Before I Knew Them

SUNDAY, JUNE 6, 1976

The phone jolted me out of a deep sleep. I looked at the clock on the night-stand—7:45, on what was supposed to be a relaxing Sunday morning.

My wife, Aliya, jumped out of bed. I put out an arm to stop her, but she was already out of reach.

"Who calls this early on a Sunday morning?" she said more than asked, heading toward the phone in the kitchen. "Something must be wrong."

"Not necessarily," I groaned, burying my head into the pillow. But this act of denial couldn't last more than a few seconds. Aliya was right. No family member or friends called unexpectedly at such a time unless there was trouble. I got up and trundled after Aliya.

"What!" I heard Aliya say as I entered the kitchen. "When?" And then a few seconds later, "Why?"

Aliya didn't cover the handpiece as she said loudly, "It's your mother. She just got a call from Martin. He's at the 61st Precinct, where he's being held on suspicion of murder."

My eyes squinched. "Murder?" I whispered, reflexively reaching for the phone. "Martin? He killed someone? Is this a joke?"

Aliya looked at me and shook her head as if to say who would joke about murder. Speaking again into the phone, she said, "Mother, I'm giving the phone to Joel. We'll be over as soon as possible. We'll catch a cab."

Aliya handed me the phone and rushed back to our bedroom. I settled into a chair at our kitchen table and took a deep breath. "Mom, what's going on? Martin's been arrested and is in custody at the 61st? Accused of killing someone? Who? What else did Martin say?"

"Very little else," my mother said, her voice catching on a sob. "Only that he did not commit this crime. Please come as soon as you can."

That strain in her voice meant—fear! I heard it as a child when my father and I would head out to the street for a bike-riding lesson, and she would say, "Please, please watch for the cars." Or when my father would slink out to the back porch for a smoke, and she would caution him each time with, "I read that bad things happen to the lungs from smoking." And especially during those few times when she would share information about how she and my grandfather had survived for six years in hiding during the Holocaust, and she would repeat, "I was only fourteen when we entered the cellar. That's when I stopped being a child."

I gripped the receiver tightly and donned lawyer mode. "Mom," I asked evenly, "could you please tell me what exactly Martin said?"

She took a deep breath. "Joel, your grandfather asked that we don't spend too much time discussing over the phone. Better he thinks if we come together at the house to go over what Martin told me and decide what to do. Aliya said you would come very quickly, okay Joel?"

Wide awake, I told my mother not to worry, hung up the phone, and walked back to the bedroom. Aliya was laying out her clothes. She had not put on any makeup, and her long hair was pinned back in her usual nonwork pony tail. I washed up quickly and hurried on a short-sleeved shirt and some light summer pants, grabbed keys and wallet, and joined Aliya as she held the door to the apartment open for us to leave.

✳ ✳ ✳ ✳

From our apartment in Stuyvesant Town, Aliya and I quickly made the three blocks to 14th Street and 1st Avenue where we could usually catch a cab. The temperature sign on the Bowery Savings Bank displayed 63 degrees with a forecasted high of 77. For a city of seven million people, the streets seemed bleak and deserted. Perhaps I felt the mood of the city facing financial collapse. Just a few months before, *The Daily News* blared—FORD TO CITY: DROP DEAD. There would be no federal financial bailout. Filthy streets. Erratic city services. The rise in crime frightened everyone. A half million residents had left since 1970. And as Aliya and I looked in all directions, we couldn't spot a cab.

"It's New York," I said, putting an arm around her shoulders. "There'll be a cab soon."

"I know. We just need to get there quickly and find out about Martin. I'm sure your mother is beside herself."

Aliya gently shrugged my arm off her shoulders and resumed pacing back and forth before pointing and shouting, "There's a cab. I think it's available."

The cab sat stopped at the light across 14th Street. We motioned vigorously. Unless it was going off duty, we had our ride. The light changed, and the cab sped toward us, screeching to a halt.

I opened the back door for Aliya and followed her in. The cabbie looked straight ahead while asking, "Where to?"

In the front passenger console area, a light jacket covered the cabbie's last name and medallion identification. I could make out his first name: Josef.

When I gave Josef the destination address, he grunted, "Brooklyn, huh. That'll mean I probably won't have a fare back. How 'bout we high flag this ride. That way you save a couple of bucks and I make a few?"

It would have been easy to just agree, but as an attorney, I was a sworn officer of the law, and Josef's request got my hackles up. While it may have been a minor ethical failing had we accepted, I knew it was illegal to "high flag," meaning riding off the meter with an unreported cash transaction. I answered, "No, on the meter please, it's the law."

Aliya touched my knee. *Was she saying? "I approve" or "You're jeopardizing our ride."*

"Have it your way," Josef snarled, smacking the meter flag down. He roared away north on 1st Avenue, not turning toward the FDR for six blocks. Aliya and I looked at each other. We both understood what Josef was doing—increasing the fare. Have it his way, I thought. Grandfather would have made the same decision.

Finally on the FDR, we headed back south passing the South Street Seaport. I saw cranes and other mechanical equipment, signs of the refurbishment and preparation for the anticipated Independence Day Bicentennial celebration parade of tall ships. We crossed the Manhattan Bridge into Brooklyn and onto the Brooklyn/Queens Expressway, where Josef increased speed and repeatedly jolted us over multiple potholes. Aliya and I remained silent in the way that Grandfather had taught us—no discussing a case when others can hear. So for 20 minutes, I turned my thoughts to Martin Ross and his relationship with my mother. He was important to her, but was there something more?

When Josef careened off the BQE to Ocean Parkway, a few minutes away from my boyhood home on Avenue P and E. 7th Street, I ended my reverie and squeezed Aliya's hand.

Josef raised the flag and muttered, "$8.30." I gave him a ten-dollar bill and asked for no change back.

* * * *

I had last seen Martin two days before at our family Friday night Shabbat dinner. It was also the second night of the two-day Shavuot, or "Festival of the Weeks" holiday. In keeping with the tradition of not eating meat on this holiday, my mother with Aliya's assistance—and some from me—had made borscht with sour cream, blintzes, noodle kugel, baked salmon, and cheesecake for dessert.

Martin joined us, as he had on several Friday evening meals over the previous eleven months. He was familiar with the rituals and comfortable in conversation, whether about politics, the arts, or even baseball. As rabid Mets fans, my grandfather and I had spirited exchanges with Martin who rooted for the Phillies. I had wondered why someone living in New York liked a Philadelphia team. I would soon find out.

Perhaps I hadn't known because I never asked him questions. I got along well-enough with him, but I felt a distance. Under cross-examination, I'd have admitted, it was my own doing. Aliya noticed.

"I think," she said gently one night after we had seen Martin at dinner with my mother and grandfather, "you're not the same with Martin as you are with just about everyone else."

"What do you mean?" I knew full well what Aliya meant.

"Joel?" she answered softly but with lifted brows.

I sat back. "Okay, I do know what you mean. It's not that I don't like him, it's not that I don't trust him, it's just that…that…"

"That you're not comfortable with your mother being in a relationship with a man who's not your father? It's twelve years since you lost him. And I'm not saying you're being childish. Rather I think you're afraid for your mother that she might get hurt, that it's up to you to protect her, maybe?"

I almost snapped back that my wife—with her newly minted Ph.D. in clinical psychology—shouldn't be treating me like a patient—putting me on the couch. But a split second of honesty made me admit, "Yes, I do feel that way. I try not to, but I can't help it."

No one else shared that tension last Friday night. Martin and my mother exchanged endearing looks, Aliya and Grandfather made Martin feel welcome by bringing him into family conversations, and I tried my best to seem pleased by his presence. And Martin, if he had any inkling that just over 24 hours later he was going to be arrested on murder charges, he didn't show it.

At dinner, we also celebrated Aliya's graduation from NYU. She was giving herself a few weeks of respite before starting work at the Stuyvesant Psychology Group, specializing in child and adolescent therapy. The graduation ceremony took place earlier in the week in Washington Square Park. When I arrived from my uptown law office, my mother and grandfather sat next to each other holding two open seats, one to the right of Grandfather and one to the left of my mother. After I exchanged hugs with various family members and friends, Grandfather motioned me to sit in the seat next to him. Soon after, Martin arrived and seated himself beside my mother. I glanced at him. *Odd that no one had mentioned that he would be attending.*

* * * *

My mother had already opened the door for us by the time we had climbed the steps to the house. When expecting a loved one, she would keep an eye out to the street. She must have seen us when the cab dropped us off.

We were hardly through the door when my mother gave each of us a hurried hug and blurted, "Thank you for coming quickly. I'm sorry I woke you so early. Zaida is in his chair."

We moved to the living room. Grandfather was in his worn, vinyl-clad easy chair, his slippered feet on a matching footstool. A kippah covered wispy, silver hair that had been receding each year. His silvery, pencil thin mustache was neatly trimmed as usual. I knew his habits. Up at daybreak, ritual morning wash and prayers, and then a light breakfast. Even though it was Sunday, he wore a white dress shirt and tie. His eyes sparkled through his glasses.

He opened his hands in greeting. We walked over and leaned down for his embrace. "Good morning, my children," he said. "It is regrettable that we must see each other under these sudden and disturbing circumstances."

"Yes," I answered as Aliya, my mother, and I took seats around him. "But what's going on with Martin?"

"There must be a mistake. It's not possible that Martin is involved with a murder!" my mother cried out.

"Malkeh, Malkeh," Grandfather said calling my mother by her Yiddish name. "As difficult as it must be for you, might we treat the next several minutes as the beginning of a case in which we employ our critical analyses skills and, as best we can, separate our emotions from obtainable facts that allow all possibilities to be examined?"

Then he added tenderly, "I know how you must feel."

My mother nodded her head slightly and said nothing in return. I wanted to dive into the fact finding, but if my mother was in pain, my grandfather, despite the calm he was exhibiting, certainly shared it. The six years he and my mother had spent together in hiding during the Holocaust had established a closeness between them, joined not just at the hip, but more so at the heart, and whatever is meant by it, at the soul. As much as I was certain that each loved me very much, I realized from early childhood that their bond was unique. Somehow, I never minded, never grew jealous.

Grandfather also said "case," as if we were convening as part of a professional investigation as opposed to a family crisis meeting. The previous July, when a few articles by Martha Brennan in *The Daily News* and one in *The New York Times* attributed the solving of the Batya Flaum murder mystery to Grandfather, he was inundated with requests for private investigator work. The requests came from as far away as California and even encompassed cold cases going back decades. But he did not take any of them, instead reverting back to working a slow succession of publicly insignificant cases. They involved investigations of the character and financial condition of future marriage partners, the financial integrity of business associates, or spouses' suspicions of infidelity.

When the case of a prominent politician murdered in Manhattan had stumped the police, the man's family asked Grandfather for help. He politely refused. "Why?" I had asked him. "It's a big deal case!"

"Please consider, Yoeli," he explained using his pet name for me, "it is not just that I am no longer a vigorous young man, and even if you were at my disposal to assist, when it comes to these cases, it is not at all like the previous cases we worked in our Jewish communities where we possessed certain inclinations, skills, knowledge, and understandings that promoted our success. As I mentioned to you and Aliya while we were working the Flaum case, if the murder had occurred let us say, in an Amish community, would we not encounter similar difficulties as any police force?"

Now, Grandfather turned toward my mother. "Malkeh, might you begin by sharing what Martin told you when he called earlier this morning?"

My mother grimaced. "He said," she began urgently, but then her voice broke, and she took a deep breath, "he said that he had been brought in last Wednesday night for—what did he call it?—an interview, regarding a murder. After, he was told to go home. Then around 10:00 last evening, police came to his apartment and placed him under arrest on the suspicion of murder."

"And who did he allegedly murder?" Aliya asked.

My mother hesitated. "I'm not sure exactly. Actually, I don't remember. Martin told me the name, but I can't recall it."

Grandfather reached for a manila folder near him. "The victim's name is Henry Casman." He opened the folder and extracted a small newspaper clipping. "I am of the habit of retaining articles I find of interest, which I did so last Wednesday when this small piece in *The Times* caught my attention. Allow me to read from it.

Detectives in Brooklyn's 61st Precinct found the murdered body of Henry Casman, 55, in his sixth-floor apartment at 1165 Ocean Parkway where Mr. Casman lived alone. The police said a neighbor of the victim had called the police after having heard an argument a few days earlier and not seeing the victim since. Upon entry, the police found the victim dead. No arrests have been made, and the investigation is ongoing.

"Eleven-sixty-five Ocean Parkway!" my mother gasped. "That's two buildings down from where Martin lives."

"Yes," Grandfather responded, looking at my mother, and added, "Malkeh, you may have heard me speaking on the telephone after you completed your call to the children?"

My mother nodded.

"Then what I will now convey may seem circuitous, but I first dialed our old friend, Sergeant Fink, at the 90th Precinct in Williamsburg. The sergeant, you may remember, Joel, helped us in our Yosele Rosenstock kidnapping case?"

"Of course."

"I dialed in hopes that he would be already present at his work, and thankfully he was. I inquired if he knew anything concerning Martin's arrest. While he did not, he was kind enough to suggest that I call our other friend, Detective Carlucci of the 61st Precinct, at his home phone, the number which the sergeant had in his possession.

"And I did so. The helpful detective told me I was fortunate to have caught him a few minutes before his departure for Sunday Mass. He informed me of his familiarity with Martin's arrest, that officers took Martin into custody last night at 10:00. A witness, who had a passing acquaintance with Martin, claims to have heard Martin and the victim arguing in Mr. Casman's apartment last Saturday evening, the night of the murder. But most incriminating, after Martin was brought in for questioning on Wednesday, he voluntarily provided fingerprints. After sending them to the State Police in Albany for an expedited comparison to the fingerprints taken from a knife, the presumed murder weapon, the police discovered a match."

My mother gasped. "No, it cannot be."

Something bothered me. I snapped, "And Martin said nothing to us about this last Friday night when he was with us? Mom, did he share with you that he was brought in for questioning?"

My mother shuddered. She looked away from me to my grandfather. "No, Martin said nothing to me."

"Mother," Aliya asked gently. "You did say that Martin denied doing it, right?"

A tear rolled down my mother's cheek. "Yes, he said he had nothing to do with a murder. Of course, he is innocent. Martin is not a murderer!"

"Mom," I asked, my voice lower. "Does he have legal representation?"

My mother looked confused. "Legal representation? I… I do not know. He said they were allowing him one call, and he waited for morning so as not to wake and frighten us."

Her voice rose. "Yes, yes, he needs a lawyer. We must make sure he has a good lawyer."

"Malkeh, Malkeh, my daughter," Grandfather said, rising and moving toward my mother. He cupped his two hands around her face. "I will investigate the matter beginning tomorrow when, Detective Carlucci informed me, Martin will be arraigned. And I have a notion for a good lawyer."

Grandfather paused and looked at me. "Yoeli, here is where I shall ask a difficult thing from you."

What might he ask? A second before he spoke, I knew.

"Yoeli. Not only am I requesting that you attend the arraignment tomorrow, but that you also appear as Martin's legal defender."

I stared at him. "But I'm not a defense attorney. I work in the Securities Division!"

Grandfather smiled. "Yes, of course I know, but your keen mind and youthful energy, which have aided in the previous cases we worked together, indicate to me an ability to provide effective counsel for Martin. And you are only two years removed from law school where you received tutelage in criminal defense practices. At the same time, we will work together, I as your official investigator paid through your billing, to seek out the truth, yes?"

"But, what if he's guilty?" I didn't want any part of what Grandfather suggested.

As soon as I spoke those words, I wanted to take them back. Aliya looked at me. And worse, my mother began sobbing.

Grandfather responded. "Yoeli, I understand your reservations. You asked, 'But, what if he's guilty?' Regardless, if you act as his defense attorney, it will demand of you every ounce of your efforts to demonstrate his innocence. And yes, usually in my profession, we do not begin a case at first assuming anyone's innocence. But a defense attorney does act on that premise. You will pursue single-mindedly Martin's innocence, while I, at the same time, will follow our well-tempered approach that employs critical analyses to shed the lights that reveal the truth."

He paused. "And hopefully Martin's innocence. Together, we will follow these processes to wherever justice will prevail, yes?"

"Yes," I answered, feeling subdued in more than one manner. "But how can I ask for a release from my work? I'm just a junior associate. Mr. Seidman, my mentor, won't like it one bit if I take off with short notice."

"Ah, Yoeli, I have taken into consideration your possible predicament. Might you construct your appeal in two ways? One, that you will cover your existing work while you extend the breadth of your contributions at the firm by taking on a criminal case and charging the firm's hourly rate. In this way, your firm will be, what is it called?–'double dipped'–on revenue. I know I may appear cavalier asking that you carry such a heavy burden for a period of time, but Martin is dear to this family, and this arrangement will allow me to work on the case."

My mother turned to me, hands clasped. "Please, Joel, I never want to make things difficult for you, but, but..."

I held up my hand. "It's okay Mom, I'll do it if Mr. Seidman agrees. But what about the fees? Where will the money come from? The rate will be $150 an hour plus expenses."

My mother answered with firmness. "The money will be found. One way or another."

"Okay," I said. Aliya's lips curved into a small smile.

I continued. "Luckily, I have Mr. Seidman's home number. I'll call him later in the day and see what he says. Mom, Aliya, are you also coming to the arraignment?"

My mother stood. "Yes, I want to see Martin. I will ask Rosa to open the store," she said referring to her manager. "She is also doing so this morning, since I am too upset to go in. After the arraignment, I will see."

"Ay, Malkeh," said Grandfather, "there is one more demand that may cause you not to travel to your work tomorrow or at least delay your arrival."

"Yes, Fotter, whatever you need of me, I'll do it."

Grandfather smiled, but the corners of his eyes were creased. "After the arraignment, I would ask that we all travel to my office where such business is properly performed, and we interview you, Malkeh. And if Martin is hopefully released on bond, then we will ask that he come to my office in the afternoon for his own interview. Yes?"

My mother's voice quavered. "I...I... Fotter, you need to interview me, officially?"

"Yes, of course, and I am sorry. But do you not know Martin so much better than we do? We welcome your knowledge of and insights into this man whom you know so well."

My mother hesitated. "Yes, of course, and I know how much you emphasize the importance of doing interviews in your office. Certainly, I'll come."

Aliya stood and put out her hand to my mother. She squeezed it in return. "I think," Aliya said, "I'll skip the arraignment, Joel. But I will come to Zaida's office for your mother's interview. That's if it's okay with you, Mother. I'd like to help as much as I can."

"Of course," my mother answered. "I welcome your presence."

"Then very good," Grandfather said. "I will telephone Detective Carlucci and ask him to convey to Martin that unless he wishes to hire a different attorney, Joel will appear as his counsel tomorrow at the arraignment. I know you will wish to have a discussion with Martin prior to the arraignment. Therefore, I will also ask the detective to please have Martin brought from the precinct to the Brooklyn Criminal Court by 8:30 for you to have a conversation and prepare for the arraignment, good?"

I nodded. *What was I getting myself into*?

"If you do not hear from me by this evening, then consider the arrangement settled. Your mother and I will see you at the courthouse, yes?"

"Yes, I know the process and building well from my law school days."

"Just one more matter," Grandfather added. "Detective Carlucci was kind enough to create copies of the police report. Joel, and perhaps Aliya, might you take the car and retrieve the copies before you return to Manhattan?"

"We'd be glad to," I answered. "It'll be good to review it before I sit down with Martin."

"Then everyone, it's time for breakfast," my mother ordered as she headed toward the kitchen. "I feel somewhat better. Thank you, Fotter, and Joel and Aliya."

Aliya said, "Joel, I'll stay and help your mother prepare breakfast while you get the reports. You should be back in under an hour. After breakfast, I'll listen in, if you don't mind, when you and Zaida strategize about the case. Then we'll head back to the apartment to get some rest, and you'll call Mr. Seidman. Okay?"

"Yes, sure," I answered. *But why wasn't Aliya coming to the arraignment or with me to pick up the police reports?*

* * * *

Detective Carlucci had left two copies of the police report at the Sergeant's Desk. With little Sunday traffic, I was back at the house in 45 minutes. My mother and Grandfather had eaten, but Aliya waited for me. I devoured not only my own eggs and toast, but also Aliya's leftovers.

We joined Grandfather in the living room where he sat in his easy chair, police report on lap, and large magnifying glass in his right hand as he examined the crime scene photos. I didn't see my mother.

"Mom's in her bedroom?"

Grandfather nodded and then pointed to a paper file on the couch. "Your copy of the police report, which I am perusing and digesting. Please take a few moments to review, and we shall share impressions, yes?"

Aliya and I seated ourselves, and I held the report where we could both see it. I squeezed Aliya's hand. "Tell me when to turn each page."

The report contained eight pages. The first, a coroner's overview, placed the murder between Saturday evening, May 29, 9:00 PM and Sunday morning, May 30, 3:00 AM. Cause of death: two knife wounds to the chest, with death surmised to have occurred instantaneously. The murder weapon, a Lamson six-inch kitchen knife, was found next to the body and removed for prints. The knife, part of a larger set of kitchen knives present in the apartment, was the only item noted as having been taken in evidence.

The second page indicated personal information about the victim, Henry Casman. The details just took up a quarter of the page. As the newspaper article reported, he was age 55. No known next of kin. Immigration papers found in the apartment indicated Casman was born in 1920 in Druya, Poland, immigrated to the United States in August, 1949, and naturalized as a citizen in February, 1956, in New York.

A note at the bottom of the page marked ADDENDUM read:

Body released on Wednesday, 2:00 PM, to Mr. Abraham Schneider representative of the Druya/Myori Aid and Benevolent Society for burial at Montefiore Cemetery in Queens, NY, in keeping with Jewish ritual practice.

When we reached pages three, four, and five, Aliya paled and took a deep breath. I glanced at her, and she nodded once. We quickly scanned photos of the victim sprawled on the kitchen's parquet floor, between the sink and small wooden table and two chairs. The victim's body lay twisted, the face turned to the side. Dried blood darkened the victim's chest and the floor to the left. From a forensics class I had taken, I knew the cause—the gravitational direction of the spurts and seepage. Since the body was found three days after death, Casman's face was grotesquely bloated. Dark flecks of blood coated the nose and mouth.

I put my arm around Aliya. As soon as I could, I turned to the next page.

When we, with Grandfather's guidance, helped solve the murder of Batya Flaum, Aliya had been shocked seeing pictures of the battered face of her best friend's mother. From time to time, she mentions how those images have haunted her into the present. Aliya hardly ever talks about the Casman pictures, perhaps because the investigation of his brutal murder may have been close to home but not as personal. But she mentions that she still remembers them, and they still unsettle her.

The sixth and seventh pages included photos of the rest of the apartment, which we looked at quickly. The last page contained the names of the people interviewed by the police:

Mrs. Mira Schnapper, neighbor who had contacted the police

Mr. Abraham Schneider, who claimed the body

Mr. William Bunch, building superintendent at 1165 Ocean Parkway

Mr. Martin Ross who was heard arguing with the victim

And then:

ADDENDUM, June 5, 10:53 PM: Fingerprints on knife match to prints taken from suspect, Martin Ross, in custody and to be charged with the murder of Henry Casman."

When we started to read the police report, Grandfather had gotten up and walked to the kitchen. Soon after, he spoke for a few minutes on the telephone. When he returned and again seated himself, we had completed our review.

"Okay, Zaida," I began, "how would you like to proceed?"

Grandfather caught each of our eyes separately, thought for a moment, and began, "Ah, my children, I wish to first ask—what are your reactions from reading the police report?"

I jumped right in. "Well, the murder weapon is a kitchen knife, part of a set that probably belongs to the victim."

"And therefore, Joel, therefore…"

"Therefore, the murder weapon was not brought in by the assailant, but was taken by the assailant as part of an unpremeditated attack on Casman, right Zaida?"

He smiled. "I would say perhaps correct. Whether homicide was in the heart of the murderer when he entered the apartment, we must be careful not to jump to any judgment. The assailant may have intended another method for the crime. Or there is still another explanation. And, Joel, might there be at least one more 'therefore' from your deduction?"

"Yes, Casman probably knew the killer. There was nothing in the police report about forced entry or any sign of it in the photos. After all, he lived on the sixth floor, and Spider-Man lives just in the comics."

"Yes," Grandfather answered. "Your surmise is appropriate. Real-life crime, its discovery and rectification, does not tie to the sensational acrobatics of a superhero."

His eyes glinted. "And am I not correct, your comparison is not completely on the mark? Is the Spider Man not, what you call, 'a good guy,' who would not climb a building for a nefarious purpose?"

A bit stung and a bit amused, I just nodded.

Aliya, who had been staring toward the window, did not react to our exchange. She turned toward my grandfather with a slight frown and asked, "Zaida, you used 'he' to allude to the murderer. How can you be sure it was a man? Or are you using 'he' generically?"

Grandfather smiled at me. "Joel, how many times have I marveled at the wisdom of your *kallah*?"

When we were first married, Aliya and I had made a bet as to how long my grandfather would refer to her as a *kallah*, the Yiddish word for bride. I estimated a year or two. "Forever," she had said. After two years of marriage, I was willing to concede the point.

My grandfather continued. "While I only have 99 percent certainty, the five- and six-inch depths of the knife wounds suggest to me the killer is a very strong man."

He paused. "But yet, there is a small possibility that a strong woman fully enraged could also be capable of such execution. So we will keep an open mind."

He took in both of us. "What else, my children, struck you?"

"Is this important?" Aliya asked. "The victim lived in a studio apartment, and everything was perfectly neat and uncluttered. The kitchen table had a napkin holder, place mat, and a cereal bowl sitting on a plate, ready for breakfast the next morning. No dishes in the sink, dishrack cleared, what looks like a Murphy bed in the wall, and bookcases with books aligned beautifully."

"Again, Aliya, a very keen observation. Two instructive factors from what you observed. First, Mr. Casman's drive toward order may be important in understanding his relationship with others. Did such a drive allow tolerance for others to behave differently? Or was there a rigidity that interfered with the autonomy of others and caused conflict? We must learn more about this man to comprehend the essence of Henry Casman and what of his essence infiltrated the mind of the person who wished to kill him."

"Or the minds of people? Perhaps more than one person is complicit in the murder?" I asked.

"Yes, good, Joel. That possibility must always be kept in mind."

Grandfather leaned over to a side table and picked up his magnifying glass. He slowly waved it at us. "The magnifying glass is not just the classical instrument associated with the private detective profession. But truly, it is a critical tool in exposing the physical environment within which a crime is committed."

Grandfather slowly rose from his chair and walked over to us. He handed the magnifying glass to Aliya, and I pressed closer to her.

"With magnifying glass in hand," he said, "please focus it on the pictures of the victim lying on the kitchen floor. Do not isolate on the body, but instead, is there anything else that demands our attention and further investigation?"

Aliya handed me the glass. We examined each photo until Aliya stopped my hand. "What's that under the kitchen table? It looks like a small piece of paper or some type of stub."

"And why would that be of interest to us?" Grandfather asked.

I answered quickly. "Because if Casman kept everything so neat and orderly in the Casman apartment, then a paper lying on the floor is an exception to the rule. Perhaps the assailant brought it in and dropped it. Casman probably would have kept it in a drawer."

"Excellent, Yoeli, excellent." Grandfather beamed.

His praise warmed me even though I tried to look nonchalant. "But the police report doesn't mention it being taken in evidence. So it may have been thrown out."

"Not necessarily," Grandfather said. "You may have heard me speaking on the phone while you were reviewing the report. I again spoke with our helpful friend, Detective Carlucci. The apartment is still closed off as a crime scene. You know from our previous work together that the examination of the crime scene is an essential step in our critical analyses process.

"So Tuesday, we must visit the apartment on the Ocean Parkway. The detective informed me that due to the building management's pressure for use of the apartment, it will be opened on Tuesday and emptied. All of Mr. Casman's possessions will go into police storage until the case is resolved because no one has come forward to take responsibility for them. Hopefully, we will find the paper under the table, and while examining the apartment also take into our cognizance other helpful findings."

"And tomorrow?" I asked. "What will our schedule be? If I'm going to talk to my boss later today, I should have a sense of chronology for at least the next few days."

"You are correct to inquire. Here is what I suggest. At 9:00, we are at the arraignment which, since it will be the court's first of the day of the week, should not last past 9:15. We will then proceed to my office to interview your mother.

"After your mother departs from us, let us say around 11:00, we will reflect on her words and then grant ourselves a respite for lunch and intro-spection. Then if Martin is granted bail, we will ask him to meet us at my office at 2:00. If not, Detective Carlucci said we could arrange to meet with Martin at that time in an interrogation room at the 61st Precinct. The detec-tive would arrange to bring him there from wherever he would be assigned in the Department of Corrections system."

Grandfather quickly glanced at Aliya. "I believe we must be grateful that the detective is so gracious to us, yes?"

Carlucci had patronized her during the Flaum case. I feared Aliya was miffed with my grandfather because of it. But she responded, "Oh, Zaida, I think I can be grateful and dislike the man at the same time."

Grandfather laughed. "Ah, Joel, have I not told you that your *kallah*,… ach, but I repeat myself."

Grandfather's eyes swept both of us. "It will be a day of intensity, stress, and hopefully some light cast onto the darkness of what occurred."

"Aliya," I said softly. "I don't know if you wanted to be in on Martin's interview, but I don't think you can. Client confidentiality extends to a pri-vate investigator such as Zaida, but it wouldn't extend to you, even if we designated you as a consultant. I'm sorry."

"That's okay." Aliya answered. "I wasn't planning on coming. I thought my being there might be an issue."

"And Tuesday at 9:00," Grandfather said, "we are expected at the apart-ment of the deceased on the Ocean Parkway. According to Detective Car-lucci, a police officer will be posted at the door who will possess instructions to let us in. Again, the good detective welcomes our presence on the case since we have a specialized knowledge of the Jewish community, which may have pertinence in solving the crime. In addition, he is kindly sensitive that the case is for us a family matter. A half hour visit, I believe, will suffice. Do you wish to come with us, Aliya?"

"Yes, I do," she answered firmly.

"Good then," Grandfather said. "And beyond tomorrow, I cannot say. Please allow me some time to digest further what we know to this point and consider the sources of other lights that will illuminate this case."

With that, his eyes raised, no doubt envisioning the murder scene in which a knife was plunged twice into Henry Casman's chest.

I may not have been envisioning anything in particular, but I asked myself, *Who was Henry Casman and what led to his horrible murder?*

Which led to my next question, *Who is Martin Ross who has captured the affection of my mother? Is he tied in any way to Henry Casman and the murder?*

Aliya rose and headed toward my mother's bedroom. She knocked and opened the door. "Mother, we're about to leave. Is there anything you need?"

I heard rustling, and my mother hurried out to us. "No, nothing, just thank you, thank you for coming and agreeing to help Martin. I feel better. Thank you."

She hugged us, and we left to take the train back to Manhattan.

* * * *

As soon as we seated ourselves on the train, Aliya leaned in and placed her head on my shoulder.

"Tired?" I asked.

"Uh-hum, I feel like it's been a full day, and what is it, just around noon?" Aliya closed her eyes until I gently prodded her as we approached the Union Square station.

Back in our apartment, I made myself a tuna on rye sandwich. Aliya said she was still full and went to lie down in our bedroom. Larry Seidman had given me his home number for weekend "emergencies." But as a courtesy to my boss who might be eating lunch, I didn't want to disturb him until after 2:00.

While I waited, I practiced my pitch in the form of a closing argument. Once I reached him, I apologized profusely for calling him on a weekend. But Mr. Seidman said, "If you thought you need to call me, then I'm sure there's a good reason."

I was almost done with my presentation based on the proposal Grandfather had laid out when he cut me off.

"Joel, I'll make you a better offer. You've been an outstanding contributor to Prentice, Walters, & Reis since you joined us two years ago. And Mr.

Reis and I are grateful to you for having engaged your grandfather to take on and, with your assistance, solve the Ori Gold murder case.

"And let's not overlook the gratitude shown by our valued client Sam Gold, who has steered several new accounts our way. So what do you think? Work with your grandfather on this murder case for your family friend. Chip Holden will cover your accounts. And let's charge for your services so it does not get recorded as pro bono. Just an accounting factor, but we'll set the rate at $75 an hour instead of $150?"

How did it sound! "Thank you, thank you," I said, perhaps a few times too often.

I can do a good job being Martin's attorney. Why not? After all, I have the training and the motivation to help the family. I felt confident and even jaunty in my new role as a criminal defense attorney. Although I needed to prepare for the arraignment, I joined Aliya in our bedroom for a short while.

MONDAY, JUNE 7, 1976

I stayed up until 2:00 reading criminal law textbooks that I'd kept from law school. I'd also skimmed my 1971 copy of the *Criminal Law Handbook of New York*. I hoped it was still current. I was cramming, as before a school test. And my nerves jittered like during the night before I started work at my law firm.

I might as well have stayed up and crammed the rest of the night because I tossed and turned until 6:00 before dozing off and waking at 6:30 to the smell of coffee. Aliya had put out a suit we called "Mr. Monday," along with a dress shirt and tie. Before I started at PWR, Aliya and I purchased six suits, naming five for each work day of the week, and one "Mr. Weekend." I arose and made my way to the kitchen.

Aliya stood over the stove. Steam rose from a cup of coffee on the kitchen table.

I walked over and kissed her. "Why are you up? Did you change your mind about going to the arraignment?"

Aliya turned and gave me a wide smile. "No, I didn't, but I thought I'd help you a bit this morning by making you breakfast. You'll need your strength for the long day ahead. I know you didn't sleep much last night."

I was about to say, "Yeah, that's an understatement," but instead I hugged Aliya and said, "Thank you."

I glanced at the stove and table. "Where's your breakfast? Too early?"

Aliya moved toward the refrigerator. "I'll have some cereal and milk and keep you company. Then I'll get a little more sleep before leaving for your grandfather's office and your mother's interview. You'll call me when the arraignments done. I'll be ready to leave for Zaida's office then."

I nodded and looked at our wall clock. 6:38. I didn't want to be late, so I planned to leave by 7:20. I scarfed down my breakfast, including a second cup of coffee, in fifteen minutes and left Aliya finishing her cereal. I jumped in the shower and was fully dressed and ready to leave by 7:20, on time. As I headed to the door, I thought one more item would add to my presenting as a criminal defense attorney. I grabbed my work briefcase and took out all the documents, leaving a notepad and pens. I was ready. I closed the door quietly behind me. Aliya had gone back to sleep.

* * * *

I hustled down 14th Street to the Union Square Station and jumped on the #5 train heading to Brooklyn, arriving 25 minutes later at Boro Hall. I walked past the entrance to my grandfather's office on Joralemon Street, took Boerum Place to Schermerhorn, and then, almost at Smith Street, I stood before the Brooklyn Criminal Court building.

I was too focused on seeing Martin, my client, to admire the building's imposing architecture. But as a law student, I'd often gazed for minutes at its ten-story structure built in the Renaissance Revival style of 50 years before. I'd admired the entrance with three arched doorways, each about three stories high, beneath an upper floor colonnade of Corinthian columns. Two metal shields topped by an American eagle set off the center door.

I walked into the two-story lobby and, as I'd always done as a student, looked up to a coffered ceiling. A bronze chandelier, almost a story tall, hung from the center ceiling panel. The shined wooden floor showed hundreds of scuff marks. The weekend buffing couldn't hide them. Straight before me, behind four two-story Corinthian columns, sat a bank of six bronze elevator doors within a marble wall.

Around me, a buzz of activity. Men in suits, lawyers I assumed, carrying briefcases rushed by. Men and women, dressed much less formally and speaking a variety of languages, walked with less assurance, stopping suddenly to look around.

I heard:

"Where do we find him?"

"¿Cómo encontramos la sala del tribunal?"

"Gut in himmel, vos hut er getton?"

I took Spanish in high school and college. Yiddish I knew from its being spoken while I was growing up.

An information desk sat in the middle of the lobby. Two women who looked like twin sisters, each with graying hair pulled back in a bun and in long-sleeved white blouses, sat behind the desk. In front of them, queues stretched ten deep.

Nearly hidden by the people on the left line, I saw a peeling paper with "A___M" stuck to the front of the desk. I guessed it referred to the last name of the prisoner awaiting arraignment. I took my place in the right line and looked at my watch—8:17. Good thing I had given myself decent leeway. When I reached the front, I quickly looked back. The line was still ten deep.

"Who ya here for, Counselor?" Mrs. Rosetti—or so her name plate said—asked in a raspy voice. She was a smoker, like my dad before the cancer took him.

"Ross, Martin Ross."

She didn't look up as she thumbed through a pile of manila folders. She plucked one out and removed a small paper clipped to the folder. "Room 11 in the basement." She looked at her watch. "They'll bring your client to you in a few minutes."

Before handing me the folder, she looked at me. "Ain't seen you before. Glad you figured out or was lucky that you got in the right line. Would have cost ya 10 more minutes to go to the back of the other line. The guards don't like it when they bring the prisoner and his lawyer ain't there."

"Thank you." I headed for the elevators.

****

I walked into Room 11 and closed the door behind me. It was the size of a cell with a concrete floor and mildew smell. I shuddered. *Was it supposed to give the accused an early taste of incarceration?*

A metal desk the size of a card table and two metal chairs presented a choice for me. Do I sit with my back to the door or face the door? I decided to face the door.

I opened the folder, took out a single sheet of paper, and got the notepad and a pen from my briefcase. The paper contained nothing that I hadn't read in the police report or heard from Grandfather by way of Detective Carlucci—my client, Martin Ross, to be charged with murder in the killing of Henry Casman on May 29 or May 30, 1976. Plea to be entered before Kings County Magistrate Judge Sylvan Black in Courtroom B, fourth floor.

My fingers drummed the table. Martin's fingerprints were on the murder weapon. I had quite a challenge before me. Waiting for Martin seemed an eternity.

Finally the door opened, and I looked up. Martin, in an orange jumpsuit, had his hands cuffed in front of him. He had a kippah on his head, but without a bobby pin that usually kept it attached to his receding hair. His bleary eyes behind his glasses indicated that he hadn't slept in days. He was my height, and last Friday night, he probably outweighed me by 30 pounds. Now, he had stubble on his haggard round face and looked a lot thinner.

A tall, silver-haired, Department of Corrections officer, with the nametag "Joseph Boykin" pinned to his gray-blue shirt, followed. I stood, and Officer Boykin nudged Martin toward the seat opposite me. I nodded toward Martin who awkwardly seated himself and placed his cuffed hands on the table.

"Good morning, Officer," I said. "Does Mr. Ross have to be cuffed while I talk to him? We are well acquainted."

Boykin's mouth turned down. "C'mon Counselor, I haven't seen you before, but even if you're new, you should know the rules. The prisoner stays cuffed until we see what happens at the arraignment. Got it?"

The officer turned to leave. "I'll be right outside if you need me."

Martin squirmed in his chair. "Joel, thank you, I didn't..." he stammered before I gently cut him off.

"Martin, my mother told me that you deny having anything to do with the murder. So in a few minutes, I'll enter a plea of "not guilty" on your behalf. And you don't have to thank me. I'm glad to do it. I'll need to bill you, though my firm has agreed to a reduced rate. Also, we'll have to bill you for my grandfather's private detective services. As an investigator within your defense team, he will also be bound by client privilege and client confidentiality. Are these terms acceptable to you? If so, they will be part of a legal agreement for you to sign. Since yesterday was a Sunday, the paperwork is being drawn up at PWR. They will be couriered to you at your apartment. If you are released on bail, please sign and return as soon as possible." If not, I'll bring them to you."

"Yes, yes, of course. Whatever the rates may be. I am grateful."

"And one more thing. I believe you know I am not a practiced criminal attorney. Are you sure you don't want to hire someone with more experience?"

Martin gave a wan smile "Joel, I think the question beneath your question is do I want to hire an inexperienced defense attorney who may also have personal reservations about me? Yes, I do. I'm a pretty good judge of character, and I believe that if you take my case, you will work hard for me. In addition, I like the partnership with your grandfather. You two have solved some difficult cases. So I am in your capable hands."

I nodded and returned his smile. *Was I pleased or displeased?* "Good, then. A few questions. We don't have much time before your arraignment. Just curious, were you brought over from Central Booking this morning?"

Martin shook his head. "No, I stayed in a single cell at the 61st Precinct the last two nights. A precinct officer brought me over this morning and handed me over to Officer Boykin."

Odd. Usually, prisoners awaiting arraignment are held at Central Booking and brought over to the courthouse from there. Central Booking was notorious, both for its crowding and violence. Perhaps my grandfather's clasped hand with the hand of Detective Carlucci enabled this special arrangement.

"I need to ask you about the murder," I continued. "Did you know the victim, Henry Casman?"

"Yes, I knew him."

"How?"

"From the old country. We both grew up in Druya, then in Poland, but now in the USSR."

"And after the War, here in the United States, did you have encounters with Mr. Casman?"

Martin hesitated. "A few times, yes."

"And how would you describe these encounters? Friendly?"

Martin pursed his lips, and shook his head slowly. "Not always. We had our differences, going back to a rivalry over a girl in Druya. I married her after the War. I think Henoch…Henry, he resented me for that."

I thought back to the police report. "Martin, a resident of Mr. Casman's building said you were in the building the night of the murder and had a heated exchange with Mr. Casman."

Martin raised his voice. "I was not in the building that night."

"Can anyone confirm your claim?"

Martin shifted and pulled at his cuffed hands. "No… I was alone in my apartment, and no one was with me," he stammered.

I also shifted. Doubt took over. "Now Martin, I need you to be straight with me. The police report says that your fingerprints are on the knife that killed Mr. Casman. Did you ever touch that knife before? If not, how is it that your prints are on it?"

Martin trembled. He held his hands to his head, "I don't know, I don't know. Might the police be mistaken?"

Now wasn't the time to discuss the credibility of forensics reports. I answered, "That's something my grandfather and I will look into."

Martin relaxed. "Thank you."

"Okay, we're running out of time. One more question. Do you have any family we should contact? I don't remember your ever bringing up family in our conversations."

"Yes, I have a stepson in New Jersey. But I prefer that he is not contacted."

I kept my head down. *Martin didn't want his stepson contacted*? I didn't have time to pursue it, but I was intrigued. Instead, I said, "That will do it for now. No time left."

I picked up the notes and the arraignment folder and put them in my briefcase. 8:52 on my watch. "If you're granted bail or ROR, that is released on recognizance, we need to see you in my grandfather's office this afternoon at 2:00. If the judge decides to hold you, my grandfather and I will arrange to visit you at the 61st, okay?"

"Yes, Joel, of course, and thank you, thank you."

As he struggled to stand, his kippah fell off. He grimaced staring down at the floor. I retrieved it and placed it back on his head, but without a bobby pin—what the authorities thought as a potential danger—it would fall off.

I grabbed my briefcase and called, "Officer."

* * * *

I rode a crowded elevator to the fourth floor. Then, I weaved through a packed hallway until I found Courtroom B. I entered behind an elderly couple speaking Spanish. The woman was crying.

The courtroom was paneled in wood. A plaster ceiling showed cracks. Worn benches for gallery attendees were nearly filled. Spindled wooden balusters separated the gallery from the well that held the plaintiff and defendant tables, court stenographer, court clerk's desk, witness box, and elevated judge's bench. Behind the judge's bench stood the flags of the United States and the state of New York. Behind the flags on a large white wall were the words—IN GOD WE TRUST.

My mother and grandfather sat in a back row, whispering to each other. I caught their eyes, and my mother waved. I waved back, took a seat in the gallery front, and looked around. Grandfather had scheduled our day based on Martin being arraigned first. All these people weren't here just for Martin's arraignment. Was Martin's case going to be called first? Odds were that Grandfather, with probably Carlucci, had worked something out.

"All rise," called the bailiff. As we did so, a man well over 300 pounds came out of a door behind the judge's bench and strode toward the chair. The bailiff continued, "This Court, with the Honorable Judge Sylvan Black presiding, is now in session. Please be seated and come to order."

With some difficulty, the judge eased into his chair. The murmuring in the gallery died down. "Quiet," Judge Black shouted. Gratuitously, I thought.

"So what bunch of delightful miscreants do we have before me today?" He picked up a paper. "First up, the state versus Martin Ross, on a charge of murder in some degree."

A side door opened, and Officer Boykin led Martin in. His hands were now cuffed behind him. I headed through the swinging center doors toward the defense table on my left. As I approached, a short man, about 35, dressed in a suit much more expensive than Mr. Monday, walked to the prosecution table to my right. He nodded at me, and I nodded back. Getting a whiff of his heavy cologne, I coughed.

Martin joined me on my left. Officer Boykin had uncuffed him. The officer moved to the side of the table.

"Well, Mr. Fried," the judge addressed the prosecutor. "Good morning to you. I see you're back for the umpteenth time before me. And you're not going the grand jury route?"

Fried smiled. "Good morning, Your Honor. Yes, the umpteenth time. And no, Your Honor, the grand jury docket is jammed up with many other 'miscreants.' So, we are all yours."

Judge Black turned to me. "And you are..." He looked at his paper, "Joel Gordon, representing Mr. Martin Ross? You're new, aren't you? Have to be. You don't look past 20. Are you with a practice?"

"Yes, Your Honor." My nervousness subsided. "I'll take your words as a compliment. I'm with Prentice, Walters, & Reis in Manhattan."

The judge laughed and whistled. "Hear that Mr. Fried. We don't see this too often. A counselor from a hot-shot law firm in the City, and he probably went to Harvard or Yale. Not like us Brooklyn College Law School guys, huh, Mr. Fried?"

"Actually, Your Honor," I cut in. "I also graduated from Brooklyn Law."

Judge Black stopped smiling. "Well, well, isn't that something. Okay, enough chitchat. Tell us Mr. Fried, why you want to send Mr. Ross away?"

Fried's summary of the charges took 30 seconds. He ended with, "and the accused's fingerprints were found on the murder weapon, a large kitchen knife."

"Fingerprints on the murder weapon. That's pretty compelling evidence," Judge Black remarked. "I think, Mr. Gordon, you'd better hire a Sherlock Holmes to help you get your client off the hook on this one."

"Thank you, Your Honor. I've already hired the best."

"Very well then, your client is pleading what?"

Martin began to answer, "I didn't…"

I put a hand on his arm. "My client pleads not guilty."

Judge Black wrote something. "Then I'll set an evidentiary hearing date for, let me see, Monday, June 21, at 9:00. I don't know if I or one of my colleagues will have the pleasure of presiding. And Mr. Fried, no games with discovery, right?"

"Of course, Your Honor."

"What is your recommendation for bail, Mr. Fried?"

"Given the severity of the crime, Your Honor, we are requesting a $100,000 bond."

A murmur went through the gallery.

The judge looked my way. "And you, Mr. Gordon, what say you?"

I didn't hesitate. "Mr. Ross is a model citizen. He has no criminal record, not even a traffic ticket, is a philanthropist, and is not a flight risk. He doesn't even possess a passport." Part of it was what I knew from previous conversations with Martin, and part, bluff. "We are requesting an ROR."

"Hmmm." The judge thought a moment. "I don't disagree with you, Mr. Gordon."

"But Your Honor," Fried interrupted. The judge waved his hand.

"Mr. Fried, has your disenchantment ever changed my mind?" Judge Black turned back to me. "But I will insist that your client, Mr. Gordon, not leave Brooklyn any time before his trial. Does he understand?"

I tapped Martin's shoulder.

He cleared his throat. "Yes, Your Honor, I understand. Thank you."

"Good then. Next case."

Martin and I rose in tandem. His kippah did not fall off. Officer Boykin came over.

"Couldn't have worked out any better for you," Boykin said with an unexpected smile, looking at Martin. "You don't want to leave wearing the Department of Corrections' finest, so come with me down to the basement. You'll have to sign some forms, and I'll bring your clothes and any other possessions they took from you at the 61st."

Boykin turned toward me. "And good work, Counselor." He placed his hand on Martin's shoulder and pointed him to the side door.

I didn't feel as if I had done much, but Boykin's words boosted my confidence. My mother and Grandfather were waiting at the courtroom entrance. I motioned them to meet me in the hallway. The court clerk called the next case.

* * * *

My mother embraced me tightly. "Thank you, I'm very proud of you."

Grandfather hugged me and shook my hand. The last time he shook my hand was at my Bar Mitzvah. "Joel," he said, "was not my confidence in you well placed?"

I blushed.

Grandfather moved nearer to my mother. "It is good, yes, that Martin has been released upon his own recognizance. Sitting in prison awaiting trial is very difficult, both upon the body and spirit."

He paused and placed his hand on my mother's elbow. "But his own recognizance may entail being a prisoner in his own home, his apartment. Newspaper articles, radio and television news programs, are carrying his name as the accused murderer of Henry Casman. It will not be easy for him to go to the store, to synagogue, for a stroll on the Ocean Parkway as he sees people staring or even pointing at him. Some may even shrink from him, and others hurl epithets. His inner strength will be challenged."

"Fotter, Joel," my mother said, encircling us with her arms, "we will help him through this. I will prepare meals, visit him, call him, and run whatever errands he requires, yes?"

I disengaged from the circle. "Mom," I said as gently as possible. *She had to understand.* "Not exactly. If we go to trial, you may be called as a defense witness. In what capacity, I'm not sure at this point—perhaps as a character witness. I'll have to ask that you have very limited direct contact with Martin. If you visit him, don't stay long. Talk over the phone. I'm sorry."

She stiffened. "If that is what's needed, then I will do as you ask. Perhaps then you, and possibly Aliya, can help him with his needs. You know, Gutman's Kosher Grocery on Avenue J. They deliver. It can be arranged. Martin is innocent. Your working with Zaida to prove his innocence is what must be our focus. I know he's innocent."

I sensed my mother's pain, but I was also Martin's attorney. I said, "Perhaps now is not the time or place to discuss it, but later at Zaida's office, you'll need to tell us why you're so sure Martin is innocent."

Grandfather quickly said, "Yes, at my office would be the appropriate location for such a discussion."

"I know because..." my mother sputtered. She stopped as Martin emerged from the crowd in the hall. While his face was still haggard and scruffy, he looked better in the button-down shirt and creased trousers than in the orange jumpsuit.

My mother's and Martin's arms opened toward each other as if to hug, but each let them fall. "Martin, Martin," my mother began. "Are you...?"

"Molly, I won't say I am fine, but I will feel better after a shower and a shave. I have faced bigger challenges in my life. I will hail a cab and go back to my apartment—if they will let me in."

"Martin!" my mother said sternly.

"Molly, Molly, it was a poor attempt at humor." He looked at Grandfather and me. "One must always find the means to fight fear and discouragement. Am I correct?"

Grandfather's eyes narrowed. "Yes, if at all possible, an equilibrium always must be maintained. Toward that end, you will try to obtain some rest before you meet with us at 2:00 this afternoon, yes?"

Martin's shoulders slumped, and he nodded.

My mother drew near him. "Martin, I'd like to speak to you for a moment in private before you go home. Fotter, Joel, do you mind?"

My curiosity was piqued, but I didn't push it. We nodded and waited while my mother and Martin made their way to a corner nook of the hallway.

"He has faced 'bigger challenges' than this?" I said to grandfather. "What bigger challenges could he have faced?"

Grandfather became grim. "We will certainly ask that question when we interview him. I would surmise they had something to do with the War."

Neglecting one of my grandfather's basic rules of investigation, I said, "Let me fill you in on my exchange with Martin before the arraignment. He categorically denies killing Casman. Despite the witness report, he said he was alone the evening of the murder, but has no way to prove it."

Grandfather waved his hand at the crowd around us. "Ah, Joel, you see we are in the midst of multitudes. I very much want to hear about your exchange with Martin, but here, in this very public place, is it wise to do so? Better, we will discuss later in the privacy of my office before we interview him. Yes?"

"Yes, Zaida, I let my excitement of the moment get to me. Sorry."

Grandfather nodded absently as he stared intently at my mother and Martin. They faced each other, with Martin leaning in and speaking rapidly in a whisper, while my mother vehemently shook her head. Martin placed his hands on her shoulders. I felt nervous. I had never seen him touch my mother before. He held her firmly and looked into her face without speaking.

After a few seconds, my mother pursed her lips, slowly nodded, and stepped away. Grandfather and I exchanged looks but said nothing as my mother slowly made her way back to us with Martin trailing behind.

Martin spoke first. "I will stay in my apartment until it is time for our appointment. I know I have said it repeatedly, but thank you, Joel, for representing me. And to you also, Mr. Wolf, thank you for your work on my behalf. I did not kill Henry Casman."

Martin caught my mother's eye. "Molly, it will be alright. You will see. We will speak soon."

My mother looked straight at him and nodded slowly.

Martin shook our hands before heading towards the elevator.

I glanced at my mother. She was pale with streaks of drying tears on her cheeks. *Should I draw her towards me and put my arms around her?* All of my life, she provided comfort. But I was in public, in my professional capacity as a defense attorney. I represented her good friend, a man I could not call her "boyfriend." I hesitated. My mother drew near my grandfather who did what I faltered in doing.

I spotted a phone booth. "I'll let Aliya know we're heading to Zaida's office." *Why hadn't I hugged my mother?* I put that thought away.

We walked out into a sunny day. Although Grandfather had on his three-piece suit with a vest, he asked that we walk the half mile to his office. My mother, who wore flats and a light jacket over a mid-calf dress, eagerly agreed. I welcomed the opportunity to take in some fairly decent Brooklyn air.

My mother put her arm through mine and addressed my grandfather. "Fotter, why don't you set the pace. We will follow."

"Gladly, Malkeh," Grandfather replied. "I find myself filled with vigor this beautiful morning. Nevertheless, let us walk leisurely."

* * * *

The walk took about 40 minutes, much longer than if I were alone. I didn't mind as it would take Aliya about the same time to come from Manhattan. When we arrived at 10:35, I saw Aliya down the street. She neared, looking more rested than she had in the previous few days.

Aliya hurried up. "I understand from Joel that things went well at the arraignment. Martin has been allowed to be free awaiting his hearing."

"Yes, my child," Grandfather answered. "The persuasive legal talents possessed by your husband convinced the judge to release Martin upon his own recognizance. He has returned to his apartment before meeting with us this afternoon."

Aliya hugged me. "I really didn't have to do much, really," I murmured. "Shall we go to Zaida's office?"

Grandfather led the way up the three flights of stairs. His pace had slowed but remained steady. My mother hovered behind him He unlocked the smoked glass door with FRANK WOLF DETECTIVE AGENCY painted on it. When we entered, I noted one difference from when we worked the Flaum murder case nearly a year earlier. Two armless metal guest chairs now flanked the padded center guest chair. We were no longer dependent on Mr. Khan from ACME Loans next door for borrowed chairs.

Grandfather had put some new order to his office. Bookcases covered every wall, filled mostly with detective works from Wilkie Collins and Conan Doyle through Sayers and Christie, to two of his favorite modern authors, P.D. James and Tony Hillerman. Harry Kemelman's "The Rabbi" mysteries were arranged in day order from "Friday" through "Wednesday." When I had last been in the office nearly a year ago, newspapers had been stacked upon his desk and in bookcases in no particular order. Now I noticed the bookcases held neatly placed selected copies of *The New York Times* and the Yiddish newspaper, *Der Tog-Morgen Zhurnal*, labeled chronologically from 1954, when he had opened the office, to the present.

Since the room felt comfortable, there was no need to turn on the air conditioner unit sitting in the room's single window that looked out to the next building's red, brick facade.

Grandfather made his way to the swivel chair behind his desk and sat.

Aliya and I moved forward. My mother remained near the door. "Malkeh," Grandfather called. "Would you please take a seat in the center chair. Customarily, it is where the interviewee sits."

My mother walked slowly to it. "Yes, where the interviewee sits," she said softly. Aliya took the seat to her left, and I to the right.

"Malkeh, my child," Grandfather began, "I am sorry that we must subject you to our questioning, but to investigate this case properly, we must speak with those individuals who know Martin well."

My mother nodded. "I will do my best to help."

"Very good," Grandfather said. He turned to Aliya. "We all have questions. Aliya, might you begin?"

I was pretty sure that Grandfather had not mentioned to Aliya that she would lead off. Aliya did not flinch. For her to have reacted with something like, "Me, Zaida?" would have put a damper on the interview right from the start. I admired Aliya's strength and loved her for it.

"Of course, Zaida, I'll begin with the obvious." Aliya turned toward my mother. "How long have you known Martin and how did you meet?"

When we worked our first case—the Joseph Stein murder—my grandfather taught me to open with a seemingly innocuous question to diminish any sense of threat. Aliya was a natural. Grandfather once compared being a clinical psychologist to a private investigator.

My mother sat back. "We met almost a year ago at a Sunday lunch given by my friend, Ruth Green."

My mother turned to me. "You know, Jonah Green's mother. You were in school together. The Greens are members of Congregation P'nai Hesed, and Martin had joined the *shul* after moving to Brooklyn. Ruth's husband, the president of the Men's club at CPH, invited him to the lunch."

I nodded, and my mother smiled. "Ruth pictures herself as a *shadchan,* always trying to match people up."

She then reddened. "I was drawn to Martin right away, and when he asked if we might see each other, I agreed."

"'Drawn' to him?" I asked.

"Joel, Counselor, dear," Aliya said. "Your mother is responding to a question. Does interrogating what she means by 'drawn' hold any relevance here?"

My face warmed. *Was separating the personal from the professional going to be more difficult than I anticipated?* "Please go on, Mom," I said.

"At first we would meet for walks, movies, and a few Broadway shows."

She had laughed, telling us about *Murder by Death,* the clever Neil Simon spoof of the classic detective story, suggesting that my grandfather should see it. And she loved *Fiddler on the Roof*, even if she had seen it three times before.

My mother continued. "Sometimes we would go together to Saturday morning services. After a while, I felt comfortable enough to invite him for Friday evening and holiday dinners."

So that explained my mother's vaguely referenced walks "with a friend." But movies, Broadway shows? How did I not know? When my mother talked about a certain show, I had assumed she had gone with a woman friend. *Why didn't or couldn't she tell me?*

"Okay," Aliya said, "Mother, could you please tell us about Martin's family?"

My mother thought for a moment. "He seems reticent to talk about his family, but he has been a widower for about three years, and he doesn't have any children of his own. He does have a stepson living in New Jersey, his wife's child by a previous marriage. His stepson's father perished in the Holocaust."

"Would this stepson be living in the southern portion of New Jersey?" Grandfather asked.

"Yes, I think in a place called Vineland."

How in the world did my grandfather guess that the stepson was living in South Jersey?

"And Martin is a Holocaust survivor?" Aliya asked.

My mother fidgeted for a moment. "Yes, he lost his whole family. He himself was in various work camps and in a concentration camp. I don't know many of the details because I didn't want to burden either of us with our wartime memories. After the War, he, his wife, and stepson came as refugees to America and settled on a poultry farm in this town, Vineland. After a few years, Martin began a poultry feed business that was very successful. Upon his wife's death, he sold his business at a very good price to a national company and moved to Brooklyn."

"Ah, Malkeh," Grandfather said, "you have provided very good information. We will explore Martin's background more deeply when he joins us. Aliya, what other questions might you have?"

"I only have one or two more questions. Mother, during the time you've known him, did Martin ever introduce you to his stepson or any close friends? Did you ever meet or did Martin ever mention Henry Casman?"

My mother put her left hand to her chin, similar to what my grandfather did when he focused his thoughts. "His stepson? I believe his name is Peter, and no, I never met him. Martin said they were distant, and he was very sad about it.

"Friends? Not really. Perhaps an acquaintance or two from synagogue on Saturday mornings. And during our walks, we would sometimes bump into a *landsman*, someone he knew from Europe before the War. I particularly remember Abe from his hometown's benevolent and burial society here in Brooklyn. The encounters were always short. Never did I hear the name, Henry Casman."

"Would the 'Abe' be Abraham Schneider?" Grandfather asked. I remembered that Abraham Schneider was named in the police report.

"Yes, I think so," my mother answered.

After a short silence, Grandfather turned to me. "Joel, would you like to ask a question?"

"Yes," I began in my new counselor voice. "Mom, I'd like to know…"

My mother shrank back. I froze for a moment. *What was I doing?* I was about to go into interrogation mode with my mother. I took a breath and started again.

"Mom, I can see how you're being eaten up by all of this. I'm guessing you and Martin were planning a future together?"

My mother blushed but did not hesitate. "Martin had not yet come to Zaida asking for his blessing, but we have been discussing the future."

My mother glanced at Grandfather. "And I shared this expectation with Zaida who did not disapprove."

My grandfather nodded.

"And did you also talk to Aliya about it?"

"Joel..." Aliya began before my mother broke in.

"Aliya, I would like to explain to my son. Yes, Joel, I have been confiding in Aliya about my relationship with Martin. Aliya is not only a wonderful daughter-in-law, but also a very good friend."

A tear rolled down her cheek. "And yes, I did not talk to you about Martin. I was a coward, afraid I would hurt you. I know how much you loved your father, how his death affected you, how much you miss him, and how much you wish to guard your memory of him. Please forgive me if you feel I have hurt or betrayed you."

I shook my head. "There's nothing to forgive, Mom. Perhaps I'm the one who should ask you for forgiveness. My attitude wasn't the best. When this case is over—successfully—let's sit down to a mother-son conversation. For now, I have another question."

My mother wiped away her tear. "Yes, Joel?"

"Obviously, you have gotten to know Martin well, and you're convinced that he is innocent. Given that a witness says she heard Martin at the time of the murder, and the murder weapon has his fingerprints on it, how can you be so sure?"

My mother's voice rose, rare for her. "Because for one, I know Martin, and he is not capable of such a crime. And at the time of the murder, he could not possibly have..."

She suddenly stopped and looked down. We waited, exchanging glances, until Grandfather said, "My child, Malkeh, please, might you finish your words? At the time established for the murder, why could Martin not have killed Mr. Casman?"

My mother shifted in her seat. "Because, because,... Oh, I cannot tell you. I promised Martin in the courthouse I would not say. I promised!"

"He made you promise not to say something that would exonerate him?" I burst out. "How can that be?"

My mother bowed her head and did not respond. Tears dropped onto her clasped hands.

Grandfather reached out both hands to my mother. "Malkeh, may I reason with you in the following way? In our religion, two situations relevant to our present predicament allow for the annulment of a vow. First, a life-threatening situation. While we no longer have in the state of New York the death penalty, Martin's serving possibly a life sentence is, from my perspective, life threatening.

"Second, and tied to the first, protecting someone's health also allows for the abridgement of a promise. As you know from your dear mother, may her memory be for a blessing, who died in the cellar while we were in hiding during the War, Martin's incarceration may easily lead to his suffering from health issues. Based on these extenuations, might you consider telling us why you are positive Martin could not have killed Mr. Casman?"

My mother's tears continued to flow. "I don't know what is right."

Aliya placed her hand on my mother's arm. "It's to help Martin. Mother, please tell us."

My mother sat up. Her face was wet, but she spoke firmly. "Martin made me promise not to divulge this information because he wanted to protect me."

She paused then shook her head. "But I'm not a child anymore. How did I ever agree to his request? Martin is in danger, and he is the one who needs protection."

I was confused. "Martin wanted to protect you? Mom, how so? In what way?"

My mother grabbed the chair arm and raised her chin. "Simply, and I will be glad to testify in court—I spent that night with Martin."

She glanced at me. I didn't look away, but I was too stunned to respond.

"At the courthouse, he begged me, made me promise not to protect him by revealing our relationship. He said my reputation would be damaged at the synagogue, in our community, and perhaps even at my business. I was weak to comply."

My mother leaned toward me and placed a hand on my arm. "Joel, employ my testimony as you must in Martin's defense, please."

Was I rattled because my mother had spent the night with Martin? Because I had no prior idea? Both? I took a deep breath. "Yes, of course, I hope it won't come to that. Perhaps we'll prove Martin's innocence prior to trial."

I stood and leaned down, pulling my mother into my arms. She held me tightly. I didn't mean my gesture to signal the end of the interview, but as I returned to my seat, Grandfather said, "My assessment is that we may terminate the interview at this point."

He made his way around his desk to my mother. He bent down and kissed the top of her head. "Malkeh, your information will help us structure our critical analyses to determine Martin's innocence. It is of immense assistance."

My mother rose and gave Grandfather a kiss on his cheek. "I'm glad, Fotter, that I can help. Martin is innocent."

She blushed and looked down. "I would know, wouldn't I? Now I will take the train into the City and my store. Working may take my mind off things."

She gave me a hug and asked, "Aliya, are you also returning to your apartment? We could take the Lexington Avenue train together."

Aliya walked over to my mother. "I don't think so. It's a beautiful day. I think it would do me and Joel some good to get out to the promenade for some more of what Joel calls 'good Brooklyn air.' Right, Joel?"

I nodded. Aliya knew that after an interview, Grandfather liked being alone to reflect on what he had heard.

After hugging Aliya, my mother said, "Don't forget to have lunch before Martin arrives. I thought of making sandwiches, but I was afraid it was too warm to carry them around. Promise?"

"Of course." I smiled.

My mother left, and I turned and looked at Grandfather. His eyes were already raised toward the ceiling, a sign that he was sorting information into various mental folders to be retrieved later.

"Zaida," I said softly, "it's now 11:15. Aliya and I are heading out for a walk and for some lunch. After, Aliya will head back to our apartment. I'll be back by 1:00 with a sandwich and something to drink for you. Okay?"

A smile crinkled the edges of his eyes. He nodded. I took Aliya's hand, and we quietly walked out.

* * * *

Aliya had in mind the Brooklyn Promenade, a 10-minute walk from Grandfather's office.

She linked arms and said, "It's a gorgeous day. How about we walk and not discuss the case. Then, we can have lunch at Bagel Town near the Nedick's on Montague? It has Kosher certification, and you can bring back a sandwich for Zaida."

It took me a moment to respond. I was thinking about my mother's interview. "Sounds good," I answered.

Aliya and I had walked on the Promenade during the Flaum murder case during a blistering July Fourth weekend. We had also taken a break from an interview at my grandfather's office. The streets had been deserted with most shops and eating places closed.

On this late Monday morning, the streets bustled with people, mainly from the nearby Boro Hall and Kings County Supreme Court buildings. Last year, the heat slowed our pace. Now crowds. Between Clinton and Henry Streets, we stopped to gaze at the old St. Ann's Episcopal Church with its Gothic Revival spires, situated on the highest point in Brooklyn Heights. It loomed over us, dark and mostly abandoned. I would have loved to have stopped at the King George Coffee House on Montague and Henry for my favorite coffee. I looked at my watch. Not enough time.

At Pierrepont Place, we entered the Promenade and headed north. Last year the plantings along the boardwalk were wild and scorched, debris littered the flower beds, and dirt and bird droppings begrimed the hardwood planks. This time, we walked along neat and vibrant flower beds planted with milkweed, asters, and goldenrods. Birds will be birds, but now we weren't traversing an eyes-down obstacle course. *Was the City making an effort to spruce up for the Bicentennial?*

We both kept our word and made small-talk about dinner plans and up-coming social engagements. My mind kept straying to the interview with my mother, but I did my part. As we neared Furman Street, our turnaround point, Aliya stopped and pointed. "Isn't that the homeless person who approached us for money last year?"

Sitting on a bench, the same man. At his feet, the same overstuffed back-pack filling a Bohack shopping cart. He had on the same olive army fatigues, wool cap, and military boots, as if he had not changed them in a year. As I thought last year, probably a suffering Vietnam veteran.

I looked at Aliya. She nodded, and I walked over to him. She was aware of my guilt in having gotten a high lottery number during the Vietnam War, thus avoiding the draft.

"Sir," I said. The man looked up. Last year when he asked, I gave him a dollar. This time, I held out two dollars. He took it slowly and said, "Thank you, mister. Kind of you."

On the way back, Nedick's, with its orange-faced man encased in a flash-ing circle, overflowed with customers, but Bagel Town next door was doing only moderate business. We found a table at the back and ordered—egg salad on a bagel for me, along with an egg cream—egg salad with greens and water for Aliya—a tuna on rye and a decaf coffee with a third of a cup of milk to go.

Our order came quickly. Before biting into my sandwich, I said, "If you want to talk about the case and my mother's interview, as I explained before, as Martin's counsel, I'm limited to what I can share with you."

"Not exactly," Aliya answered. "I want to talk about how you might be taking what your mother told us."

My face heated, and I looked away. I wasn't ready for that. "You mean about how she met Martin and what she knows about him?"

Aliya gave me an exasperated look. "Joel!" The couple at the next table glanced at us.

I clenched my jaw. "Okay, okay, you mean about her...spending the night with Martin, and how I feel about it."

Aliya reached across the table and placed her hand on mine. "Yes, *chamudi*, I'm not Sigmund Freud. I'm your wife and best friend. I know you're hurting."

She only called me *chamudi*, Hebrew for "honey" or "sweetie," once in a blue moon, when I was hiding my emotional pain behind a defensive barrier. My first instinct was to pull back further. But Aliya had been right in the past. When I did so, matters always got worse.

My throat tightened. *Why did I feel like crying?* "I'm feeling confused. It's hard for me to say what's bothering me."

I met her gaze. "Aliya, what are you thinking?"

Aliya squeezed my hand and spoke slowly and softly. "Let's see what might be bothering you? Let's start with what might be the most important— that your mother was in some sort of illicit relationship with Martin?"

I winced and bit back a rebuttal. She was right. *Why did I want her to be wrong?* I didn't respond.

As I struggled, Aliya continued. "Are you feeling that she was violating a religious prohibition?

"That she has been violated?

"That she cheated on your father, may he rest in peace?

"That she had an affair with a man accused of murder?

"That the community will learn about her behavior, and she will be shamed?

"That the family will be shamed?

"That you had no clue about the nature of their relationship?"

I looked down and thought for a long moment. Her rapid burst of possibilities shook me. "I'm honestly not sure. Maybe all of them."

I shook my head and went on. "And there's one other possibility—what about the pain that Zaida may have experienced as my mother was talking about it?"

Aliya sat back. "Oh, for heaven's sake, Joel! You think Zaida didn't have a clue when his daughter, who he loves more than life, is not at home all night? Do you think your mother would just return in the morning and not say a word about where she's been? Or lie? Of course Zaida knew. Don't backpedal. Don't hide from the truth by involving someone else in your own issues."

I stared at her. "And he's okay with it?"

"I can't tell you if he's okay or how okay he is with it. Only he knows how he feels. But I'm sure he puts it in perspective. He hasn't cast your mother out into the wilderness or railed about her moral turpitude, has he?"

I shook my head. "Okay, what 'perspective' are you thinking about?"

Aliya smiled. "So tell me, if you heard a widower was in such a relationship, how would you be feeling? The same? And let me remind my onetime high school Casanova about your own past. Girls talk. No moral turpitude back then was there?"

I laughed, the tensions in my shoulders easing. "Aliya, did you know this about my mother and Martin?"

"'This'? No, not this particular 'this.' I knew how much she liked Martin and I thought she might be falling in love. Nothing about spending the night. But I did suspect. Why do you ask?"

"Most of the things you ticked off trouble me. Two more than others."

Aliya placed her hand back on mine. I continued, "First, I feel I was the only one in the dark. And I get it. Everyone knew that I wouldn't take it well, especially given my reaction to Martin coming around."

"And second, Joel?"

I sighed. "I'm Martin's legal defender. I'll fight for his exoneration, despite my personal issues, even if I can't let go of the idea that my mother has given her affection to a man who might be a murderer. It's going to be difficult."

Aliya squeezed my fingers. "You can do it."

I placed both my hands on hers. "Thank you, *chamudati*."

Aliya laughed. "You know that's the first time you ever called me, *chamudati*. I like it." She looked at her watch. "It's getting late, and I'm sure you want to get back to Zaida to process the morning events. And he's probably getting hungry."

Ten minutes later, I had finished my egg cream but had eaten only half of my sandwich. The reverse had occurred. Aliya's plate was clean.

* * * *

Grandfather took a sip of his drink and unwrapped his lunch. "Joel, I see you know my tastes well. The mixture of milk and coffee is very much to my liking. While I nourish myself, might you summarize your conversation with Martin prior to the arraignment? Then we will proceed to review our conversation with your mother, yes?"

I nodded, but first there was something I had to ask. "Zaida, when Mom said Martin had a stepson in New Jersey, how did you guess he lived in South Jersey?"

"Ah, Joel, you say 'guess,' but conjecture did not figure in my deduction. Did not Martin manifest several times that he is a Phillies fan? What region of New Jersey is close to Philadelphia? Is it not the southern portion of the state?"

I smiled, "Of course." *Grandfather could really give Sherlock Holmes a run for his money.*

"Good, then Joel, might you proceed in the order I mentioned? First, a summarization of your conversation with Martin prior to the arraignment."

I picked up my briefcase and took out my notes. "'Summarization.' Here goes. He emphatically denies killing Casman. I know Mom's words serve as an alibi, but how does he explain the fingerprints on the knife? I asked him, and he said it must be a 'mistake.'"

"Nuh, nuh, Joel," Grandfather interrupted. "Are we not proceeding ahead of ourselves by bringing in your mother's statement? And this early in our investigation, are you not exhibiting a scoffing tone regarding the possibility of the fingerprints results being in error?"

I grudgingly nodded. Grandfather was theoretically correct, but not much of a chance that the prints were in error.

I continued, "Despite my lack of criminal defense experience, Martin really wants me to be his attorney and for me to work with you toward his exoneration."

I held up my hand. "Yes, I'm aware, Zaida, that your objective is to establish the truth and not to exonerate your client. But I'm his lawyer, and you're working with me as my private detective. Aren't we both then supposed to work for his exoneration?"

Grandfather smiled. "Yes, and in this case, we will work toward each of our objectives which, I hope, will converge in the end. Please continue."

"He has no problem with the billing arrangement. He didn't even ask what the PWR rate will be. Mom did say that he is well off. I know I've included Mom's comments, but do you think his financial situation plays in any way on his case?"

"At this moment, Joel, all information is relevant for exploration. Do you have anything in mind? It is satisfactory if you do not at this time."

I shook my head. "It's just that when it comes to murder, money often plays a role. But for now, I'll go on and somehow bring up his financial state when we interview him.

"Martin admitted he knew Henry Casman, knew him going back to the 'old country.' Here's the thing Zaida. They didn't get along. Martin said it had something to do with a girl back home who Martin married after the War. I really didn't have time to get into it with him."

"Joel, your then time constraint is completely understandable. Martin will be here in 40 minutes. We will, as you say, 'get into it' with him when he is with us."

I nodded. "Independent of Mom's corroborating statement, he also claimed he was not in Casman's building 'that night.'"

"'That night'," Grandfather asked. "Did he employ those exact words?"

I looked at my notes. "Yes, I have his statement in quotes. Why, Zaida?... Oh I see where you're going. 'That night,' suggesting he may have been in the building another night."

My grandfather smiled. "Or...?"

I finished his question. "Or, he might have been in the building earlier in the day."

Grandfather's smile broadened. "I will surmise that there was intensity in his voice when he made the statement?"

I gave a weak smile. *How could I have missed this possibility?* "Yes, and we know why. His mind was on protecting Mom and not the larger implications. He emphatically insisted he was alone the night of the murder."

The corners of Grandfather's eyes creased. "Yes, we understand. For an investigator, the more intense a denial, the more one is attuned to the protestation of too much. Is there more, Joel?"

I took another look at my notes. "Just one more thing. His only family is that stepson in South Jersey, but Martin didn't want him contacted. I think we need to dig further."

"I agree. Perhaps Martin will enlighten us, but I suspect we will have more to investigate concerning his stepson."

Grandfather thought for a moment while drumming his fingers. "If there is nothing additional from your pre-arraignment discussion with Martin, I would like to call Detective Carlucci to request phone records of the last month for Martin and Mr. Casman."

"Yes, good, Zaida. I was going to ask for the same." I rose and stretched while Grandfather dialed.

After explaining the situation to Carlucci, Grandfather concluded, "You believe you can have the phone records for us at the time we visit the murder scene tomorrow morning? That is helpful and very good of you, Detective." After another minute of small talk, Grandfather hung up and smiled.

"The good detective is very cooperative with us, is he not, Joel?"

I returned his smile but couldn't help remember Aliya's struggles last year with Carlucci's "helpfulness."

* * * *

After hanging up with Detective Carlucci, Grandfather said, "Joel, might we establish a demarcation between your discussion with Martin and what we heard from your mother?"

I returned to my chair. "We still have 25 minutes. Sure."

Grandfather pinched the bridge of his nose and closed his eyes. He took a deep breath and exhaled slowly. I sat down and fidgeted. I wanted to complete this discussion as soon as possible. *Try to relax—work with Zaida.*

After a minute, Grandfather opened his eyes. "Yoeli, it is a difficult situation for you, and I admire your fortitude. I am always available for a talk with you, but I believe your *kallah* serves well as a source of reflection."

My shoulders stayed tense. "I know, Zaida, I appreciate your understanding…but, but, this is Mom."

Grandfather came around the desk and sat next to me. For a short moment, he held his hand to my cheek. "Yoeli, what is your foremost thought this moment about your mother's words?"

I blinked and swallowed. "Zaida, if it was any other interviewee, would we accept her claim that she was with Martin the whole evening as the absolute truth? Or would we suspect she might be lying to give him an alibi? Or, God forgive me, would we consider her also a suspect or somehow complicit? Zaida, do you hate me? I think I might be hating myself."

Grandfather pulled me toward him. I didn't resist. When I was a kid, especially after my father died, he would embrace me this way when I was very upset.

He lifted my face and said, "You surely know this without the words being spoken, but I will place them on our record—I could never hate you, and certainly not for performing your job so well. The fright of considering that a loved one is capable of a major transgression is enormous. And you are frightened for this reason, no?"

I put my hand atop Grandfather's. "You're right, Zaida, I'm also scared Mom will be hurt, especially if Martin is guilty. After all, regardless of Mom's alibi, he was seen, and left his fingerprints on the murder weapon."

Grandfather eased himself back into his seat. "Then I will say what is in both of our hearts, that I would never express if it were not your mother. I am exonerating your mother from deception as one basis for determining if Martin is innocent or guilty. And while I am on the record, I vow that if I am mistaken about your mother, I will resign myself from this profession forever. I know I am being dramatic, but I wish to convey strongly how much I trust your mother."

I shook my head. "No, no, no! Zaida, please retract your vow." I leaned forward. "When I was a kid, you always chided me about needless promises. I completely believe Mom, not just as a factor in defending Martin, but because I'm her son who knows her well."

I paused. "I think I was more frightened that I believed she could be lying than about a possible lie itself."

My grandfather tousled my hair and returned to his desk chair. "Joel, what other information your mother provided was of interest to you?"

I silently reviewed my mother's responses. *What else had she said that caught my attention?* "What strikes me, Zaida, is that Martin is not only— what did Mom call it—'distant' from his stepson, but he also doesn't have any close friends—just acquaintances. He might be shy, but not with Mom, clearly, or with us. Is he avoiding people for some reason?"

Grandfather stroked his chin. "A very salient question, Joel. But are you prejudicing your analyses by assessing Martin's fault in being 'distant' from his stepson as opposed to saying, 'Martin and his stepson are distant from each other'. It is an area of interest for us, along with his overall relationship with others besides our family members, yes?"

I barely nodded when I heard a knock on the door. I looked at my watch—1:50. Martin was a few minutes early.

* * * *

"Please come in," Grandfather called.

After the door opened, Martin did not move forward. Grandfather motioned him to enter and pointed to the guest chair. Martin settled into his seat, I to his right. I already had my pen in hand and notepad open.

He wore a blue pin-stripe suit, burgundy tie, and white shirt. His kippah was bobby pinned on his head. Even though he was cleaned up, shaven, and nicely attired, he appeared physically bedraggled with bags under his eyes. He looked worse than when I spoke with him before the arraignment. Prior to his arrest, he showed, for what I considered his age, a litheness and confidence in his movements. Now, he moved with a stiffness that I couldn't write off to a few nights on a 61st Precinct cell cot.

He had to be scared about his arrest—Might this interview be adding to his fright?

He sat and looked from Grandfather to me. "Mr. Wolf, Joel, I am grateful…"

Grandfather waved his hand and leaned forward. "Please, Martin, you need not express such gratitude. It is true you are a family friend, especially close to my beloved daughter. Nevertheless, we are here to engage with you in a professional capacity. You are accused of murder. You have agreed to a contract with Joel's law firm for our services. Know completely that Joel will work tirelessly to acquit you of this charge, and I am supporting him in my role as a private detective."

I nodded. "I will, Martin. I promise."

Martin pivoted toward me. "I am confident that you will fight for my innocence."

He turned back toward Grandfather. "But I wish for more, Mr. Wolf. I wish you both also to believe I did not commit this crime as you work for my exoneration."

Grandfather thought for a moment. "Ah, Martin, I will aid Joel in his efforts, but as I have previously explained to Joel, my objective will be to search for the truth—which I hope will bear out your innocence. Are you satisfied with my answer?"

Martin looked down. "Yes, I must be satisfied, must I not?"

Grandfather leaned back. "Good then, we will proceed with the interview. Joel, might you begin?"

In law school, professors had complimented my mock criminal client interviews. But this was the real world, and my mother's happiness was at stake. Despite that burden of responsibility, I felt ready. I planned to begin indirectly and see what emotions triggered.

I cleared my throat. "Yes, of course. Martin, my mother told us you sold a thriving business in South Jersey and moved to Brooklyn. Are you living off the profits of that sale, or do you make a living in other ways?"

Grandfather put his hand to his mouth and gave a slight nod. Martin turned sharply toward me. "I am not sure of the relevance of your question since I committed to the financial terms of my defense. Nevertheless, I will answer your question."

His response had irritated me. "My question," I said keeping my voice neutral, "isn't meant to cast doubt on your ability to pay. Rather, I'm trying to get a full picture of the person I'm defending, beginning with information about your current living situation."

"Very well, then," Martin said, "I am comfortable. Yes, I started a poultry feed business in Vineland, New Jersey, in 1955, and operated it along with my farm. Even though the egg business by the late fifties was in decline, still my feed business made money as I expanded into other animal feed and agricultural products. I easily bought out competitors. In 1966, I did not hesitate when a national animal feed company offered to buy a minority stake in my company. In 1973, after my wife passed away, I sold out entirely. I made some good investments along the way. Now, as I said, I live comfortably."

"Might you," Grandfather asked, "provide us with a picture of how you spend a typical day?"

Martin fidgeted. "Mr. Wolf, I can assure you that I employ my time productively. I keep up with my investments, with current events, with all things American. I have observed that you do also, Mr. Wolf."

My grandfather did not respond. But an image of his starting most mornings with his Sanka and *The New York Times* flashed through my mind.

As to Martin, his tone seemed snappish—different from the tone I knew from our previous encounters. *Is the questioning annoying him? Is it just that he's scared?*

Martin looked from Grandfather to me. "You see, since coming to this golden land, I have been determined to separate myself from the filth and horrors of what occurred in Europe."

He shook his head. "I read best-selling books as recommended by *The New York Times*. I seek out worthwhile movies and shows, and now find myself fortunate to have someone to accompany me. I make it a habit to exercise for at least an hour most days. I enjoy American sports—I follow my favorite clubs avidly."

If it weren't such a serious moment, I may have smiled. He was right about how not only our family took to many things American, but also so many of other Jewish immigrants—especially to baseball. Even some members of ultra-Orthodox Jewish groups in Williamsburg rooted for the Yankees.

Martin laughed slightly. "Even today, in the circumstances I find myself, I checked the standings. My Phillies are ahead of your beloved Mets by eleven and a half games."

I turned toward Martin, ready to defend my "beloved" Mets. I took a breath and looked away.

Grandfather answered neutrally. "Yes, the Philadelphia club is very good this year."

He cleared his throat. "May I ask, have you established any friendships since moving to Brooklyn? Of course, besides my daughter and her family."

Martin sat up straight. "Friendships, you ask? I...I have met many people, at the synagogue, in my building, at the Kings Highway Library. I have made several acquaintances."

Martin paused. "And of course I count you both as friends."

Friends? I couldn't say I was, or had let myself be, Martin's "friend."

Grandfather remained poker-faced. "You gave us your history beginning in 1958. I assume you first came to Vineland as part of the larger migration of Jewish refugees as poultry farmers to that area in the late 1940s and early 1950s. Might I be correct? And we welcome a brief history of your life before the War."

Martin flinched. "Yes, my wife and I and her son came to Vineland, as you say, to be chicken farmers in 1950. Although we knew nothing of such work. I was just a farmer until I also started my poultry feed business in 1958."

Grandfather nodded. "And before the War?"

Martin hesitated, gripping his chair's armrests. "Before the War! Is it really important to bring up that period in my life? There is not much to say."

Not much to say! What was I to make of his reluctance? The horrors caused many survivors to be reticent. Was there more going on with Martin?

"Yes," Grandfather said. "We understand the difficulty it must present, but even a response in brief will be appreciated."

Martin closed his eyes. "Then in brief, Mr. Wolf, I will share the following. I am the youngest of five children born to Yechiel and Esther Rossinsky of blessed memory. We lived happily in a small town called Druya in what was then eastern Poland. My father owned a dry goods store. Then the Russians came in 1939 as part of the German-Soviet Pact that divided Poland. They confiscated the store and sent my father to Siberia as a *kulak*. After two letters, we never heard from him again. That is a summary of my life before the War."

"And during the War?" Grandfather asked gently.

Martin took out a handkerchief and wiped his glasses. "In the summer of 1941, the Germans came and placed us in a ghetto. I believe I do not need to describe the conditions we lived under. You both certainly heard enough stories. But because I was young and strong, an athlete in those days, the Germans sent me first to local work camps and then to work camps in Germany and other parts of Poland."

Martin held up his left arm and pushed up the shirt and suit sleeves exposing tattooed numbers on the outer side of the forearm. "Then, gentlemen, as you can see, I was sent to a concentration camp. That was in March, 1944. I somehow survived the ten months until liberation."

I swallowed hard. Growing up, I had seen such tattoos on survivors.

He opened and closed his fists. "Then, then, after the War ended, when I... I made my way back to Druya, I learned that my mother, brother, and sisters, other family members, neighbors, friends—twelve hundred Jews— were murdered on June 17, 1942, when the ghetto was liquidated."

He looked at the far wall. "Is that enough of my history?"

Grandfather responded. "Your pain is felt deeply by us. One does not need to have suffered as deeply as you to experience the enormity of your pain."

"And of yours and Molly's, Mr. Wolf?" Martin broke in.

I wasn't sure I agreed with my grandfather. The few times I listened to my grandfather and mother talk about their six years in hiding during the Holocaust, I felt the pain of their suffering and wanted to flee. With difficulty, but also with a sense of obligation, I had read narratives of Holocaust survivors. But it wasn't the same as my having gone through the horrors. How could someone like me experience their days and months and years of suffering? In addition, extraordinarily, I had watched them come back to life and be productive human beings. How could they do it? I couldn't imagine myself being able.

My grandfather's voice broke my reverie.

"Yes, Martin, we share a tragic bond." Grandfather breathed in deeply. "But Joel and I must continue to ask some clarification questions. Is it acceptable to proceed?"

Martin nodded.

"Good then. Joel, might you continue?

"Yes. After the War, Martin, you married an old sweetheart you knew in Druya?"

I watched his face. *What emotions would I see as he spoke about his wife?*

He looked down. "Sweetheart? Yes, Dora. And I will tell you now. Henoch...Henry Casman and I, right before the Nazis stormed in, we were rival suitors for her hand. If truth be told, we were rivals in many ways. In sports, in our studies. But Dora, she was a beauty with a sharp wit who looked kindly on both of us, gave hope to both of us. Yet back then, her choice would have been as much up to her parents as to Dora. So Henry and I were also rivals in playing up to her parents."

Martin shook his head. "We had so many hopes. And then the Nazis came."

"How did Dora survive?" I asked.

Martin looked from me to Grandfather. "Again, may I ask, does this question have anything to do with my defense?"

My grandfather leaned forward. "I believe Joel's question is most relevant. The inception of a murder that does not appear to be the result of another crime such as robbery is often found within the web of relationships that have starting and interlacing points, with spaces of light that help us view a victim's life."

Grandfather paused. "And in your case, the life of a man accused of the victim's murder. You stated that you and Mr. Casman were rivals in many ways. Might not the prosecution become aware of such conflicts and exploit them as a factor in his murder? Therefore, please answer Joel's question."

Martin sagged and muttered, "Everything that occurred back then is difficult to relate."

He lifted his chin and said with a stronger voice, "My wife, Dora, along with a few other young people, was secreted out of Druya a few days before liquidation. Some of the guards were bribable. Many families wished to remain intact, not wanting to believe what the Germans would do. But not Dora's parents. They sensed what would occur and told her she was young and healthy and had a chance to escape the doom."

Martin looked at me and shook his head. "Many young people today don't understand. They ask why we didn't fight back. Why we meekly marched to the slaughter."

His voice rose in anger. "The young people today were not there. Then, the young felt a need to stay and protect their elders, as well as they could. With my father taken away, my brother and sisters would not leave my mother. And so many of the elders wanted to believe that there was a higher risk of death trying to escape." He swallowed hard. "May they continue to rot in hell. The Germans made sure to hold public executions each day, with no logic behind who was chosen to die."

I placed a gentle hand on Martin's arm. "I'm sorry that we must ask these questions."

His voice had become raspy. "Let's stop for a minute," I said. "I'll get you water." I took a clean cup from Grandfather's desk and left the office for the hall water cooler. I was back quickly. Grandfather smiled when I returned.

Martin took the cup and drank. "Thank you, Joel, the water is helpful. As for Dora, she made her way to a Jewish partisan unit. And here is what you need to know. She was extraordinarily brave. Because she was light-haired with no obvious Jewish facial features, she was sent on reconnaissance to surrounding areas to help plan sabotage missions or to determine the identity of collaborators. She carried various Polish identification papers which were forged in the camp. She even made her way into taverns where she flirted with the German soldiers to obtain information."

He looked at Grandfather. "There are no words for how brave she was."

"Yes," Grandfather answered. "It is difficult to find words to describe many things that occurred in the Holocaust. But Dora, she was with child while with the partisans, yes?"

Martin grimaced. "Yes, she fell in love with a man named Notke Zimmer the way many couples did in the partisans so as to not feel alone while they fought, while living with the knowledge of what had happened to their families. Notke was from Brody, about 450 miles from Druya. He was in Druya visiting family when the Nazis invaded. He also escaped the ghetto before liquidation and wound up in the same partisan unit as Dora. They had a *partisaner* wedding and…"

"'A *partisaner* wedding?'"

Martin gave me a wan smile. "There were no rabbis in most of the camps, so a ceremony was officiated by the person at the camp who had the best knowledge of the Jewish wedding rites. Whatever paper was available served as the *ketubah*, the wedding contract. The wedding rings were hammered together from bits of metal."

"And the glass to step on?" I asked.

"No glass. The groom pounded the earth with his foot to symbolize the utter lack of joy. Sometimes he could not stop and had to be pulled away from his frenzy."

Grandfather asked, "And Dora became with child, yes?"

"Yes, Mr. Wolf, soon after the marriage. But before she gave birth, Notke was killed during a mission. He threw himself on a grenade to save the lives of three comrades."

Grandfather shook his head. "Ay, ay, ay, a very brave man. And your wife survived as a partisan until the end of the War?"

Martin sighed and shook his head. "No, she did not. After the baby was born, she went back to going on missions. The baby was watched after at the camp by others until she returned. But in July of 1944, she was caught, given over to the Gestapo, tortured for information which she did not provide, and then…"

He stopped and looked down for over a minute. He was breathing hard. I opened my mouth to ask if he was all right, but my grandfather put a finger to his lips. Finally, Martin lifted his head and looked straight ahead.

"Because she…Dora had medical training before the War, the *mamzerim* sent her to a hospital in Germany to help with the injured German soldiers. She would not talk about what she did there. I do know that she was fed very little. At liberation, she weighed 85 pounds. While most refugees were fleeing toward the west when the War ended, Dora by rail, by wagon, by foot made her way east back to Druya hoping to find her son. To her great relief, she found Payshe—Peter—in a Catholic orphanage, left there by her partisan unit fleeing from a German assault after Dora was captured. In her way, after their miraculous reunion, Dora never stopped keeping an eye on her child."

Was it sweat or tears streaming down Martin's cheeks? He retrieved his handkerchief and mopped his face. "Just a few more questions," I said gently. "I want to build the best defense possible, and answering these difficult questions helps me."

Grandfather nodded. "With your permission, Joel, a few more questions from me related to what Martin just told us. Then Joel, you will ask your questions?

"Yes, of course."

"Good then. Martin, after the War, how did you find Dora and Payshe?"

Martin's eyes showed a spark of happiness. "In the DP—Displaced Persons—camp in Bavaria. One day in the communal dining hall in early 1947, we saw each other. We fell into each other's arms, and three weeks later we married."

Grandfather said, "I wish not to assume, but together, you and Dora did not have any children?"

Martin looked down and shook his head. "No, God did not bless us with our own children."

"And how would you describe your relationship with your stepson?"

Martin winced. "Cordial at times. Combative at others. Overall, I would sadly call it distant." He looked at me, and his eyes narrowed. "Perhaps Payshe also felt I was an illegitimate father replacement."

I stared at him. *Did Martin really say that? 'Also'!*—As if he was comparing his stepson's attitude to the way I felt about him! Was he taking a jab at me? I caught my grandfather's gaze, which counseled patience. I took a calming breath. Perhaps I was overreacting. He could mean that, in addition to other things, Payshe did not see him as a father. And if so, what were those other things?

No matter. He was my client, and his hearing was just a few weeks away. I needed to plow ahead to build a defense that made sense to a jury. I had to get at the heart of the evidence against Martin.

"You have an alibi for the time of the murder. My mother told us she was with you, that she will testify on your behalf, and that there is not to be any debate about it. She worries more about your staying out of jail than any consequences for her. Can we proceed on that basis?"

His face reddened. "She is a wonderful woman, your mother." Martin turned toward Grandfather. "I was hoping I could be exonerated without her testimony, without any embarrassment to her. Yes, I can proceed on that basis if you, Joel, can also proceed?"

It was my turn to flush. "Your relationship with my mother won't get in the way."

"Thank you, Joel. I am…I believe I have an excellent lawyer."

I smiled a bit at his words. I still had to understand my client better. Perhaps I had let my own resentment get in the way of a fair assessment. I looked forward to the post-interview discussion with my grandfather.

I pushed on. "Although my mother will testify that you were with her, the prosecution will invalidate the importance of her testimony as tainted by your relationship. They may even say that she was asleep, and you snuck away for a short while. So we must talk about the heart of the evidence against you—the fingerprints on the knife."

He opened his mouth, but I put up my hand. "And while there's a possibility that the fingerprints analyses by the police are in error, we must go on the basis that they are accurate."

Martin's hands rose as he shouted. "Then I do not know, I do not know. I never touched the knife. I did not kill him."

"Okay, okay, Martin," I said. "Let's keep working this through. Did you have an encounter with Casman anytime on Saturday, May 29?"

Martin gripped the arm rests. "I did. I saw him around 5:30 that afternoon."

I waited for him to say more, but he didn't. Hadn't Grandfather talked about Martin's evasive response pre-arraignment.

"Where did you see him and why?"

Martin's eyes narrowed, and his lips pinched. "Where? In his apartment. I came unannounced. Why? Because I wanted to reason with him."

"About what?"

Martin's voice rose again. "About his not allowing me into our town's benevolent society so I can eventually be buried at Montefiore Cemetery near my *landsleit* from Druya. What is it called in America? Blackballing me! It takes only one member to be opposed."

Grandfather said, "So that is your reason for interacting with Mr. Schneider?"

"Yes, he is the president of the association."

Why was I getting frustrated? It was my first criminal defense case—was pulling teeth typical?

I asked. "How would you describe your exchange?"

"He was his usual hateful self. He refused to listen. He didn't want me to come in past his foyer, but I walked around him to the kitchen, sat down at the table, and said, 'Henoch, let us sit and, over a glass of tea, discuss like two civilized human beings. And do you not see, the door is open? Do you want the neighbors to hear?'

"He would have nothing of my plea. He shouted for me to get out and moved toward me. I thought he would attack me. 'Henoch, I beg you, do not let the differences of our past rule our behavior today.' But he spat curses at me until I got up and fled the apartment."

I waited, but Martin didn't continue. I leveled my voice. "You haven't told us why Casman was so opposed to your being allowed into the association."

"Because…" Martin hesitated, frowning. "I think because he came out of the War a very bitter man, and his dislike for me from the years before took him over. He didn't believe that I rightfully survived. Along with cursing, he shouted, 'How is it that someone like you is here and better people died?'" Martin glanced at me, then looked away.

I didn't get it. Did Casman really hate Martin so much because of some stupid rivalry years before? He said "better people?" *What did he mean by "better people"?*

I leaned forward. "And he thought that way because of your rivalry before the War?"

Martin placed his hands over his eyes. "That man, he judged survivors on how much he thought they suffered during the War. I cannot say more."

Or you won't say more. I decided to let it go. I wanted to hear what Grandfather made of Martin's statement. Perhaps my grandfather had the same thought, but before I could continue, he said,

"Might I inquire? In what language did you quarrel with Mr. Casman? English, Yiddish, both?"

"What language?" Martin sounded surprised. "Yiddish, of course."

"Thank you." Grandfather nodded for me to proceed. *Why did my grandfather ask that question? What difference did the language make?* My mind raced as I asked, "Did anyone see you come or leave?"

Martin shrugged. "I did encounter a lady in the hallway who I think I met before. Anyone else, I am not sure."

"And after you left Casman, did you go back to your apartment?"

He shook his head. "I walked along Ocean Parkway until it was time to meet your mother…at the apartment…at eight."

I closed my notebook. "Okay, I have no more questions for now. I'm sure I will have more as we continue to prepare for the hearing. Is there anything else you'd like to tell us?"

"Nothing else," Martin said as he rose slowly. He shook my hand and then walked over to my grandfather, took Grandfather's hand with both of his, and shook firmly. He then gave me a weak smile and slowly left the office.

* * * *

After Martin closed the door, I got up and walked over to the window and stared over the air conditioner at the next building. My body sagged. How wearying this interview had been compared to any others I had done with my grandfather. When I turned to Grandfather, he held both hands to his forehead.

"Ay, ay, ay, Yoeli, a very difficult case, no? What I sense we have discovered from our discussion with Martin is that the web within which Mr. Casman's murder was spun may go back to the Holocaust. And that possibility imposes sensitivities, barriers, and, yes, deceptions that will create difficulties. Martin is a tortured man. Each survivor carries within some element of personal pain which is never fully revealed, even to loved ones. But it is now our unfortunate duty to bring to the surface the demons and, yes, even the lies I sense that Martin conceals. And I am afraid that the revelations may be greatly hurtful to Martin and to others."

"Zaida, you're thinking of Mom?"

"Yes, Yoeli, and of others, you and I included. During our previous cases, you noticed at times that I experienced a sadness emanating from darknesses that pervade the human condition. And now we will be dealing with the enormity of the Holocaust darkness which is also so very personal to our family."

Grandfather straightened himself. "Nuh, but there is no desisting from the task before us. Let us examine what Martin conveyed and, importantly, what he did not. Might you begin, yes?"

I took a minute to review my notes. "To start, Zaida, I still don't get why Casman hated Martin so much. Because of a childhood rivalry before the War? Because of Dora? That's why Casman said 'better people' than Martin died? There's got to be more to it."

"Unquestionably, Joel, yes. What were Martin's words? 'I cannot say more.' You yourself may have immediately thought—does he mean, will not? You will go on, please."

"Well, Martin never really addressed any substantive reason why Casman was blackballing him from membership in the benevolent society. And what about the others in the association? Why didn't they object?"

Grandfather's eyes lit up. "Yes, yes, such a thing occurs when one has no friends, but rather…"

"Acquaintances," I finished Grandfather's sentence. "Yes, that made sense. According to Martin, our family constitutes his only friends."

So Martin has acquaintances but not friends. The benevolent association isn't fighting Casman's blackball. If I were to defend him properly, I needed to put it all together.

"What, Joel, struck you about how Martin survived the War?"

I thumbed through my notes. "Let's see. Labor camps and then in a concentration camp for ten months. Did I get it right, Zaida?"

"Yes, you did. But do you have his exact words?"

I looked at my notes before shaking my head.

Grandfather continued. "He said, 'I somehow survived the ten months until liberation.' We can imagine much from what has been reported about life in the concentration camps. But is it not his choice of the word 'somehow' that is intriguing and must be pursued?"

I considered my grandfather's point. *'Somehow'! Was it just a random choice of a word?*

I nodded. "'Somehow,' as opposed to the greater detail that he gave about how Dora survived?"

Grandfather's eyes narrowed. "Yes, the greater detail and lack of detail. Martin said he was in a concentration camp but did not say specifically, Auschwitz, correct?"

My grandfather was right, but… "Zaida, how do you know he was in Auschwitz and not some other concentration camp?"

"Ah, Joel, we must be aware that prisoners allowed to survive were tattooed only at Auschwitz and not at other camps. Do you remember Martin's number?"

I shook my head and shifted in my seat. Had I recoiled from the sight of the tattoo and missed an important indicator? I didn't know much about the tattoo system at Auschwitz. *Was it just a random number?*

"Yoeli, do not feel aggrieved for not remembering or recording the number. It was 'A 1.911.' Therefore, the question we must ask…"

"Is why he didn't say Auschwitz directly the way others do?"

Grandfather smiled. "Yes, is it an understandable flight from a terrifying past? Might it be evasion of some sort? Are there other explanations? And the second question, Joel?"

"I…I don't know, Zaida, what's the second question?"

Grandfather pointed at the phone on his desk. "After you leave, I will call Detective Carlucci and ask him to review Mr. Casman's morgue pictures. Does he also have a tattoo and, if yes, what is the number?"

I smiled. "And if the numbers are close, that might tell us they were at Auschwitz around the same time."

"Yes, Joel, a strong possibility that we must pursue. As for what he told us about Dora, let us examine the detail. Her escape from the ghetto. Her joining the partisans. His extolling her missions. Her first marriage. The birth of her child. Torture at the hands of the SS. But then an odd story with superficial detail. That the SS did not execute her after she refused to inform, odd, yes? To manufacturing plants, to mines, to munitions factories, slave laborers were sent. But that she was sent to work in a German hospital? I am not an expert, but in my readings, I have not come across such an occurrence. Yet, we must keep an open mind as we investigate, yes?"

As I jotted notes on what my grandfather had just said, my eye fell on words I had underlined. "What did you think, Zaida, about the swipe he took at me when describing why his stepson and he didn't get along."

Grandfather placed his hand to his chin and leaned forward. "Yes, I believe he wanted to make a point with you. But is there more of import to his assessment? Did he not, in various instances during the interview, reveal much about his relationship both with his wife and stepson?"

"Well, Zaida, he gave a brief, factual rendition of how they met and made their way to Jersey. But," and I tried to find the right words, "it was matter-of-fact. There was no…no emotion, was there?"

Grandfather smiled. "I hope you do not mind my saying that your perspicacity grows every day. I, too, sensed no emotion. I had the impression, and again that word, that he was 'distant' from his wife and stepson. Did Martin ever say 'my son'? I believe not. What were his exact words? 'Dora never stopped keeping an eye on her child.' Does he use 'we' or 'our' when mentioning their family structure? How did he enunciate coming to Vineland? 'My wife and I and her son.' Most telling, is it not?"

My face grew warm. *How could my grandfather's memory be so much better than my note taking?* What did a "distant" relationship with Martin's wife or stepson have to do with Casman's murder? My grandfather's "critical analyses" approach in which no thread in the web is ignored always worked in the past. We would have to dig into Martin's family relationship after the War. But for now, I had to ask about something else.

"Zaida, I'm really curious. Why did you ask in what language Martin and Casman argued? What difference does it make?"

"Ah Yoeli, it may be a small stone, but it must not be left unturned. What now appears to be a nuanced piece of information later may have great bearing on a case, no?"

"Yes," I said. "In previous cases, a small piece of information or a fragment of an event played a part in the resolution.

I asked. "Anything else, Zaida?"

Grandfather took off his glasses and rubbed his eyes. "For now, Joel, nothing else. It has been a most exhausting day, no? We both have much reflection to occupy us. Tomorrow morning at 9:00, we will visit the scene of the murder, and your *kallah*, if I remember correctly, will be with us. I will remain here a while and then return home. And you now will be on your way?"

I walked over to Grandfather and hugged him. He squeezed my hand.

"I'll call Aliya and tell her I'm coming home," I said. "We'll see you tomorrow at 9:00."

As I left, I saw that Grandfather had raised his eyes toward the ceiling. He was constructing the web in which the murder occurred, weaving and unraveling, part by part, examining where gaps existed and where the web knotted.

* * * *

Forty-five minutes later, I arrived at our Stuyvesant Village apartment. I mulled over what I didn't know about Martin. How vulnerable would his defense be as a result? If only I had my grandfather's discipline. We were at the beginning of the case with much still to discover. During the Flaum murder investigation, hadn't I counseled Aliya with "Patience, my love, patience."

Aliya sat at the kitchen table with a stack of books and our Underwood manual typewriter. "Hi," she said, jumping up to give me a tight hug. "I'm getting ready for my first day at work. Preparing calms me down."

She released me. "How are you, and how's Zaida? Is Martin holding up?" She looked at her watch. "Wow, it's 4:45. You must be exhausted."

I pulled her back for another hug. "I'm okay, and Zaida seems to be okay. And Martin? I don't know, but really that's about all I can say about him to you."

"Attorney-client confidentiality, I know, I know. I have no intention of pushing against those boundaries.

"Are you still coming to the murder scene with us tomorrow?"

"Yes, I'd like to come with you tomorrow." She paused. "Unless I'm not feeling well."

"Not feeling well? What is it, Aliya?"

"Oh, I'm sure it's nothing. Just some sort of bug, I guess. Don't worry."

"Okay, but you won't let something go because you're about to start a job? Right?"

Aliya laughed. "I won't let anything go, I promise. You're probably hungry. I'll fix you something substantial. For me, I have a yearning for cottage cheese and fruit. Change, and we'll eat."

I loved Aliya for her understanding. I headed to the bedroom. There was nothing more I wanted to do than to shed Mr. Monday.

TUESDAY, JUNE 8, 1976

I spent a restless night. At 6:30, I put on shorts and a tee and ran over to the newspaper kiosk at 14th and 1st. I bought a copy of each of the three dailies. All had short, buried stories about Martin's arraignment. Henry Casman's murder did not carry the front page attention in *The Daily News* as when we worked the Batya Flaum murder case. The disappearance of a Yonkers politician made page one. A multi-car collision on the Major Deegan took the cover of *The Post*. On page one of *The Times*, the top headline predicted Jimmy Carter's winning the Georgia primary and nearing the Democratic nomination for President. A seven sentence story on the murder appeared in the A2 section.

I had no need for my Mr. Tuesday suit. The forecast warned of a sweltering day. I changed into light summer trousers, a button down short-sleeve shirt, and cordovan loafers. Aliya dressed in a loose-fitting blouse over a knee length skirt. We both had shredded wheat and milk for breakfast.

We were about to leave to meet my grandfather at Casman's apartment building when my mother called.

I answered. "Everything okay, Mom? Zaida?"

"Zaida is well, and I'm…I'm fine, Joel. How is Aliya? And you?"

"Good and good."

"I called to tell you I am leaving for the City and will drive Zaida to the Ocean Parkway building. I don't wish him to walk over a half mile on a hot day. Also, Gutman's does not wish to deliver groceries to Martin's apartment. The person said 'it might not be good for business.' Somehow, I'll take care of it."

I said goodbye, hung up, and the phone rang again—Martha Brennan, the chief crime reporter for *The Daily News,* who had helped us with the Flaum case. She and my grandfather had struck up a friendship, and in return for her assistance, we had given her some scoops.

After a few moments of chit-chat during which she asked after Aliya, Brennan said, "I won't keep you long, but I was going over the court records for that Ocean Parkway murder and saw that you're the defendant's attorney. Not a slight, but aren't you more of a financial sector lawyer than criminal defense? And your wonderful granddad, is he also working the case?"

My mind wandered to the ribbing I got from Aliya when I had denied thinking Brennan attractive. Did this humorous recall curb my annoyance when I responded, "I've been specializing in securities law, but branching out now. And yes, my grandfather will be working with me as my chief investigator."

"Sounds great, Joel. Anything special you might give me?"

I thought for a moment. I didn't want to give her anything at this time, but I was pretty sure my grandfather would want to maintain the relationship.

"Not right now, but possibly further into the case."

"Good, stay in touch."

* * * *

Aliya and I picked up the Q Train and headed for the Avenue J station in Brooklyn. There were plenty of seats. Aliya put her head on my shoulder. But after a few minutes, she sat up.

"Joel. Are you nervous about visiting the murder scene?"

My initial male reaction was to say, "No, not at all, I've now been to several crime scenes." But I told the truth.

"Yeah, I am. It's not just because we'll see the murder which upsets me, but also what we find…or don't find…will affect my job as Martin's attorney. By the way, how are you feeling this morning?"

"Okay. But because of Martin's attorney-client confidentiality, I'm sitting back after this."

I smiled. "Yes, whether you want to or not. Do you?"

She squeezed my hand. "Let's just say overall it's for the best."

How did I feel about losing Aliya's assistance and advice? She really helped with the Flaum case. But she hadn't been herself lately, and that worried me. Also, was I afraid that in a moment of pillow talk I'd betray something I shouldn't as Martin's lawyer.

We descended the steps of the station to E. 16th Street and headed west on Avenue J. A few blocks down, the black marquee of the *Midwood Theater* rose up. The theater was showing second run movies. The marquee featured *Dog Day Afternoon*, which we had already seen.

Crossing 13th, Aliya pointed. I expected to see the *Bezalel Judaica* shop, which had been part-owned by the murdered Batya Flaum. Her partner, Marcia Gelb, had been a suspect. Now, the windows were grayed, and only the stenciled letters of the store's name remained on the glass door. A cardboard "For Rent" sign hung from the door's inside.

I shook my head and touched Aliya's elbow. "Had you heard that it closed? One of the casualties when the tangles surrounding a murder are undone."

Aliya nodded and pursed her lips. "Yes, I guess so. I hadn't heard. Let's keep going. We don't want to be late."

Aliya was fending off memories of that horrific murder.

Seven blocks later, we reached Ocean Parkway. I looked at my watch. 8:35—We would easily be on time. As a kid, I always loved Ocean Parkway. Even though it's a six-lane major urban road, somehow I always felt relaxed there, a feeling of well-being as I pedaled car-restricted bike lanes besides pedestrian paths. When I walked, triple rows of trees provided shade to benches and game tables just 25 feet away from whizzing traffic. High rise apartments dominated the two service roads and sidewalks—I ignored them.

We turned south on the parkway and walked two avenue blocks past the eastern edge of Washington Cemetery and its 100,000 graves, one of the largest Jewish cemeteries in the U.S.

I gestured toward the gravestones. "A fitting way for New Yorkers to be buried, one very near to another," I said.

Aliya nodded with a "Hmmm."

I changed the subject. "You know we're ten minutes early, but…"

Aliya laughed. "But your grandfather will already be there."

"And he'll be pacing back and forth, surveilling the street, the building, the buildings around it, and the people going in and out."

We linked arms. I spotted Grandfather down the block.

* * * *

Not pacing. Instead my grandfather stood still, craning his neck in our direction. A black, rectangular camera bag that contained a Polaroid hung over his shoulder. Grandfather was enamored with the technological breakthrough the Polaroid offered investigators—instant photos. We waved to each other.

"Good morning," he said as he hugged us. "You are early. It is merely 8:45."

I laughed when Aliya said, "But exactly on Zaida time."

Still smiling, he said, "Yes, good, my children, there is much work before us."

The smile disappeared. He motioned toward the entrance. The black awning showed 1165. "There is much to discover inside, as there is no lock on the entrance doors, no doorman to note who comes and goes, and no security cameras which are increasingly present in commercial buildings in Manhattan to record entries and exits. The information security cameras hold will soon be of great assistance to my profession, will they not?"

Aliya and I nodded as we followed Grandfather toward the entrance.

1165 Ocean Parkway was a brown, six-story brick building erected in the Brooklyn Renaissance style of the 1930s—emphasis on symmetry. The awning protruded from a white, horseshoe-shaped doorway, framed on each side with a rectangular column rising to a balustraded balcony available to the residents of the second floor. The unit on the first floor, left of the door, indicated "JEROME BRESSLER, DPM," and the unit on the right, "MARIO BUSCOMO, DDS." Each unit from the second to the sixth floor, to the left and right of the center apartments, were similar in appearance, with air conditioners and black iron-railed fire escapes in the same locations.

We entered a small, dimly lit lobby. Four identical wrought-iron sconces decorated the walls at each corner of the lobby. The candle bulbs in two were out. A matching eight-bulb candelabra chandelier also had two non-working bulbs. A chipped, black wooden bench sat along the right wall. Built into the left wall, six rows of gold-colored metal mailboxes, ten to each row, displayed apartment numbers and resident names. Two elevators took up the far wall.

What a contrast to the well-maintained harmony of the building's exterior. I shook my head. "I'm surprised at the disrepair."

Grandfather's jaw tightened. "Yes, Joel, I am also surprised."

The murder had taken place in 6D, but as Aliya and I walked toward the elevators, Grandfather stopped in front of the mailboxes. He scanned each row of the cluster before rejoining us. "Yes, 6D. We will proceed to examine Apartment 6D."

I pressed the UP button. As an elevator arrived, I heard a nearby door open. A man with a mop and bucket emerged from the back corner. Grandfather put out a hand for us to pause.

"Good morning," Grandfather said.

The man, thin with pale skin, a creased, angular face, and graying, blonde hair, wheeled the bucket toward us. *What was wrong with his dark, brown eyes?*—The left eye was smaller than the right. The white overalls he wore over a blue work shirt displayed *William Bunch—Building Superintendent*. As the "Super," he maintained the building, performed repairs, and was the point of contact between the residents and building owners.

"Can I help ya folks?" He took out the mop from the bucket and leaned with it. His squinting eyes darted among us, lingering longer on Aliya.

I took out my business card and handed it to him. "My name is Joel Gordon. I'm defending the man accused of killing your resident, Henry Casman, in 6D. The police have given us permission to examine the apartment."

Bunch double gripped the mop handle and looked from Grandfather to Aliya. "An old man and a pretty young thing working with y'uns, well, isn't that a hoot. Can't say I ever have any such help."

What a creep. Aliya glared. Grandfather's expression remained neutral as he stepped forward. "Mr. Bunch, I assume that you were acquainted with the murder victim, yes?"

"'Acquainted,' you say? Yeah, if that's what y'uns call it. I knew what a piece of work he was, right from the beginning. I'm also the building's rental agent, and why I let him take 6D, I don't know to this day. Around four years ago, he signs the lease, the way everyone does, and shows up with his stuff a week later to move in. I tell him nicely the first month's rent and one- month deposit money was short fifty dollars. He starts hollerin' that I'm wrong and shows me the receipt I gave him for four hundred dollars. I tell him he's short the fifty because he forgot to include 'welcome money' for the Super."

Bunch shook his head. "Y'uns know that we got a custom called 'welcome money' where another fifty is expected for the super. But he just points a finger at me, and in his foreign English, tells me where I can go. Couldn't stop him from movin' in. Welcome money ain't in the lease, but everyone knows it's the right thing to do. It's a good thing he ain't ever needed any repairs because I woulda' had a 'super' way to fix what he wanted."

I clenched my fists and took a deep breath. I had my job to do. But I promised myself to report him later for the illegal rent practice.

I asked, "So what interaction did you have with Mr. Casman after he moved in?"

The left side of Bunch's lip curled up. "'Interaction,' that's a fancy word, Sonny. Maybe y'uns can call 'interaction' passing by the guy and him never saying "good mornin' or 'how ya doin.' Only tenant that never gave me a Christmas present. And I wasn't the only one he ignored. Never saw him exchange a word with any of the other tenants. Always walked by with his head down and hate on his face. I had reason to dislike him, but what he was hatin' about, who knows and now who cares."

"I have a question," Aliya said firmly.

Bunch snickered. "Well, shoot then, young lady."

"On the date of the murder, Saturday, May 29, did you see Mr. Casman either by himself or in the company of someone? Did he have a visitor to his apartment? But just a minute before you answer."

Aliya pulled the police file from her bag and quickly took out a photo of Martin. "In particular, did you see this man?"

He looked quickly and shook his head. "Saturday, that's a day the Jewish folks come in and out visiting each other and gabbing in the lobby and outside of the building. I stay in my apartment on those days and pretty much take the day off. Just too many of them all dressed up and lookin' alike. Even if I saw Casman with someone, I probably couldn't't've told one from another, including if I saw that guy in the picture who looks Jewish to me."

My stomach turned. Aliya placed the photo back in her bag, her hands slightly shaking. But I had to say it. "Thank you, Mr. Bunch, a police officer is expecting us."

"Glad to help. Tell your client that if he did it, I get it."

An elevator door stood open. We rode up to the sixth floor in silence.

* * * *

Cooking and laundry smells met us as we left the elevator. The direction indicator on the wall under a burned-out bulb indicated 6D to our right. We turned down the worn, carpeted hallway and saw a uniformed police officer in front of a yellow taped door.

I recognized Officer Coleman from the 61st Precinct. We'd met him during the Flaum murder case.

"Good morning, sir," he said looking to Grandfather, and "nice to see you again," nodding toward me. "Miss." He tipped his hat to Aliya.

He handed a large envelope to Grandfather. "Detective Carlucci instructed me to give it to you and let you into the apartment. In about an hour, a crew's coming to remove all the contents to evidence storage until the case is resolved. So, I'll let you in, and you can stay until they arrive, if you want."

"Thank you, Officer Coleman." My grandfather handed the envelope to me. I saw written on it, "Phone Records" and "Autopsy Photos."

"We will open it after we complete our examination of the apartment, yes Joel?"

I nodded. *Zaida wants to spare Aliya from seeing the photos.* She gave him a smile—she understood, too.

Grandfather added. "But before we enter, please allow me a few minutes to perambulate the hallway. I will not be long."

He stopped for several seconds in front of the other five apartments on the wing, culminating at 6I across from us, where he lingered a bit longer. *Was the door to 6I open a crack?*

We entered 6D, and the officer closed the door behind us. We crossed a tiny parquet-floored foyer with a carpeted living area to our right which contained a red fabric sofa, glass coffee table, and a black dresser. A finely lacquered desk held a paper tray with rubber-banded envelopes, pencil holder, and a manual Olivetti typewriter in a protective cover. Four black bookcases took up much of the apartment's wall space. A Murphy bed was attached to the far wall near a door to a bathroom. A makeshift clothes rack held suits, trousers, and shirts.

We headed toward the kitchen area, where, on the floor between the sink and small wooden table and two chairs, the black marker outline of Henry Casman's body on the floor stopped us. And on the counter near the sink sat a six piece, wood block knife set, with the largest slot empty.

Grandfather handed the Polaroid to me and fished out from his suit jacket three pairs of latex gloves and handed one pair each to us. He pointed under the table. "We are very eager to retrieve that small piece of paper, yes?"

I pulled my gloves on. "I'll get it, Zaida."

I carefully picked up the paper and showed it to Aliya and my grandfather.

Grandfather took the paper and held it up. "Nuh, nuh, my children, what have we discovered? What is this scrap of paper?"

"It's a ticket," Aliya said slowly, "a bus or train ticket for a company called Bridgeton Transit for travel between New York and Vineland." Aliya's eyes widened. "Vineland! Isn't that where Martin lived in New Jersey?"

"Yes," Grandfather said, "your memory serves you well."

"But what does Bridgeton Transit have to do with Vineland?" Aliya asked.

"Ah," my grandfather answered, "that may be an easy question to answer. Just yesterday, I perused a map of southern New Jersey. Bridgeton is a town approximately fifteen miles southwest from Vineland. I surmise that this transportation company originated in Bridgeton, therefore the name. And the mode of transportation would be bus as I believe no trains run directly between Vineland and New York."

My lips tightened. "Unfortunately, it implicates Martin since he has a connection to Vineland."

My grandfather's eyes narrowed. "Yet, are there no other possibilities? Could Mr. Casman himself have been the traveler?"

"Probably not, Zaida," Aliya said. "At least not with this ticket."

She gestured in all directions. "As I mentioned when we were examining the police report photos, Henry Casman doesn't strike me as the type to come home and not put away or discard the stub. So, to my mind, it came from his assailant."

My grandfather put his hand to his chin and nodded. "I tend to agree with you for one other reason." He handed me the paper. "Joel, might your young eyes validate my older ones? How do we know the terminus points of the traveler?"

"Hmmm, it says here 'Round Trip: 'Vineland—New York' and 'New York—Vineland'."

I shrugged and looked from Aliya to Grandfather.

"Nuh, nuh, Joel, Aliya, why was the traveler probably neither Henry Casman nor Martin Ross?"

It hit me as Aliya said excitedly. "Because then the ticket would have said New York—Vineland and Vineland—New York."

Grandfather's smile broadened. "Yes, exactly, it does not exculpate Martin, but it also does not incriminate him further."

Grandfather's smile faded. "One other question concerning the paper. Joel, is there a date on it?"

I looked carefully. "Uh-huh, there's stamped that—it's blurry—I think it reads, '5/28/76.' That's a day before the murder."

"Yes, indeed so, and it is another knot in our thinking that we must unravel. But one more thought to investigate. Is there at least one other individual of whom we are aware with a connection to Vineland?"

"Of course," I said. "Martin's stepson, what's his name, yeah, Peter, or Payshe, his Yiddish name. And he would be going from Vineland to New York and back."

Aliya closed her eyes and rubbed her temples.

"Are you all right?" I asked.

She gave me a tentative smile. "My head hurts, that's all."

Aliya's cheeks looked pale. *Why did her head hurt? She had never complained of a headache before.* I put a hand on her shoulder.

"You mean from all of the confusion around the case?"

Aliya hesitated briefly. "Yes, Joel, from the confusion around the case. And of course, because it involves Martin. Don't worry, I'll be fine soon."

I let it go and patted her shoulder.

Grandfather said, "Ay, ay, ay, yes, there is much confusion and possibilities that we must investigate. In a building that presents symmetry and order, and in an apartment that held precision and order, terrible disorder has occurred. We must shed light on the darkness in which this disorder occurred, must we not?"

"Yes, yes," we said simultaneously.

"Good then, Joel. You will please take a few pictures of the ticket stub. We will place the stub in a plastic bag I have with me and request the good officer, upon our departure, to bring them to Detective Carlucci."

Grandfather turned away from the kitchen. "Then shall we proceed to examine the rest of the apartment?"

I placed the stub on the kitchen table and took out the camera. "Certainly, Zaida."

* * * *

After I took the pictures, we all moved out of the kitchen. My grandfather put a finger to his lips. We didn't speak as we moved about the rest of the apartment. What an incredibly neat unit—except for the ten days of dust. Grandfather stood for a few minutes before each of the bookcases, not once touching any of the books, neatly lined up with the edges of the shelves. When I sensed he was at the end of his inspection, I said,

"Zaida, we should look into the dresser and desk drawers. Also the bathroom cabinet."

Grandfather hesitated. "Yes, we must do so. We are working on behalf of your client and for the sake of a complete investigation. Thus, we must violate Mr. Casman's privacy. Joel, Aliya, please do so. I wish to examine further the bookshelves."

We started in the bathroom cabinet. Spotless—the usual toiletries and over-the-counter medications tidily stored. The dresser only held assorted garments which I patted down—nothing but fabric. Besides a sheet of stamps and white envelopes, chronologically sorted cancelled checks going back seven years, filled the desk drawers. No outstanding bills—Casman probably paid them as soon as they arrived. We weren't going to go through all of the checks, but I made a mental note to request bank records going back a year.

"Zaida," I said. "I was hoping as part of our search to learn how Casman made a living. We really don't know, do we? And it might link to the murder."

"Maybe we do," Aliya said pointing to the desk. "The answer may be on top of the desk and not inside. I quickly thumbed through the envelopes in the wooden tray. I'm pretty sure they're pay statements since there are no stamps on them. The recipient is 'Henry Casman' with no address, and each is from the German Reparations Office in Manhattan."

I put my arm around Aliya and had no intention of hiding my proud smile. "Zaida, is there something you'd like to say about my *kallah*?"

My grandfather grinned. "I think you know my mind, and you have just spoken for me. An excellent discovery, Aliya."

Aliya blushed.

"But back to business. Zaida," I said. "The German Reparations Office are the folks who are negotiating with the German government to pay damages for the losses victims experienced during the War, right?"

His eye brows furrowed and his jaw clenched. I had rarely seen that look on him.

"Ay, ay, ay, Joel, you are correct if you are paraphrasing their stated mission. I do not mean to take away from the work they are doing, but the reimbursements are to the pitiable number of survivors for their losses and not to the more than six million who were murdered. Of course money payments can never be calculated for the dead. What dollar amount for a baby just born who will never take his first steps? What is the worth of his murdered mother, a young scientist ready to bring wonderful life-saving research to the world? And what value can be assigned to the baby's grandfather, having reached Shakespeare's 'sixth age' of his life, he eager to go down on his hands and knees in play with a grandchild. All never to be."

Grandfather looked down for a moment before meeting my eyes. "You will excuse my anger, please?" He waved his hand. "We must continue with our current task, as we do overall in life. Joel, might you later call the Reparations Office to determine if Aliya's conclusion is accurate. And if so, may I suggest you take a trip to their office for an interview concerning Mr. Casman?"

Shaken, I pointed to a telephone in the kitchen. "I…I can call now. It's probably their business hours."

"Please, no, Yoeli. We do not have permission to use the phone. There will be, after all, message units charged to…to, I surmise, to Mr. Casman's estate. Please call from a phone booth or from home."

I nodded. "Okay, I will."

"Good. Let us then survey the room together. Does anything particularly strike you?"

I motioned toward each area of the apartment. "The bookcases, they dominate this small space, don't they? Casman was quite the reader."

"That is a good starting point, Joel. And what of the books in them?"

I answered quickly. "They're all alphabetized by author. I checked one row, and not one book's mis-shelved."

Grandfather nodded. "Might you have taken note of the subject matter of the books?"

I looked at Aliya. Where was my grandfather going? What did I miss that was apparent to him?

My grandfather motioned toward the nearest bookcase. "Please, my children, go over to that bookcase and tell me if there are any titles with which you have familiarity. Yes?"

We went over.

"*Man's Search for Meaning,*" I said quickly, pointing to the end of the top shelf, "by Viktor Frankl. I read it for a philosophy class in college. Frankl was a concentration camp survivor. I'll never forget one quote from him. Something like, 'Forces beyond your control can take away everything you possess except one thing. Your freedom to choose how you will respond to the situation.'"

Grandfather nodded vigorously. "I was well acquainted with Viktor and the Frankl family in Vienna before the War. Professor Frankl is a brilliant thinker."

Aliya pointed at a book on the second shelf from the top. "*The Reawakening,* by Primo Levi. We were assigned that book and *Death in Auschwitz* junior year in high school. I couldn't finish either after I learned Levi survived the concentration camp but killed himself after the War." She wiped her eyes. "The horrors were too much for me."

"Aliya, your reaction is fully understandable. What else, my children?"

"*The Last of the Just* by Andre Schwartz-Bart. We read it senior year in high school, not as Holocaust but as 20th century European literature." I took Aliya's hand and squeezed it gently. "It also was a tough read."

"Yes," Grandfather said. "It is a great novel that follows eight generations of a Jewish family to the family's end with the Holocaust."

I looked down at the bottom shelf. "I see *The Night Trilogy—Night, Dawn*, and *Day* by Elie Wiesel. Also, not the easiest books to read."

Grandfather shook his head. "They are not. And if you carefully examined each book in that particular bookcase, you would see that they are all fictional renditions or memoirs from people who lived through the Holocaust, mostly Jews and some non-Jews. For instance, there, on the bottom shelf, is a riveting autobiography by the Polish writer Seweryna Szmaglewska, *Dymy nad Birkenau,* or in English, *Smoke Over Birkenau*, written right after the War. Mr. Casman's edition is in the original Polish, which I am sure he spoke fluently."

I stared at my grandfather. He probably had read every book in Casman's apartment. I didn't remember any of these titles in the small bookcase in my grandfather's bedroom. But he was a constant library borrower, often going to the 42nd Street Library in the City. He would quote Einstein, who said, "The only thing that you absolutely have to know is the location of the library."

"Please, let us move to the next bookcase," Grandfather said.

Aliya and I scanned for a few moments before Aliya said, "There's *Death in Auschwitz*. I wonder why it's in this bookcase and not the other one?"

"Ah, my child, a very salient question. Most of the titles are not in English, am I correct? But regardless of the language, do you see any words in common?

We took a few minutes. I said, "There are a few titles in French and I think two in Italian that have '*collaborateur*' and '*collaboratore.*' Meaning 'collaborator,' right?"

Grandfather nodded. "And do you see the German '*mitarbeiter,*' and one instance of the Dutch '*medewerker*?" They also translate to 'collaborator.' And there is one book in Hebrew with *mishatef peulah*, also meaning the same. "Is there any other word that stands out?"

Aliya pointed toward a book with an Italian title. "I see a few books with 'K-A-P-O', *kapo*—am I saying it right?—in the title."

"Yes, you are pronouncing it correctly, Aliya. You are both familiar with the term, 'kapo?'"

We both nodded. Aliya said, "It's those Jewish people who collaborated with the Nazis in the ghettoes and concentration camps?"

"Yes, for now, my child, your definition is acceptable, except we should qualify by saying 'accused' of such activity. And that brings us to your question of why Primo Levi's book, *Death in Auschwitz*, is in this bookcase."

I jumped in. "Because as I remember, his book discusses the Jewish collaborators at Auschwitz."

"So this whole bookcase, my children is, is given over to..."

"Kapos or other types of Jewish collaborators during the Holocaust." I finished my grandfather's sentence.

"Yes, but not just Jewish. There were also non-Jewish collaborators in the camps and throughout the conquered German areas. And as for 'Jewish' collaborators, we are just beginning our analyses of what it meant to be one. Even 30 years later, it is a raw issue, and writers are hesitant to address it. I feel the immediate future holds more honest and intense discussions on this subject. However, for the present, with our allowed time growing short, you may have noticed that many titles in the third bookshelf contain 'Nuremberg,' where the trial of Nazis and accused collaborators right after the War was held, along with extended annals from the Belsen trials and the Jewish kapos trials in Israel."

"And the fourth bookcase," Aliya offered, "is only half full. I saw Malamud's *The Magic Barrel,* Wouk's *Marjorie Morningstar,* and a whole bunch of Yiddish books by Sholem Aleichem, Isaac Babel, and others who wrote before the Holocaust."

"So," I said, "Casman was much less interested in the type of books on that shelf as opposed to his interest, or should I say obsession, with the Holocaust."

"You will pardon me, Yoeli, but in reference to a Holocaust survivor, I do not believe we should ever use a word such as 'obsession' with its negative connotation to describe such a survivor's state of mind. Perhaps we might say immersed in or with a compulsion to read Holocaust literature. Yet, despite the word you use, how does your thought contribute to our understanding this man who was brutally murdered?"

I shuddered. I understood Grandfather's question. Aliya dropped onto the sofa, head down, hands around knees, jaw clenched, and body stiff. I touched her shoulder. "Are you going to be sick?"

She shook her head. "No, I just need a moment's break."

I patted her shoulder. Then, as I did when I was a child and needed comfort, I moved closer to Grandfather. "Zaida," I stammered, "we said that… Casman may have been with Martin in the concentration camp. Do you want to open the envelope Carlucci sent and see what the autopsy photo shows of his arm?"

He looked at Aliya. "I do not at this moment. We will look later."

Aliya raised her head. "I fully understand. I shouldn't be around if you discover something confidential about your client."

I said, "In one way it's too late. Aren't' we thinking…uh, conjecturing, that Casman hated Martin because…because, he thought he had been a kapo, some kind of collaborator with the Nazis!"

I clenched my fist and thought about my mother. That she may have given her affection to a murderer was bad enough. I had no conclusive evidence, but to a Nazi collaborator? And I had committed to defending him? I wanted to scream!

Grandfather's eyes narrowed even more. "Joel, I trust I do not have to remind you of your responsibilities as Martin's defense attorney. We will discuss your conjecture later, but consider for the moment that at this point we only have fragmentary information. Please do not declare Martin guilty in your mind, including his being a collaborator, prior to further investigation. Yes?"

I swallowed hard and nodded. Though my grandfather was right, I couldn't bring myself to say it.

We left the apartment with ten minutes to spare. Officer Coleman took the plastic bag with the bus stub, and we removed our gloves. Grandfather started toward the elevators, and I held Aliya back. I had tightly entwined her arm with mine.

"Martin may have been a kapo," I whispered.

"For now, don't even think it," she whispered back.

* * * *

Aliya and I sat with my grandfather on a bench at the front of the building, shaded by a large maple tree. Two men, both about Grandfather's age, were bent over a stone table chess-board about five feet away. Although traffic hummed up and down the parkway, the bicycle lane and pedestrian path, with mothers strolling with carriages or holding on to toddlers, gave a sense of retreat from a large city's bustle.

Grandfather inhaled deeply. "Ay, ay, ay, my children. Ay, ay."

Aliya touched his shoulder. "I'm going to leave now, Zaida. I have an appointment in the City, and you and Joel need to talk. I'm also meeting your mother, Joel, at the store and we're going to lunch."

Appointment? Did I know about an appointment? Aliya's going out to lunch with my mother wasn't uncommon. Maybe I'd forgotten about the appointment. My mind quickly went back to Martin—had he been a kapo?

"I'll walk with you until Avenue J. There's a phone booth, and I'll call the Reparations Office to make an appointment to see them. Okay with you, Zaida? I'll be back in about 20 minutes."

My grandfather nodded slowly. His eyes were raised skyward. I laughed to myself. *Was that the sound of a UNIVAC computer?*

A block down the avenue, Aliya grabbed my arm. "Joel, remember…"

I snapped. "Yep, that it's just a conjecture I drew from one visit to Casman's apartment. I know, I know."

Aliya's mouth tightened and eyes widened. I softened my tone. "Okay, I have a sworn duty to defend Martin with my best efforts, regardless. I will. It's just…I'm so shaken."

She nodded. We walked the rest of the way to Avenue J in silence, holding hands. When Aliya turned down J toward the subway, I closed the door to a phone booth, looked up the reparations office number in the directory, and dialed. A woman who identified herself as Mrs. Saperstein answered.

"You say you have questions about Henry Casman? Would you hold, please?"

When she said Casman's name, she hadn't said the Jewish equivalent of "May he rest in peace" or "May his memory be for a blessing." I would have to mention that omission to my grandfather. Two dimes later, she returned. "Are you able to come at 3:00? Mr. Bloch, our director, can see you then."

"Yes, thank you. 145 W. 24th Street, Room 304?"

"Yes," she said and hung up.

I ran. It took me just five minutes to get back to my grandfather. He still had his gaze to the clouds.

* * * *

I related my conversation with the woman at the reparations office, including that Mrs. Saperstein uttered no traditional words of sympathy for Casman.

Grandfather pursed his lips and slowly shook his head. "That is a salient observation, and a sad one, but it continues the description of Mr. Casman as a disliked man. Regardless, this negative sentiment should not in any way temper our work. We are seeking the truth as to what happened and why it happened. A disliked person brutally murdered also deserves justice and an understanding of why it occurred."

I shrugged. "Sure, Zaida," I said. Ironically, seeking justice for Casman was the easy part for me. But how well could I compartmentalize my new feelings about Martin given the suspicions lurking in my gut?

I nodded toward the envelope on my grandfather's lap. "Have you looked inside?"

Grandfather motioned for me to sit down. "No, Joel, I wish for us to examine the contents together."

He knew what interested me the most. He extracted a photograph. I looked down—a chill shot through me. Not because of the forensic picture of Casman's left forearm by itself, but because of the tattoo. I easily made out, 'A 1.890.'"

"You are thinking, what Joel?"

"I'm thinking… I'm thinking that with Martin's serial number so close to Casman's—21 apart, there's a good chance they were at Auschwitz at the same time."

"Yes, I believe they were at the camp at the same time. And they were probably liberated at the same time."

"And Martin may have been a kapo at Auschwitz, right Zaida?"

Grandfather lifted a finger. "Sha, sha, sha, Yoeli. Your conjecture is not misplaced at this time, but we need to delve more deeply with questions to others and then ask Martin directly."

"We're going to ask him if he was a kapo during the War?"

I thought for a moment and answered my own question. "Well, why wouldn't we? I know I have to defend him regardless of his answer, but we must ask."

He put an arm around my shoulder. "Good, then. Shall we look at the last four months of phone records Detective Carlucci sent for Martin and Mr. Casman?"

Grandfather withdrew his arm and took out two sheets of paper. He examined them for a few minutes before handing them to me.

I looked them over and asked, "Where's area code 609?"

"Ah, why do you wish to know?"

Grandfather knew why I asked. But as part of his "critical analyses" investigative method, he employed Socratic dialogue to stimulate the thought process. "Because," I said, "both Martin's and Casman's phone records show calls between a number in area code 609 and their numbers here in Brooklyn."

Grandfather said, "The 609 area code is for the southern portion of New Jersey including Vineland."

I turned sharply toward my grandfather. "And I can pretty much guess to whom that 609 number belongs."

"Yoeli, one need not guess. After we depart from this location, I will call Mr. Hoskins at the 42nd Street library. He is the head of the reference section. I have known him since the time I worked at the library over twenty years ago. It is possible, because many people here in New York have connections to friends and relatives in that area of New Jersey, the library contains a current Vineland phone directory."

My pulse quickened, and I winked at my grandfather. "Dollars to one of your cheese danishes that the number belongs to Martin's stepson."

Grandfather laughed. "Ah, but in this case, I do not accept your wager. Yes, Joel, that would not surprise me."

I scanned the log for Martin. Four calls over the last three months, each spaced about a month apart, to the same 609 number. I took a breath. All for five minutes or fewer. "I can understand calls between Martin and his stepson. But why would there be calls between his stepson and Casman?"

"Yes, Joel, and how many, and what are the dates of the calls?"

"Let's see, the first, March 28 of this year. It was from Casman to the 609 number. It lasted 41 minutes. The second, on May 11, lasted five minutes and came from the 609 number. The third, oh gosh, May 24, four days before the date on the bus ticket stub and five days before the murder. That call, from the 609 to Casman, lasted seven minutes. How did they even know each other?"

"A good question. And we will find out. I believe, Joel, a short trip away from Brooklyn is in our future."

I thought back to the dorm murder case when my grandfather and I traveled to Connecticut—which turned out critical to our investigation. Going to Vineland? That's what my grandfather must mean. Well, the only part of Jersey I knew was Fort Lee, across the bridge from Manhattan, where Aliya's sister and her family lived. With high-rises and heavy traffic, that part of New Jersey certainly didn't reflect as "The Garden State." But South Jersey, perhaps there I would see lush fields of vegetables and bucolic farms with cows in the pastures and chickens running around barnyards.

"I'm ready for a bus trip, Zaida. When do we leave?"

"Ah, but we have some sleuthing to be done which must precede our journey. You will be going to the reparations office this afternoon, yes? And tomorrow morning, I would like to visit Mr. Schneider at the burial society to which Martin sought admission. While you are in Manhattan, I will attempt to contact him. And, of course, we must once again question Martin. Let us establish the time to see Martin after I speak to Mr. Schneider.

"And as to our probable trip to the southern portion of New Jersey, I will research if there is a bus leaving New York tomorrow in the late afternoon or early Thursday morning, yes?"

I gently poked Grandfather on his shoulder. "You've got more energy than me. But I think I can keep up with you. I agree to the plan. It's 10:45, and not too hot,… yet. How 'bout we take a leisurely walk to Kornblatt's for brunch, and then I'll walk you back home? I've got plenty of time before I head to the City."

"Ah, the brunch suggestion entices me, but we must pay one more visit to someone in this building."

What was I missing? "In this building, Zaida?"

"Yes, do you remember from the police report a Mrs. Schnapper who says she heard Mr. Casman and Martin arguing right before the murder. In what apartment does Mrs. Schnapper dwell?"

I smiled. "In 6I, across from the murder scene. That apartment had its door open a crack while we were there."

Grandfather smiled. "And I will surmise that Mrs. Schnapper was watching us while attempting to listen to our conversations. Let us make our way back and question her about her witness statement."

"You mean, just barge in on her? She might not like it."

Grandfather shook his head. "'Barge' is not the correct word for how we will behave." He smiled. "We will not force our way into the woman's apartment. Rather, we will ring her bell and politely ask to speak with her. And she will let us in."

How could he be so sure? I trusted my grandfather, and anyway, the lady would be a key witness against Martin if we went to trial. At some point, she had to be interviewed. I rose. "Zaida, I'm ready when you are."

Grandfather stood up and linked arms. He pointed to the entrance. "Then let us, in our most *unbargeful* fashion, make our way to Mrs. Schnapper's apartment."

* * * *

We stood in front of 6I. No yellow tape by 6D any longer. Men were going in and out, removing the contents of Henry Casman's apartment. The door to 6I was still open a crack, held shut by a small latch chain. I rang the bell.

Immediately, a woman responded in a thick, European accent, "Yes, who iz dis?"

Grandfather motioned me to let him answer. In Yiddish, he said, "My name is Frank Wolf, a private detective, and I am with Mr. Joel Gordon, who is representing the man accused of murdering your neighbor, Henry Casman."

Growing up, I'd often listened to my mother and grandfather speaking German and Yiddish. I understood both languages well enough, but when I tried to speak either, out came a mixed patois. So, I rarely spoke them, and took Spanish in high school and college. Now, my grandfather would carry the questioning. Anything unanswered by the end, I'd jump in.

First, the door closed, and I heard the latch being moved. Then, the door opened. A short, thin, white-haired woman in a gray house dress looked us over, stopping at Grandfather. She also spoke in Yiddish. "I know you from the newspaper, Mr. Wolf. I read *The Forverts*. But I did not know how distinguished you look in person."

I almost laughed. *Another lady taken with Grandfather?* Was he still keeping company with Mrs. Wachter whom he'd met during the dorm murder case? Maybe Aliya was right—I should pay better attention to some things.

"And you, the lawyer for my neighbor's murderer, you are handsome." She pointed at Grandfather. There is a resemblance. You could pass for Mr. Wolf's grandson."

Motioning to come in, she said, "*Kiem arine*. There are enough people in the hallway."

We entered a small foyer. Grandfather almost closed the door, keeping it slightly ajar, and slid on the latch. He quickly peeked out to the hall.

"I thought you would wish the door left in the same position as you had it when we unexpectedly rang your bell," Grandfather said.

She flicked her hand. "That is thoughtful of you. Expected, unexpected, it is good to have company. It is now three years since my Mendel, may he rest in peace, passed away. My two boys are in California and Florida. They are busy with work and families. I understand they don't have time to visit their mother. So, I am often alone."

We moved into an apartment with a small kitchen to the left, followed by a door that led to another room. Probably the bedroom. A dining/living room area stretched the length of the apartment, straight ahead and to the right. Mrs. Schnapper directed us to sit on a green fabric sofa. She sat on a matching chair on the other side of a coffee table piled with photo albums.

"You are very observant, Mrs. Schnapper," said Grandfather, "Mr. Gordon also happens to be my grandson."

She lifted her brows and smiled at me. "Ah, I see from your ring, you are married. That is too bad because I could speak a good *shidduch* for you."

I fidgeted. *What should I say?*

My grandfather got me off the hook. "Yes, Joel would be a good match for anyone, and perhaps that is why he is married to a wonderful *kallah*."

"Nuh, nuh, nuh," Mrs. Schnapper smiled. "That is the way the world goes round. But that is not why you gentlemen are here, correct?"

My grandfather leaned forward. "Again, you are observant. We are here to understand better the witness statement that you gave to the police. But first, from where did you come before the War?"

"From where, you ask? Ah, a *shteteleh* called Kolchin, then in *Rusland*, which," she laughed, "is now in *Ukraina* which is still held by *Rusland*."

Grandfather also laughed. "So, you are a *Galitzianer*, yes?" He was referring to a now obsolete name for a region in Europe that before World War II spread over Russian and Polish territory. It also designated a type of Yiddish accent.

Mrs. Schnapper laughed. "Yes, I am and proud of it."

I grinned. I didn't know what this banter was about, but I was sure Grandfather had a plan.

"And how long, Mrs. Schnapper, have you lived across from Mr. Casman?"

"How long? We have been here since 1960, and he moved in about four years ago. But to tell you the truth, whether seeing him in the hallway or in the elevator or coming in and out of the building, we never talked except for an occasional '*Gitten tag*' between us. Not a friendly man like the Menshkoffs in 6E."

"Apparently, not a pleasant man. Please tell us, when you were interviewed by the police, did you speak to them in English? Or in Yiddish, and there was a translator?"

She laughed. "In English. A broken English, and I tried my best."

Grandfather nodded. "We are sure you did try your best, but could you please tell us everything you remember about Mr. Casman and his accused murderer, our client, Mr. Martin Ross, on the day of the murder?"

She put her hands to her temples. "Even in my old age, I still have a good memory."

We nodded, and she went on. "Your client was here, I think, twice. The first time around 5:30, as I was preparing to leave for *shaleshudes* at the Young Israel." She was referring to the traditional third meal of the Sabbath eaten communally at a synagogue or at a home.

"I heard them arguing in the hallway—I should say, my neighbor was hollering and your client was speaking in a lower voice."

I breathed rapidly, steeling my nerves. *I could do a simple sentence in Yiddish.* "Could you hear what they were saying?"

Mrs. Schnapper's eyes lit up. "Ah, you can speak a little Yiddish. It is good that the younger generation can do so. Could I hear what they were saying? Not everything, but it had something to do with a burial society. More, I could not tell, especially when they seemed to have gone into the apartment. A few minutes later, I came out, and there was your client backing out of the apartment with Casman pushing at him and shouting.

"I was a bit frightened, but I calmed down after your client had the decency to look at me and wish me a Sabbath greeting." He then walked quickly to the elevator. Without a word, Casman went back into his apartment and slammed the door behind him. By the time I got to the elevator, your client had already gone down."

"Very good, very helpful, Mrs. Schnapper," Grandfather said. "A question, please. How is it that you knew to identify our client as the man who may have murdered Mr. Casman? Did you know Mr. Ross previously?"

She shook her head slowly. "Know him? Not as a friend of even an acquaintance. I am familiar with many people at the building where he has an apartment, and they introduced him a few times when he passed by as we sat on the benches and talked. Nothing more. But I remembered his name—Ross—or at least that is what he is called in America. Also, a few days after I spoke to the police, they came back with a picture and asked if he was the one I saw on the day of the murder. It was of your client."

"Then the second time you saw him?"

She paused. "The second time, yes, the second time was around 9:30, Saturday night. I had come back from *shaleshudes* an hour before, changed, and was watching the *Newhart* man show which, when I understand, there is much to make me laugh. I heard a doorbell ring. I was not sure if it was mine which made me frightened—who would ring my bell so late at night—or the neighbor's?"

I snickered inside. *Couldn't tell her bell from the neighbor's. Really! What an excuse to snoop.*

"It turned out to be by Casman's apartment. I looked out and saw a man at his door. Casman opened it, and the man said '*A gitten ovent.*' Immediately, Casman began screaming at him, 'What do you still want from me? I told you not to come. I will not change my mind.' And other not nice words.

"The man seemed calm, and I couldn't hear exactly what he said, but somehow Casman let him into the apartment with the door closed. After five minutes, I heard a scream from Casman. I am sure it was Casman's voice, 'What are you doing?' and then a thud. A few minutes later, the man came out, closed the door slowly, and I heard the ring of the elevator which told me he had left."

Right away it struck me. Why had she called the alleged killer, "the man" and not "your client" or "Mr. Ross?" If Grandfather would not ask, then I surely would.

I needn't have worried. He did. "Mrs. Schnapper, I will share an assumption with you, and please tell me if I am right or wrong. The hallway was dark, you were looking through a crack, and you did not have a clear vision of who rang the bell, yes?"

She looked down. "You are not wrong."

"Then why did you tell the police that you saw Mr. Ross?"

Mrs. Schnapper furrowed her brows. "I never told the police who were asking me questions that I absolutely saw Mr. Ross. I told them I saw a man who sounded like Mr. Ross as they argued in the hallway. But no, I did not clearly see the man's face."

"Ah, it is good of you to clarify your testimony. Another question. Did you notice if the man carried anything?"

She thought for a moment. "Let me see. 'Carried,' no nothing in his hands. But I believe on his back he wore—what do they call it in English—a *beckpeck*, yes?"

Grandfather nodded. "Yes, we understand, a 'backpack.'"

He smiled broadly. "A big thanks to you, Mrs. Schnapper. Should there be a trial, Mr. Gordon will certainly ask you to be a witness for, as it turns out, and not against Mr. Ross."

"Yes, yes, but will I be able to speak in Yiddish?"

"I can arrange for a…*an iberzetz mensch*, a translator," I said in broken Yiddish and using the English word just in case.

Perhaps a last question, Grandfather said. "Are you sure the man said '*a gitten ovent*' and not '*a gutten ovent*'?"

Mrs. Schnapper tightened her lips. "My memory is as good today as it was when I was 20. He said '*gitten*.' For sure. Why are you pressing me?"

Grandfather shook his head. "No, no, no, it is not that I don't trust your memory. It is just I wanted to make sure I heard you correctly."

"Nuh, good then. All is understood," she said.

Grandfather rose, and I followed. I had no other questions.

Grandfather bowed. "Then we will say goodbye and thank you for your graciousness in welcoming us into your home and answering our questions."

Mrs. Schnapper moved closer to Grandfather. "It was a pleasure doing so, Mr. Wolf. And if you are ever of the mind, please pay me a visit. I am usually home."

* * * *

During the half hour we spent with Mrs. Schnapper, it had become much hotter outdoors.

"Zaida, are you still okay to walk to Kornblatt's?"

My grandfather lifted his fedora and replaced it. "Yes. Shall we walk in a leisurely fashion while we take a hiatus from our case and discuss the Mets, or the upcoming bicentennial, or the not too distant presidential election? Then, in the coolness of the delicatessen, we will share some reflections and what lies ahead for us. Good?"

I nodded and let my grandfather set the pace. He immediately brought up the election.

"I saw in the paper this morning that Mr. Carter will be the nominee of the Democrats. A fascinating development, no? A man little known to the public rises from obscurity while Mr. Humphrey, a known man, declines to enter the race and Mr. Jackson, also a known man, is disliked by a strong faction in his party."

I said, "Carter really did well in the primaries, didn't he?"

"Ah, a keen observation, Joel. This man, a peanut farmer from Georgia, saw what a Mr. Udall did not see—a new political process through the primary system—for better or worse."

I smiled. "And it seems the one-time host of *Death Valley Days* also understands how the process has changed." I referred to Ronald Reagan's mounting a challenge to President Ford's nomination. "Do you think Ford will hold him off?"

Grandfather thought for a moment. "Yes, I believe our president will prevail. But I sense Mr. Reagan is rising, and we will see more of him in future years."

When we came to Avenue J and the phone booth from which I had called the reparations office, my grandfather stopped.

"Joel, I apologize for interfering with our walk, but I wish to give Detective Carlucci a call concerning our conversation with Mrs. Schnapper, particularly her imparting to us that she did not clearly see Martin in front of Mr. Casman's door near the time of the murder."

"Good idea." The mediocre play of our Mets could wait while Grandfather made his call. Besides, we had another ten minutes before we got to Kornblatt's. Grandfather dove into his trouser pocket, brought out a coin purse, and entered the booth, keeping the door open. After dialing, he asked for Detective Carlucci. Grandfather drummed on the booth wall as he waited while three minutes went by and another of his dimes fell through the slot.

Finally, Carlucci came on. My grandfather said, "Yes, detective, it is Frank Wolf, and welcome back from your week's vacation. I hope your niece's confirmation ceremony was a happy family event."

A few seconds later, "Ah, good, detective. Unfortunately, there are two matters related to the murder of Mr. Casman I wish to bring to your attention."

For the most part, I couldn't hear Carlucci. Grandfather told him that he had sent the bus ticket stub with Officer Coleman and our assessment of the stub's import. I was half listening when Grandfather said, "I am pleased you have it for examination."

After Grandfather reported on our interview of Mrs. Schnapper, I heard yelling from the other end and snapped to full attention. Grandfather repeated three times, "Yes, detective," before ending the conversation with, "I understand and am very sorry for your upset. And I am glad you have an officer who speaks Yiddish to re-interview Mrs. Schnapper. I am eager to hear if the new interview bears out what we heard."

After a few exchanges of pleasantries, Grandfather emerged from the booth, shaking his head.

"Ay, ay, ay, Joel, I didn't know that the detective could be such a *schrier*," using the Yiddish word for "screamer."

"What was he upset about?"

Grandfather shook his head. "That his homicide colleagues were, what he called, 'inept,' in not seeing the stub under the table and, worse, for the superficial way Mrs. Schnapper was interviewed in English. He is immediately sending out a Yiddish speaking officer to interview the lady."

I gently poked Grandfather in the ribs and said, "It is good then that he also has Frank Wolf on the case, yes?"

Grandfather blushed, but I saw the twinkle in his eyes. "Let's us return to our own disappointment—our Mets, yes?"

* * * *

The lunch rush at Kornblatt's always began a few minutes after noon. We were still able to find a red vinyl booth toward the back where we could speak without being overheard. Along with Aliya, we had sat in that same booth during the Flaum murder case.

Standing near the swinging kitchen doors, the same waiter from last time, with his full head of gray hair tufted in the middle and the worn white velvet kippah with "Mo" stitched on the front, waved to us. He stopped another waiter passing by and pointed before moving our way.

Mo nodded at me and addressed Grandfather. "Well, well, well, Mr. Wolf, nice to see yuh again. Guess yuh solved another one last year, the rabbi's wife murder. Sad thing it was, but are yuh now workin' another case?"

Grandfather leaned toward Mo. "It is also nice to see you. But you certainly understand that we cannot divulge business. We can tell you that we are not, as it was last time, here to question you or any other member of the staff. But we appreciate your interest and are here mostly for your excellent offerings. I would like your salad with salmon and a glass of Sanka coffee. And you, Joel?"

I may have been only moderately hungry when we entered the deli, but the smell of freshly baked breads, barreled pickles, and cooked meats spurred me to ravenous. "I'll have pastrami on rye and a Coke." Mo took out a stubbed pencil from behind an ear and scribbled our orders on a small pad. "Yuh got it, gents. And by the way, Mr. Wolf, the Sanka is on the house."

My grandfather did not argue. We talked about the Mets until Mo returned with our orders. My pastrami, heaped high, obliterated sight of the bottom bread slice.

We began eating. I spoke in a low voice. "Zaida, the waiter's having an accent made me think about the way the building's super spoke. "Have you ever heard someone saying 'y'uns' before? What type of accent is that?"

Grandfather smiled. "Ah, I had never heard it spoken, but when I worked at the New York Public Library, I had much time to read. I wanted to acquaint myself with all regions in America, Therefore, I perused a book on American dialects and accents. I remember that Mr. Bunch's accent and his use of 'y'uns' is associated with Western Pennsylvania and some Appalachian areas."

I got up, put my hands on Grandfather's shoulders, and planted a kiss on his forehead. "You're amazing, Zaida," I whispered. "But I wonder what brought Bunch to Brooklyn?"

"What a nice boy," an elderly lady at a nearby table said loudly.

The corners of my grandfather's eyes crinkled. He went on. "It may be simply that he, like so many others, reversed Mr. Greeley's earlier call to 'go west' and came east for the opportunities a city such as New York offers. But we will keep your 'wonder' in mind as we deploy our critical analyses probes."

I nodded and changed the subject. "But back to Mrs. Schnapper, if it bears out from her re-interview that she can't conclusively state she saw Martin near the time of the murder, I'm going to file a motion to Judge Black to dismiss the charges."

Grandfather stroked his chin. "Your initiative has merit, Joel. Except…"

"Yep, I know, Zaida. Except there's still the matter that Martin's prints are on the murder weapon. It's worth a try, and if nothing else, it sets up in the record the line of questioning I would use with Mrs. Schnapper if we go to trial."

Grandfather sighed. "It is worth a try."

Just then, Mo approached and placed another large glass of hot water, a Sanka packet, and non-dairy creamer before my grandfather. "I thought yuh can use another one, Mr. Wolf," he said. "Also on the house."

"Very gracious of you and very welcome, Morris. Thank you." Mo bowed and left.

Grandfather took a sip of his coffee. "Is there anything, Joel, you would like to bring up from our conversation with Mrs. Schnapper?"

"I do have a question for you," I said quickly. "That exchange you had with her—when you asked if she remembered correctly if the man she saw at the time of the murder said to Casman, '*a gitten ovent*' or '*a gutten ovent*.' What was that about?"

"Ah, Yoeli, would you know in what Yiddish accent the people speak who come from the Druya region, Martin's home of origin in what was then Poland?"

My knowledge of Yiddish accents was shaky. I shook my head.

"Ah, the Jewish people who come from that region speak with what is called a '*Litvak*' accent. Mrs. Schnapper clearly saw Martin in the hallway. She told us that he gave her 'a Sabbath greeting' which would have been a *Litvak sounding*, '*a gutten shabbos*'."

"And," I interrupted, "the man in the second instance said, '*a gitten shabbos*', with a *Galitzianer* accent. Therefore, the "man" Mrs. Schnapper heard at the time of the murder, presumably, but very presumably, would not have been Martin."

Did I hit on something important? I continued, "And, and if so, then it's evidence that it wasn't Martin the second time, right?"

I took a breath. "I was thinking of adding this information to my motion. Zaida, do you think it's too confusing?"

"Ach," my grandfather said, "not only confusing, but perhaps the judge may also find it sophistry and esoteric misdirection. He may think," and Grandfather lifted a finger, "as we must also hold the possibility, that Martin was sly enough to fake the accent in the second instance to mislead a neighbor who speaks Yiddish and wishes to know everyone's business. But as we continue our investigation, we will hold this difference in accents closely in mind, yes?"

My lips tightened. "You're right. I'll leave it out of my motion. That's my only follow up to our conversation with Mrs. Schnapper."

Grandfather had finished his salad. He hadn't touched his second glass of Sanka. I had finished eating several minutes before.

I said, "Zaida, unless you have something else to discuss, I'll walk you back home and go on to the City to talk to the person at the reparations office."

My grandfather put out his hand. "I do not have any other matters to discuss. But lunch has invigorated me, and I would like to go to the subway station with you for travel to my office. My office is my favored place to review the case and make necessary calls. I do not wish to trouble you by asking that you return to Brooklyn since you will be already in Manhattan, but might you call me upon the completion of your interview? But before we leave, allow me to finish my second glass of Sanka so not to make the waiter feel that he was needlessly gracious."

"Okay, we'll leave when you finish that generous glass of coffee."

He smiled. "And let us tip Morris handsomely for his generosity."

* * * *

Grandfather said that he would walk the five minutes from the Jay Street stop to his office, so we both took the F train from the Avenue J station.

Before we got on the train, I said, "Zaida, let me give Mom a call to see if she's back from lunch with Aliya."

I entered a phonebooth, deposited a dime, and dialed. Rosa answered. My Mom had not yet returned. After lunch, Rosa said, they were headed for an appointment. There was that word again, "appointment." Aliya never did say what the "appointment" was for. I'd be sure to ask her when I got home.

On the train we spoke little—the subway's din made it hard to hear. My grandfather got off at Boro Hall, and I rode on to West 23rd street in the City, a block from the reparations office on West 24th.

The German Reparations Office was on the top floor of an early twentieth-century, red brick building wedged between two modern high-rises. Five gargoyles snarled down from a concrete cornice. A candy store with a luncheonette counter took up the bottom level. I entered through a glass door to the left of the store and bounded up the stairs to the third floor.

I stopped before room 304 with GERMAN REPARATIONS OFFICE written in black on the frosted glass door. I knocked. When a woman's voice called, "Yes," I stepped inside.

The small, high-ceilinged office had three large, rectangular windows against the right wall. An air conditioner stuck out from the middle window and loudly labored to cool the room. Overflowing bookcases and open file cabinets of various sizes took up the left wall. Tables on each side of the door held stacks of telephone books and file folders. Five gray steel industrial desks cramped the room. Four of these desks had mishmash arrangements of folders with files protruding piled high. Four middle-aged women sat before vintage typewriters, tapping with two fingers.

No one sat at the fifth desk, toward the back right corner. It held an old typewriter, neatly piled folders, a stapler, wooden in and out trays, and four pens symmetrically laid and pointing in the same direction. *That had to be Casman's desk.*

The woman closest to the door looked up and gave me a faint smile.

"Are you Mrs. Saperstein?" I asked.

She nodded toward the woman at a desk behind her. "Rachel, a man here to see you."

What a contrast to the typing pool at my firm, where 30 young women took up half a floor, touch-typing over 100 words a minute on IBM Selectrics. I moved toward Mrs. Saperstein.

"Hello, I'm Joel Gordon. I spoke to you earlier today about Henry Casman, and you told me to come at 3:00 to see Mr. Bloch." I looked at my watch. "I'm afraid I'm ten minutes early."

The woman eyed me. "You're a lawyer! They make them younger and younger. And I didn't know lawyers dressed that way during a business day."

I smoothed out the wrinkles in my light, summer trousers. She was referring to my not wearing a suit. *Should I have worn a suit?* I reached for my wallet and took out a business card and handed it to her. "Yes, as you can see, I'm with Prentice, Walters, & Reis, and, as I mentioned on the phone, I'm the defense attorney for my client, Martin Ross, who is accused of killing Henry Casman."

She jerked her head toward the back of the room where a door to an inner office read, Solomon Bloch, Director. "Just knock once and walk in. He is expecting you, Counselor."

I did as instructed. Solomon Bloch sat behind a large wooden desk piled with files, newspaper clippings, and open envelopes. An air conditioner, quieter and performing well, stuck out from a single window on the right. The left wall had closed paper and steel file cabinets marked by the name of countries. I spotted US, Israel, and France. On the wall behind him hung a portrait of President Ford and a map of Europe with dozens of pins. An American flag hung from a pole in the room's left corner.

The man motioned me to a wooden arm chair in front of the desk. He closed a folder, took off his glasses, stood, and offered me his hand. He was thin. A thick mustache accented his face. A bald pate, illuminated by the fluorescent overhead light, shone between two well-barbered rows of brown hair.

Sleeve garters around his upper arms held his loose-fitting, green pinstripe shirt in place, and a belt on its final notch, held up his baggy beige trousers. On this hot day, he wore a yellow, buttoned sweater vest.

"Solomon Bloch, Director, how can I help you Mr....?"

I took out another card and handed it to him. "Joel Gordon, from Prentice, Walters, & Reis. I am defending Mr. Martin Ross who is accused of murdering your employee, Henry Casman. He was your employee, correct?"

We both sat. Bloch smoothed his mustache and hunched forward. "Yes, Henry was employed by our office, but on a part-time basis—twenty hours a week. But I cannot think of anything that will help your defense?"

I took a breath. Start slowly, allow Bloch time to adjust to my questioning. "Mr. Bloch, my client categorically denies his guilt. I am interviewing people who were acquainted with Mr. Casman to get a sense of his personality and learn about any factors that may explain why he was murdered and by whom."

I paused and opened my hands. "So if I may, how long had Mr. Casman worked in this office?"

Bloch eased back in his chair. "Henry had been with us for five years. You used the term, 'acquainted,' and that's the deepest I would describe any of our relationships with him. Was he married? I don't know. How did he get through the War? No idea. Did he ever accept an invitation to dine with any of us? Never. So what I can tell you is only from a supervisory perspective."

I nodded. "What kind of an employee was he? How was his work?"

Bloch picked up a pencil and twirled it as he spoke. "Unfortunately, given the exceedingly important work that we do, we ask our investigators—those ladies on the other side of the door—to close cases on a quota basis per the hours of work they put in. Most struggle to achieve their goals. But Henry...Henry would come in for his five-hour day, four days a week, and meet his goal within three or four hours."

"Then he worked on additional cases? I asked.

Bloch snickered and shook his head. "He did not. Although for the sake of many elderly survivors who are struggling to make ends meet, working additional cases would have been greatly helpful. But he did not."

Bloch halted and raised his eyes.

"Instead..." I said.

"Instead, he reviewed files that were not assigned to him to 'learn more about the War.' Those were his words, but I knew what he was doing."

I leaned out. "And that was...?"

Bloch put the pencil down and rubbed his eyes. "He was Nazi hunting, looking for information, I am convinced, on where to find those beasts who have, to this point, evaded accountability for their crimes."

He pointed to himself. "And how did I know this? I saw on his desk correspondence from Simon Wiesenthal. You know the man who helped track down Adolph Eichmann in Argentina. Not that I was snooping, but as I would pass by his desk in my official capacities, I saw envelopes. And they were always gone after he left."

My stomach churned. *Casman was a Nazi hunter. If he was closing in on someone, could that person have found out about his work and killed him? Was there an organization of escaped Nazis hunting the hunters?* I had to stay on track and find out more.

"Did Casman ever appear as if he feared for his life?"

Bloch shrugged. "I don't know. I never heard of such fear coming out of his mouth."

"Is there anything he did say, Mr. Bloch, that has stayed with you?"

He thought for a while and said, "No, I don't…well yes, one thing."

When Bloch hesitated a few moments, I prompted him. "Please go on, what did he say?"

"I wish to be precise, Mr. Gordon. All of us in this office are either Holocaust survivors or have relatives who perished. At lunchtime, we often are together, eating our home-made lunches, and we share bitter thoughts about the War and about the pitiable rectifications and reparations for which we work. In its way, we find it therapeutic to let out our emotions.

"Mr. Casman never participated, except once. About four months ago, he surprised us when he shouted, 'And the kapos, those Jews among us who helped the Nazis, they too must be identified and punished.' He never joined us again in our conversations."

Bloch frowned and looked away. Puzzle pieces were interlocking, but I had many pieces to go to see a full picture. Bloch was partially correct. It wasn't just Nazis—Casman was also hunting Jewish collaborators.

"Did he ever mention anyone by name, anyone he thought of as a collaborator, a kapo, perhaps?"

Bloch resumed pencil twirling. "Hmmm… No, not that I remember. Perhaps he mentioned a name to the ladies, but I doubt it. I'll check with them after you leave and call you if someone remembers a name."

"Thank you. Please call me at my home number. It's on the card."

I stopped, leaned forward, and asked slowly. "Did he ever mention my client's name, Martin Ross?"

Bloch did not hesitate. "Never. I would recall if he did. Is there anything else?"

"No. Thank you for your time."

I rose, shook hands, said goodbye, and left his office, closing the door behind me. "Ladies," I called, trying not to shout. "Did Henry Casman ever mention the name, Martin Ross?"

They looked, one to another, each shaking her head. Mrs. Saperstein said, "But he must have known him, Counselor. After all, you are defending this Martin Ross for Henry's murder."

* * * *

My visit to the reparations office took only thirty minutes. I was in a cab headed to my PWR office on 54th and Lex by 3:30. I would have taken the subway, but I wanted to get my motion for dismissal to Judge Black and the Brooklyn DA's office prior to the PWR courier's leaving at 5:00. Before hopping into the cab, I stopped at a phone booth and called Detective Carlucci to see if Mrs. Schnapper had been re-interviewed.

"Big time case, you're on, Joely, good for you," Carlucci said. He sounded sincere. "Nice that you have your grandpa in your corner. He really knows his business, especially when it comes to you Jewish folks."

"Yes, thank you, Detective. I was wondering if you had an opportunity to…"

"To interview that neighbor of Casman's with a Jewish speaking officer? Yep, sure did. Got the typed report right in front of me."

Carlucci laughed. "And in English. Says right here, the lady wasn't able to say absolutely that the man she saw arguing with the victim near the time of the murder was your client."

I thanked him and hung up. Then I called my office and outlined my argument to Julie, the paralegal for our team. When I arrived at 3:55, she met me with a draft. I dictated finishing touches to her. I almost made it to my office without anyone else seeing me, but as I unlocked the door, I heard, "Dress code, sport?"

I very well knew Chip Holden's Harvard-by-way-of-Andover voice. I'd respond with Brooklyn class. I turned.

"Nice to see you too, Chip. Thanks for covering for me while I work my criminal defense case."

I didn't wait for a response.

* * * *

My desk clock read 4:45. Was my grandfather still at his office? I dialed his number.

Grandfather answered on the second ring. "Joel, I am pleased that you are able to call before I departed at 5:00. That I should not forget, we have an appointment with Mr. Schneider in his office for the Druya/Myori Benevolent Society in Boro Park tomorrow morning at 9:00. His address is 1365 56th Street. I spoke to the gentleman, and he is eager to see us. Does that time accord with your schedule?"

"Yeah, sure, Zaida. I'll also call Martin and have him come to your office at, say 11:30? How about I meet you 8:45 at 13th Avenue and 56th, and we can 'perambulate' the street together?"

Grandfather laughed. "Yes, 11:30 tomorrow with Martin and yes, Yoeli, a pleasant proposal for our perambulation. Although the modern generation is not so much taken with leisurely walks that allow for reflection, I believe I will make you into a 'perambulator,' nevertheless.

"But as much as we would like to jest, we have pressing business at hand. How did your interview at the reparations office proceed?"

"Great, Zaida. I think we have some new and important information. While Casman worked part-time as a reparations investigator, he used the files in that office for another purpose."

I paused. "He was a Nazi hunter. And, from something I heard that he had said to others in the office, you might guess, he was also a…"

Grandfather said quickly. "Mr. Casman also sought out the identities and locations of Jewish collaborators and kapos, yes?"

"Yes, I'm pretty sure. But that information leads me to the following. If he was a Nazi hunter, might his murder be the act of a hidden Nazi, or a secret group of Nazis, who felt he was closing in on one or more of them?"

Was my grandfather as equally excited as I by my news and theory? I waited.

He spoke slowly. "I am digesting your information as I respond back to you. It is possible what you hypothesize may be so. We are hearing often from reliable investigative reporting that escaped Nazis, especially in South America, have joined together in hiding each other's identity and in mutual protection—especially after Eichmann's capture sixteen years ago.

"Yet, from the analysis of the facts you presented, I am surmising that Mr. Casman's murder is not out of the mold of a Frederick Forsythe novel such as *The Odessa File*, but rather the entanglement of individuals known to each other dating back to the Holocaust."

I squeezed the receiver. "Are you saying you know who killed Casman. "Or are you saying you think Martin did it?"

"Sha, sha, sha, Yoeli. I do not at this point know the identity of the killer. And while I cannot demonstrate with certainty, I do not believe Martin is the murderer. But allow me to postulate why I do not believe an organizational cabal is behind Mr. Casman's death.

"First, Mrs. Schnapper heard the probable murderer speaking Yiddish as he forced his way into Mr. Casman's apartment. Now is it possible the killer was capable of assuming a convincing *Galitzianer* Yiddish accent? Perhaps. But a German speaking Yiddish tends to have a *Litvak* accent as you hear from me or from your mother. Could someone Jewish with such an accent be a hired murderer? It is again possible. But did not Mr. Casman, according to Mrs. Schnapper, shout, 'What do you still want from me? I told you not to come. I will not change my mind.' So Mr. Casman knew his killer from a previous interaction and addressed him in Yiddish."

I switched hands holding the phone. Grandfather was right. I had let a moment of Hollywood-induced plotting get the best of me. But I had my own counterargument in support of Grandfather's view to offer. "And Zaida, there's still the fact that Martin's prints are on the knife. Even if it's possible to counterfeit fingerprints, why would whoever planted them choose to frame Martin? For me, the complexity of such intrigue is too much to be plausible."

"No, Yoeli, you say 'too much to be plausible.' At this point, let us keep open the possibility of such an 'intrigue.' And yes, ay, ay, ay, Martin's prints on the knife. I will guess that when you hear back from Judge Black on your motion to dismiss, he will not please you with his response. Therefore, we continue on, yes? Was there any other intelligence gained from your visit?"

"Well, nothing new when I say that Casman, when he wasn't Nazi or collaborator hunting, did his job well and did not interact with the others socially. I'd say he was not liked, but certainly not disliked enough for anyone there to wish him harm."

"Good then, I have spoken to your mother. She wishes to help us in our endeavors surrounding Martin and insists that she will drive me to Boro Park tomorrow morning on," Grandfather laughed, "her circuitous way to work."

"What time did you speak to Mom?"

"What time?" Grandfather thought for a moment. "I had looked at my watch. It was at 2:45."

So by 2:45, after being out for about three hours, my mother and Aliya had returned from lunch and the "appointment." My mother rarely took off that much time from work. I lost track of what Grandfather was saying.

"Joel, are you still there?"

"I am. I was just distracted for a moment. Thinking about the case. I'll see you tomorrow morning."

"Yes. Try to achieve some relaxation this evening. There is much on your mind."

I dialed our apartment. Aliya answered. "Hi. Where are you? I've started preparing supper. I had a nice few hours with your mom. Came home and felt like cooking. Chicken Paprikash, from your mother's recipe. When will you be home?"

Aliya was feeling better, but I would still ask about the "appointment" when I got home. "In the office, about to leave after I make one more call. See you in about 45 minutes."

* * * *

My next task weighed on me. I sat at my desk and dialed Martin's number. He picked up on the first ring. His "Yes, how are you?" came out slowly.

"Good, Martin. My grandfather and I would like to ask you a few more questions tomorrow at 11:30 at his office. Does that work for you?"

Martin sighed deeply. "I guess in my situation, meeting with my defense team is not a matter of having any higher priorities."

He stopped breathing heavily. I waited. Then, "I apologize, Joel. I am not myself. Of course I will be there at 11:30 tomorrow. But might you share with me what other questions you have that I did not address yesterday?"

How much to share at this time? For the most part, my grandfather did not like to tell an interrogee the questions before a face-to-face interview. But did Martin's being my client dictate that I act differently? Did my being a rookie defense attorney jeopardize his defense? My hesitation didn't go unnoticed. "Joel, are you still there?"

I took a breath. Doing it my grandfather's way seemed the right approach for now. "Yes, yes, I am. Some things came up in our investigation today that need clarification. It'll be better if we talk about them tomorrow in my grandfather's office. Okay?"

Martin didn't push further. We'd see each other tomorrow.

I rushed out and took the #6 train to 14th Street, jogged to Stuyvesant Town, and arrived in the time predicted.

* * * *

The smell of the Chicken Paprikash, with it slow-cooked onions, garlic, and paprika greeted me as soon as I walked into the apartment. I loved that dish growing up. Grandfather had told me that although it originated in Hungary, the Viennese upper classes adopted it around the turn of the 20th Century, and it soon became a favorite of all classes. The Jewish cooks in Vienna's Leopoldstadt neighborhood replaced the lard with oil or chicken fat, and it became a staple of Sabbath-eve meals.

Aliya was in the kitchen humming Paul McCartney's "Silly Love Songs."

"Just in time," she called. "Supper is almost ready. Want to help me put together a salad?"

I hugged her from behind. She turned and carefully moved a spoon of Chicken Paprikash sauce toward my mouth. I licked the spoon.—*Delicious. My mother would be proud.* But I had one thing on my mind.

"I never did have a chance to ask. What appointment did you go to with my mother after the two of you had lunch?"

Aliya blushed, hugged me, and whispered in my ear. "You know, Joel, it's one of those girl appointments, and it was nice that your mother accompanied me. It was to a ladies' doctor practice at NYU Langone, on First and 32nd."

She released me, looked me in the eye, and smiled. "And everything is wonderful. Not to worry. Okay?"

I exhaled and smiled back. "Okay, I admit I was a little worried. Thanks. And I'm hungry. I'll get going on the salad."

"Before you do, is there anything you can share about today?"

"Hmmm," I said. *What could I tell Aliya while still upholding attorney/ client confidentiality?* I gave her a summary of the rest of the day including the visit to Mrs. Schnapper and to the German Reparations Office.

"Great, great," Aliya said. "I won't push for details." She shuddered and shook her head. "But nothing in either visit explains Martin's prints on the knife? You don't have to answer."

But I did answer. "Nothing."

I started preparing the salad. *Happy Days* and *Laverne and Shirley* were on at 8:00. I needed a break from the day's tensions. *Except.* I asked Aliya, "Should I call my mother when she gets home from the store and update her on what I can about the case?"

Aliya nodded. "Yes, I think your mother would appreciate it. Will it be hard to figure out what you can tell her?"

"I've made up my mind about what *not* to tell her—about any suspicions that Martin may have been some sort of a collaborator. I don't know what he's said to my mother, but at this point, it's premature for me to tell anything about it."

I'd try to call my mother at 7:30, after *The CBS Evening News* and before the sitcoms at 8:00. I also wasn't going to mention that Martin was coming to Grandfather's office tomorrow for another interview. If Martin wanted to tell her, that was up to him.

WEDNESDAY, JUNE 9, 1976

I had set the alarm for 7:15. The phone rang at 7:00.

"I'll get it," I said to Aliya. "I'm about to get up, anyway."

I ran to the kitchen and grabbed the receiver on the third ring. "Good morning, Joel," my grandfather said.

"It's Zaida," I called to Aliya.

"Good morning, Zaida."

"I have just taken a call from Detective Carlucci. Perhaps he should have contacted you directly, but he informed me that William Bunch, the super in Mr. Casman's building, is in custody."

My heart pounded. *Bunch, in custody! Has he admitted to killing Henry Casman?* "Zaida, Bunch is being charged with the murder?"

"Ah, Yoeli, I, too, had such a first thought, but the detective quickly disabused me. No, it seems Mr. Bunch's fingerprints were found in Mr. Casman's apartment. They matched arrest warrants for burglary and an unlawful flight from Butler County near Pittsburgh that go back many years."

My hope hung by a thread. I held on. "But he might have killed Casman, right? What was he doing in Casman's apartment?"

"Ah, the detective has clarified this question. It seems besides Mrs. Schnapper, a different neighbor heard disturbing sounds from Mr. Casman's apartment and decided to ring the doorbell around fifteen minutes after the sounds subsided. When no one came to the door, the neighbor called Mr. Bunch and suggested that he see if there was anything amiss."

My jaw tightened. "And he did go in, didn't he? He would have had a master key. And he must have seen Casman dead if he wasn't the one who killed him. And he didn't call the police? Incredible!"

I couldn't remember what the law was in New York for not reporting an obvious crime, what's called "misprision of a felony."

My grandfather took a few seconds to respond. "Unfortunately, the actions of human beings when they carry an internal darkness, or when a societal darkness covers them, no longer spurs within me a sense of incredibility. But I digress. Our detective friend believes that Mr. Bunch had nothing to do with the murder. He bases his conclusion on the sequence of events reported by the two neighbors, Martin's fingerprints on the knife, and Mr. Bunch's own recount of his behavior in the apartment, including taking fifty dollars from Mr. Casman's wallet as rightfully his for never having received 'welcome money.' Mr. Bunch has waived an extradition hearing and will be taken back tomorrow to Pennsylvania."

As I surveyed my dashed hopes, Grandfather sighed. "Ay, ay, ay, Yoe-li. We do our best in a sordid world. Today at 9:00, we will visit with Mr. Schneider in Boro Park as we persist in our investigation and defense of Martin, yes?"

"Yes, as we agreed, we'll meet at 13th and 56th. By the way, how's Mom?"

When I spoke to my mother the night before, she listened and did not ask any questions. She just thanked me for the call. "Joel," my grandfather said, "your mother is a strong person. She should not be underestimated. I know she was very appreciative that you had the consideration to call her. I will see you in a few hours."

I didn't need to leave for another forty-five minutes. By the time I was off the phone with Grandfather, Aliya was scrambling eggs. She had an appointment at 9:00. But I knew about this one—she was meeting her director at the Stuyvesant Psychology Group, a fifteen minute walk away, to discuss her responsibilities when she began work in just under two weeks. After that meeting, she'd head to an all-day orientation session.

I again decided not to wear a suit, but I did put on a long-sleeve, button-down shirt along with a wide, floral Kipper tie that I never wore to the office. At 7:45, I was in the bedroom preparing to leave. The phone rang again. Aliya answered. After a brief exchange, Aliya called me. "It's Julie at PWR." She handed me the receiver.

"Mr. Gordon," Julie began, "a courier just delivered an envelope from Brooklyn Criminal Court. Do you want me to open it?"

I quickly said, "Yes, please, and tell me what's in it."

I heard paper rustle. "Mr. Gordon, it's from Judge Black. Here's what's written: 'Nice try, Counselor. I would have expected nothing less from a fellow Brooklyn Law grad. So the snoop next door can't clearly identify your client as the man who was arguing with the deceased at about the time of the murder. A point in your favor. But…'"

Julie hesitated and said. "The next sentence is all in capital letters. 'WHAT COUNTERS YOUR ARGUMENT ARE YOUR CLIENT'S FINGERPRINTS ON THE MURDER WEAPON.'"

She hesitated again. "Back to upper and lower case, 'I remember suggesting that you get yourself a Sherlock Holmes detective to help you. When your Sherlock can explain how your client's prints are on the murder weapon and he didn't do it, then send me another motion for dismissal. For now, Counselor,' again in upper case only, 'MOTION DENIED.' I'm sorry, Mr. Gordon."

"It's okay, Julie. It was a long shot. Thanks for letting me know."

I hung up and called to Aliya who had gone to the bedroom. "No surprise. The judge declined my motion for dismissal."

Aliya came out and hugged me. "You tried." She looked at the kitchen clock. "It's nearly 8:00, so you better get going."

I ran out of the apartment and jogged to the Union Square Station. Subway luck was with me. A #4 train heading toward Brooklyn had just pulled in. I switched to a waiting D at Atlantic Avenue and got off at the 55th Street stop at 8:43. My cordovan loafers weren't the best shoes for running, but two minutes later, I was at 13th Avenue and 56th. Grandfather, of course, was already there.

* * * *

My grandfather took my shoulders and gave me a quick hug. "You are red in the face, Yoeli, as if you have been running, yes?"

I saw the twinkle in his eyes. I said, "Uhumm. Shall we walk down to 1365?" As we walked, I told him about the rejected motion to dismiss.

"As anticipated," he remarked.

The address was halfway between 13th and 14th Avenues. Houses were identical-looking duplexes with ten-step stoops and thin, black wrought-iron fences that separated one, small front yard from the next. Most duplexes had a pear or oak tree in front of both units, but 1365 had its own, small linden tree in its fenced-off area that shaded most of the dry grass.

We slowly climbed the concrete steps to a tiny landing. I pulled open the storm door, and Grandfather rang the bell. A heavyset, jowly man opened the door, looked us over, and smiled. A large felt kippah covered his wide, balding head. He wore a buttoned, short-sleeve white shirt with ritual fringes looping out of both sides of black trousers into side pockets.

He reached out his hand to Grandfather. "*Shalom aleichem*," and then in accented English, "You are the detective, Mr. Wolf, who called me yesterday." And to me, "And you are Mr. Gordon, the lawyer for the murderer of Henoch, or should I say, Henry Casman?"

I flinched. Why was the man so sure Martin was the killer? After all, he didn't say "accused murderer" or Martin's name which he certainly knew. Nevertheless, I joined my grandfather in responding, "*Aleichem shalom*."

Grandfather followed with, "Yes, we are who you say. It is nice to meet you, Mr. Schneider."

We shook hands, and Schneider motioned us in. Grandfather swept his fingers over the mezuzah, two-thirds the way up on the right door frame, and put his fingers to his lips. I followed, and we both entered.

We stood momentarily in a small entry foyer with a descending staircase on the right and one ascending to the left. Schneider motioned us to the right, and we followed him down carpeted stairs to an open room. A sign on the

wall behind a large mahogany desk said DRUYA/MYORI AID AND BE-
NEVOLENT SOCIETY. Each block letter consisted of an individual piece
of paper on a long string.

Schneider beamed. "I see you are admiring the work of my seven-year-
old son who made the sign. Quite good work for a boy his age, no? He is my
youngest. I have six others, all good children."

He waved his hand toward two metallic folding chairs in front of the
desk. Schneider seated himself on a swivel chair behind the desk.

"May you continue to receive much *naches*," Grandfather said. "It is
wonderful taking joy in the accomplishments of our children."

"A dank, a dank." Schneider's beaming smile subsided. Fully turning to
my grandfather, he said. "You have questions for me?"

Grandfather took off his hat. A kippah remained on his head. "Yes, we
do. Thank you for welcoming us into your home and office. Do you wish to
speak in English or Yiddish."

"Ah, my preference is in English, for two reasons. The first, my children
speak English among themselves, so I wish to learn to speak better by speaking the language whenever I can."

He turned toward me. "And second, I am not sure how well Mr. Gordon
understands Yiddish, so it may be better for him."

My grandfather gave me a nod. "While Mr. Gordon does understand
Yiddish, your first reason has sufficient merits to proceed in English. Joel, do
you wish to begin?"

I exhaled. I had prepared my opening question. "Mr. Schneider, what do
you do for a living?"

His eyes lit up. "What do I do for a living? My name answers your question. You understand at least some Yiddish. What does a 'schneider' mean in
Yiddish?"

I was about to answer when he went on. "A 'schneider' is a tailor, and
when one has seven children with endless ripping of their clothes and growing out of their clothes, one after another, it is a good profession to be in.
Today, I will open my shop at 10:00 on the 13th Avenue. It is only a few
minutes' walk. We have no need to hurry."

My shoulders relaxed. I said, "And how long have you been president of
your society?"

Schneider thrust out his chest. "How long? Ask me how long the society has been in existence. Since 1956, twenty years. I have always been
president. Who else would want a job where there are 20 members and 30
opinions on many matters? But someone must do it, no?"

"Yes," Grandfather said, "it is important work you do. I am sure the
members are grateful."

Schneider snickered, but before he could say anything, I asked, "What exactly is the purpose of the society?"

He leaned back. "Ah, as we wrote down our purpose when we formed, to be a charitable organization which at first gave financial aid to those in need who came to America after the Holocaust from the neighboring communities of Druya and Myori which, before the War, were in Poland. If they had money problems, we would do for them what we could. We would provide loans to help them start a business, or gifts, no questions or repayments asked. What has become more and more important to us, to obtain several plots in one place at the Montefiore Cemetery in Queens for those who wish to be buried amongst their *landsleit*."

Schneider looked at me. "*Landsleit*, you know this word, yes?"

I pressed my lips together. I felt patronized. "Yes," I nodded. "Those who come from the same town or geographical area."

He turned to Grandfather. "Ah, you are right, he knows. Good. And one more reason for the society. Most of us like each other. We, what do they say in America, we 'socialize' together. Once a week, the men play Canasta or Casino, and the women, sometimes they play cards, but mostly they talk."

I tapped my fingers on my thigh. *Should I get to the meat of our questions or wait a little longer?* Grandfather solved my dilemma.

"Mr. Schneider, you say there are about 20 members. Kindly tell us if all members like to 'socialize.'"

Schneider waved a finger at Grandfather. "Ah, Mr. Wolf, I believe you have two questions. First, Henoch Casman…did he also 'socialize?' He did not. He refused invitations, and after a short while, we stopped asking. We did not mind. He was not a pleasant man."

"And the second question?" I asked.

"Yes, the second, young man, I am sure you also want to know about Moshe Rossinsky… Ah, excuse me, we are now in America… Martin Ross. When he arrived in Brooklyn a few years ago, he wished to socialize with us. At first we did not stop him, but when he was with us, the air, no—What is the word in English?— Ah, the 'atmosphere' was…uncomfortable. Perhaps he understood why. After a while, he stopped coming."

Grandfather crossed his legs and leaned back. "We did, Mr. Schneider, have those questions in mind. But please allow me two other questions. To begin, what made Mr. Casman 'not a pleasant man?'"

Schneider, elbows on desk, slowly rocked back and forth. "Henoch, ach, again, you know him as Henry, was always angry. We call each other by our first names, but because of the way he behaved, we addressed him as 'Casman.' If it wasn't about the amount of our dues, it was him wanting an accounting of every penny that we spent and arguing about the totals. But mostly, he was bitter and angry about the War. You see, when we come together to play cards and talk, we wish to be away, at least for a short while, from those memories."

Schneider looked at me. "What is it called these days? Our few minutes of 'therapy?'"

"Yes, 'therapy,'" I acknowledged and asked, "Was there anything in particular that he was angry about?"

Grandfather gave me a quick smile. Schneider continued to rock.

"In particular, yes, in particular, he was angry about the collaborators who helped the Nazis, may they rot in hell. And when I say 'collaborators,' yes, those who were not Jewish, but he was most angry with those among us who he felt cooperated with the *mamzerim*."

"Which leads to my second question," said Grandfather. "From the little we are putting together so far, are we correct that Mr. Casman thought Mr. Ross to be a collaborator because Mr. Ross was a kapo when the two of them were together at Auschwitz?"

The rocking stopped. Schneider paled and leaned forward. "Hear me, now, please. With my own eyes, I cannot say that I saw Moshe collaborating or that he was a kapo in the camp. The rest of us in our society survived by either being in the Partisans or by being hidden by a righteous gentile. Casman, at one of our business meetings with all members in the room, screamed that Moshe should not be allowed to be in our society. He shouted that Moshe's actions had led to the death of many Jews and that he despised him."

Grandfather narrowed his eyes. "And how did Mr. Ross respond?"

"He was calm and said quietly, 'You know, Henoch, that if I had not been forced to become a kapo, someone else would. Maybe even you.' With this, Henoch exploded and while screaming words that should not be said in public, started moving toward Moshe. A few of the men held him back. 'Never,' Casman roared, 'never would I have become a kapo. They could have shot me on the spot. Never.'"

Schneider shook his head and again rocked. "And Moshe, I remember word for word because he said the same thing at other times, answered, 'Henoch, I beg you, do not let the differences of our past rule our behavior today.'"

He paused and raised his eyes. "Moshe then added, 'You know I did much to help the prisoners. You were there, Henoch.'"

I said, "What did Mr. Casman say to that?"

Schneider placed both palms on the edge of the desk and pushed forward. "Casman shouted a date, 'October 7, 1944,' and stormed out."

He looked from Grandfather to me. "In private, one day, I asked Casman the meaning of the date. I, the others, were not familiar. Do you know the meaning of the date?"

I said, "No," and looked at my grandfather. *Should I know*? I racked my mind for a connection.

Meanwhile, Grandfather bowed his head and slowly said, "It is the day when there was a revolt of the prisoners at Auschwitz, is it not, Mr. Schneider?"

"Yes, yes, Mr. Wolf."

Grandfather raised his head. "Many know nothing of this occurrence. Only in the last few years has there been a recognition and a historical recording that counters the notion that those prisoners forced into labor such as the *Sonderkommandos*, who disposed of the bodies of the more than a million killed in the gas chambers, or the so-called kapos, who were chosen by the SS to perform supervision of orders and administrative tasks, acted passively and even brutally to save themselves."

My grandfather sat up straight and gripped the armrest of his chair. "No, what occurred on October 7, 1944, shows a different reality. These very same people, along with many women who were working in a nearby ammunition factory and who smuggled out dynamite for the revolt, rose up and fought their tormentors."

Grandfather opened his hands to Schneider. "Oy, oy, my friend," and then to me, "Oy, oy, my child, sadly the revolt achieved none of its objectives. Yes, a handful of Nazis were killed, but the larger result was the execution of hundreds of *Sonderkommandos* and kapos. A dozen women from the factory were shot dead. They had revolted from within and against the darkness that oppressed them. That date, October 7, 1944, must be known and remembered."

I gripped the sides of my seat. Grandfather's words unnerved me. I hadn't remembered his voice ever being so forceful. I wanted to raise my fist. I wanted to flee. I wanted to shout. But I didn't know what to shout.

I cleared my throat. I needed to focus on the case and keep questioning. "So, Mr. Schneider, Mr. Casman, for some reason, blamed Mr. Ross for... for what exactly?"

Schneider pushed himself back and thought for a moment. "The truth is, I do not know exactly. I can guess as much as you can, but for sure I cannot say."

Grandfather said. "That is a very reasonable response, Mr. Schneider. Joel, do you not also think so?"

I understood. We were going to interview Martin in just a few hours. There was no point guessing when we could ask him directly. "I agree, completely."

Schneider stood. "Then, gentlemen, soon it will be ten o'clock, and I must hasten to my shop."

My grandfather and I also rose. I raised my hand. "May I ask one more question? Mr. Casman opposed my client's obtaining a burial plot in the society's cemetery area. All other members agreed with him?"

"Ah, Mr. Gordon, you are not from the old country and maybe don't understand. Our wanting to be buried together is a final statement of our being reunited in holiness as a community in the memory and shadow of all the others who we lost. We declared clearly in the beginning that those who lie together in the end must lie in peaceful acceptance by everyone in the society. Henoch never changed his mind, and although the others did not agree with him, so it was to be."

"Thank you for your time," I said.

"And if you will provide me with your business card from your tailor shop," Grandfather said. "I am often on the 13th Avenue seeking bargains, and I may need, from time to time, your services."

Schneider took a card from his desk, bowed, and handed it to my grandfather. "*A dank und a gutten tog tzu eich,*" he said in Yiddish—"Thank you and a good day to both of you."

Grandfather bowed back. "*A gutten tog und a dank tzu dir eichet*"—"A good day and a thank you to you also."

* * * *

We took the D to Atlantic Avenue and switched to the #4. One stop later we got off at Boro Hall and walked the few minutes to Grandfather's office on Joralemon. We hardly spoke. Not on a train with the noise and people around. And besides, I was lost in my own thoughts.

I gripped my briefcase firmly as we rode. Walking from the station, I switched it from hand to hand. As we started up the three flights to his office, I said, "It's going to be hard interviewing Martin this time."

Grandfather stopped on the second floor landing. No one else was around.

"Joel, do not think that just because you are working on your first criminal defense case, it will be hard. For obvious reasons tied to a past darkness that we do not yet fully understand and, let us not deny, our own family relationships, I, too, sense nervousness in myself. But we have taken the case, and together we will proceed, yes?"

Had I appeared so agitated? What a question. Since I was a little kid, my grandfather always knew my emotions. "Yes, of course. It's 11:05. We've got some time to go over what Schneider told us and prepare for Martin."

Grandfather never left his office with the air conditioner running. He often said, "Who is to say that the world's energy is limitless?" Then with a twinkle in his eyes, "And a lower bill from Consolidated Edison is a good thing too, no?"

So when we entered my grandfather's hot office, the air fetid, I rushed to the window air conditioner and turned it on. Grandfather took a handkerchief from a desk drawer and offered it to me. I wiped the heavy stream of sweat from my face. I sat down in the middle guest chair and faced Grandfather behind his desk.

I leaned forward. "Slow me down, Zaida, if you think I'm racing ahead, but we now know that in Schneider's quoting Martin's own words, Martin admitted that he had been a kapo at Auschwitz."

My grandfather put up his hand. "But, Joel as I said earlier…"

My agitation kept revving. "Yes, yes, I did hear you, that not all kapos were automatically collaborators, that some did what they could to help their fellow prisoners. But now we have October 7, 1944, and what happened that day at Auschwitz, and what Martin may have done…or not done as part of the revolt." My leg tapped. I wanted to get up and move. Walk around the office. Something to channel my nerves.

My grandfather leaned back and placed his palms on the desk. I also leaned back and took a breath.

"So, am I right, Zaida, it's time to ask Martin directly about his being a kapo and zero in on what happened during the revolt?"

Grandfather nodded. "Ay, ay, ay, Yoeli, I will not patronize you by asking you to be less agitated. At this moment, you are assessing how the answers to these questions may affect your defense and how, fraught with our own emotions, they will influence your reactions to your mother's relationship with Martin, and how those of us who love your mother will behave around him."

He shook his head again. "But ay, ay, ay, in a few minutes from now, we must ask him. Yes, we must. And there are other questions, are there not?"

Other questions. Other questions. Certainly there must be. But what specifically did my grandfather have in mind?

"I'm sure there are, Zaida, but with time short, please tell me what you're thinking."

Grandfather took out a file folder from a desk drawer and removed some papers. I recognized the phone records for Casman and Martin that Detective Carlucci had given us.

"Zaida," I said, "you want to review the phone records again before we talk about our visit to Mr. Schneider? There may not be enough time for both."

"Yes, a quick perusal, as time is short." He took a quick look at each sheet and said, "The calls between Martin and his stepson are infrequent and brief. Martin made four calls to his stepson, Peter, and not one over five minutes. Mr. Casman has three phone conversations with Peter, one of them for 41 minutes. That is an expensive call. Joel, do you remember who called whom between Mr. Casman and Peter?"

"I do. That long call last March was from Casman to Peter. The other two, each much shorter, were close together in May before the murder and were from Peter to Casman."

"Yes, yes, good memory. Please consider what we have. Martin initiates calls to Peter, possibly to foster a relationship. The short calls suggest lack of success? Perhaps."

I interrupted. "And someone who for all we know was a total stranger to Peter, but who may have shared a dislike for Martin, speaks to him for over 40 minutes and again twice in the week before he's murdered."

"But those last two calls are significantly shorter, are they not?"

"Yes, one seven minutes and one five minutes."

"So, Joel, with every unravel, we come across another knot. And who can help us most at this point?"

"Martin," I answered.

As if on cue, a knock on the door. I looked at my watch. 11:30.

"Come in," I called.

* * * *

Martin closed the door behind him. I moved to the chair on the right and motioned him to sit in the guest chair I had just vacated.

"Mr. Wolf, Joel, *shalom aleichem*."

We returned his greeting.

He wore a blue blazer over a white dress shirt, open at the collar. His beige trousers could have used a pressing. Behind his glasses, his lower eyelids sagged, as if dragged down by the large bags under them. He still hadn't gotten much sleep since I saw him two days ago. He walked slowly to his seat.

"Gentlemen, you have additional questions for me?"

"We do," Grandfather said. "Thank you for coming on such short notice. We will try not to keep you long."

Martin gave each of us a wan smile. "I am a jumble of nerves these days, and when Joel called me, my state of anxiety drove me into some irritation. Of course you would have additional questions. And now that I am here, I feel glad to be with friends, out of the seclusion and depression of my apartment, even if you are also my inquisitors."

Inquisitors? Had he really used that word? As if it were 1492 Spain and not his legal team trying to free him from a life sentence. *Should I let it go?* Yet… It could also have been the misuse of a term by an immigrant not totally aware of nuance and connotation. *Nothing to be gained by challenging him*. I looked at Grandfather. He nodded for me to go on.

"Martin, we'd like to construct some timelines to help us in your defense. To start, you have been a widower for three years? When exactly did your wife pass away?"

Martin's eyes narrowed. "I do not know why this question also irritates me. Perhaps because I do not see its relevance. But I will answer—February 27, 1973, the 25th of Adar in the Hebrew calendar."

Grandfather said, "Although it is now over three years, may you still be comforted through your memories over her loss. May I inquire, since she was young, did she die from the cancer?"

He winced. "Yes, the ovarian cancer, a terrible cancer. She suffered greatly in the months before her death."

I waited a few seconds. "And when did you move to Brooklyn?"

"In August of 1973."

"We understand," Grandfather said, "before moving to Brooklyn, you sold your poultry feed business. Do you still own the farm where you lived?"

Martin shifted in his seat. His eyes narrowed as he looked at my grandfather. "Again, I do not understand the relevance of your question, but I will answer. I no longer own the property in Vineland. Right before I moved, I sold it for one dollar to my stepson, Payshe, or Peter, as he is called in English." He rubbed the back of his neck and shifted in his seat again.

Something was bugging Martin. Was he anticipating having to explain his having been a kapo? There was still time to get to it.

"So, you gave it to him as a gift," I said. "That was very generous of you."

Did Martin just huff a dry chuckle? He said, "I did not need the money, and from the time he was a little child, my stepson loved the farm. You know he went to the Rutgers Agricultural College in New Brunswick to learn about modern poultry science. There he was a star student. Yes, you may call it a gift."

Grandfather said, "And was he grateful for the gift?"

Martin hesitated. "He was not against it. He signed the papers."

"And how often do you speak to each other?" I asked. "When was the last time you visited him in Vineland or he visited you in Brooklyn?"

Martin bit a lip. His voice rose. "We have short exchanges over the phone from time to time. Calls are expensive. When did I see Payshe last? Hmmm… I saw him late in March of this year and then again in mid-April."

Grandfather leaned back. His eyes narrowed. "I surmise that your visit in late March coincided with the *yahrzeit* of your dear wife, and that is why you remember the date so easily?"

What a great piece of deduction. My grandfather continued to amaze me by tying that visit to the yearly Hebrew calendar anniversary of Martin's wife's death.

Martin nodded.

"And the second visit?" I said.

Martin's face relaxed. "Ah, I found it surprising when a few days after my first visit, Payshe called me and invited me to come see some of the innovations he had put into the farm. I was pleased for the interaction, and, of course I went for two days."

Grandfather leaned forward. "On your second visit, what 'innovations' did Payshe present to you?"

Martin shrugged. "One was a new switch mechanism that tied all the chicken feeding tracks together in the coops, and the other a new model incubator for the chick house. To tell you the truth, but I did not say it at the time, the 'innovations' were not so grand. I acted enthusiastic, because I hoped that the request to visit was a sign that Payshe wanted to improve our relationship."

"And did it?" I said.

His shoulders slumped. "I think not, because since then, we have gone back to a monthly call of a few minutes."

"I am sorry," Grandfather said. "But may we go back to your first visit in late March? Was Henry Casman also in Vineland on that date?"

Martin's head tilted toward Grandfather. His eyes widened. "Why yes, he was. You have very good instincts, Mr. Wolf. But why did you guess so?"

My grandfather closed his eyes briefly. "I cannot explain to you exactly, but such a surmise came over me, and I thought I would ask."

What a talent my grandfather possessed! *He knew exactly why he was asking.*

Grandfather continued. "And how did Mr. Casman behave during the visit?"

"How did he behave?" Martin voice rose. "He behaved his usual self. Angry, accusatory, made a scene at services at the Plum Street Synagogue where I and Payshe came to say the mourner's *kaddish*."

Was it now time to ask the kapo question? I would wait a moment longer. Perhaps Grandfather had additional follow up questions about the visits to Vineland. Would he ask details about the scene Casman made?

"Thank you, Martin," Grandfather said, "just a few short questions. First, did you take a bus to Vineland from New York? If so, was it on Bridgeton Transit?"

"Yes, both times and on Bridgeton Transit."

"And second, where did you stay on your visits?"

"Stay? The first at the East Landis Motel, and the second at my old house on Forest Grove Road. Payshe insisted I stay there."

"And finally, Martin, you had meals at Payshe's house?"

Martin lifted his head quickly. "Meals, yes, of course. Payshe is a good cook, and although he is in many ways not observant, he does keep a kosher house in honor of his mother's observance."

My grandfather leaned back and coupled his hands. For some reason, he hadn't asked about the "scene" Casman made at the synagogue. He gave me a quick nod.

I took a deep breath and turned slowly toward Martin. "We visited Abraham Schneider of the Myori/Druya Benevolent Society."

Martin sank back, pursed his lips, and shook his head. "Joel, I can easily guess what he told you."

His voice rose again, and he sat forward. "Yes, I was a kapo at Auschwitz for about eight months until liberation. Henoch Casman was also there during that time. He held it against me and considered me a collaborator. I was not, I tell you. I did what I could for the prisoners."

Suddenly, Martin stood, his hands clenched at his side. Was he going to do something violent? I got up, just in case. Grandfather put out his hands and motioned me to be seated.

Then Grandfather turned toward Martin. "Sha, sha, sha, Martin. Please, please be seated. We wish to hear fully from you, as upsetting it must be to recall what you went through."

Breathing hard, Martin walked behind his chair and placed his hands on the back. "You will forgive me. In a minute I will sit. I am… I am sorry. The accusation that I was a collaborator causes me much pain. It makes me crazy. You must understand—please—there were few men at Auschwitz who would not have been kapos given the opportunity as much as we despised the *mamzerim*."

He waved a hand toward me, toward Grandfather. "No, I tell you, not just for their own benefit, which was a short, uncertain extension of life, but also because what they could do for the others. Yes, there were thieves and even murderers who the Germans on purpose placed as kapos. They acted like beasts, like their *mamzerim* bosses. But many I swear to you, like me, brought extra pieces of bread to the prisoners. We kept, as best we could, the sick from work details that meant sure death."

His voice wavered. 'We gave the overseers misleading numbers to account for…extra scraps of food."

He blinked, his eyes damp with tears. "We put our lives at risk, shot on the spot if found out."

Martin sat and wept. Tears flowed down his cheeks. He wiped them away, almost angrily. "I do not wish to make myself out to be a hero. I survived. Millions did not. But I was not a collaborator. If you wish, I can give you the names and addresses of a half-dozen prisoners in the barracks to which I was assigned who will tell you that what I am saying is the truth."

"Yes," I said, "their names and addresses could be helpful in preparing for trial."

Clashing thoughts raced through my mind. Martin was the guy courting my mother. He loved America. He loved baseball. I should like him. But... but, he was a kapo during the War. Even if he was a decent kapo, he still was one. Maybe Casman was right about always saying no to the Germans. *Yet, I must keep in mind that Martin is my client.* Any negative feelings I might have shouldn't get in the way of his defense.

I kept my voice soft and asked, "In the ten months you were at Auschwitz, is there any particular event or date you remember?"

Martin took a deep breath and exhaled. "Joel, we do not need to go around a circle to get to what you really want to know. You have interviewed Abe Schneider. I am certain he informed you about the venom that Henoch carried for me not only for being a kapo, but in addition, for the way I acted surrounding the October 7, 1944, uprising. Am I correct, that is what you are after?"

I nodded. "Yes, it may also become part of testimony at trial, which the prosecution will use to reinforce motive for your killing Casman. They'll say he embarrassed you. He maligned your reputation. He blackballed you from your society's burial right. They'll say his accusation of cowardice before and during the revolt drove you to murder him."

His face reddened. "No, not so, I was not a coward. I was not a collaborator. A few months prior to the uprising, a secret council met late at night to plan the revolt. We rotated where we would meet in certain barracks where the prisoners and kapos could be trusted."

Martin stood up and started pacing. "The objective was to blow up at least one crematorium. Henoch, he...who was one of the healthier prisoners, pushed hard for the revolt."

Martin stopped behind his chair. His voice lowered. "In the end, I was the only one to vote against it. I understood the motivation, to strike back, to assert one's dignity through standing up to the monsters. But I thought it desperate, poorly planned, certain to fail with many deaths as a result. I begged not to go forward. I said the signs were there that liberation was not far off, that more will die from the revolt than from the daily attrition until the Russians arrived."

"You knew the Russians would arrive soon?" I asked.

Martin looked at me. "Yes, we had means of knowing that the Russians were very close. We could hear the anxiety in what the guards said among themselves."

His voice tensed. "But Henoch insisted that anyone who did not support the revolt was a coward and a collaborator."

Tears welled again in his eyes. "I do not say it with any glee, but because the revolt was planned in haste, one of our plotters acted too early in shooting a guard, and soon the revolt was crushed. I can tell you that I protected the men in my barracks from being identified with the revolt—even those few who were participants. None was shot."

Martin sank down in his chair. "That is all I wish to say about October 7, 1944."

"You need say no more," Grandfather said gently. "I am certain Joel will do his best to convey your point of view in a trial."

My grandfather cleared his throat. "May I question you about a different aspect of your life?"

Martin sat up. "Please proceed, Mr. Wolf."

"Your wife, Dora, you said, was also from Druya, yes?"

He nodded.

"Then did she have no interest in being buried in the society's burial plots?"

"You are correct, Mr. Wolf. She did not. We discussed it toward the end of her days. She insisted that she be buried at the Alliance Cemetery outside of Vineland so that Payshe could visit her grave regularly."

I knew what question my grandfather would ask.

"Then you do not wish to be buried next to your wife?"

Martin paled and looked away. "It is, Mr. Wolf, not that I do not wish to be buried next to my wife, but I wish more to be buried among those others I spent my youth with in Druya."

Grandfather, his eyes greatly narrowed, stared at Martin. I knew that look of disapproval. "May I at this time say what you said to Joel earlier. 'We do not need to go around a circle.' Would I be accurate to say your marriage was not always happy?"

Martin bowed his head and closed his eyes. After a few seconds, he said, "Not always. I loved Dora, but after we were married, I did not like her. But in my defense, during the six months in which she suffered before her death, I was steadfast in caring for her."

What did Martin mean? He loved Dora, but after they were married, he did not like her? I expected a clarifying question from my grandfather. Instead, he made a statement.

"Martin, what led to your dislike has to do with what happened to Dora after she was questioned by the Gestapo."

Martin covered his face with his hands and shook. He whispered. "Yes, it did."

Grandfather pushed on. "Dora was not sent to a hospital in Germany where she assisted in treating wounded German soldiers, yes?"

Martin raised his head and rapidly looked from side to side. *Was he about to flee the room?*

His entire body tensed, went rigid. He looked straight at Grandfather. "She was at a hospital yes, Mr. Wolf, but not to treat German soldiers. She... she..." He closed his eyes.

We waited while he collected himself.

After a few moments, he opened his eyes and continued. "She was at a hospital where experiments were done on Jewish and Gypsy women which left...which left..."

"It is all right, Martin," Grandfather said. "Take your time."

He looked past Grandfather. "Which left Dora sterile."

I understood. Martin didn't dislike his wife because she was sterile but because she didn't tell him before the marriage. In a voice as soft as possible, I asked him if it was so.

"That is right, Joel. After a couple of years, she did not become pregnant. Then one day as I was lamenting our bad fortune, she told me what had been done to her. I vomited a few minutes later. I insisted to myself that what troubled me was the torture she had endured, but things were never the same after that. A distance set in. I also realized that she did not love me—rather she was still in love with Notke Zimmer, Payshe's dead father. Her marrying me was out of fear and convenience. If she had bumped into Henoch Casman or some other man she knew at the DP camp, she would have married him. I felt sorry for myself, and the more my self-pity grew, the more I disliked Dora."

A single tear rolled down his cheek. "And you would be correct in assuming that I also did not like myself."

Grandfather faced Martin and opened his arms. "You are very brave and strong to answer these difficult questions, particularly about your relationship with your wife. Please allow one more question in this area. How did your feelings about your wife affect your interaction with your stepson?"

"My relationship with Payshe? I am sorry to say that it hurt our relationship. I wanted to adopt him. Dora would not allow it. She made it clear that he was her son and not in the least mine. She doted over him, called him *mein tattelle*. Joel, in case you are not familiar, *my little father*, as he was named in memory of her father who perished in the Holocaust. When we married, Payshe was five-years-old, and from that early age, Dora would tell him about his father, especially stories of his bravery as a Partisan. Whether she meant it to make it so or not, a distance developed between Payshe and me."

I said, "Did you ever tell her about your having been a kapo?"

Martin flinched. "No, I did not. So I am also guilty of having kept a secret between husband and wife."

"We are not here to judge you, Martin," my grandfather said. "Rather, we asked these difficult questions to better understand you and those who have been close to you. In this way you help your own defense."

"Thank you, Mr. Wolf." Martin grew paler. His shoulders slumped. "If there are no more questions, may I go? I do not feel well."

Grandfather looked to me. "Joel?"

"I do have one question. Prior to that uncomfortable encounter with Mr. Casman around your wife's *yahrzeit*, did you ever see him before moving to Brooklyn?"

"No, not once. I knew of our benevolent society over those years, but before moving to Brooklyn, I never attended a meeting or knew that Henoch was an active member."

"And I now have one final question," Grandfather said. "Did you or your wife apply for German reparations?"

Martin's eyebrows rose. He tilted his head. "Reparations? I did not want anything after the War from the Germans. But Dora, she said why shouldn't they at least pay money for what they stole from our lives. She applied and received modest settlements for herself and Payshe along with small monthly payments as long as she was alive."

Grandfather rose and shook hands with Martin. I followed. With a brief goodbye, he left the office.

* * * *

After watching Martin close the door behind him, I turned toward my grandfather. Tears filled his eyes.

I stood, shaken. I could count on one hand the number of times I had seen Grandfather cry. I hurried over to his desk and placed my hand on his shoulder. "Zaida... Zaida, are you... I... I... Are you okay?"

Of course he wasn't okay. I didn't know what to say—what to do.

He took out a handkerchief and dried his eyes. "Forgive me, Yoeli, but at times the darkness that we fight in our world overtakes me. I feel the personal darkness of the Holocaust that overtook your mother and me, the darkness that overtook Martin in losing his entire family and becoming a kapo at a death camp.

"The darkness that pervaded Henry Casman, body and soul, and made him Martin's enemy, and the darkness that overtook Dora as a result of human beings thinking that they have the right to experiment on young Jewish and Roma women.

"There are darknesses of the past that travel years into the future, and, as in our case, lead to murder. Ay, ay, ay, Yoeli, but we push on to find the light that will explain this particular murder. That is as much as we can do as individuals—persevere to untangle the cloak of darkness that immediately surrounds us."

I closed my eyes for a moment. I had mostly understood. I said, "Yes, we will, Zaida, But there's my own confusion. For instance, Martin feels he bears no guilt since he was 'good kapo.' How do you feel about how he excuses himself?"

Grandfather leaned his elbow on the desk and placed his hand on his chin. "Ah, my child, a profound question. On the one hand, we are prone to rationalize when we look back on our actions that another judges as wrong. Is rationalization a blessing or a curse? I believe that Martin is a good man, and whatever motivations he had in accepting the kapo position, we will never know, and perhaps Martin also does not fully comprehend. But to proceed within his own darkness, he must believe that as a kapo he helped others—and he may have done so. It is only when we clearly have done wrong, and when that wrong continues to occur, if then we rationalize away any accountability or the need to make amends or learn from the experience, then it is a curse."

I closed my eyes and thought for a moment. "I'm saying to myself, Zaida, 'relevance, counselor?' What difference does it make because I'm fully committed to defending Martin, but a part of me feels that Casman was right when he said no prisoner should have agreed to be a kapo. Maybe he was right."

"Maybe, and maybe there is no certain truth to this conundrum, no certainty, no one answer. Perhaps it is a matter of personality of how two people in a similar situation see the matters before them differently. No, Yoeli?"

I nodded vigorously. "Yes, that's what I see in everyday life, let alone in a concentration camp. In the same way, there's no answer as to who was right when it came to the revolt in the camp. I'm beginning to think the outcome dictates right or wrong. Had the revolt in any way succeeded, Martin would have been wrong."

Grandfather sat up. "Yes, a cogent observation. And the 'relevance, counselor,' is tied to our understanding the web of personalities and their actions that engendered the murder of a man so that you can defend your client."

He stood and pulled up the knot on his tie. "Is there not, based on our interview, an individual entwined in this web of whom we have little understanding?"

I responded immediately. "Martin's stepson, Peter—Payshe—who exchanged calls with Casman. He also had recent interactions—spotty as they may have been—with Martin."

"Yes, as I previously mentioned the possibility, it is now incumbent upon us to take a trip to…"

I knew exactly where. "Vineland, New Jersey," I smiled, "and on Bridgeton Transit? When?"

Grandfather laughed. "Yes, Bridgeton Transit, if it is acceptable to you, I had previously checked the schedule, and there is a bus from Port Authority tomorrow morning at 8:30. It is scheduled to arrive in Vineland at 12:15. We will return Friday. You see, it is already Thursday tomorrow, and if we delay, we will not be able to go until Sunday or Monday because of the Sabbath. I would suggest we do not lose so much time. Yes?"

I'd check with Aliya first, in case she'd planned something I didn't know about. And she hadn't been feeling well lately. I wanted to make sure she'd be okay.

"Yes, tomorrow, Zaida at 8:30. If it's acceptable to you, I'll meet you at Port Authority on the main level at 8:00 to buy our tickets. I'll call you to confirm after I speak to Aliya tonight. She's at an all-day orientation session for her upcoming job."

Grandfather laughed. "Ah, you are emulating speech components from your beloved grandfather. And may I say how delightfully cultured you sound."

I smiled. "Then shall we both traverse the few blocks to our respective trains? You to return to the house, and I to Stuyvesant Town."

It felt good sharing a brief moment of humor. There hadn't been much of that the last few days.

Grandfather looked at his watch. "Joel, it is merely 12:30, and I should remain in my office during most of the stated business hours. But in addition, I wish to perform research at the nearby Grand Army Plaza branch of the Brooklyn Library. You proceed home, perhaps obtain some lunch for yourself, and I will partake of the meal your mother packed for me. Good?"

What sort of research? "Would you like me to accompany you to the library?" I asked.

Grandfather shook his head and smiled. "It is not necessary. After all, you have hired me as your investigator, have you not? Does not an investigator do research? We have a long day tomorrow. Some rest will prove beneficial to you. I promise I will not exert myself exceedingly."

Tomorrow, he would tell me about the research. "Okay then, Zaida. I'll call you later."

* * * *

I changed my mind when I reached the Boro Hall station. I decided to treat myself to a cup of my favorite coffee at the King George Coffee House nearby on Montague and Henry. The King George wasn't busy, so guilt-free, I lingered for over an hour reviewing notes from the interviews and mulling various approaches to Martin's defense. It hit me why my grandfather asked

Martin whether his wife had applied for reparation benefits—in reviewing files, Casman could have come across Dora's history and address in America, and even that she had died and the date of her death. He very well might have figured out when her *yahrzeit* would be.

I also had a moment of guilt. Along with two more cups of coffee, I had a package of Drake's Ring Dings as my lunch.

I arrived home at 3:30. I planned to surprise Aliya and make dinner—Chicken Marsala, a favorite dish of hers. The chicken lay defrosted in the refrigerator, and the wine, mushrooms, non-dairy margarine, and spices lay at hand. Over an hour later, the dish, along with pasta and a salad, was ready just as Aliya walked through the door.

"Chicken Marsala," Aliya said loudly, while still in the foyer. "Smells delicious, and today I'm really hungry." She rushed in, looked at the table set for two, and kissed me. "Thank you, thank you, orientations are so long and tedious. Tell me what you can about your day."

I recounted the visit to Abraham Schneider and how we had learned that Henry Casman was not only a constantly angry man, but also a Nazi hunter. I said nothing about his also lashing out against Jewish collaborators and concentration camp kapos. I also kept mum about our second interview with Martin. Aliya did not press me.

As we cleared the table after dinner, I said, "Grandfather and I need to go to Vineland tomorrow morning to talk to Martin's stepson. We would stay until Friday. Bus from Port Authority at 8:30. Are you okay for me to go?"

Aliya took me by the shoulders and cocked her head. "Why wouldn't I be okay? You've got a job to do. And it's Martin you're defending."

"Well...because...you haven't been feeling well. And there was that doctor visit yesterday. I wanted to make sure you'd be okay."

Aliya tightened her grip. "Joel, go, and I'll make breakfast because you'll need to pack and leave by 7:20 to play it safe."

She drew closer and gave a wide smile. "Everything is good doctor-wise, and, you know what? After we finish cleaning up, I'll have some good news for you. Okay?"

I could use some. "Well, if it's 'good news,' sure, okay."

I wrapped my arms around her. "I know it's early, but after I call Zaida to confirm, let's get to bed, you tell me the 'good news,' and maybe we watch some dumb shows?"

We kissed, and Aliya picked up a dishtowel. "You wash, and I'll dry. And then to bed."

* * * *

We sat at the edge of the bed. Aliya took my hand "Joel, we're going to be parents in early January."

I froze and melted in quick order. "You're…we're going to have a baby! That's why you went to the doctor's appointment with my mom?" I hit my head. How could I have not known? It was right there in front of me. "It's… it's wonderful."

I clutched her and, after a kiss, I stood up. I sat down. I asked, "You're feeling okay? I remember you said… I remember…that everything is fine. You're…the baby is fine?"

Aliya took back my hand. "Yes, just as I told you, the doctor says everything is fine."

I thought for a moment. "But you start work soon. Should you? And if you do, you'll have to take lots of time off when the baby comes. Is it worth even starting work?"

Aliya released my hand. Her eyes narrowed. She cupped her hands around my face. "Listen, Joel, husband of mine. I'm starting work as planned, and God willing, I'll work until the baby comes. Then I'll take the necessary time off to be with our baby. And it will work out well. Do you know why, Joel?"

"Why?" I asked tentatively and immediately added. "Well, because it will. No reason to think it won't."

"And," she prolonged the word, "because the two of us together will assume care for the baby right from the start, even if it means your taking some time off here and there at PWR. With our two salaries, we'll be able to afford good child-care. Sound right to you?"

I smiled and hugged her again. "Sounds very right. I may have suggested it myself."

I was going to be a father!

We talked non-stop until 11:00, when Aliya said, "Time to turn in, Counselor. You're off to the wilds of New Jersey tomorrow morning."

THURSDAY, JUNE 10, 1976

The ten minutes went by in a flash as I jogged from our apartment to Union Square. Thoughts of parenthood filled me—mostly glee and worry. Would it be a boy or a girl? Did it matter? I said it didn't—but a boy to shoot baskets and play stickball, that would be… But if a girl—I'd teach her, too.

Baby's name—we started talking about it last night—if a girl, for sure she would be Rebecca—Rivkah in Hebrew, named after my grandmother who perished in the Holocaust. If a boy, Harry, and Gershon in Hebrew, after my father. Both Aliya's suggestions.

Due in January! NYU Hospital was only a dozen blocks away down First Avenue. But what if it snowed hard when we had to go? The roads icy and cabs unavailable? Do I call an ambulance? To prepare for the worst case, in the next few months, I'd go over to the 42nd Street Library and read about how to deliver a baby at home.

And then the matter of my taking off from work. *Of course*. Why would it have to all fall on Aliya? She also had a career. I would talk to Larry Seidman and try to work things out. I tried to remember—any other men doing it? I didn't care. I wanted to take care of the baby. *Then why was I feeling uncomfortable*?

I carried these thoughts, along with my overnight bag, onto an N train headed to Times Square. I nearly missed my stop. I followed a throng of commuters up the stairwell to 42nd Street and Seventh Avenue and headed one block west toward the Port Authority Bus Terminal. Once on the street, the sight of New York City's decay cut into my euphoria.

People walking at a crisp pace jostled each other. I didn't hear a single "excuse me." Even though it was the height of rush hour and the street recently cleaned, I smelled the stench of urine, vomit, and rotting garbage. A few homeless men sat or lay stretched out against storefronts. Each held, or had attached to clothing, a cardboard sign asking for money. I stopped and gave a dollar to one dressed in army fatigues. He took off his woolen cap and dipped it toward me.

Electronic goods shops lined the street. They promised great deals on the latest calculators, digital or video cameras, Sony Betamax recorders, and Atari Super Pong consoles. Two 24-hour movie theaters enticed customers.

One marquee displayed last year's top movie, *Jaws*. The other, *Blonde in Leather*.

As a teenager, I had come with friends a few times at night to experience the excitement of Times Square, away from our placid Flatbush neighborhoods. The street offered reduced-price electronics, liquor, drugs, guns, and girls. We gawked, we played at being grown up, but in the end, we never bought. The lure, fun enough.

I neared Eighth Avenue. The multiple glass doors to the block-long Port Authority Bus Terminal across the avenue never closed completely as individuals rushed in and out. 7:55 on my watch. The terminal was built 25 years before and touted as an architectural marvel. Now, according to an article I had recently read in *The Times*, New Yorkers considered it the city's "ugliest building." It was also a dangerous place, especially at night, rife with muggings, drug marts, and prostitution. Was my grandfather safely inside? He was always early. We planned to meet at 8:00 at the Bridgeton Transit ticket window on the main concourse. Knowing the reputation of Port Authority, I should have left earlier.

Inside the well-lit main concourse with bright-white wall tiles, I relaxed somewhat. Except for tourists who wandered about looking befuddled, some confused and clutching one another, the commuter crowd hurried out the exits or toward ticket windows and the lower level where the busses waited. Escalators from the roof parking level brought down well-dressed men in suits carrying briefcases. Several pairs of NYPD officers in dark blue uniforms walked the corridors, each with a hand on a nightstick.

Shops selling books, candy, jewelry, leather goods, and higher-end electronics were already open, along with sandwich shops and a *Nathan's* hot dog kiosk. Above the din of the crowd, pigeons fluttered and cooed as they flew around the ceiling's rafters. I laughed to myself. *They probably rode the escalators down from the roof and up from the basement*. A cleaning woman removed droppings as I gingerly walked by.

I started at Window 1 and moved along until I saw the sign for Bridgeton Transit at Window 18. It was 7:57. I didn't see my grandfather. Could I really have arrived earlier than him? My stomach knotted. I did a complete turn. *Where was he? Should I buy our tickets*?

A tap on my shoulder—I jumped. I turned and faced my smiling grandfather.

"Joel," he said after setting a suitcase and burlap bag down, "I seem to have startled you, for which I am sorry."

"Zaida, no, no, it's all right. I was looking for you. I...I just didn't see you."

I flung my bag over my shoulder and gave him a bear hug.

My grandfather exhaled deeply, repositioned his fedora, tilted his head, and raised an eyebrow. "Yoeli," he said softly, "are you somewhat out-of-kilter this morning? It is just I thought with a long trip before us, I would avail myself of the lavatory. We do not know if the bus has such a facility."

"Out-of-kilter!" I hadn't heard my grandfather use that term since I was a kid overreacting to a minor inconvenience or setback. The funny term, which I only heard from him, always calmed me. I'd wonder how one gets into a kilter? That would refocus me then, as it did now.

I grinned. "Sure, we don't know if there's a restroom on the bus." My smile broadened. "Yes, Zaida, I may be a bit discombobulated this morning since…really since last night when Aliya gave me some good news. You see, Aliya is… Aliya and I are…"

I stopped. The corners of my grandfather's eyes crinkled. It hit me. *He knows.*

I kept smiling and took a half step back. "Aliya and I are going to have a baby." I wagged a finger at him. "But you already knew, didn't you? Mom certainly knows. Probably even Rosa at Mom's store knows. How did I miss the signs? But I don't care. I'm going to be a father."

Grandfather beamed. "Yes, your mother informed me, but we concluded that it was for Aliya to tell you. I wish you and Aliya—I wish all of us—a *mazel tov.*"

I kissed him on his cheek. "Yes, it's wonderful for all of us."

Grandfather nodded and took out his wallet. His smile departed. "Now that you have come out of your discombobulation, we are back to the difficult task at hand." Out of his wallet, he removed two ticket stubs, giving one to me.

"I have already purchased our tickets. It is now 8:05. Shall we go down to the lower level where our bus awaits us at Gate 30?"

I nodded and looked at the ticket. The same paper and format as the partial ticket stub we found at Henry Casman's apartment. In two parts, it indicated a round trip—New York to Vineland and Vineland to New York.

I took his suitcase before we went down the escalator, where we rode from light to a darkened netherworld. The walls on the lower level were also white-tiled, but everything from well-drawn flowers to vulgar graffiti covered their length on both sides of the passage. I hesitated when I saw orange tape on the floor in a few corners indicating where the homeless may sleep. Several were occupied, one person sitting or lying within each designated rectangle.

Bus engines roared. Carbon monoxide fumes choked the air. Grandfather coughed along the few minutes stretch until we arrived at our gate which said, "Vineland-8:30."

Grandfather put a handkerchief to his mouth. "I see we are permitted to board," he said. "Perhaps the air inside the bus is less noxious?"

I followed him out the door to where the bus driver stood taking tickets. 8:20. Just ten minutes, I hoped, before we took in more breathable air.

* * * *

We seated ourselves in the mid-section of the bus. Grandfather took the window seat, his fedora on his lap, and I sat by the aisle. He had put his handkerchief away. We settled in for the nearly four hour ride. The bus left on time, but it would take another twenty minutes until the air quality improved. We followed other busses out of the terminal into West Side traffic toward the Lincoln Tunnel. As we went underground, the bus crawled in the right lane, while cars, traveling no more than 30 miles per hour, passed on the left.

A catwalk lined the tunnel walls on both sides. Every few hundred feet, a Port Authority policeman sat in a small booth monitoring traffic. *How could they do that job? Did they just get used to the claustrophobia? How well did the closed booths shield them from the exhaust fumes? Could fresh air be pumped in? Their health certainly had to suffer.*

Finally, the bus emerged into bright daylight. Warehouses, factories, and multi-ethnic shops dotted these sections of Weehawken and Union City, New Jersey. Signs for German, Italian, Irish, Jewish, and Cuban eateries filled one billboard after another.

The bus broke out of traffic and wound its way from one highway exchange to another until we entered the New Jersey Turnpike. Around Newark Airport, a plane about to land flew low over our heads. The air smelled better. The respite lasted until we came to Linden, fifteen miles south of Newark.

Massive oil and gas storage tanks lined each side of the turnpike and extended into the eastern and western horizons. The tanks were marked ARCO, Hess, Cities Service, Exxon. A few still showed, ESSO, Exxon's former name. I detected an unpleasant odor that nauseated me for the next five-miles.

As we neared Exit 9—New Brunswick—my grandfather pointed to a Rutgers. The State University sign. "A fine place of learning," Grandfather said. "Their agricultural college is one of the finest in the world."

Rutgers! I thought for a moment. "Zaida, that's the school Martin mentioned that his stepson, Payshe, attended, right? And it was in the agricultural college where Payshe excelled and learned a lot about improving poultry farming."

"Yes, you remember correctly. I surmise that Payshe is well acquainted with chemical formulations and mechanical advances that apply to poultry health and egg production—and perhaps other applications."

My grandfather took a deep breath. "While we are on the subject of agriculture, I would like to share a brief history of Jewish farming in southern New Jersey and what I learned at the library yesterday about Vineland itself."

Other than the conversation we had with Martin about his farm life and business in Vineland, I knew nothing else about Jewish farming in South Jersey nor about the town. In all of the previous cases I had worked with my grandfather, his knowledge of the historical and geographical backgrounds to the crimes helped unravel the mysteries. While the murder of Henry Casman took place in Brooklyn, Martin had lived in Vineland. His stepson, Payshe, still lived there. Casman had visited Vineland just a few months before his death and had a confrontation with Martin. I needed to understand more about this Jewish farming community.

My voice rose. "Okay, Zaida, how far back does this history go?"

"Ah, an excellent opening question." He paused. "In the latter half of the nineteenth century, there was a notion among well-meaning philanthropists throughout the world that immigrants living in the teeming tenements of large cities would benefit physically and spiritually by moving to rural settings and farming the land. It was termed the 'back to the soil movement.' So, in 1882, 43 Jewish individuals and their families living in the Lower East Side of New York took land gifts to farm ten to fifteen acre lots in the countryside surrounding Vineland.

"The soil was poor for planting most crops and for the pasturing of livestock, but the poultry business, including egg production, appeared possible. It was a hard life. To begin, the settlers knew nothing of agricultural methods. Markets for eggs such as in Camden and Philadelphia were nearly 40 miles away. The men focused on the poultry work, while many of the women performed sewing tasks that allowed the families to survive financially. At least for about 30 years into the 20th century."

My grandfather touched my shoulder. "But then, Yoeli, what do you think caused this first chapter of Jewish poultry history in the southern portion of New Jersey, for the most part, to come to an end?"

I thought for a moment. "Competition from other farmers? The inability to have enough labor? What, Zaida?"

He put his hands together. "Joel, your second conjecture is close to the mark. Their offspring, young people like you, went away to colleges and did not return. It is an interesting irony, is it not, that the next generation wished to reside in the congestion and pollution of Philadelphia or New York rather than the salubrious atmosphere of the country?"

"Well, maybe," I said. *What would I have done in that situation?* I didn't say it, but I was fairly certain I would have also taken the get-away option. "And the next chapter, Zaida?"

"Ah, the next chapter is a short one. But may I divert a moment and recount how Vineland itself came to be? You will see it coincides with the idealistic inception of the Jewish farming communities in and around that town."

I turned toward my grandfather. With all my education, undergraduate degree, law school completion, if there were such a thing as a measure of knowledge, I stacked up well short compared to him. He had an enormous curiosity about all subjects and amazingly retained what he had learned even years before.

"Sure, go ahead, Zaida," I said.

He closed his eyes for a moment. "In the early 1860s, as the Civil War raged, a utopian philanthropist named Charles Landis bought up thousands of acres of land in southern New Jersey and laid out a town according to his specifications and rules that included temperance. Those who bought plots at discount prices in his community were required to farm the land in some fashion. They also were to allow spaces between homes for the planting of flowers and shade trees. Thus, you will notice when we arrive that the roads of the town follow a 90-degree grid of north-south and east-west, with street names such as Oak, Wheat, Cherry, Grape, and other such appellations."

Grandfather laughed. "And here is an amusing irony. While the town in its early years did not allow for alcohol consumption, the one crop that seemed well suited for its soil was grapes. So Mr. Landis offered much larger parcels of land at reduced cost to buyers, particularly recent immigrants from Italy, who would tend vineyards and cultivate the vines for the production of wine in an alcohol-prohibited area. And thus, Joel, the town was named…"

"Vineland! You're right, Zaida. That's really funny." I waited a moment. "So now back to chapter two of Jewish farming in the…" I enunciated very slowly, "'Vine—land' area?"

His smile receded. "A very short, a very sad chapter, with a slight modicum of amusement. In the 1930s, when the Nazis rose to power in Germany along with the *Anschluss*, the annexation of Austria by Germany, many Jews from there fled to the United States and other countries. Many were professionals—doctors, teachers, lawyers—whose credentials were meaningless in this country when they first arrived. So with the help of agencies still dedicated to farming as a utopian solution to a refugee dilemma, these immigrants came to the Vineland area and tried to learn the poultry business."

Grandfather smiled briefly. "But within this tragedy of their displacement, there is a moment's levity. I remember seeing a picture of these men in three-piece suits, ties, dress shoes, and hats dressed for work—that is, laboring in the midst of their chicken-tending endeavors."

I half-smiled and glanced at my grandfather who hadn't gotten out of Austria in time and had come as a refugee after the War. Daily, he dressed similarly to the refugees he had just described. Today's temperature was predicted to go up to 95. He wasn't heading out to feed chickens, but still, would he have done so? No, not my grandfather. Nevertheless, I pictured him dressing similarly and hid a smile.

I asked, "And chapter three is the post-Holocaust arrival of more than a 1000 survivors and their families that we discussed with Martin? That chapter is pretty much at its end, right, Zaida? And it's the last chapter?"

He nodded. "But not quite over, as some individuals such as Martin's stepson are still involved in the poultry business. But yes, for the most part. The Jewish refugees of this chapter did well enough, adapting to chicken farming during the 1950s when there was a demand, from Philadelphia to New York, for local eggs and chickens. Sadly, the prevalence of the refrigerated railroad cars in the 1960s enabled large farms in our southern states to send their eggs to the north. Philadelphia and New York buyers no longer depended on New Jersey eggs, and prices dropped. Many of the farmers went bankrupt or sold out as best they could. And as history repeats itself, the offspring, those your age, have not wished to be farmers. They also are off to the cities. There are very few Jewish farmers left."

"But it seems Payshe is thriving," I said.

"Hmmm, yes. From what Martin told us, he appears to be a very interesting young man—smart, innovative, and industrious. Upon meeting, we will attempt to understand him and how, if in any way, he fits within the puzzle of Henry Casman's murder."

I turned fully toward Grandfather. "But what if he won't see us? By the way, did you try to call him to arrange a meeting?"

He shook his head. "I did not call him, nor do I think we should let him know that we wish to see him. From my experience, observing how a person behaves when surprised provides unfiltered information about the person and what he wishes to convey. In some cases, a detective sends notification of arrival to unsettle the individual to make the person more vulnerable to questioning. In other cases, as I suspect with Martin's stepson, if the individual is tightly wound, prior notification gives him time for anticipation of the questions. It is a risk, yes, that he may not be home when we arrive, or will not wish to speak with us, but a risk worth taking, no?"

"I hope so," I said. *Was I?* I looked past Grandfather through the window. The bus had just left the turnpike at the Bordentown exit, and we were pulling into a Howard Johnson on Route 206.

The bus driver left the engine running while he stood and shouted, "Listen up, everybody." He looked at his watch. "It's 9:55. We're stoppin' for fifteen minutes for you to see to your business and get somethin' inside the HoJo. Remember, fifteen minutes don't add up to sixteen or seventeen. Most of ya are past the third grade. We leave promptly at 10:10 with or without ya. And if you're not on, you can hitch the rest of the way to Vineland or just wait for the next bus comin' by at around 5:30. And now I gotta take care of my own business."

I cringed and blurted, "Oh, for heaven's sake."

My grandfather laughed. "Nuh, , Yoeli. The man is trying to make the best of a difficult job. I find that a bit of humor attached to an imperative prompts positive reactions. Let us take advantage while the bus is stopped to retrieve the refreshments your mother prepared for us." He pointed above to the luggage rack. "Sandwiches are in the bag I carried with me. With the fourteen minutes left, we will use the restroom and purchase some drinks, time willing. When we come to Vineland, we should, as quickly as possible, make our way to the farm. Eating while the bus travels is good usage of our time, no?"

I nodded and smiled. "Yes, Zaida, much can be accomplished in fourteen minutes. I'll lead the way."

We were back on the bus by 10:07, with a Mountain Dew for me and a decaf coffee for Grandfather. We had around two hours before we arrived in Vineland. Unhurriedly, we ate the egg salad sandwiches my mother had sent with Grandfather.

Route 206 south and then Route 54 took us through forested areas interspersed with small, bungalow-style homes, some just a few feet off the road. In other stretches, I viewed the promise of New Jersey being the "Garden State" with barns, silos, large pastures, and crops dominating the land.

At the end of 206, the bus pulled into the parking lot of Scaffidi's Diner. "Ten minutes if ya want to get off the bus while we pick up a few more passengers," the bus driver called. "But then again, you can almost walk to Vineland from here if you ain't back."

We both laughed. "We are in Hammonton," Grandfather said, "I believe still 20 miles from our destination. I do not need to partake of this establishment's facilities. And you, Joel?"

"No, I'm fine. And I don't want to risk a five-hour walk to Vineland."

Grandfather nudged my shoulder. "And one more bit of history to share—Hammonton was also founded by Mr. Landis prior to his Vineland venture. And for many years into our present, the town has been called the 'Blueberry Capital of the World.'"

A few minutes after the bus departed the diner, we entered Route 54. On both sides of the two-lane rural road, seemingly endless fields of low-lying bushes dotted with blue filled my eyes. Men and women in sombrero-like hats were bent over, reaching toward the blue and placing their pickings in buckets. I loved blueberries, but did I once wonder how they came in abundance to our local Waldbaum's supermarket?

Route 54 became Wheat Road. "If I remember my map correctly," Grandfather said, "we are on the outskirts of our destination and just a few miles from the farm where Martin's stepson resides."

I heard what my grandfather said, but at the same time, my attention was drawn to a male voice at the back of the bus. "Hey, Mr. Driver, can you let me off when you get to Brewster Road?"

"Sure can," the driver responded.

I poked Grandfather. "Wow, Zaida, you can just ask to be dropped off in the middle of a route?"

My grandfather chuckled. "Yes, Joel, is it not marvelous to explore the larger world?"

I laughed. "Yes, Zaida, it's not Machu Pichu, but it sure isn't Brooklyn."

* * * *

The bus stopped along a curb in front of a booth-like enclosure. Small letters at the top of its one door said, Vineland Bus Terminal. *What a difference from Port Authority!* I took down my overnight bag and Grandfather's suitcase from the luggage rack and waited our turn to leave the bus. My grandfather held the burlap bag that had held our lunches.

I followed Grandfather onto a narrow sidewalk and looked around. Street signs indicated that we were on SE Boulevard between Landis Avenue, a major thoroughfare, and a much smaller, Elmer Street. Railroad tracks divided the boulevard between east and west. Toward Elmer Street sat an almost empty large parking lot next to a run-down building marked in faded letters, FOOD FAIR, and below, in more visible markings, PANTRY PRIDE.

Hmmm. *FOOD FAIR or PANTRY PRIDE*—I'd never heard of them. Like Bohack or ShopRite in Brooklyn, I assumed. Across the tracks stood a metallic structure in the shape of a train car with Boulevard Diner in large red-painted letters. Two men in white uniforms and paper soda jerk caps stood at its side smoking cigarettes.

In front of the bus sat an old Buick Electra with a dark blue body and white hardtop roof. We owned the exact model for the three years before my father passed away in 1963. Except—atop the roof sat a sign with gold letters reading Bucci Car Service and a phone number. Bracketed to the trunk, symmetrically placed between the fins, hung a white rimmed metallic, rectangular sign with *Ortlieb's—The Wet Beer* centered in an oval border next to a picture of a four-pack carrier with the proud declaration of Throwaway Bottles.

The driver's door opened. A large man with wispy brown hair and a jowly face got out and approached. Slightly askew wire-rimmed glasses framed smiling eyes. A faded black tee shirt covered his body down to khaki shorts.

"Good afternoon, gents. John Bucci at your service. Might you need a ride somewhere?"

I glanced at my grandfather. He nodded.

"Yes," I said. "We'd like to go to a property on Forest Grove Road. We don't have an exact address, but it's a poultry farm. Peter Zimmer is the owner. Do you know it?"

The man chuckled. "They're just starting to assign numbers to houses along that road. But no problem. I know where Pete lives. We're not that big of a town. I've driven a lot of folks out there who've come to talk to Pete about his chicken feed formulas and machines for poultry farming. Two folks from Purina were here last week to throw money at him for his pellet formula."

He paused for a moment to wipe sweat from his face. "And those baby chick incubators that he designed and built himself—couple of months ago, two executives of Massey-Harris from upstate New York were at the farm, hat and money in hand, to buy Pete's patent. Heard he told them to take a hike. Pete's been written about a few times in *The Vineland Times Journal*, our local newspaper."

The driver narrowed his eyes. "You folks strike me like college types. You down from New Brunswick to talk with Pete about his research?" He tilted his head slightly. "Or maybe you're family? Ain't seen much of family since Pete's stepdad left town a few years ago."

"Uh, no," I said, "we're not relatives, and we're not from Rutgers. We're here to see Pay... Peter on other business. If Peter is there, we'd like you to please drop us off and come back an hour later. Then we'll need to go to the East Landis Motel."

The driver walked over and picked up my bag and Grandfather's suit-case. "Sure can. I'll drop you off and go across the road for that hour and visit with my cousin, Bobby DeCarlo. I might wake him because he works the night shift at Wheaton Glass on the Boulevard. But that's okay—we've been annoying each other since we were kids."

"Thanks."

He pointed to the Buick. "Hop in—I'll put these in the trunk and take'em out when we get to the motel."

Grandfather and I got into the taxi's backseats. I reached for a seatbelt. There wasn't one. I shook my head. Grandfather lifted his hands slightly and smiled. The man slowly settled into the driver's seat and started the engine. He turned onto the Boulevard for about twenty-five yards and signaled a right turn on Landis Avenue. "We'll be going through the center of town now," he said. "It's the more touristy way. Won't cost you any more."

My grandfather leaned forward. "Mr. Bucci, from your words, might I be correct in my assumption that Mr. Zimmer is somewhat of a town celebrity or even a hero?"

Bucci drummed on the dashboard waiting for the signal to change. "Celebrity? Maybe. A hero? I don't know about that? A hero around here is the quarterback who throws a last minute touchdown pass to beat Millville High during the Thanksgiving Day game. Better yet, the guys who gave their lives during World War II or the Korean War. And let's not forget about our veterans who were in Nam and came back, a few seriously injured. We treat 'em like heroes—not like how some other towns turned their backs on 'em."

I thought about my being exempt from service during the Vietnam War due to my high draft number. I thought about the war's veterans strewn on the streets of New York to whom I would give a dollar or two, here and there.

We turned on Landis Avenue. On our left, I saw a storefront sign for Goldstein's Delicatessen and Market with Kosher below. I tapped Grandfather and pointed to it. "Yes, Joel," he said in a low voice, "we may avail ourselves of their delicacies for dinner tonight, yes?"

Bucci said. "If you folks need the special food that Jews eat, kosher, I think they call it, then Goldstein's is the place for you. Not that I've ever eaten there, but I hear it's good. Me, I go for my cold cuts to my cousin Angie's deli on Chestnut and 2nd." He laughed. "You can't get Genoa salami and provolone on Italian bread at Goldstein's."

"That is good to know," Grandfather said. "What else can you tell us of Mr. Zimmer?"

He shook his head. "No, Pete's not a hero. More of a town character who makes us proud from time to time. And if there are a couple of words for him, it might be 'town eccentric'."

Grandfather leaned forward. "Ah, Mr. Bucci, you say he is a 'town eccentric.' We would be curious how Mr. Zimmer has earned that designation. If you don't mind telling us."

Bucci laughed. "Don't mind at all. If Pete was with us, I'd say it right in front of him." He cleared his throat. "To start. He ain't got any friends in town. Never did. My boy, Joey, went through school with him, and he stuck to himself from kindergarten through Vineland High. On the other hand, his workers who usually last a month or two on other farms, they've been with him for a few years now. They'd deck anyone who said a bad word about him. Matter of fact, his foreman, Luis, who frequents the Grove Tavern, never got into a fight about some of the stupid guys calling him a *spic*—oh, excuse me, that's someone with a Spanish heritage—but Luis did beat up a guy who called Pete 'a dirty Jew.' Guy wound up in the hospital for a week. Police came, but when Sherriff Mastrianni heard what caused the fight, he didn't press any charges against Luis."

I laughed, probably too hard. I wanted to hear more about what he had to say. "So, Peter's a loner, except for the relationships he has with his workers?" I asked.

"Well, let me say this. Yes and no. He don't socialize much with folks outside the farm, doesn't have a beer with anybody as far as I know. On the other hand, when the North Vineland fire station's siren goes off, he's always the first one to report for duty. And, oh yeah, in the winter when it snows, he hitches a snowplow to the front of his Ford Bronco and clears out the driveways of elderly neighbors up and down his neck of the woods."

Conundrum—wasn't that the word Mr. Levine in tenth-grade English taught us when we had to read *Oedipus Rex*? That's how the taxi driver was describing Martin's stepson—a "conundrum" making him hard to understand as we applied my grandfather's critical analyses to unraveling the facts and emotions within the web of Casman's murder. *How does rationality deal with a "conundrum?"*

We stopped for a light, and Bucci put on a left turn signal to turn on East Avenue. On our right, the vertical neon sign for the three-story East Landis Motel caught my eye. Attached to it was a one story eatery with the simple title of Restaurant. Across East Avenue on the right loomed a wooden, multi-roofed building with Adamo Feed Co. brightly sketched on the second level. Had it been a competitor with Martin's company? Perhaps Martin had bought it and kept its name.

On the left, across Landis Avenue, the marquee of the Landis Movie Theater displayed *Robin and Marian*—and stacked underneath, Sean Connery—Audrey Hepburn. A smaller sign advertised a 2:00 Wednesday matinee for $1. Straight ahead on the other side of East Avenue, a large red brick edifice dominated the horizon. At the top of its far end sat a steeple with a cupola bedecked with a stone cross. Must be a Catholic church. My certainty increased when I saw a small group of teenage boys in white shirts and ties and girls in knee-length plaid skirts crossing East Avenue and heading toward the church. *A Catholic school must be nearby.*

We turned onto East Avenue heading north. Bucci hadn't spoken for over a minute—until, "Uh, let me ask you somethin', gents. Does Pete know you're coming?"

My grandfather and I looked at each other. Grandfather, who had settled back, leaned forward again. "Mr. Bucci, do you pose your question because you feel that Mr. Zimmer's not knowing that we are coming may be inappropriate?"

Bucci circled his head against the car's backrest. "'Inappropriate?' Well, I'd say not the best thing to do. Pete's a very private person. And he guards his farm like it's Fort Knox."

Against what? "You mean because he's afraid that some industrial spies might try to steal some of his secrets?" I asked

Bucci didn't answer for a few seconds. "Well, that may be one reason. But Pete acts every now and then like he's back in Europe fighting the Nazis during World War II. Let me tell you what happened soon after Martin moved away."

"Yes," Grandfather said. "We would greatly appreciate hearing."

"Yeah, glad to, but first real quick," Bucci pointed ahead, "this here is our own Park Avenue where the richer folks in town live—doctors, lawyers, car dealers, construction company owners—Catholics, Baptists, Jews, they've all built new homes along this stretch in the last few years. Been upscale for almost a century, but these days with a newer look."

He coughed and motioned toward the right as we crossed Park Avenue. "No offense, I hope, gents, but I'm guessing you're of the Jewish persuasion. There's a synagogue down there where, I'm told, the upper-crust Jews pray. The others pray at the ones on Plum or Grape Street."

I cringed. *But why tell us?* Was it because of his easy identification of our being Jewish? His identifying a segment of the Vineland Jewish community as being "upper crust?" Both?

But Grandfather said neutrally, "Mr. Bucci, no offense has been taken. Thank you for that interesting information."

We had passed other fruit-named streets such as Pear and Peach with ranch or older wooden bungalows on small lots—most with one-car garages. Now I spotted several multi-level brick homes on large lots and manicured lawns with two-car garages—one even had a circular driveway.

Bucci refocused my attention. "So back to Pete and his—call it, 'guarding his privacy.' Maybe more than that. Throughout the years Martin and his wife still lived on the farm, every so often there'd be jerks who did nasty stuff like scrawling swastikas on the house or even throwing dead cats onto the property at night. Jerks are too nice a way to describe those morons."

Dead cats thrown onto the property. My stomach turned. Killing animals to exhibit contempt? I'd never come across that ugliness.

Grandfather put his hand to his face. "Mr. Bucci, and after Mr. Zimmer's stepfather left?"

"Yeah, well, right after, Pete woke up one morning and saw a swastika scrawled on the house's front. He called the police, and the chief himself, Mastrianni, came out. Everyone knew who done it. When they got drunk, the trash McKenzie clan, especially the brothers, Rob and Dennis, who live next door to Pete's farm, had over the years bragged about what they'd been doing. The chief told Pete he'd pay them a visit. But Pete told him to hold off, and that he hisself would pay the boys a neighborly visit and ask them nicely to stop.

"I guess the chief agreed because this here's what my cousin Bobby told me. Bobby heard that Pete sauntered over to the McKenzie house and waved a handgun in their faces. Told them that if there was another such incident, he would come after them—didn't care if they done it or not or about any consequences to himself. Pete left, and there hasn't been no incident for over two years now."

My grandfather settled back with arms crossed. His brows furrowed as he looked out his window. "Although we will arrive unexpectedly, I hope Mr. Zimmer will welcome us when we explain our business."

Bucci sighed. "I hope he does."

We passed through longer stretches of road between cross streets—Oak, then Wheat, then Garden, then Forest Grove Road. Homes sat farther apart. Some appeared abandoned along with their flat-roofed chicken coops, tar sheets hanging down to the ground over open wood windows. As we eased to a stop at Forest Grove Road and East Avenue, I noticed a field of blue-tinged low-lying bushes. Straw-hatted, dark-skinned women in rows that striated the field bent over plucking from the growth.

"Mr. Bucci, blueberries?" I said.

He laughed. "With all the time we've already spent together, don't you think it's time for you to call me, John? Yes, blueberries. Hammonton ain't the only town around here that grows 'em."

He turned left and drove about two hundred feet to the first house on our right, then pulled into a gravel horseshoe driveway that encircled a two-story red brick house. Four vertical white windows, two on each side, flanked a narrow front door, and three similar windows symmetrically set off the second story. An air conditioner protruded from an upper window. Two cedar trees on the well-maintained, green lawn rose high, dwarfing the house.

John stopped the car at the back of the house, halfway into the first leg of the horseshoe.

About 25 yards up from the house, a single-story building with seven units reminded me of one-story motel designs I had seen on television commercials. Thick, green grass spread over the property. A well-worn dirt path wound beyond this structure to a series of low-lying buildings which I took to be chicken coops. In the distance, I spotted a corn field, green stalks bending to a light wind. To our right, lush, dark green lilac bushes with their heart-shaped leaves showed remnants of lavender flowers that had probably been in full bloom two weeks earlier.

John turned off the engine. "Those, there," he said pointing to the nearest building, "are the living quarters for Pete's workers. Each unit got its own bathroom and shower. None of the other farms, the ones that are left anyway, got anything like it. Some just an outhouse and a shared outdoors shower. Shall we get out, gents, and see where Pete might be?"

My grandfather and I exited the cab and joined John. A rhythmic din flowed from down the dirt path. *Chickens clucking symphonically?* At the back of the house, a small concrete patio led to a screen door.

John pointed to the screen door. "You gents are lucky. Pete's home. Gotta be around here somewhere."

"Because the main door inside the screen one is open?" I said.

"You got it. Pete would never leave the door open if he was away. And only he and Luis has the key."

I pivoted to take in all of the farm. But a squeaking noise pulled my attention back to the screen door. A lanky man, dark-haired under a paper-thin white hat with "Lerman Oil" across the front, wearing light-blue overalls with no shirt underneath, sauntered out. His right hand held what looked to me from my brief class on arms history during law school to be a Sten gun, its barrel pointing down at a 30-degree angle. He stopped a few feet short of us. His angular face carried a few days of stubble. I tried to gauge the look in his deep brown eyes. *Menacing? Strong curiosity? Anger?* It must be Payshe. I stepped in front of my grandfather.

A grin spread over the man's face. He kept his gaze on Grandfather and me as he slightly dipped the weapon toward John. "So John, who have you brought me this time?"

* * * *

John took a few steps toward the man. "Now, Pete, nothin' to get excited about. I'm pretty sure these gents mean you no harm. No need to scare 'em with that ancient gun of yours. Unless you're gonna tell 'em to get out right now, I'll be leavin' and goin' over to Bobby's for a little while before I come back and take 'em back to town. Okay, buddy?"

I walked over to where John stood, keeping my eye on the gun—glad it was still directed toward the ground. I pointed to my back trouser pocket and said, "Might I take out a business card to show you? My name is Joel Gordon, and I believe you're Peter Zimmer. I'm representing your stepfather, Martin Ross. I'm not sure if you know, he's been accused of murdering a man named Henry Casman in Brooklyn."

"Accused of murder, is he?" the man said. "Well, well, well."

I took out my wallet and walked toward the man. I handed him a card and extended my hand. He took the card, hesitated for a moment, and then shook. I motioned toward Grandfather. "And this is my investigator helping with Martin's case, Frank Wolf—he's also my grandfather." I stepped back.

The gun angled even further toward the ground. I relaxed a bit. The man stared at Grandfather. A glint appeared in his eyes. "He's an investigator? And he's your grandfather?"

Zimmer turned to the driver. "Well, John, I guess you've brought me a different type of business than those connivers you usually bring."

With his free hand, Zimmer motioned to me and Grandfather. "But two things, Mr. Lawyer and Mr. Investigator. One, I didn't know you were coming, which is rude—I do have a phone, and I'm listed in the directory. And two, what does my stepfather's defense have to do with me?"

My grandfather moved forward. "Ah, Mr. Zimmer, we must offer you our profound apologies for failing to call to establish an appointment for our visit. No excuse on our part will suffice."

Grandfather coughed. "As for your question related to your stepfather's defense, we are in hopes that you would wish to help us in our efforts, as he vehemently proclaims his innocence. Do you not?"

"Martin 'proclaims his innocence,' does he? Well that's none of my business. Do I want to help? I can't say I do, I can't say I don't. But talking to the two of you about what Martin's accused of might be interesting."

Zimmer looked at his watch and turned to John. "Okay, John, it's now 1:40. I've got a delivery coming at 2:30. You know Bobby's probably asleep, but what your family does to each other is none of my business. Just be back by 2:20 to pick up these people, and everything will be all right."

John gave Zimmer a mock salute and walked to the car. Zimmer, in turn, indicated with his head for us to follow him toward the screen door. "Won't be offering you any refreshments. You've got around 40 minutes. Let's see what's on your minds."

* * * *

The screen door opened to a small mudroom jammed with a washer and dryer from the 1960's, shoes and boots tidily stored on a wall rack, a wooden bench, and labeled glass bottles filled with powders and liquids along the floor edges.

We took one step up into a yellow linoleum-floored kitchen with a sink, counter, and white cupboards framing a large window on the left, a gas stove and refrigerator straight ahead, and an arched entryway on the right to an oval dinette set with a red Formica table and four red and white cushioned steel chairs. A red plastic napkin holder centered the table.

Peter, as he entered, had placed his gun atop the counter. He motioned us to sit, but indicated not on a chair closest to the kitchen entryway. The chair was pushed in close to the table with an apron carefully folded over its back. *Why was that chair special?* He then took the seat facing me, Grandfather to his right.

My grandfather gave me a nod to start. *Ease into the conversation.* I sensed this man was not one for a deposition or interview approach.

I smiled at Zimmer. "May I call you Peter, or Payshe?"

Zimmer leaned back. His dark eyes bored into me. "Hmmm, my step-father calls me Payshe. That's how he must have referred to me when you spoke to him. Do you speak Yiddish?"

Why ask that question? Grandfather did not hesitate. He responded in Yiddish. "I came to America after the War. I, of course, speak Yiddish, and Joel speaks some but understands much."

Zimmer shrugged his shoulders and answered in English. "Well then, call me Payshe. That's what my real father, *zichrono l'bracha,* would have called me had he had not been killed by those *besterds.*"

That Zimmer used the Yiddish expression for "May his memory be for a blessing" made sense. But why would he refer to the Nazi murderers of his father in a Yiddish-accented "besterds," when he had no other accent? I cast a quick glance at my grandfather. His face showed no tension or confusion.

The gun on the counter gave me an idea. I pivoted and pointed at it. "Payshe," I said. "Is that an old Sten gun?"

Payshe's eyebrows raised and his eyes widened. "You're into guns? Yes, you might think it's a Sten gun, but it's a Błyskawica, a Polish-made version of the Sten given to only the best resistance fighters. My father had one in his Partisans' unit. My mother told me. For several years, I looked far and wide for one. Finally, in 1967, before the rules for purchase got stricter, I found one in a World War II gun catalogue, being sold by a guy in Poland. I snapped it up. Didn't care what it cost. Paid a good amount for the shipping, too. All registered and legal now."

I smiled. "And you keep it loaded?"

His eyebrows remained lifted. He tilted his head. "You think I came out with the gun for show? Of course I always keep it loaded. The world's full of bastards that are looking to hurt people."

"Bastards," he had said—not "*besterds*." *What was going on? Why the distinction?* I quickly looked at my grandfather—still a neutral expression. But I had a segue. "Yes, it's sometimes a terrible world. That's what's brought us here to talk with you about your stepfather being accused of murder. As my grandfather mentioned, we were hoping that you might have information that could help him."

Payshe's two fists hit the table softly. "Help him? Let me be straight with you. He's my stepfather and not my father, and I don't particularly like him—never did. But even if I had a liking for him, what would I know about this murder accusation? Martin moved away three years ago. I don't know what his life's been like or what trouble he's gotten himself into. So what else can I do for you?"

I couldn't lose the momentum. He was taking the offense and driving to end our visit. I said quickly, "Did you know Martin had been arrested for murder?"

He shook his head. "No, how would I know? I don't read your New York newspapers, just *The Times Journal*, and I didn't see anything in there." His eyes narrowed. "And I really don't hang around with the town's *yentes* who might have heard something."

He was still trying to maintain the offense. So I redirected. "Then did you know the victim, Martin Casman?" I asked.

Payshe's eyes narrowed, and he glanced a few times from side to side. "Know him? That might be too strong of a term. First I came across him was a few months ago when I showed up at the Plum Street *shul* for my mother's *yahrzeit,* and he was also there. Said he learned of my mother's death a few years before, and he wanted to honor her memory. Seems he knew Mama as a young man in Druya before the War. And just so there are no games here between us, I'm sure you know he made a scene about Martin's having been a kapo at Auschwitz. That's about it for how I knew of Casman."

Grandfather opened his hands toward Payshe. "If I may ask, Mr. Zimmer, you stated that you never liked your stepfather. What was the cause or causes for the dislike? Is it that he somehow treated you unfairly?"

Payshe frowned and snickered. "Unfairly? Ha! More like too fairly."

His eyes moved from me to Grandfather. "You are looking at me as if I'm a *meshuganer*. Here's the thing. He tried too hard to be my father, and that wasn't going to happen."

He grabbed the edge of the table and leaned forward. "He wanted to adopt me, have my last name changed to his—my mother wouldn't have it." His sneer deepened. "She told me from the time I could understand that I was the son of Notke Zimmer, a true hero who gave his life fighting so I could live."

He waved a hand. *Was he banishing the thought of his being adopted by Martin? Or dismissing Martin as a father?* Payshe continued, "And I was named after my mother's father, Payshe Rappaport. She always called me '*mein tattelle.*' I belonged to my mother and real father whose name I would always honor. 'You will forever be your true father's son,' my mother, who was a saint, would say to me. 'Never forget this.' The more Martin tried to be nice to me, to build a relationship as if I were his own, the more I hated him for it."

Payshe's lips tightened and jaws clenched. *Was he actually raging about Martin wanting to care for him? How much of a 'meshuganer," a nut, a less than stable person, was he? How do I figure him out?* I was glad my grandfather spoke up.

"It is wonderful, Mr. Zimmer, to hold such reverence for a parent. I understand your father was a true hero and why you are attached so strongly to him."

Grandfather coughed. "Yet, based on our interview with Martin, it appears you do not wish to exist in a completely adversarial relationship with your stepfather. Just a few months ago, you graciously invited him to visit with you to observe some of your advances in poultry management. Is my assumption correct?"

Payshe's face reddened as he scowled and fidgeted. His voice rose. "Well, I'm not a completely ungrateful taker." His eyes darted back and forth between Grandfather and me. "Martin did teach me a lot about farming. He probably told you that he let me have the farm for a buck. So every once in a while, I think I should show him what I've done better with what he started."

He again waved a hand. "But that doesn't mean I have any affection for him."

"So I take it," I said, "you've never visited Martin in Brooklyn? Never drove or took the bus?"

Payshe glared. "If Martin told you I came to see him in Brooklyn, he's lying."

My grandfather put up a hand. "No, no, Mr. Zimmer. Martin not once said you had come to see him in Brooklyn."

Grandfather took a moment to remove his hat and place it on his lap. "Mr. Zimmer, on a different subject, I do not wish to conjecture, but I am curious. How did what Mr. Casman said at your mother's *yahrzeit* observance about Martin having been a kapo strike you? For instance, were you surprised? Perhaps angry?"

Payshe crossed his arms. "The best words to describe it would be increased contempt. I told myself, maybe it wasn't just something personal between him and me? Maybe I had always known the real man behind the front? Maybe that's why I never liked him?"

"'The front'?" I asked.

His eyes blazed. "Yeah, the front. Meaning the guy who was religious, wore a hat or *kippah* around the farm, contributed to all sorts of charities, gave in to all requests for extended credit from his customers—that guy, from what Casman said, that guy was also nice to the Nazis, a collaborator, a kapo at Auschwitz. Yeah, I had no trouble believing it."

I tensed and took a breath. I hadn't ever come across someone like him. I couldn't let my anger compromise the interview. "But Peter, you yourself said Martin was kind to you. And I'm trying to understand how the kindness caused your very opposite emotion. Regardless, might there be anything you can share with us that might help Martin's defense?"

"Help him? Didn't they find…" He scowled. "I mean the police must have some solid evidence for thinking Martin did it. No, I can't think of anything."

Didn't he just say, "didn't they find .." What was he going to say? Definitely something to discuss with my grandfather, later. For now, we had to keep up our momentum. Grandfather may have been thinking the same. "Then, Mr. Zimmer," Grandfather said, "is it possible you could shed some more light on our understanding Henry Casman, the murder victim, yes? After your encounter with Mr. Casman at the *shul*, did you ever see or speak to him again?"

Payshe turned directly toward Grandfather. His eyes narrowed. "Didn't I say 'no games between us?' I'm sure you have phone records for the dead man. And you know I spoke to him long-distance three times. The first, a few days after the scene at the *shul*. He called one night and asked a ton of questions about my mother. About what she told me about her life in the Partisans, her arrest, how she survived until the War ended, and how she came to marry Martin. He also wanted to know about my father and said he thought he knew him before the War when my father would visit an aunt and uncle in Druya."

He looked down. "That's why my father found himself in Druya and not in his Ukrainian home town the day the Nazis stormed in. And how he wound up with that particular Partisan unit after he made his escape from Druya at the same time as my mother."

Payshe looked up. "That was the first time I spoke to him on the phone. I couldn't wait for his questions to end."

"But after, you called him two times, right?" I said.

He nodded. "Yes, both times I wanted to clarify some of the things he told me about life in Druya before the War." He smiled. "You know I may write a book someday about my mother and real father. I just wanted to make sure I had the facts right."

"Ah, Mr. Zimmer," Grandfather said, "your own clarifications are most helpful. Thank you."

Payshe tilted his head. *Was he confused about my grandfather's claim that his "clarifications" had been "most helpful?"* I was. But I had seen Grandfather being disingenuous to our advantage in previous cases. Yet, Payshe could be feeling that my grandfather was "playing games" with him.

Grandfather looked at his watch. "Ah, Mr. Bucci will be here in another ten minutes. Mr. Zimmer, I do not know if it will please or irritate you when I tell you that Martin is very proud of your achievements in the Rutgers University agricultural school."

With furrowed brows and tightened lips, Payshe was clearly irritated. He snapped, "Well, la di da. He's proud of me, is he? Well good for him."

Payshe paused, then slowly nodded. "But he's right. I did really well at Rutgers. Not just in The School of Agriculture. People call you an Aggie and think you majored in corn husking. First two years, I took the same courses as the Arts and Sciences boys. I majored in chemistry, you know. Graduated magna cum laude, period."

He crossed his arms and leaned back. Grandfather nodded vigorously and smiled.

"Yes, despite the irritation it may have caused you, and I am speaking for myself and not for Martin, what you describe is quite an achievement, no?"

Payshe returned a wan smile. My grandfather went on. "I, too, along with my interest in philosophy at my Vienna university, possessed a secondary specialization in chemistry. Thus, might you excuse my enthusiasm as I ask my next question? I noticed corn growing in the distance. Do you by any chance mix carbon powder in the soil to increase the size and vitality of the corn?"

Payshe leaned forward and uncrossed his arms. "Yes, yes I do. You know your stuff—nutrients."

"Ah, very smart," Grandfather said.

Were Payshe's eyes crinkling—his jaw muscles relaxing and his smile widening? "Mr. Wolf," he said, "do I have it right, that's your name?"

Grandfather nodded, and Payshe went on. "Not only that, Mr. Wolf, but I used to get my chicken feed from Adamo Feed. Gaspare, Mr. Adamo, is a good man, fair prices, but a few years back I started making my own mash from the corn I grew. And guess what? Because my corn has more nutrients and I also added ground soybeans for protein to the mash, my chickens are bigger, stronger, and lay more eggs than on other farms, especially those outfits that keep the chickens in cages."

The man is smart and creative. I had to admire this aspect of the guy.

He chuckled. "I trust the two of you not to tell the folks at Purina what I just told you. Haven't made the time yet to file a patent."

He laughed loudly and looked toward the gun. "Now I don't want to come after you."

Just then we heard the sound of car tires on gravel. Payshe jumped up. "Well, that's gotta be John come for you. Your visit turned out to be alright. But don't ever come unannounced again."

I put up my hand. "We won't come unannounced again," I said. "We promise."

Payshe shook Grandfather's hand. He nodded at me.

I hoped that we would never have to return.

As we were about to depart through the mudroom, Grandfather stopped, turned to Payshe, and spoke in Yiddish. "Ah, Mr. Zimmer, the farmer's life is not easy. I hope you have good helpers. I noticed that you maintain lodging for your workers. Did I correctly see *zeks* units?"

Payshe's voice rose. "*Zeks, nein, ich hub ziben.*"

Grandfather answered in English. "Thank you. Seven and not six, as I miscounted. Very impressive, Mr. Zimmer."

I didn't say anything. My grandfather was not one to miscount the number of units when he was eying something. Seven, not six, Payshe had corrected him. *What was my grandfather after?*

* * * *

"Ah, Mr. Bucci," Grandfather said after we had settled into the taxi, "I hope that your unannounced visit to your cousin did not cause unwanted irritation?"

John laughed. "I'd say it caused wanted irritation. Bobby and I were born a few days apart, and we grew up like brothers. We teased each other, wrestled, played stupid jokes. We're both now forty, and to the great, what did ya call it, 'irritation' to our wives, we're still at each other. Bobby slung some Italian cuss words at me when I woke him, and then we had a beer together."

He lifted his head toward the rearview mirror. "But don't you worry, gents. Just one beer. East Landis Motel, right?"

My grandfather and I laughed. "Yes, the East Landis Motel," I said. "And John, we trust your driving."

"Good. You can. I take my profession serious." He chuckled. "And I see that Pete didn't harm a hair on your heads, him gun-totin' and all."

I smiled and looked at my grandfather. His jaws tightened, his lips tightly pursed. "No, thank God, we are well," Grandfather said. "But when a firearm is displayed in the fashion Mr. Zimmer exhibited, then various consequences, including the unintended, may occur. Therefore, yes, I say we are well, thank God."

For the remaining few minutes, we rode in silence. Bucci took the same route back on East Avenue as we had come. My grandfather leaned back and closed his eyes.

We crossed Landis Avenue, and Bucci pulled over near the southeast corner of East and Landis. He took out our bags and walked us down Landis to the motel's entrance.

"A pleasure, gents. You know how to find me should you have the occasion again."

My grandfather and I shook hands with him. "We will certainly do so," said Grandfather. "You have been most helpful."

* * * *

I pushed open the heavy glass door entrance to the East Landis Motel and followed my grandfather into a darkly lit, well-trod carpeted lobby with a front desk enclosure, wooden phone booth, and an elevator with a metallic scissor gate door. A young, thin man wearing a white dress shirt and wide paisley tie sat behind the front desk. To our left, through open double doors, a brightly-lit large room with a checkered green and white linoleum floor held six white-clothed tables, each set up for up to six diners each. A long, buffet table with empty chafing dishes, beverage dispensers, and serving utensils took up a wall. Toward the far end against gray velvet draped windows, a man in a white apron stood drying glasses behind a long bar with at least ten wooden stools, all unoccupied. He waved to us.

A wall clock atop the front desk enclosure showed the time—2:40. *Maybe the dining area and bar would be filled with patrons later in the day.*

The taciturn front-desk clerk checked us in. After I gave him the ten dollar room charge, the clerk turned to a cubby hole at his back and retrieved a folded paper. "You're Gordon?" he asked, looking at me.

"Yes," I said, taking the paper. I looked quickly. A message from Julie at my office asked for me to call Detective Carlucci at the precinct number she had included. "Everything's okay," I said to my grandfather, fearing he's worried. And then in Yiddish, *"Shpeter."* It could wait until later.

The man gave me a large key and told us to follow him to the elevator. He slid the accordion gate into its side pocket and pulled the elevator door open. "You're on the second floor—room's right across from the elevator."

He closed the door and turned a lever on a side panel toward the number 2. The whining elevator rose slowly, until it rattled softly to a stop once the man, after a few attempts, lined it up with the door. He pushed the door open. "I think it's good," he said. "But watch your steps anyway."

We got off, and he pointed to our room. No number showed on the door. "That's it. Like I said, right across from the elevator."

He turned back and before pulling the door behind him, said, "Oh yeah, dining room and bar opens at 5:00. Case you're interested. And TV is a quarter for each half hour."

We had to pay to watch TV? I'd never heard of it.

"Not bad," I said entering the room and seeing two double beds. When Julie had made the reservation, she told me that though she had requested double beds, the reservation person couldn't guarantee it. "Depends what we got when you check in." It wouldn't have been the end of the world, but I worried I would have to share a bed with my grandfather—which I hadn't done since I was eight and ran to his room after awakening from nightmares.

In addition to the beds, it had a sink in front of a wall mirror. To the right of the sink, a small room with a toilet. I had seen a sign labelled **shower** in the hallway. A table with a lamp that provided the room's only light separated the two beds. A long, wooden, brown-lacquered writing desk with dresser drawers below and leg space and wooden chair in the middle stood along the wall opposite the beds. Near the desk, stood an aluminum assembly with five paper-covered hangers showing the name of a local dry cleaner. Another wooden chair sat near a paint-flaked window housing a small air conditioner, humming loudly.

On a metallic stand at the foot of the far bed, a seventeen-inch, black and white RCA television. A small device attached to the television's side. Wires from the device led to the back of the TV. Atop the TV, a slot for quarters. So that's what the clerk meant. I shook my trouser pocket. I had a couple hours of quarters on me.

My grandfather took off his hat and hung up his suitcoat. He settled himself in the desk chair, facing me. I stood with folded paper in hand.

"Nuh, Yoeli, might *shpeter* have become *itster*? I am eager to know the contents of the phone message."

I smiled, understanding his use of the Yiddish word for now. "Detective Carlucci called my office and left a message for me to call him back." I looked around. No phone in the room. "I'll run down to the lobby and call him from the pay phone. I'll also check in on Aliya."

"And you will ask Aliya to let your mother know that we are safely arrived? And while you are downstairs, I will unpack and take a rest as I review in my mind our visit to Martin's stepson."

My grandfather's eyes rose toward the ceiling. I wondered if he really would unpack before I returned. Or would he spend all of the time in his mind back at the farm visualizing and reviewing every sighting, gesture, and word spoken?

* * * *

The lobby phone booth was unoccupied. Through the operator, I charged the call to my PWR corporate account. An Officer Sanchez answered, putting me on hold while he tried to find Detective Carlucci. Ten minutes passed. I wondered if he had forgotten me. Boy, the long distance charges were piling up.

Finally, Carlucci came on. "Hello, Counselor. A bit of news for you. Forensics got back to me on the ticket stub you found in the victim's apartment. They were able to lift a partial print. There's no match to your client, but it's only a partial anyway, and partial matching don't stand up in court."

Carlucci paused. "If I'm guessin' right, you don't think it would match to your client, even if it was a full print?"

Of course, not. Even though I hadn't thought much of the ticket stub since sending it along to Carlucci, still I hid my disappointment that a match would identify the real killer. "You're guessing correctly, Detective," I replied.

"Oh, well, sorry I don't have better news, but I thought you'd want to know right away. How's your granddad? Quite an investigator, he is. Send regards from his favorite detective. And oh, I'll see you and, I guess, Mr. Wolf, at your client's evidentiary hearing on the 21st."

"Yes, great, see you then. And thank you for calling." I hung up.

I called Aliya and asked that the charges be reversed. It didn't feel right for the firm paying. Would Aliya be home? She answered on the first ring and accepted the charges.

"Yes," I answered after greetings, "I...we're both fine. And so far, we'll be arriving back at Port Authority around 12:15 tomorrow afternoon.

"Quite an encounter with Martin's stepson just a little while ago. But I'll tell you all about it tomorrow when I get home. Let's keep this call to around three minutes, long distance charges and all."

My voice rose. "But how are you? How's the... How are you feeling?"

"I'm fine, Joel. Not to worry. I've been reviewing Stuyvesant Group policy and going over some readings from grad school. You know, I start on the 21st—that's just a week from this Monday."

"The 21st—that's..." I mumbled.

"Is there something wrong, Joel, about my starting on the 21st?"

"No, not really, it's just that Carlucci reminded me that Martin's evidentiary hearing is on the 21st, and I'd hoped you'd be there. But no big deal."

Neither of us spoke for a moment. Then Aliya said, "I know, I know, it's your first criminal defense case. I'll be there in spirit, though."

I hesitated. My head said it wasn't a big deal. And after all, it's her first day of work for which she had been preparing since she entered grad school. But my heart wanted her to see me in my first day as a defense attorney. The right thing was not to press her. "Sure, of course, it's okay. Zaida will be there, and I'll tell you all about it afterwards. I don't know about Mom. I guess I wish she wouldn't come. It's hard on her."

Aliya's voice grew firm. "But you won't tell her not to come, right Joel? It should be up to her. And speaking of your mother, unless you've already done it, I'll call her at the store and let her know you and Zaida are well and at your motel."

"No, I haven't called her. Thanks, and I love you."

I didn't want to leave it at that. *The Wizard of Oz* was one of our favorite movies, and we would often play on phrases from it. I couldn't resist. "You know what I discovered, Aliya?"

"What, Joel?"

"That I have a heart, you know why?"

Aliya said quickly. "Because it's breaking for some reason?"

I laughed. "Now let's not get overly dramatic. Just sort of. Because it tells me I miss you. Good enough?"

"I'll take it, Joel. Say hi to Zaida. See you tomorrow."

We hung up.

My grandfather was sitting as I'd left him. But an emptied suitcase lay on a bed. "Aliya says hi, Zaida. And she's calling Mom to let her know that we're safe and sound."

He motioned for me to take the spare chair and sit near him. "Yes," he said, "after our disturbing moments with Martin's stepson, it is good to state that we are 'safe and sound.'"

I told him about my conversation with Carlucci.

"Ah," Grandfather said, "then the lack of a full fingerprint does not present doubt as to Martin's involvement in Mr. Casman's murder nor does it add to the evidence against him. Yet, the presence of even a partial fingerprint may help our case. I must dwell more assiduously on this finding before I am comfortable sharing a certain thought with you."

What was Grandfather thinking? I knew from years of hearing him say he needed more time before sharing something that there was no prodding him to come out with it.

"All right. When you're ready. But can we now talk about our visit to Payshe?"

He leaned back as far as the small chair would allow. "Yes, yes, Joel. I also would like to review what we saw and heard. And permit me to expand on our immediate plans. Upon the completion of our review, might we walk the few blocks to the Goldstein's Delicatessen that your young eyes spotted earlier today? It is kosher, and as we ate our combined breakfast and lunch on the bus, we will soon be ready for an early dinner, yes?"

I nodded. "Yes, I'm already hungry. And after?"

"We return to our accommodations, watch local and national news at 6:00, and as we come, at least for the present, to some settlement with our own thoughts, we remove ourselves from this wearying day into sleep or some other quieting activity such as your watching a baseball game should Martin's Phillies be on the television tonight, yes? And tomorrow morning, as planned, our bus returning to New York departs at 8:30. Good?"

"Yes and good," I said, slapping my trouser pocket. "If a game's on, I've enough quarters to go deep into extra innings."

Grandfather smiled. "Watch as long as you wish. The television's sound will not prevent somnolence descending upon me."

He cleared his throat. "Now, Joel, what struck you about our visit?"

I hadn't taken notes—once we were in the house with Payshe, I didn't think that would be the right approach. Should I now try to order my thoughts or just say the first thing that came to mind? What's to think about? He's my grandfather and not a law professor or a judge. I let out, "Zaida, do you remember when Payshe said, 'Didn't they find...'"—hesitated, and then made a generalized statement of how the police must have solid evidence to accuse

Martin? I'm pretty sure he was going to say he knew the police had found Martin's fingerprints on the murder weapon."

Grandfather nodded. "A good starting point for our review. His blurted words and quick recovery are seared into my memory. Which means what for us, Joel?"

Means? Means? I'd not overthink it. Sometimes the simplest answer is the best. "That he lied and had heard about Martin's arrest. That he somehow has information about the case."

I hesitated. "But how? The New York newspaper accounts didn't say anything about the police finding Martin's prints on the knife. And I doubt that Payshe knows an informant at the 61st."

My grandfather chuckled. "Yes, I doubt that Detective Carlucci has a mole in his midst. Let us place in abeyance that mystery as you convey what next comes to your mind."

I was prepared. "Did it strike you, Zaida, that when he said 'bastards' one time in reference to the Nazis, his accent was Eastern European and sounded like 'besterds?'"

Grandfather looked up. "I did, Yoeli. And I suspect that you noticed that when he spoke the word at another instance, his pronunciation was not accented. Yes?"

I wanted to stand and pace around, but I remained seated. "I did, I did. What do you make of it?"

Grandfather looked up. "Let us together make something of it."

Grandfather put a finger to his temple. "Think for a moment. In what context was the word accented and in what context without an accent?"

"Easy, on the first part. He had an accent when he told us about his father being killed by the Nazis. The second time? I might remember if I gave it some thought, but please tell me."

Grandfather shifted in his seat and sat up straight. His gaze drifted beyond me. "I am picturing the moment, so you will please allow me to jog your memory. You had just asked him if it was his habit to keep the gun loaded. His reply was?"

Just a moment's thought. "That he did, and if I'm quoting correctly, because 'the world's full of bastards that are looking to hurt people.'"

Grandfather looked at me and smiled. "Yes, you are quoting directly. And what is it that you make of this differentiation?"

"I'm thinking that when he's talking about the Holocaust and referring specifically to Nazis, he puts on, for some reason, an accent. But if he's generalizing about people, he doesn't."

"I believe, Joel, you are close to the mark. But must it be that he is 'putting on' an accent?"

I frowned. "How else?"

My grandfather opened his hands to me. "Ah, Joel, please permit us also to hold that question as you share any additional observations."

"Hmmm. Besides the way he greeted us with a loaded submachine gun, I find him to be a *meshuganer*. For heaven's sake! He hates Martin because Martin was 'too fair' to him? Because Martin tried so very hard to be a good parent? Am I off base, here, Zaida?"

Grandfather laughed. "This particular baseball metaphor implies that one has already reached base for one to be 'off base.' But for now, let us continue for a few moments longer. Is there another observation you wish to share?"

I rubbed my forehead. "Just one, and it's a question. I know you too well, Zaida. You didn't miscount the number of units in that workers building. What was that all about?"

My grandfather wagged a finger. "Ah, you know me too well. Allow me to answer your question with a question. You understand Yiddish well enough. In Yiddish, therefore, how many units did Mr. Zimmer, indignantly and proudly, tell me he built?"

"I remember, exactly. He said, 'zhiben,' seven, right?"

My grandfather shook his head. "Not 'exactly,' Yoeli. Mr. Zimmer said, 'ziben,' with the same opening sound as in 'zoo.' Are you comprehending my clarification?"

I stood, stepped toward my grandfather, then stooped and put a hand on his shoulder. "Zaida, I think I get it. You and I, Mom, Martin, we've all got a *Litvak* accent and say 'zhiben' for seven, with the opening sound for that number the same as, say, the French name Jacques, as in Cousteau. And certainly Martin's deceased wife from his hometown would have said 'zhiben,' yet Payshe didn't." I straightened and paced, frustrated. I shook my head. "I'm getting parts, Zaida, but the whole is really confusing me."

"Joel, please sit. A few moments of calm reflection will aid in our analyses."

I sat, and Grandfather continued. "Allow me to merge your observations into a unified inference regarding an instability in the character of Martin's stepson. From this inference, let us explore implications for our case."

My grandfather grimaced. "You alluded to him as a '*meshuganer*,' translated into the English parlance of today, a 'nut,' yes?"

"Yes, that would be right, Zaida."

"Therefore, our critical analyses calls upon us to examine his 'nutty,' or, might we characterize it, his irrational behavior as we unravel our mystery, yes?"

I nodded. "Makes sense."

"Mr. Zimmer greeted us with a gun in hand—for me, the most extreme of the irrationalities. Why?"

I put up my hand. "But that could have been for show, just to demonstrate who's in charge."

Grandfather waved his hand. "Perhaps. And before we sat down at his kitchen table, what do you remember?"

The chair with the apron draped over it. "Payshe motioned us away from the chair with the apron over it. Of course! It must have been where his mother always sat. He's made it into a shrine."

"Very good. I like very much how you extricated its meaning."

Grandfather's eyes narrowed. "Then back to his use of an accented '*besterds*' in one pronouncement and without an accent just moments later."

When I was a kid, my grandfather would guide me in putting together a difficult jigsaw puzzle. His voice would be measured, focusing me, encouraging patience. So I just nodded. "Go on, Zaida."

"Your ascribing irrationality to hearing Mr. Zimmer explain his growing dislike for Martin because Martin wished to do well by him is understandable. But for Mr. Zimmer, this reaction is natural and rational."

How could that be? How could "nutty" behavior be rational? I would wait for Grandfather to explain, while I added, "And we have why Payshe speaks in a *Galitzianer* accent when he grew up with *Litvak*-speaking parents."

My grandfather grimaced. "Again, I believe the answer to these questions lies within what occurred during the Holocaust. The evil perpetrated by the Nazis and their henchmen cast a darkness over the world. Yes, after many years, they were beaten back, and some light returned to us. But consider that some of the darkness settled into the minds and hearts of individuals who survived the onslaught."

Grandfather spread his hands. "For instance, there is Martin and his shame of having been a kapo, even as he insists he did the right thing. Mr. Casman and his innate propensity for anger that was magnified and focused by his Holocaust experiences. Dora, Martin's deceased wife, who lost the man she truly loved and then, finding herself alone and physically maimed, married a decent man, but one who did not measure up to the husband she had lost. Each carried a darkness impermeable to any light that may have alleviated their oppression."

I shuddered. *How does one live through that horror of a never ending darkness. I couldn't imagine myself doing so.* I opened and closed my fists. I shook my head. "But that didn't happen to everyone. It didn't happen to... to..."

My grandfather rose and approached me. He took my face in his hands. "You are about to say, you believe the darkness did not envelope me or your mother, or even many other survivors. In this, you would be partially correct. I am afraid I must say that some darkness exists in all who survived the

War—in our minds, in our hearts, in our bones. But most, accepting that the elimination of total darkness is not possible, have made it their life's efforts to push forward, to let the light in that calls for the building of a better world for themselves, for their offspring, for their larger communities."

Grandfather returned to his chair. I relaxed. I did have in my own family examples of individuals who fought against the darkness, making the world brighter. I was grateful. "Yes, Zaida, go on."

My grandfather exhaled deeply. "Ah, Yoeli, but there is additional distress that emanates from the darkness—in some instances, it also infiltrates the next generation. As it has happened with Payshe Zimmer."

Payshe Zimmer, yes. I was getting it. *But what about myself?* Had some darkness also settled into me? Had I ever examined myself as to how my being the son and grandson of Holocaust survivors affected me? Right now, I had a job to do—my client's welfare was at stake. But when this case was over, I'd talk to my mother—talk to my grandfather. I wasn't a kid anymore running from anything more than a skeletal rendition of what had happened to them.

"Yes, as with Payshe?" I asked.

My grandfather's eyes reddened at the edges. *Were they also watery?*

"Ah, yes, with Mr. Zimmer," Grandfather said, sighing. "Consider that from the time he was an infant, he was filled with stories about, how does he term it, his 'real' father, the Partisan hero who died on a mission against the Nazis. His mother tragically lost her husband shortly after they married and he was conceived. He called his mother a 'saint,' and he her 'little *tattelle*.' He was not to be in any fashion Martin's son who could never achieve equal status with her first husband. Thus, he was nurtured with an ardent love for a saintly mother and a father he could never have in his real life, along with a revulsion for the man who could have been a worthy surrogate parent. Even into his adulthood, he went to great efforts to obtain the exact model gun his father carried in the Partisans."

My grandfather's puzzle construction was interlocking, but some pieces were still missing. "But why does he have a *Galitzianer* accent?" I said. "He said 'ziben' and not 'zhiben.' The way we say it."

"Nuh, , Joel, might you recall how his father found himself in the same Partisan unit as his mother?"

I closed my eyes. "Yes, I do. Payshe told us his father was visiting relatives when the Nazis took over Druya."

Grandfather's eyebrows rose in a wan smile. "Exactly. Notke Zimmer was not from Druya. He was from…"

"Ukraine," I let out. And Yiddish-speaking people from Ukraine had a *Galitzianer,* not a *Litvak* accent."

"Yes, Joel, they did."

Was what my grandfather suggesting credible? Would Payshe's drive to be one with his father go so far? He would've had to practice constantly to overcome his innate accent. But having encountered the man, I couldn't say that it wasn't possible.

"So where I think you're going, Zaida, is that Payshe developed a split personality?"

"Ah, Joel, Aliya may wish to comment on that conjecture, but I do not believe that he has a split personality in the fashion of a Dr. Jekyll and Mr. Hyde. No, it is not so dramatic where a personality transformation occurs."

I recalled the movie version of Robert Louis Stevenson's book that starred Spencer Tracy. "Not only 'personality transformation,' Zaida, but physical changes to the face and body."

Grandfather smiled. "Not in the least with Mr. Zimmer. Any transformation is moment-by-moment, dependent on the context of what is occurring for him."

Grandfather's smile disappeared. He closed his eyes. "Consider that in general he is a complicated individual. You heard Mr. Bucci describe him as the 'town eccentric' who lives a mostly isolated life and feels threats everywhere—thus, the gun always at his ready—yet he also performs acts of goodness for the community."

Grandfather slowly shook his head. "And consider how much effort must have taken for him to feel one with his father?"

He chuckled. "I remember well when the television show, *Combat*, was popular, how you and your friends would emulate the American soldiers fighting the Nazis. Our living room was often left in shambles."

I laughed. The difficult part of the make-believe with my friends was that no one wished to play the Nazis. Viewing the beat-up living room, my father would chastise me, but my mother and grandfather never said a word. I did have help putting the room back together. "I remember, Zaida. Go on."

"But for Mr. Zimmer, such emulations must have been a daily drill until all aspects of what he conceived to be his father's personality, behavior, response to threats, heroics, and even Yiddish speech patterns became integrated within Payshe's own self, at the ready when a certain situation prompted appearance. Might we imagine the struggle and difficulty of changing one's accent when the people around him spoke in a certain way?"

I would ask Aliya what she thought of my grandfather's theory. I'd also ask Martin about the difference in accents. Part of me felt what Grandfather was saying made sense. Another part thought it preposterous. And yet... I shuddered. *What if he was correct?*

"Zaida," I asked, "the person Mrs. Schnapper said she heard outside of Casman's apartment the night of the murder had a *Galitzianer* accent. You mentioned implications coming out of your analyses. We know that Payshe has a *Galitzianer* accent."

"Yes, and that implication must remain with us as we probe further. There are many individuals with such accents. And one might, in a compacted occurrence, simulate an accent. And while at this moment, that factor is important to us, it will not be exculpatory for Martin without additional proof of his innocence."

I nodded. "I agree. We'll hold on to it. And there's another oddity we haven't fully discussed. That's Payshe's slip that he knew Martin's fingerprints were on the murder weapon. What's your take on it?

"Ah, Joel, I do not yet have a well-formulated 'take.' It is a central puzzle piece lacking surrounding connecting pieces. Perhaps the implication is not so much that he knows of Martin's fingerprints but that he was imparting that they were not his own fingerprints. Are you following my reasoning?"

Was I following? And was the implication of implications that my grandfather thought Payshe was the murderer?

"Without hemming and hawing, Zaida, do you think Payshe killed Henry Casman?"

My grandfather pursed his lips. "Nuh, Joel, it is not a matter of 'hemming and hawing.' I can tell you directly that we have the matter of Martin's fingerprints being on the knife. Mr. Zimmer's prints are not on the knife. Yet, I will also tell you, I do not believe Martin is the killer."

Grandfather exhaled. "And I will tell you directly that I suspect Mr. Zimmer is the killer. But what would have been his motive? He had only recently met Henry Casman. Why did he speak to him three times on the phone? And if the murder was not planned, perhaps in the spur of a certain moment as many are, why would he find himself in Mr. Casman's apartment for the crime to have occurred?"

Grandfather's shoulders slumped. "Mr. Zimmer may be at times irrational or disturbed. But he is also shrewd. If I am correct, and he is the killer, we must supply the proof or have he, himself, proffer an admission."

Grandfather rose. "There is still much work ahead of us. But for now, we are both hungry, no? Might we as planned make our way to the Goldstein's Delicatessen for our early dinner?"

I had gone from hungry to starving. I stood. "Zaida, let's go. It's a short walk, but it's blazing hot outside. Do you need your suit jacket?"

My grandfather reached for his jacket. "While your observation is perfectly reasonable, I will feel more at ease with my jacket upon me. I am in hopes that the delicatessen is air-conditioned. Shall we go?"

* * * *

We crossed Landis to the avenue's north side and turned left. As we passed The Landis movie theater, the Tradesmen's Bank, and a modern post office, the town's appearance stirred memories of the Old West I'd seen on television. Cars were parked at an angle to the sidewalk, like horses once tethered to hitching posts. The day being so hot, there weren't many people walking—and those who were, walked slowly and nodded to us as we passed. A few turned to look—we were strangers in town. One woman stopped us and asked if we needed directions.

We passed 8th Street, and as we approached 7th, my grandfather put his hand on my arm and pointed to his left across the avenue. Just off Landis, I saw a sign for *The Vineland Times Journal*.

"Yes, Zaida," I said, "that's this town's newspaper the taxi driver and Payshe mentioned. Why are you pointing to it?"

"Ah, Joel, it is not only in connection to what was imparted to us, but the gentleman who is its editor-in-chief, a Mr. Ben Leuchter, has a certain renown not only in this local area but also in the larger Jewish community of the United States. I read an article in *Der Tog-Morgen Zhurnal,* my Yiddish-language newspaper, that reported on the man and his paper. The article lauded his integrity, his journalistic excellence, and his generosity in welcoming and easing the transition of immigrants, not only Jewish, into the Vineland community. I subsequently asked my friend, Mrs. Raymond, the head of periodicals at the 42nd Street library, to obtain a few copies of the paper. I believe Mr. Leuchter deserves a Pulitzer Prize for his daily column, 'Keeping Up With The Times,' and if there is a special prize for a small town newspaper, *The Vineland Times Journal* deserves such an accolade."

There must be a reason he was going on about the newspaper and its editor-in-chief. *Patience, Joel, patience.* Meanwhile, I scanned through the stores we had been passing. F.W. Woolworth and Kresge department stores I knew from New York. But we mainly passed smaller shops such as Dunn Shoes, Silverman's Men and Boy's, and Crosby Jewelers. Soon after crossing 6th Street, we came to Goldstein's. The unadorned glass front showed the deli's name, a Kosher sign, and Under Supervision of Rabbi E. Poupko, Philadelphia.

We entered, and at the first gust of cold air, I closed my eyes and breathed deep. The smell of pickles in two barrels at the store's front could give an appetite to someone who had just eaten a five-course meal. Before us stretched a narrow aisle with a glass counter to the right and three square tables with black Formica tops and sculpted metal legs straight ahead. No other customers were there.

What a difference from Kornblatt's in Brooklyn, with its hanging array of salamis, bolognas, corned beefs, pastramis, tongues, liverwursts, roast beefs, and turkey breasts. At Kornblatt's, the deli case held prepared foods such as stuffed cabbage with ground beef, schnitzel, goulash, chicken with mushroom sauce, chicken and vegetable barley soups, noodle and potato kugels, and stuffed derma. The smell of freshly baked ryes, pumpernickels, Russian black breads, bagels, and bialys competed for attention with the pickles.

Here, at Goldstein's, a few salamis, bolognas, and liverwursts labeled Foremost Kosher hung from ceiling hooks. The deli case featured a bowl of coleslaw, a bowl of potato salad, a plate of stuffed derma, and a short stack of sliced turkey breast. Three breads in white paper bags labeled Palace Bakery sat atop the counter. And the square, red Coca Cola vending machine beyond the tables tempted me to take out a few bottles and open them using the attached metal opener at the machine's side.

Two men stood behind the counter—one short, bald, and in glasses, and the other a foot taller with a full head of hair. Each wore white cotton shirts and matching trousers, with a white apron tied at the front.

The short one spoke. "Hello, gentlemen, what can we get you? I'm Al, and this is my brother, Sammy."

He laughed and said what he probably said over and over again to new people. "But you can call us Mutt and Jeff."

Grandfather tipped his hat, and I said 'Hello."

"It is nice to make your acquaintance," Grandfather said. "We wish to partake of your offerings. I would like a turkey breast with mustard sandwich on pumpernickel bread, if you have, with a glass of water.

"Al answered. We sure do, Mr...."

"Wolf, Frank Wolf. And this is my grandson, Mr. Joel Gordon. What would you like, Joel?"

I didn't have to think long. At Kornblatt's I would have had my usual pastrami on rye. But I didn't see any pastrami, so I gave into a weakness. "Salami with mustard on rye." I lifted the bottles of Coke in my hands. "Also some mixed pickles."

My mother and Aliya had pestered me not to eat salami. "No nutrition, too much fat, chemicals, and bad for the health," both would say. But today, *what choice did I have?*

"Okay," Sammy said. "Do you want the sandwiches made for you, or do you want to buy the meat by the quarter or half pound and the bread separately? Cost you fifty cents more if we make them for you."

I'd never come across being asked if I wanted the components separately. I looked at Grandfather who was smiling.

"Made as sandwiches for us." Grandfather said. "It would be most helpful if you do so."

Sammy moved off to prepare our food. Al spoke again. "You two are from New York, right?"

"Yes," I answered and laughed. "What gives us away? Our accents?"

Al also chuckled. "That and other things. What brings you to town?"

Grandfather took a step forward. He did not pursue what "other things." Instead, he said, "We have business with a resident of your town. We are here just overnight, leaving on the morning bus tomorrow."

"What type of business?" Sammy asked loudly as he hand-sliced bread for our sandwiches.

I glanced at my grandfather. He didn't hesitate. "Personal business with a gentleman named Peter Zimmer. Might you be acquainted with him?"

Al snorted. "Acquainted" Everyone in Vineland is acquainted with Pete. He's a town character. But I heard you say 'personal business,' and when I hear that, it means to me, don't ask any questions."

"Ah," Grandfather said, "Your sensitivity is much appreciated. I assume you see Mr. Zimmer from time to time?"

"Hardly ever," Al answered before Sammy added. "Albert, you weren't here about two weeks ago when Pete surprised the hell out of me. I'm pretty sure it was a Friday morning because I was deciding what to put away before we closed at 3:00 for Shabbos. He came in and wanted a sandwich made up. Said he needed it for a trip he was taking. Then I saw him down the street getting ready to board the bus to New York."

Payshe had lied about not traveling to New York. I gave a quick glance at Grandfather. His eyes remained neutral as he pointed to the middle table. "We will take a seat, Joel, yes?"

Sammy brought us our order. Grandfather ate slowly and I with gusto as we discussed the National League race with the brothers, ardent Phillies fans excited about how well they were doing. The salami sandwich was delicious but, yes, quite salty. I took out another Coke and asked that the fifteen cents be added to our tab, which came to $4.85. As I prepared to pay, I looked at Grandfather. He knew what I was asking and shook his head. No tip.

We walked silently back to the motel. A few people had drifted into the restaurant. Bobby Darin's *Mack the Knife* drifted from the bar area. The same clerk operated the lift for Grandfather and me. I looked at my watch—5:07. I took out the key and unlocked our door. Once we were inside our room, Grandfather said not a word until after he hung up his coat and hat.

"In a moment, Joel, you will allow me some privacy, please, as I change into my night clothes. Perhaps you might sit in the lobby for a few minutes, no?"

"Yes, certainly. But what about what we heard at the deli?"

"I take your meaning to be the revelation that I would surmise the Friday, a day before the murder, Mr. Zimmer traveled to New York?"

I nodded.

"It holds great significance. It adds to my certainty that he somehow was involved in the murder. But again, why Mr. Casman? One would think

Martin would have been his homicidal objective. But I must reflect more deeply into what I saw, heard, and learned about Mr. Zimmer. If I am correct, we must, as many of the great American detectives would say, 'flush out' the suspect. Let us suspend discussion until we arrive back in New York tomorrow, yes?"

Was I too tired to argue that I'd love more immediate discussion? Well, why not wait a day? My grandfather himself must certainly be weary. And his practice when facing a quandary was to be alone for a while with his reflections.

"I'll go down to the lobby and be back in about fifteen."

I took the steps down. The clerk ignored me as I sat in an easy chair and picked up a copy of *The Vineland Times Journal*. I headed straight for the Sports section. A columnist named Del Brandt rapturously discussed the Phillies drive for a pennant. I looked at the standings. The Mets were mired in third place, twelve and a half games behind the Phillies. And the Phillies were playing late on the West Coast against the Dodgers and not on TV. Too bad. I could have used a baseball game to relax.

When I returned to the room, my grandfather was in bed under the covers. The air conditioner was running well. The clerk had permitted me to bring up the newspaper. For a while, we discussed all of the baseball standings. We both predicted the Yankees to win the AL pennant. At 6:00, I put in two quarters, and the television came alive allowing me to choose a channel. We watched local news until 6:30 when Walter Cronkite and *The CBS Evening News* came on Channel 10. The lead story was an assassination attempt on Idi Amin, the flamboyant President of Uganda. Eric Sevareid provided commentary on the battle for the Republican nomination. The TV switched off at 7:00. I did not add any more quarters.

My grandfather read all the sections of the newspaper, including the comics. He loved "Peanuts." I asked him if the paper had "Peanuts." It did.

Around 8:00, he asked if the lights could be turned off. I agreed. I could toss and turn for a while until sleep came, while at the same time, mulling the same questions over and over—*If Payshe was the killer, why did he kill Casman and not Martin? What happened between Payshe and Casman after that explosive encounter at the Plum Street synagogue when Casman berated Martin? And how did Martin's fingerprints get on the murder weapon.*

FRIDAY, JUNE 11, 1976

I was up at 6:30.

"Good morning," my grandfather said, smiling at me from his bed. "I have awaited your awakening. I hope you are not over-rested due to my forcing an early sleep upon you?"

I laughed. "Not at all. Nice to feel like a teenager again."

"Very well, then," he said, "I do not know the exact amount of time I slept, for I spent the early part of the evening reviewing a plan in my mind for how we proceed next."

In my undershirt and pajama pants, I jumped up and swung my feet to the side of the bed. "What is it? I didn't fall asleep for a while either thinking about the case and Martin's defense."

"Ah, Joel, I request forbearance. Our bus leaves at 8:30. Might we allow relaxed time for our morning ablutions and prayers before we pack and walk the short distance to the bus station? Not far from the station, as the Goldstein gentlemen mentioned to us yesterday, is the kosher Palace Bakery. Do you remember the location?"

I nodded. "Down Landis to the Boulevard and to the right. About a block from the station."

"Yes, that is also my memory. Might you attend to yourself first and then make your way to this bakery to purchase pastries. I noticed a sign indicating the restaurant below offers coffee in the morning. In this way, we will fortify ourselves for our journey."

Grandfather sat up and stretched. "Then, upon our arrival in New York, I suggest we make our way directly to my office where I will convey, in detail, my thoughts. Yes?"

"Okay." I quickly washed up, dressed, and left.

Vineland, itself, was also just rising. A few cars lined Landis Avenue. I encountered a couple of passersby as I went into jog speed. I walked into the bakery. The smells of its freshly baked breads and pastries coaxed the purchase of two large almond danishes for myself, and a cheese danish, my grandfather's favorite. Back and forth in 25 minutes. At the hotel restaurant, I picked up a large regular coffee and a decaf Sanka.

Grandfather was dressed and packing when I made it back to the room. "Cheese danish and a Sanka," he laughed. "As you can see, the world outside of Brooklyn is not so different."

At 7:45, we checked out. The same clerk as yesterday. When did he sleep? Grandfather purchased a copy of *The Vineland Times Journal*. "Reading makes the time on the bus go more quickly," he said.

The clerk took the key and muttered, "See ya next time."

I carried my grandfather's suitcase the four blocks to the bus station. 7:55. A few people sat in cars at the curb opposite the station enclosure. Dropping off riders, I guessed. No sign of John Bucci or his cab. I wouldn't have minded saying another goodbye.

The bus left right on time. The return trip to New York matched the previous day's ride in reverse. Same route, same driver, same stops, and same "don't get left behind" warnings.

* * * *

My grandfather and I came off the bus and into the basement arrivals area at Port Authority. I startled, seeing my mother as soon as we got off the bus. I nudged Grandfather and pointed. *What was my mom doing there?* My heart pounded. *Was she okay? Aliya, and the baby! Did Martin do something stupid?*

Grandfather wasn't fazed seeing my mother. He walked up to her and hugged. "Malkeh," he said, "what brings you away from your store in the middle of the day? Regardless, it is a most pleasant surprise."

My mother motioned to me. I put down Grandfather's suitcase and my bag and gave her a hug.

She took my face in her hands. "My Joel, you look ashen. All is well. Aliya told me that you would be on this bus. I am guessing that your Zaida wishes to go to his office." She looked at Grandfather. He nodded. "So I made sandwiches and thought we would go to the nearest Horn & Hardart for beverages and have lunch together."

I breathed out deeply. "Great plan, Mom. Yeah, I was a bit worried. And I am hungry." I gave her another hug.

"Malkeh," Grandfather said, "it is most thoughtful and gracious of you. Thank you."

The nearest H&H was at 46th and Sixth, a fifteen-minute walk. My mother had made tuna sandwiches. The automat was lunch-time crowded, but we found a table for ourselves. I brought over a decaf coffee for Grandfather, tea for my mother, and two Mountain Dews for me.

Before beginning to eat, I tried calling Aliya from a pay phone. She wasn't in. I left a message on our answering machine telling her when I anticipated coming home. I also called Martin to let him know about the partial fingerprint on the bus ticket stub. In a tired voice, he said, "Thank you for letting me know. If it will help my case, I am glad." He didn't ask for elaboration, and I didn't want to stay on for long. I ended with, "I'll call you Thursday to prep for the hearing." I then returned to our table where my grandfather and mother leaned toward each other in whispered conversation. They leaned back when I approached and smiled.

"How've you been, Mom?" I asked as I sat down.

My mother sighed, even as she kept smiling. "It has been difficult, going to the store, making sure that Martin has everything he needs, and…"

I waited. She hadn't finished her sentence. Was she hesitant to tell us something? "'And,'" I prompted. "Mom, you were about to say more?"

She looked down and then at my grandfather. "It's just…just the…I guess the tension. Martin is depressed. He is agitated which he tries to suppress. And the tension…the tension when we are together and the tension when…when we are not together. It's difficult. I don't sleep well, and as you will notice, I don't have the best appetite."

During the Batya Flaum case, Aliya had observed that we tend to see our moms as figures who don't change from day to day or even year to year. Now, I saw dark circles under her eyes. Her face was thinner. I flashed back to the three months before my father's death when we knew he was terminal. I shut my eyes for a moment. I wasn't going to cry in front of my mother and make things worse.

My grandfather laid a hand on my mother's hand. "Malkeh, we are moving forward with our investigation. I can share with you that I believe Martin is innocent, as you have corroborated his statement that he could not have been in Mr. Casman's apartment at the time of the murder. I cannot tell you that in time all will return to normal when we finish with this case, but life will assume a more acceptable equilibrium."

I wished I shared my grandfather's certainty on all counts.

My shoulders hunched. "Mom," I said, "our trip to New Jersey was helpful. We learned a lot about Martin's stepson, and Zaida has a plan which we'll discuss in his office."

"You are making progress, and I am glad." She looked from Grandfather to me. "If you please, I don't wish to hear—not at least at this moment—details about your trip related to the investigation. But I'm very interested to hear about your travels and accommodations and about the southern portion of New Jersey which," she laughed, "is a foreign land to me."

We also laughed. My shoulder muscles relaxed. I didn't want to talk about the case either.

Instead, I told her about the bus ride, the bus driver, the countryside, the town of Vineland, our helpful taxi driver and tour guide, and our meals. She expressed interest in every detail. Grandfather didn't say much. His head tilted up.

Where was he within the contours of the case? Perhaps Vineland, perhaps Brooklyn, perhaps traveling back and forth, as he planned our next steps. Soon we would be in his office, and I'd hear his thoughts. Meanwhile, I kept up the conversation with my mother until she remarked that she needed to return to the store.

On the street, my mother embraced Grandfather and then me. "Joel," she said, "I already mentioned to Aliya that I would like to have a family Shabbat dinner tonight. She said she could come, but it would be up to you because you may be tired. Are you able to come?"

I could've used a night in our apartment because coming to dinner meant staying until the end of Shabbat, tomorrow night. But I couldn't say no. "I'm not that tired, Mom. Of course, we'll come. If I know Aliya, she'll want to help you get ready, so around 5:30?"

My mother nodded.

"Mom," I asked, "will Martin be there?"

Her eyes narrowed, and she looked down before looking up at me. "Yes, I invited him, and he is coming. I thought it a good way for him to get out. Why do you ask? Is there a problem with your representation if you have dinner with your client?"

"No, not at all," I rushed my answer. "I was just curious. No problem for a defense attorney to have a meal with his client."

I hugged my mother again. She turned north on Seventh Avenue toward 49th. Grandfather and I headed south toward the 42st Street Time Square IRT station. We got on a #2 train to Brooklyn Boro Hall. Forty minutes later, we were in his swelteringly hot office.

My grandfather took off his suit coat and hat. I put the air conditioner on full blast and sat down in the guest chair. My grandfather, seated behind his desk, leaned forward.

"Joel, there is much complication in this case. We will need assistance, primarily, as I mentioned yesterday, in flushing out the suspect."

I tilted my head. "The 'suspect'—Payshe, I assume? And 'assistance'—? Zaida, who's going to assist us?"

Grandfather's eyes crinkled at the edges, and I saw a twinkle. "Yes, at this moment, Mr. Zimmer, to my mind, is our primary suspect for the reasons we discussed yesterday. And 'assistance,' that would come from two good friends to our investigations, Martha Brennan and Detective Carlucci, with further 'assistance' from *The Vineland Times Journal*."

I opened my mouth to speak, but my grandfather held up a hand.

"Please allow me to explain what has been percolating in my mind."

* * * *

I stared at my grandfather for a few seconds. "You want me to call Martha Brennan and ask her to do what? Zaida, let me see if I got it right."

My grandfather smiled. "Ah, Joel, I believe I have taken you off guard in my plan to flush out Mr. Zimmer as a means to determine if my premise that he killed Henry Casman is correct—or come to terms with an error in my analyses. Please proceed."

I leaned forward. "You want me, as Martin's attorney and lead in this case, to call Martha Brennan and tell her that a partial fingerprint, possibly other than from Martin, was found at the murder scene, and that I would present this finding at the evidentiary hearing on the 21st? And that she can quote me to say that 'in my mind the finding presents sufficient doubt as to Martin Ross's guilt?'"

Grandfather's smile widened. "Yes, to this point, to use your parlance, you 'got it right.' And, Joel?" he prompted.

"And ask Martha to send the story as a courtesy to *The Vineland Times Journal* in case the editor would find it interesting for his Vineland readers, right? Payshe said he hadn't seen any mention of Martin's arrest in the Vineland paper. I guess the paper didn't pick up anything about the murder from an AP wire, or AP didn't bother with the story. So Martha sending them her story hopefully covers the miss."

"Yes, precisely. It would seem that you 'got it right' on both parts."

I coughed. "But…but what I don't get, and you didn't explain, is how you hope it flushes out Payshe?"

Grandfather nodded. "Ah, yes, the intent of this gambit, I did not explain." He opened his hands. "Let us critically analyze the character of Mr. Zimmer. He is brilliant, and he is resolute. Yet, he is also impetuous and taken with himself. He knows that the authorities have strong evidence against Martin, and it will be infuriating to him to read that the charges against Martin may be dropped. And, I am hypothesizing, that he will want to observe the proceedings."

Grandfather drummed his fingers on the desk and continued. "Would you not conjecture that Mr. Zimmer knows that he lost his return bus ticket somewhere and worries that it may have occurred in Mr. Casman's apartment? When he reads about a fingerprint being found, other than from Martin, his agitation will increase. He cannot count on more information being printed in the Vineland newspaper. Yes, all combined, I believe his agitation will drive him to attend the hearing. He will wish to observe and know the outcome immediately."

I grasped the arms of my chair. "So, bottom line, getting to flush him out means getting him out of Vineland, out of his element, and to Brooklyn where he is accessible and more vulnerable. But, Zaida, even if he comes, he's not going to want to sit down with us again for questioning."

My grandfather's lips tightened. "Yes, you are correct. I partially rest my hopes on Mr. Zimmer's exhibiting some sort of offensive behavior during the hearing such as an obdurate refusal to remain still so that he may be assisted out of the courtroom and taken into custody. And if he does not, that is where our friend, Detective Carlucci, may be of assistance."

My mind was swirling. "Yes, you mentioned that Carlucci would help. How?"

A twinkle returned to Grandfather's eyes. He said, "I will have a conversation with the good detective and suggest that based on an eyewitness who saw Mr. Zimmer getting on a bus to New York a day before the murder, Mr. Zimmer should be brought in for questioning. Such a request is in order, is it not?"

I nodded. "It is, it certainly is. But then what? How will you get him to tell the truth? He was pretty cagey yesterday on the farm. And Carlucci doesn't have enough to hold him, even as a material witness."

"Ah, that we will see. And there will be another component contributing to Mr. Zimmer's discombobulation, which will be a boon to our questioning." The twinkle grew. "And you, Joel, shall have a major role in this aspect of our plan."

"Me?" I placed a hand on my chest. "What have you got planned for me, Zaida?"

He laughed. "Ah, for you. First, permit me a question. Is it allowed for the charged person, Martin in our case, to testify at an evidentiary hearing?"

I thought for a moment. "It's not usual, but it's allowed as long as the defendant is given his rights and told he doesn't have to testify. Why?"

Grandfather coughed. "Because with your agreement, during the hearing, I would like you to put Martin on the stand and ask him a litany of questions pertaining to his deceased wife, Mr. Zimmer's mother, particularly as to the behavior she exhibited prior to the War when she was courted by both Martin and Mr. Casman. I am hoping for an outburst from Mr. Zimmer which will give Detective Carlucci an excuse to take him into custody. This approach is somewhat unsavory, but I believe necessary as we seek Martin's exoneration."

Unsavory. That may be one way to put it, but thinking about my first criminal defense trial, I foresaw Fried objecting for "relevance" and the judge sustaining the objection. With ten more days until the hearing, though, I'd give it a lot of thought. Meanwhile, I said, "Okay, let's discuss my line of questioning next week."

"Yes, of course, Yoeli," Grandfather said. "I know that not fully comprehending the workings of another person's plan can be difficult, and I thank you for your forbearance."

I slowly nodded. I did trust my grandfather—the years I spent growing up under his loving care and his own "forbearance" made it easier. But still, my muscles tensed and I felt weary as I prepared to call Brennan. Also, another uncomfortable task faced me. "Okay, I'll call Brennan, and you'll call Carlucci. But I also have to call Martin and fill him in on our trip to Vineland. And I want to ask him about Payshe practicing a *Galitzianer* accent. That's so weird. And I'd like to do it before we see Martin tonight at Shabbat dinner."

Grandfather stood, pointed at the phone, and motioned me to take his seat. "I will allow you some privacy with your client, as I must make my way to the hallway bathroom."

I rose and put out my hand. "Zaida, Zaida, you're part of the defense team. I can speak to Martin in front of you."

"Joel, I am aware. But I must attend to my needs and you may be more comfortable speaking in private. Good?"

I moved to Grandfather's chair. "Okay," I said. "See you in a few minutes. You don't have to stay out longer than you need." Grandfather left.

Martin picked up on the first ring. I would've been surprised if he wasn't home. In short order, we exchanged pleasantries. I gave him a two-minute overview of our visit with Payshe. I did not mention my grandfather's plan.

"I am glad he is doing well," Martin said. "And I do know he exhibits his gun to strangers. The people in Vineland tolerate him. He is often a helpful neighbor."

I said, "That's the general feeling I got from the way people talk about him. But does anything surprise you about his devotion to his biological father?"

Martin's voice rose. "Surprise me, not at all. Boys growing up need idols, and with Dora's constant talk of Notke's heroics, there is no surprise that Payshe idolized his dead father."

How understanding. Martin's description might have fit, as a kid, my idolizing Gil Hodges, the Brooklyn Dodgers great first baseman. I pushed on. "And you're aware that Payshe speaks in a *Galitzianer* Yiddish accent. Growing up, did he practice speaking this way so he'd sound like his dad?"

Martin answered quickly. "Yes, I thought it somewhat excessive when for several years he practiced speaking like a *Galitzianer.* But Dora beamed and said how wonderful her little *tattelle* was to want to be so much like his real father. She even coached him, and after a few years, it came naturally to him."

Why didn't Martin react more strongly? Payshe had expressed disgust for Martin's constant indulgence of Payshe's repudiations. Was I falling into a similar reaction?

One more factor contributed to my discomfort. Martin hadn't reacted when I told him about Payshe's being spotted getting on a bus to New York the morning of the murder. Not a word. I had to follow up.

"Martin, both grandfather and I feel that the possibility that Payshe was in New York on the day of Casman's murder is a big deal. And as I mentioned, we found a return bus ticket stub to Vineland with a partial fingerprint on it at the murder scene. What are you thinking?"

Martin responded with a flustered voice. "Thinking? What do you want me to say? Payshe didn't call to tell me he was coming to New York—didn't ask to stay with me. You say he took the morning bus. Maybe he had a business meeting and went back home that evening. He does not observe the prohibition against traveling on the Sabbath. Or, perhaps he went from Port Authority when he arrived straight to a bus to New Brunswick to discuss his research at the university and stayed overnight in New Brunswick. Payshe does not like to drive long distances."

Martin stopped. *Why had he so quickly rationalized away any connection between Payshe's trip to New York and the murder?* I shook my head and waited.

Martin went on, his words coming through what sounded like clenched teeth. "I will not, Joel, even though my well-being is at stake, jump to any conjecture that Payshe was involved in Casman's murder. He is my stepson—he is Dora's child. I will not go to where, I believe, you wish to lead me, and assign guilt to him. And as you so often remind me, my fingerprints, not his, are on the knife, regardless of any other findings."

I took a calming breath. *Joel! Stifle your annoyance. Work with your client taking into account his personality and wishes—not on the basis of how you'd like him to be.*

I had done my job keeping Martin abreast of developments and asking questions. Also, Martin's coming to dinner tonight. How would that go? For now, I said, "Okay if you don't have any questions for me, I'll see you tonight?"

After a brief hesitation, he said, "I do not have any questions. I will see you tonight."

A minute later, my grandfather returned. I had already gone back to my chair.

"Nuh," Grandfather asked, seating himself. "It went well with Martin?"

"Fairly well. I asked him about Payshe's learning to speak in a *Galitzianer* accent, and he confirmed that he practiced daily until it became natural. Martin doesn't think it was weird at all."

My grandfather's brows turned down. "And I also do not think it is 'weird,' which is a word I would use only in the instance of extraterrestrials or ghosts. But as for an aspect of human behavior, especially as we understand the forces playing on Payshe's psyche, perhaps 'unusual' would be more fitting."

Was Grandfather saying that if one assesses the background to a human's actions, one may think it "unusual," yet understandable? How often did I, or my friends, call something "weird" when we came across something different?

I still had to call Martha Brennan before I left. "Grandfather, could you please give me Brennan's number?"

My grandfather took his beat-up address book from his desk. He read me her number at *The Daily News*. As I expected in calling the paper's newsroom, a man answered and asked, "What's it about?"

"The Casman murder case in Brooklyn," I responded. "Please tell her it's Joel Gordon."

After a few minutes, Brennan came on the line. She greeted me warmly and asked, "You have something for me on the Casman case?"

"Yes, you said if I had something 'special,' to call. So here it is." I told her about the partial fingerprint "of interest" found at the scene and relayed Grandfather's request for her to write an exclusive story on the finding and send the story on to *The Vineland Times Journal*.

She said, "Consider it done, if my editor agrees. Thanks for the scoop, and thank your lovely grandfather for me. Let's see—it's Friday. If I get agreement, probably in the Monday morning edition? Then I'll send it on to that Jersey paper."

"Perfect," I said and thanked her.

"My pleasure," she said. "My love to your granddad. He's something 'special' too." Brennan laughed and hung up.

I smiled as I lay down the phone.

Grandfather's eyebrows rose. "Something amusing with Ms. Brennan?"

"Not really. She sends her best wishes. And she'll do as we ask, if her editor agrees. She'll try to get her piece in the Monday morning edition. She'll also send it to the Vineland paper." I stood. "Time to go? We've had a couple of intense days. Sort of looking forward to Shabbat."

"Only 'sort of?' Why such a qualification?"

Martin's coming to dinner! I said, "No, you're right. Looking forward to a restful Shabbat. Shall we go?"

Grandfather shook his head. "Joel, you go. I will need to spend a few more minutes in my office trying to contact Detective Carlucci. I will see you in a few hours. Yes?"

"I'll see you at the house, Zaida." I left hoping my grandfather would also leave soon. If I felt tired, how much more might he be. I waited ten minutes for a #4 Train at Boro Hall. Twenty-five minutes later, I arrived at our apartment in Stuyvesant Town.

"Hello," Aliya called as I came in. "I'm here."

I dropped my overnight bag in the kitchen and walked to the bedroom. Aliya was taking down a suitcase from the bed. "Should you be doing that?" I rushed over and grabbed the suitcase. "Are you all right?"

Aliya placed her hands on her hips. "And hello to you, Joel." She came over and opened her arms.

I put down the suitcase and hugged her. "Yes, hello, I love you, but should you be lifting a heavy suitcase?"

"And I love you, but please drop the over-solicitous behavior. I'm pregnant—not ill. I'll let you know if there's a problem or when I need help. And you'd better get back to your exercise program if you think that suitcase is heavy. Just a single change of clothes for each of us. Now, can we agree to what I just said?"

"Of course."

She hugged me more tightly and gave me a long kiss. I gently released her. I said, "I'll start working out again."

I turned and flopped onto my side of the bed. Aliya pointed to my shoes and tssked. I kicked them off quickly and patted the area next to me.

Aliya hesitated and lay down. "You know, it's already 3:45. If we don't want to pay for a cab, we need to leave soon. Your mother could use our help with dinner."

I opened my arms for Aliya to nestle against me. "I know. Just a few minutes as I relax a bit and tell you about the last couple of days. You know, last night was our first night apart since we were married."

Aliya snuggled closer. "I know. I thought about that last night. But we can be more sentimental later. I want to hear about your trip."

Time was short so I gave her a summary narration with little color commentary. I told her about our interaction with Payshe, his having been spotted getting onto a bus to New York the morning before the murder, and my grandfather's plan for luring Payshe to the evidentiary hearing to "flush him out." I didn't mention my conversation with Martin.

Aliya listened with few questions. When I finished, she asked, "Do you think it'll work, Zaida's plan, to get Payshe to come to the hearing? I wish I could be there, but it's my first day at the Stuyvesant Group. I'm not sure you'll be able to reach me there to tell me how it went as soon as it's over. I'll be on pins and needles until I see you."

Don't be a baby, Joel. I was disappointed that Aliya wouldn't be at the courthouse to see my first day as a defense attorney. But it was also the first day of her new career.

"Honestly," I said, "I have doubts about Zaida's plans." I laughed. "But he's a pretty good detective, so I'm gonna trust his instincts."

Aliya also laughed and glanced at the bedside clock. "And so will I. Shall we go?"

I put a hand out. "One more thing before we go. I want your learned opinion."

Aliya frowned. I knew why. I said, "Okay, forget 'learned,' just your opinion."

"Go on."

"You know how people our age use the word, 'weird,' a lot?"

She nodded.

"Well, Zaida didn't like it when I described Payshe's obsession to be just like his biological father as 'weird'—he'll accept 'unusual,' but not 'weird.' What do you think?"

Aliya sat up and looked at me. "Easy one, for me. And maybe because of what I did learn and observe about people's behavior in grad school, I agree with Zaida. 'Weird' is for what cannot be explained such as the occult. Zaida's assessment of Payshe's personality can be explained. If Zaida's got it right or wrong remains to be seen. But for a detective or a defense attorney to consider it 'weird' would be to throw up one's hands and say, 'Oh well, I don't get him. What do I do now?'" She edged off the bed. "Ready to go?"

There are different ways someone loves another person. In this moment, I loved Aliya for how well she understood people, free of her own judgment or frustration. It wasn't because she was "learned"—she was that way before graduate school. My grandfather and my mother quickly came to adore Aliya because, among various reasons, she, unreservedly got them, understood their nuanced beings, and accepted them for who they were, even as they were so different from her parents and others she grew up with. My grandfather was right—Aliya would always be my *kallah*, my bride, my friend, my confidante, my love.

I wanted to pull her back to me, but instead jumped up and said, "Yep, ready to go." I quickly put on my shoes and picked up the suitcase. I bent an elbow and offered her my arm. "The Q Train to Brooklyn awaits you, my queen."

* * * *

Rush hour commuters packed the train. I did my best to get in between Aliya and others pressing against her. "I'm okay, Joel," Aliya said when I may have been too aggressive in making space for her. We took the train to the Kings Highway Station and walked the half mile to the house. My mother opened the door before we rang the bell.

After hugs, my mother thanked us for coming early. Did she give a quick glance at Aliya's belly? Since Aliya told me the news, I had found myself furtively doing the same. Aliya headed immediately to the kitchen. My mother said, "Your Zaida is in his easy chair. He appears somewhat gloomy. Perhaps it is just weariness from his trip. You will keep him company, Joel, while Aliya and I prepare dinner?"

"Sure," I said. We headed in two different directions.

I frowned. *Grandfather gloomy? Was my mother overreacting? She sometimes did so when it came to my grandfather's health? Even when I thought he must be feeling down, I couldn't always tell.*

Perhaps my mother was right. Grandfather sat slouched in his easy chair, arms folded, and sections of *The New York Times* lying on his lap. His mouth was turned down, and his eyes narrowed looking straight ahead. He looked up when I moved into the room and opened his arms to me. I came over and gave him a hug. "You are somewhat refreshed, yes?" he said.

I nodded. "I am. But what about you, Zaida? You seem tired."

My grandfather sat up. "Ah, Yoeli, your mother also commented on my demeanor. It is not so much that I am tired as much as I am worried."

"About what?"

He took a deep breath. "That I am wrong about Mr. Zimmer's guilt in the murder, that my plan for luring him to Brooklyn is illusory, that…"

He hesitated, and I said in a whispered voice, "That Martin may be guilty?"

My grandfather shook his head. "No, that Martin may be guilty is not a part of my apprehension. I was about to say that I am worried that I may be too taken with myself and our previous successes."

I shook my head. "C'mon, Zaida. You're a top-notch detective. I have every confidence in you."

He closed his eyes briefly. "But repeated success can breed error. If I don't question my own thought processes, then I am not doing my most effective job. I ask myself, am I so sure that Martin is innocent because guilt would hurt your mother immensely? Thus, is my thought process steering me toward finding a different suspect? We do our best employing critical analyses, but we must question, question, question. We will continue with our plan—in which I have some confidence—yet remain open to other possibilities and revision, yes?"

I didn't share my own doubts about Martin. No, I would proceed as if there was no other suspect beside Payshe Zimmer—no other plan. I just nodded.

"So, Joel, the Sabbath is soon upon us. We shall put away the case, as best we can, and talk about sports, and politics, and opera? And later you will accompany me to my Quentin Road *shtiebel* for Friday evening services, yes?"

"Opera?" I spluttered and then smiled. He was pulling my leg. I knew nothing about opera. Only that Grandfather and his lady friend, Mrs. Wachter, had gone to the Met several times over the last couple of years. Grandfather laughed and motioned me to sit.

"Opera, oh, please," I said feigning annoyance. "Yes. I'll go with you to the *shtiebel*."

The beginning smells of our traditional Sabbath eve dinner began to waft my way—noodle kugel, chicken soup, brisket, stuffed cabbage, and string beans. Certainly, we would have compote and mandel bread for dessert with tea in glass cups. My mother was a great cook with a wide repertoire, but Friday night dinners were consistently the same. She had once told me that it honored the memory of her mother who cooked that way in Vienna before the War.

* * * *

Around 7:50, Grandfather and I returned from Friday evening services. I was glad we had gone to the Oseh Shalom *Shtiebel*—the "little house synagogue of making peace"—just a few minutes' walk from the house. Without the two of us, there wouldn't have been a minyan, a minimum of ten persons quorum, to perform services. So many of the elderly members had passed away, or moved to warmer climes, or to live with children scattered all over the country. How long could this small synagogue remain open? It would be sad for Grandfather when it closed.

When we returned, the dining room table was fully set, along with silver-filigree candlesticks holding lit candles on trays. My mother and Aliya, wearing white lace head coverings, greeted us with "Shabbat shalom," and we answered in kind. Aliya had changed into a flowing summer dress.

I looked around the room. "Martin's not here, yet?" I said.

My mother's lips pursed. "No, he's not. I'm sure he will be here soon. He said he would join us."

"Let us await him in the living room," my grandfather said motioning us to join him. Just then, the doorbell rang. My mother briskly moved forward. "I will open the door," she said.

I heard the door open and the exchange of "Shabbat shalom" greetings. Nothing more. My mother led Martin into the dining room. We welcomed him, but a sudden heaviness descended in the room. Hurried glimpses replaced eye contact. Everyone spoke more slowly than usual. Grandfather's blessings over the wine elicited subdued responses. I sang the blessing over the challah. Throughout dinner, moments of silence followed sporadic statements. My mother and Martin, who during many previous dinners would exchange smiles and glances, hardly looked at each other.

Some of the discomfort may have been my fault. Early on, I said, "Martin, I imagine it was hard not attending services tonight at P'nai Hesed your usual practice?" Aliya blinked a few times and gave me a quick glance.

Martin looked down. "Yes, I did not attend services tonight."

I waited for something more from Martin, but it didn't come. I could've left it at that, but I added, "Hope soon you'll be able to go." I didn't sound convincing. After, I said very little.

My grandfather-led discussion around the week's Torah portion garnered little interaction, except for the moment when Grandfather described the part of the reading that dealt with the *nazir*, the biblical person who abstains from drinking wine and lets his hair grow long.

"I would not mind being young again and partaking of that status for a while," Martin said with a hint of a smile. "To escape from the world's troubles and never go to a barber again. I could live with not drinking wine anymore. And what is described, is it not called being a 'hippie' today?"

Martin did not laugh, but everyone else did, perhaps too loudly. "Yes," Grandfather said, "there is much that the Torah teaches us about our modern world."

I helped clear the dinner dishes, preparing for dessert. When I returned from the kitchen, Grandfather motioned me to sit. "Joel," my grandfather said, "even before dessert, Martin has requested that we say our grace after meals so that he may depart from us as he is much tired."

I sat and mindlessly sang with the others the grace after meals. Martin stood and bowed toward everyone. "You will please excuse my early departure. My current situation hangs heavily over me, and I tire easily. Good Shabbos." He turned toward my mother. "And Molly, I hope to see you soon."

My mother looked at Martin quickly. "Yes, good Shabbos. I will walk you to the door."

The front door opened and closed. I heard no conversation. My mother returned and said, "We will now have dessert. Joel, you'll help me to bring it out?"

In the kitchen, I stole glances at my mother. Her face had thinned. The darkness under her eyes frightened me. Was there a slight tremor in her hand as she placed the mandel bread on a tray?

When Aliya had first met my mother, she had said, "Your mom is very pretty." I was surprised, not used to associating looking "pretty" with my mother. Had I been blind to her appearance all my life? And now, the situation with Martin was taking its toll.

After a quick dessert, I said, "Aliya, how about you and I clean up, and we'll let Mom and Zaida get some rest?"

"The two of you also need to rest," my mother said rising quickly. "The three of us will clean up and then retire? I am not planning to go to services at P'nai Hesed tomorrow morning. Joel, you will accompany your Zaida to the *shtiebel* in the morning? Perhaps Aliya and I can spend a leisurely morning, just talking."

Aliya and I both answered "Yes."

In bed, before tiredness took us into sleep, I asked, "What did you think about dinner tonight?"

"It was quite different from the past," Aliya answered, "wasn't it?"

I laughed. "Yeah, it was—I was about to say 'weird,' but that's not the right word,"

"No it's not," she answered kissing me on the forehead. "And you don't have to be 'learned' to understand why it wasn't 'weird.' Rather predictable, given the circumstances and the relationships. Good night, my love."

SUNDAY, JUNE 13, 1976

On the train returning home from Brooklyn the previous evening, Aliya and I decided that tomorrow we would take the whole day off. "We haven't seen Shoshi and her family for a few weeks now," Aliya said referring to Shoshannah Marcus, her best friend since elementary school. Shoshi's mother, Batya Flaum, was murdered in her home in Flatbush sixteen months before. Aliya and I had worked with my grandfather to solve the case.

"I'm all for it," I said, savoring the thought of a stickball game against Ben Marcus, Shoshi's husband—a worthy opponent.

Back in the apartment, Aliya had immediately called the Marcus home. "It's 10:15," she said, while dialing. "I hope it's not too late." It wasn't. After a few minutes of conversation in which Aliya said, "Yes, Shosh, I'm perfectly fine. I've started eating for two," Aliya hung up. "Joel, it's all set. Brunch at their apartment at 11:00, and then if you and Ben want to join 'mad dogs and Englishmen' and play stickball in the 'midday sun,' it will be up to you. Shosh and I will stay with the boys in the apartment or find some shaded area outside."

"Wonderful." I twirled my right arm in a pitcher's warm-up motion. "Wonderful."

* * * *

The next morning, before leaving I called to see how my mother and grandfather were doing. My mother answered. After a brief exchange, I heard my mother's muffled voice. "Fotter, it's Joel. He called to say hello. They are going to visit with Shoshannah and her family in Midwood."

After a moment, my mother laughed. "Your Zaida wishes me to tell you that since you have no interest in the opera, he has taken the initiative to invite a friend to accompany him to a performance of *Aida* this afternoon at the Met. He says perhaps you will consider for next time."

I snorted. "Hah," I said. "Very funny. So is this friend Mrs. Wachter?"

"Yes, Joel. I will tell Zaida you will take into consideration his next invitation."

So my mother would be alone today? Was she planning to see Martin? I said, "So you'll be home all day until Zaida returns."

"Yes, I will," she snapped. "I have books to read, correspondence to take care of, and store accounting to keep me busy."

She softened her voice. "Please say hello to Aliya and have an enjoyable day. Goodbye, Joel." She hung up.

* * * *

Aliya and I took the Q Train to the Avenue M station, a block from the Marcus apartment. The Dime Savings Bank across from the station showed 90 degrees.

The Marcus children, Uri four and Tzvi nearly two, greeted us raucously when we walked in. Tzvi grabbed my ankles, and I winced as Uri nearly bowled Aliya over. After a bagels and lox brunch, Ben went to a broom closet and took out three balls and two sticks. "Three brand new Spauldeens," he said holding the balls in one hand. In the other, he held out two sticks. "Broom handle or the real thing from Joe Torre's sporting goods store. Thought I'd throw him some business."

I laughed. "Real thing. Let me see it."

Shoshi, who had been herding the kids running with food in their mouths, said, "Okay, if you two are *meshugah* enough to play in this heat, how 'bout you go down the block to the Kolbert Playground? There's a shady area there where Aliya and I can be with the boys. We must get them out of the apartment for a while after we clean up."

Ben gave a sheepish grin. "Good idea. Don't clean up. I'll do it after we get back. Or I'll look after the boys."

Ben slaughtered me. We usually had close games, but this time, as much as I wanted not to think about work, I just couldn't. I kept thinking about my grandfather's plan. How would my questioning of Martin on the stand during the evidentiary hearing be central to Payshe's losing control. I kept telling myself—*leave it alone for now*—*I'll meet Grandfather at his office on Tuesday to discuss the questioning. There's time enough. Concentrate, Joel, concentrate. Get it out of your head.* But I let one pitch after another go down the middle without swinging. Strike after strike. Normally, I would hit them onto E. 18th Street.

At one point, Ben yelled, "Joel, what's with you? Are you okay?" I just waved the stick at him and told him to keep pitching. It ended 12-1.

On the subway back to Manhattan, Aliya leaned in on me and said, "I'm not going to say, 'You can't win 'em all' because I'm sure your mind wasn't on the game. Correct?"

I squeezed her closer. "Nope, it wasn't. And you were thinking about your upcoming first day too, right?"

"Uh-huh, but those two boys keep the mind focused. If we don't keep an eye on them, they wind up in Queens. So, in a way, I had an easier time."

We rode in silence for a few minutes before I turned and said, "I keep thinking about tomorrow and *The Daily News* piece Brennan said she would try to get into the morning edition." I shook my head. "It's the first move of Zaida's gambit."

MONDAY, JUNE 14, 1976

At 5:00 in the morning, I started watching the bedroom clock inch its way toward 6:00 when the newspaper kiosk at 14th and 1st would open with the morning editions. At 5:50, I slowly edged out of bed and threw on shorts and a tee. I quietly left the apartment and hurried down to the street. There was Nick, who ran the newspaper stand, cranking open the shutters. Three roped stacks of *The Daily News* lay at his feet. "Good morning," I said, pointing to a stack. Nick nodded and took out a box cutter. He cut the rope and handed me a *Daily News*. I gave him a quarter and ran back to our building.

I opened the door slowly. Aliya greeted me from the kitchen. "Good morning."

"Oh, you're up," I said. "I tried not to wake you."

She was in pajamas, standing over the steaming water kettle. "You didn't," she said, coming over for a hug. She pointed to the paper I'd placed on the table. "Well, is it in there?"

"I haven't looked, yet." I opened the paper from its full front page picture of a mass casualty auto pileup in Acapulco. On page 5, top left, I found a picture of Henry Casman, and underneath, "New Evidence Calls into Question Who killed a Nazi Hunter" with a Martha Brennan byline.

"Wow." I pointed to the photo and headline.

Aliya picked up the paper, took a quick glance, and said, "Should I read it out loud?"

I nodded. "Slowly please."

Aliya began:

Sometime in the evening of May 29 last, the murdered body of Henry Casman, 55, was found in his Brooklyn apartment at 1165 Ocean Parkway. He had been stabbed to death. A few days later, Martin Ross, who lived a block from the victim, was charged with the murder. Ross's fingerprints were identified on the murder weapon, a large kitchen knife belonging to the victim. At his June 7 arraignment, Ross pleaded 'Not Guilty.' An evidentiary hearing is set for June 21 at the Brooklyn Criminal Court.

But new evidence has been discovered that puts in question Ross's guilt. In speaking to the defendant's attorney, Joel Gordon of the Prentice, Walters, & Reis law firm in Manhattan, a partial fingerprint, other than from the victim, was also discovered. Detective Anthony Carlucci of the 61st Precinct, who is leading the murder investigation, corroborated this finding.

Gordon believes that the new evidence has significant bearing on the case. He said 'In my mind, the additional fingerprint presents sufficient doubt as to my client's guilt.' Gordon plans to introduce this new evidence at the hearing.

Renowned detective, Frank Wolf, who has solved several crimes within the New York Jewish Community, is working with the defense.

Ross did not respond to several attempts to reach him. A neighbor said that 'a lady' visits him and delivers groceries.

The victim, Casman, worked part-time at The German Reparations Office in Manhattan, performing clerical duties. His co-workers reported that they believe he also was a Nazi hunter.

Aliya closed the paper and laid it down with a slap to the table. "'A lady' visits Martin? Brennan had to drag your mother into her story?"

"I don't like it much," I said, "but at least she didn't mention Mom by name."

Aliya's eyes narrowed. "I may not like the way she sensationalizes stories, but she's quite a good reporter—I'll give her that. How'd she know about Casman working at the German Reparations Office? We knew because of the envelopes I saw in the Casman apartment. It was cleared out a few days ago, so she couldn't have seen them there. Seems she's got eyes and ears everywhere."

I laughed. "And then to go down to the Reparations Office and talk with the staff! She's just taken an ordinary story that *The Times* wouldn't go back to after their initial report and jazzed it up with the possibility that Casman was killed by one of his Nazi targets. Well, she's not going to get a *National Enquirer* Pulitzer for this one—Zaida convinced me that her conjecture is highly improbable."

After I filled in Aliya on my grandfather's logic, we ate breakfast. I planned to head to my office to read up on New York criminal defense process and check in with Chip Holden about the accounts he was covering for me.

I was about to put on Mr. Monday when the phone rang. Aliya had eased back into bed for another hour's sleep. I ran to the kitchen.

"Good morning, Joel," Grandfather said cheerily. "I imagine you have been awake for a while and have read Ms. Brennan's piece, yes?"

"I have. What do you think?"

My grandfather chuckled. "It is quite an article, no? Ms. Brennan is not only a brilliant reporter, but also one filled with imagination. But the story serves our purpose well."

"Did Mom read the story?"

Grandfather hesitated. "Yes—she is not pleased."

"About being the 'lady' in the story?" I interrupted.

"Hah, not at all. Yet without providing details, I informed her that the story would help us in Martin's defense. That explanation seemed to assuage your mother's upset."

"Good, I hope Brennan followed through on sending the story to the Vineland paper."

He gave a short laugh. "Joel, you may take back your 'hope' for future use. Ms. Brennan was kind enough to call me a few minutes ago to let me know that she, indeed, has wired a copy to *The Vineland Times Journal* requesting the courtesy of being wired back any story on the murder appearing in their paper."

I smiled to myself. How the ladies took to my grandfather. She could have called me, but no. Perhaps in time I would grow into my grandfather's charm. Most importantly, Brennan had come through on both requests. Before hanging up, I said, "Zaida, thanks for letting me know. Let's see if the Vineland paper follows with move two of your gambit. I'll see you tomorrow at 9:00 in your office to discuss Martin's questioning.

Martin did not read *The Daily News*. I called him to let him know that the paper had published a new piece on the murder. I gave him a summary, to which he said, "Then what is new is the tabloid interest in Henoch as a 'Nazi Hunter' and the discovery of the partial fingerprint—which the police made public. Are you planning to use both in my defense?"

I took a deep breath. "I'll be giving the 'Nazi Hunter' angle some thought, but the partial fingerprint, we'll probably make use of it to establish doubt."

I thought back to my religious training when my teachers would discuss not only lies of "commission" but also "omission." *Why hadn't I told Martin that I was the one who had informed Martha Brennan about the partial?*

Martin replied. "As I have often stated, I trust you, Joel."

I squirmed and gave Martin a cheery, "Goodbye."

TUESDAY, JUNE 15, 1976

The #5 train taking me to meet my grandfather at his office halted at the Bowling Green Station in Manhattan for twenty minutes. No explanation given, and no air conditioning. By the time the train pulled out, my t-shirt showed sweat stains. The train pulled into the Boro Hall Station at 9:12. Twice, I tried calling Grandfather's office from the first phone booth I saw to tell him I'm running late—busy signal after each. Despite the heat, I jogged the few blocks to his office.

After taking three flights of stairs, I rushed in, closing the door quickly behind me. *What a relief !* I took in the cold from the air conditioner, on full blast. Drops of sweat rolled off my face. "I'm sorry, Zaida, the train was delayed," I sputtered. "I tried to call, but your phone was busy."

My grandfather rose and held his hands open. "Please, Yoeli," he said, motioning me toward a chair, "sit and regain your bearing. Your delay did not in the least cause a loss of productive time." He smiled. "I have been on the phone with Ms. Brennan."

I sat down in the guest chair. "Brennan," I said. "She called?" I slapped the side of my head. "Don't tell me—she heard back from the Vineland paper? They published a story on Casman's murder?"

"But I will tell you," Grandfather said, laughing. "Ms. Brennan, indeed, did communicate to me that very same news. A story did appear in this morning's edition of *The Vineland Times Journal,* albeit on a back page. It is small, but hopefully effective for our purpose. Ms. Brennan was kind enough to dictate it to me. Shall I read it to you?"

I leaned forward and nodded vigorously. "Yes, I really want to hear."

My grandfather picked up a sheet of paper and cleared his throat. "First, the headline." He brought the paper closer to his eyes. "Former Vineland Resident Arrested in Murder of Brooklyn Man." Grandfather paused. "It will seem that the headline dwarfs the story itself. But I continue.

"Martin Ross, previously of Forest Grove Road, Vineland, has been charged with the brutal slaying of a Brooklyn man, Henry Casman. The killing occurred in the victim's Brooklyn apartment. Both Ross and Casman are Holocaust survivors. The victim is a known Nazi hunter. Ross has pleaded innocent. An evidentiary hearing is scheduled for Monday, June 21, to determine Ross's indictment. Joel

Gordon, the accused's attorney, is confident that new evidence to be presented at the hearing will clear his client."

I sat back. "Perfect. The article's ending saying that new evidence will clear Martin really works for us. Payshe just might want to attend the hearing to see first-hand if Martin's let go."

Grandfather placed the paper in a folder. His eyes softened as he looked up. "'Perfect?' I do not know, but as I stated, good for our purpose. We wait in anticipation for Monday morning. And now for our business today—your examination of Martin on the stand should Mr. Zimmer be present. And, Joel, only if he is present, yes? Otherwise, there is no reason to subject Martin to the ordeal of testifying."

I nodded. Everything about our plan counted on Payshe attending the hearing. *If he didn't, then what?*

There were other matters to consider before discussing my strategy for questioning Martin on the stand. I said, "I'll also spend time this week preparing my cross-examination of witnesses that Fried will call. He'll ask Mrs. Schnapper to testify about the argument she observed—or should I say, heard—between Martin and Casman a few hours before the murder."

Grandfather's eyes narrowed. "No, don't worry," I continued. "I won't bring up the nuanced difference between Martin's *Litvak* accent and the *Galitzianer* accent of the man who confronted Casman at the time of the murder. Even if it's not Judge Black, I won't do it. It would make it seem I was using some sleight of hand as my defense."

Grandfather relaxed. "Ah, Joel, again, your probity is admirable. For whom else will you be preparing a cross-examination?"

I took a notebook from my briefcase and thumbed through a few pages. "I've made a list based on who I think Fried will call to the stand—Again, Mrs. Schnapper. I'm pretty sure I can get her to admit that she never actually saw the second man at the time of the murder. And to eliminate the chance that she will fumble her response in English and not be understood, I asked my paralegal at PWR to send in a request for a Yiddish translator to be present.

"Then there's Abe Schneider, who Fried will call to establish motive for Martin killing Casman, based on their confrontations at the *Benevolent Society* meetings. My cross-examination will point out that Martin never exhibited any violent tendencies toward Casman."

"Joel," my grandfather said, frowning. "You must do as you must, but it will come out from Mr. Schneider's testimony, with next day mention in the newspapers, that Martin was a kapo."

I crossed and uncrossed my legs. It hit me. Would my mother be there on Monday? I hadn't asked her. Had Martin told her about his having been a kapo? My mother hadn't said a word to me. To Aliya? Surely, Aliya would've told me.

"Zaida," I said, "you're thinking about Mom. Has she said anything to you about knowing that Martin had been a kapo?"

He shook his head. "She has spoken little about Martin since his arrest—principally to inform me when she is bringing groceries to him."

I hated the thought, but I knew what I had to do. "Zaida, as hard as it's going to be, I'll talk to Mom in the next few days. Either Martin has already told her, or I will have to when I see her. She can't hear about it for the first time if she attends the hearing."

Grandfather's eyes moistened. "Yes, your mother is already filled with much sadness. She should not experience such a shock in a public place." He lifted his glasses and dabbed his eyes with a handkerchief. "Someone else, Joel?"

I looked at my notes. "Yes. Brennan found her way to the reparations office. I'm guessing that Fried's team also talked to people there and got similar information about Casman's non-work-related activity as a Nazi hunter and his hatred of Jewish collaborators. So I'll prepare for Bloch's—or someone else's from that office—testimony, which, added to Schneider's testimony, will strengthen the prosecution's assignment of motive to Martin."

Grandfather placed fingers to his lips. "Yes, such additional testimony will do so. What is it you wish to bring out in your cross-examination of such a witness?"

"As we learned from Bloch, I'll have him—or whoever—go on record that Casman never mentioned Martin by name when he spoke of Jewish collaborators." I shrugged. "Maybe it'll serve as a small wedge against motive if and when we go to full trial." I lifted a finger. "Which, Zaida, I anticipate will happen if our plan doesn't work out."

My grandfather placed his palms on his desk. "Yes, I have engaged in some readings about evidentiary hearings, which, unlike a grand jury, allow for cross-examination, albeit short. Nuh, Joel, are you planning for any other witness cross-examination?"

I shook my head. "No, is there someone else?" I glanced at my notes again.

He opened his palms. "Ah, yes, let us not forget about our friend, Detective Carlucci, who will be called to present police and forensic evidence."

"Sure, I know he will be called, but I didn't plan on any questions. I think he will mention finding someone else's partial fingerprint on the ticket stub, and that establishes some doubt without my pushing it under cross exam. Hopefully, it'll be enough to upset Payshe, if he's present. What else, Zaida?"

"Ah, if I may strongly suggest that you also ask the detective if it is possible to place another person's fingerprints on an object. Accept any response from Detective Carlucci. And please do so if Mr. Zimmer is present or not, yes?"

It sounded outlandish, but I nodded. Planting fingerprints! Wasn't that a form of science fiction from paperback detective stories? In a law school forensics class, we were told that it's theoretically possible, but would take a great deal of expertise. Grandfather would've elaborated if he had wanted to explain more now. He had a reason. I'd have nothing to lose except for a possible sneering redirect from Fried who would make it sound if I was taking a desperation shot. So be it. If Zaida thought it that important, I'd ask, whether Payshe was there or not. I'd have to do some digging to see if there was any more research on planting fingerprints since my law school days. Maybe there was new info that might help if we went to trial.

"Okay," I said, "reviewing the prosecution's anticipated testimony has been really helpful. But I mainly came to discuss putting Martin on the stand, which is highly irregular in an evidentiary hearing." I swallowed hard. "Oh, no, you don't want me to have Martin testify about his being with Mom at the time of the murder?"

My grandfather waved a finger. "I very much do not wish you to do so." He leaned forward with his hands to his temples. "I would like you to call Martin under the pretext that before the judge makes a decision about indictment, that he understands how given Martin's model character, he could not be a murderer." Grandfather again, held up his hand. "Yes, I know it is what you young people today call 'lame,' but quickly ask Martin how he was first acquainted with Mr. Casman in the old country and use a form of the following terminology—'So you and Mr. Casman in your youth were rivals for your wife's hand?' And when Martin acknowledges that it was so, ask: 'was she flirtatious with both you and Mr. Casman at that time?' Then, Joel, find a way to exit quickly from your examination."

Grandfather slumped back. So did I. As nervous as it made me, I thought I understood—the last move of our gambit. Either Payshe fell for our moves, or we were in checkmate.

I had to start thinking about my trial strategies because every one of our moves had to work. Would Payshe see the article in the Vineland paper? If so, would he decide to come to the hearing? At the hearing, would he do something not only to allow for his being taken in for questioning but also held? And even if he did, how to get a confession out of him?

"Yoeli," my grandfather said softly. "This case is exhausting for all of us. Thank you for coming to my office for this discussion. It has been helpful to me—and for you I hope."

Was I exhausted? During my first year at PWR, I had worked 60-plus hour weeks. Almost every night I went to sleep tired and immediately fell asleep. But this was a different type of exhaustion that wore down not only the mind but also the body and spirit. Since Martin's arrest, I had gone to bed each night exhausted but had trouble falling and staying asleep. The news of the baby exhilarated me. But then there was my mother's torment. And thinking of my mother, I said, "Zaida, I'd like to call Mom at the store."

Grandfather smiled and pushed the phone forward.

Rosa answered and called my mother over. "Mom," I said after a quick, 'Hello.' "Are you free to have a mother and son lunch tomorrow? I was thinking the Bernstein on Essex Kosher Chinese Restaurant? I've never been to a Chinese restaurant. I'll be at PWR tomorrow morning. I'll meet you at the store around 12:00, and we can take a cab to the restaurant. My treat."

Good to hear my mother laugh on the other end. "I would love to have lunch with you. But I am your mother which means now I don't bathe you, I don't check on your homework, but I still wish to feed you. So yes, lunch tomorrow, but it will be my treat. We can share the taxi fare."

I laughed out loud. "I can live with those conditions. See you tomorrow at noon." I hung up.

My grandfather looked at me with raised eyebrows. "Nuh, Yoeli, if it is not private, might you share the humorous exchange with my daughter?"

Well, that was true. His daughter was my mother. "Sure," I said and recounted my mother's conditions for the lunch.

Grandfather said, "I may have bathed you on occasion, and there were times you came to me for assistance with your homework, but I had little to do with feeding you, therefore...therefore if you at any time wish for us to dine together, I will have no hesitation in allowing you to treat me."

Grinning, I stood and returned the notebook to my briefcase. "Well, then, on our next excursion, your glass of Sanka and cheese danish are on me."

WEDNESDAY, JUNE 16, 1976

We didn't have to give Vasily, our taxi driver, the exact address for Bernstein On Essex. "I make many trips to that restaurant every day, except Saturday," Vasily said in a thick Russian accent. "I have you there in fifteen minutes. I take FDR." He laughed. "Of course, only if no pileup on the FDR. You are having deli or Chinese?" He laughed again. "Or maybe gentleman deli and lady Chinese? Or other way round?"

Smooth sailing down the FDR. Vasily stopped at 135 Essex Street besides the restaurant storefront with its vertical yellow and red neon sign that proclaimed Bernstein on Essex and a red canopy entrance with We Parcel Post Anywhere over its front overhang. Most of its patrons still called the place *Schmulka Bernstein's*, referring to its previous name as just a kosher deli before it introduced a Chinese menu in the early 1960's. It still was the only kosher establishment in the City that offered Chinese food. Many of my friends who didn't maintain a kosher diet had eaten Chinese and raved about the tastes. I looked forward to my first bite. As we eased out of the cab, two men in summer suits took our place.

We entered, pushing by a large group leaving. A short man in a white shirt and black vest, a black apron over black trousers, and a blue velvet kippah over tufted gray hair, asked, "Two?"

Before I could get a "yes" out, he had turned and scanned the room. "Care if you sit with another couple at a table for four?"

I shook my head. "We'd rather not. How long before a table for two?"

He again scanned the room. "I'd say ten minutes. You're in luck. That party of eight that just left—we can break down their seating for a party of two. For now, stand aside."

While waiting, I looked around. The restaurant was packed. I'd heard that *Schmulka Bernstein's* devotees came for a Chinese lunch and a Jewish deli dinner. At first, the place reminded me of Kornblatt's in Brooklyn with its deli case, hanging cured meats, pickle smells, and the aroma of freshly baked breads. But the traditional smells of a Jewish deli had competition. The smoky smell of frying oil drifted in from the kitchen area behind the deli and bread cases. "It must be the Chinese food," I said to my mother as I caught sight of a placard on a wall that read: "Where West Meets East for a Chinese Feast and Kashruth is Guaranteed." And then further down: "Authentic Chinese Cuisine."

The man was true to his word. Under ten minutes to be seated at a small table at the back where my mother and I could speak privately and easily hear each other.

After a few minutes, a man who reminded me of Mo at Kornblatt's, came over. Except, and I held back a laugh, instead of a kippah, he wore over his bald head a red-tasseled Chinese cap with, I assumed, Chinese letters. All of the waiters, men only, wore similar caps with their white shirts and black trousers. He placed two glasses of water before us. "You want the Jewish or Chinese menu?" he asked in a Yiddish accent. "Or maybe, both?"

"Just Chinese?" my mother answered, looking at me. I nodded.

The waiter handed us each a red vinyl-covered menu with a red tassel similar to the one on his cap. The cover also showed a gold, metallic oriental symbol in the shape of what looked like a Chinese character.

My mother and I discussed the menu. "It appears to me," she said, "from what I hear from my staff who often eat at Chinese restaurants, that dishes where shellfish, pork, or ham are staples at non-kosher Chinese restaurants, here, they have been replaced with veal, pastrami, or a kosher fish such as flounder or sea bass. Since I am the treater, I am allowed to splurge and order the sea bass with slivered scallions, ginger, and steamed vegetables. I know, at $6.50, it is quite expensive. And you, Joel?"

I had no idea. Friends often talked about hot and sour or egg drop soups, but this menu only offered chicken noodle, which I had eaten all my life. The names of dishes stumped me. Except, "Aha," I said. "I think an egg roll as an appetizer. What do you think I'd like for my main, Mom?"

She smiled. "As opposed to what I heard about other children, you always loved chicken livers, in one form or another. So I suggest *Lo Mein Bernstein*, which I see has fried chicken livers, egg noodles, mushrooms, broccoli, carrots, and snow peas in a soy sauce as the Chinese flavoring. All for $3.95, which includes soup and dessert. And it is fairly healthy. So we will both order, I imagine, the chicken noodle soup, and for dessert...?"

"What is this lychee fruit?" I asked.

"Ah, it will be good to try something new. Shall we both order it?"

The chicken noodle soup was ordinary, compared to my mother's. But then I took my first forkful of the Lo Mein dish. Was it just plain delicious or was it the new taste that I loved? Regardless, after the first few swallows, I felt even more hungry. I devoured my dish in five minutes. *Aliya and I would have to eat here from time to time. We could walk on a nice day. Even stroll with the baby.*

My mother chatted while we ate. "So I believe you like it?" she said. "Do you want to order another serving?"

I laughed. "Yes, but I won't. It really was different and delicious."

A few minutes later, my mother had finished her sea bass. A busboy quickly removed our dishes, followed by our waiter who placed two bowls on the table, each with three pinkish-red golf-size balls with leathery peels. He also brought two small cups and a pot of jasmine tea. I pointed. "Lychee fruit? Mom, do you know how to eat them?"

"Yes," she answered picking one up. "Use your thumbnail, like this, to pierce the peel. Then slowly, like an orange, peel the skin away." When she had finished peeling, my mother separated the whitish flesh and removed the pit. She then broke off a part of the flesh and handed it to me. "Taste. Do you like?"

It sort of smelled like a rose, and the texture was like biting into a sweet grape. But the taste, more like a strawberry, or a ripe pear, or an orange, or a mixture. Whatever, I liked it. I followed my mother's instructions in eating all three of my fruits. *How did my mother know how to eat lychee fruit?* I'd never seen it in our house.

"Just wondering, Mom, when had you eaten lychee fruit before?"

My mother reddened and looked down. "I was here with Martin a few months ago. He showed me. He joked that when he had gone with business associates to a non-kosher Chinese restaurant, he could only order some desserts, usually the lychee fruit."

The waiter came over. "Anything else?"

We shook our heads, and he left. I couldn't delay any longer. "Mom, speaking of Martin, I have a question for you."

My mother gave a wry smile. "I did not think that out-of-the-blue, you just wished for a mother-son lunch date. I imagined that you had something on your mind concerning Martin." She caressed my face. "But, I don't mind. I am happy to spend time with my son. What is it you wish to know?"

No point beating around the bush. I'd get right to it. I placed my hand over hers on the table. "At the hearing on Monday, it'll probably come out that Martin was a kapo at Auschwitz. Did he ever tell you?"

My mother's face paled. "Yes," she said softly, "he told me a few days ago when I was delivering groceries. He too said it might soon come out publicly." Her face glistened with tears.

My free hand trembled. My poor mother's torment. I leaned forward. "How'd it make you feel?"

She took a deep breath and placed her other hand atop mine. "How did it make me feel? I will not lie to you. It made me feel terrible. I made what Martin certainly recognized as an awkward excuse to leave. I have not seen him since."

"You mean his having been a kapo really bothers you, that it's unforgivable?"

She leaned forward and whispered. "There is much for me to consider. No, it is not that he was a kapo, per se, which is a factor in my thoughts. But your Zaida has said at times that if the Holocaust survivor did not commit an overtly evil act, then who are we to judge how the person survived? Martin insisted to me that he tried to do good in his position, and the Nazis would have found someone else, perhaps with cruelty, as a kapo. I can understand that reasoning in the moment he had to decide and in his looking back."

"There is a 'but,' isn't there, Mom?"

She took a breath and nodded. Color had come back to her face. "The 'but' is that he never told me before this terrible business arose. How, I ask myself, does one not share this important information with a person to whom one is expressing affection? Can I get over my resentment? I very much want to, but I don't know if I can."

My mother looked straight at me. "You see, my Joel, I realize that I do not love Martin the way I loved your father—the way I sense you love Aliya. With such a love, there is more the possibility of forgiveness."

She stopped and thought for a moment. "Perhaps, perhaps if it was your father, I very well might have forgiven him for my feeling betrayed if he had not told me about having been a kapo. I care for Martin greatly, but it is not love. And his having been a kapo and his not telling me weigh on me terribly."

The waiter came over and placed the check on the table.

"I think I get it, Mom. I'm really sorry. We can talk anytime you want. I asked in case Martin hadn't told you, I didn't want you to be shocked if you were planning to attend the hearing."

We released hands.

"I wasn't planning to come, Joel. I will hear from you and Zaida after."

I moved the check in front of my mother. I had snuck a peek. $13.55, including the tax.

"Thanks for the lunch and instruction. Let's see if Vasily or one of his taxi colleagues is out front to take us back to your store."

One more caress to my face. "I love you, Yoeli."

THURSDAY, JUNE 17, 1976

Earlier in the week, I had scheduled a meeting for today at PWR with a couple of our criminal defense guys. I'd pick their brains for anything I might have missed in my preparation for Monday's hearing. The meeting with Jeff Lewis and John Langston started at 9:00. After I gave them background, and they understood that we weren't yet going to full trial, their interest cooled. Jeff, the head of the PWR criminal defense division, said, "Your client's sure to be indicted from what you told us. Don't expend much energy, and keep your powder dry until you go to trial. And remember, judges at evidentiaries don't like long-winded witness examinations. Don't alienate—the same judge may preside over the trial."

I nodded often—asked a few questions to which I suspected I knew the answer. I learned nothing different from what I had been taught in law school and from my own research. Several times I almost told them about my plan to put Martin on the stand. *Why didn't I?* Because of what Jeff had said about "long-winded witness examinations?" More simply—Could I defend a negative response from them? *How odd, they would've thought, if I told them I was going along my grandfather's thinking.* I asked if we could meet again "if we went to trial."

"If?" John Langston snapped. "Your boy's going to be indicted. There's no 'if' with his prints on the murder weapon." I thanked them and shook hands. I received back two half-hearted "good lucks."

In my office at 9:30, I muttered to myself a quote that had stuck with me since I saw in high school my first production of *Macbeth.* "If it were done when 'tis done, then 'twere well it were done quickly." I had to call Martin and let him know that I wanted to put him on the stand—might as well get it over with. I took a deep breath and dialed.

"You wish for me to testify at the hearing on Monday?" he challenged. "Is it not unusual for a defendant to take the stand in his defense during a trial, let alone at an evidentiary hearing?"

I thought quickly. Was I heading toward another "lie of omission?" *You can't lie to your client, but is a truth that happens to not fully expose all aspects of a statement a lie?* "The thing is, Martin, I'm worried that the prosecution may ask ROR to be revoked, and the trial won't be scheduled for several weeks. There's a city-wide push to be tough on anyone indicted for murder by refusing bond or release on one's own recognizance. I want to keep you on the outside while we wait."

He said nothing for a few seconds. "Thank you, Joel, but I do not understand. What will I say on the stand that will help keep me free until the trial?" Then, in a stern voice, "I do not wish to mention that I was with your mother the night of the murder. Please do not ask me to do so."

My heart pounded. If the case went to trial, my mother would insist on testifying in Martin's defense.

"Let me tell you I have no plans at the evidentiary hearing to ask anything about you and my mother. Rather, I'll pose a few background questions to establish you as a good family man who was in love with his wife going back to when the two of you were young adults. I'll also ask about your rivalry with Casman for your wife's hand in marriage. That it turned out that your wife married you and not Casman, that'll work against your having a motive to kill him. After all, it was Casman who would have been angry with you."

I could hear his breathing. "Joel, I cannot say that I understand fully, but I find myself in your hands, and I have confidence in those hands. Yes, okay, I will take the stand."

Could Martin hear me exhale? I spent the rest of our conversation instructing him on what to expect from the prosecution, including the witnesses that I expected Fried to call, and how I expected to refute their testimony.

"Yes," Martin said, "it does make sense from what you had previously told me that they would ask those people to make the case against me. I am certain you will cross-examine very effectively."

"Do you need anything?" I asked.

"No, thank you," he said, "your mother has seen to my needs quite well."

We hung up.

I pulled up my sleeve and looked at my watch. Just 9:50 in the morning. Why did it feel like I'd already put in a full day's work?

SUNDAY, JUNE 20, 1976

A few more fitful nights went by. I'd lie down in bed, kiss Aliya good night, and tell myself to go to sleep and stay asleep. My orders would go unheeded as my mind played with various scenarios that might occur on Monday. Aliya also slept poorly. She insisted she felt fine, but the sounds of my mind, she told me, kept her awake. I could take the humor—glad to be the fall guy, even if I knew she was doing her own worrying about the start of her job.

Ben Marcus called at 10:00. "Are you up for another seven innings of stick ball?" he asked. "Thought you might want to reclaim your reputation after last week's walloping. And truth is, Shoshi wants to get out of the house and visit with Aliya, if it's okay with her."

"I'll ask her," I said muffling the receiver. *Was I up for another round with Ben? Would I be able to relax any better? Did I feel prepared for tomorrow?* I convinced myself that I could regain my form. Aliya readily agreed to seeing them.

"Good," Ben said. "How 'bout we meet at Tompkins Square Park at 10th and Avenue A? We'll drive over from Brooklyn."

Forty-five minutes later we met the Marcus family at the park. Uri and Tzvi took off for the swings with Shoshi and Aliya behind them. Ben and I waited ten minutes for a court to be available. I brought my favorite stick and three Spauldeens we'd used when I'd beaten Ben a few weeks back. I played better than last week when I was crushed, 12-1, but still, enough distractions interfered with my concentration. Not too bad—lost 6-4.

Ben and Shoshi left quickly after our game to drive back to Brooklyn—lunch with Ben's parents and siblings.

"You hungry?" Aliya asked as we linked hands and turned toward 14th Street.

"Very," I said. "What are you thinking of having?"

She squeezed my hand. "I'm thinking," she laughed, "that the other day, you made my mouth water talking about how much you loved eating Chinese with your mother at *Schmulka Bernstein's*. I wouldn't mind walking over there for lunch. That was your first time eating Chinese, but my parents would take my sister and me there several times a year. I loved the *Moo Goo Gai Pan*. What do you say? It might relax both of us."

Drenched in sweat, the sun blazing hot, I couldn't think of a better idea. "Then we'll watch the end of the Mets game, when we get back?"

"Yes," Aliya laughed harder. "Then supper. And we watch Rhoda, Kojak, go to sleep, and I get to eavesdrop on your mind. Hope it'll be about sweet dreams."

MONDAY, JUNE 21, 1976

The radio alarm set to WPIX, the top 40 and oldies station, woke me at 6:30 to Carly Simon's "You're So Vain." I stretched—Aliya was already up.

"Good morning," Aliya said as she entered the bedroom. "Our plan for relaxing last night seemed to work. I eavesdropped and heard only good vibrations."

I laughed. "Then it should have been The Beach Boys rather than Carly Simon's false accusation."

Aliya leaned over and kissed me. "Better yet, I should have ordered Carole King's 'You've Got a Friend.'" She poked my ribs. "You really do have a friend, who has a suggestion." She pointed to a suit hanging on the closet door.

I looked. Had my "friend" made a mistake by putting out Mr. Tuesday instead of Mr. Monday?

Before I could say anything, she put up a hand. "I didn't confuse the days. Just two weeks ago, at Martin's arraignment, you wore Mr. Monday. What if you have the same judge today who saw you in that suit? Besides, a change of routine might be energizing."

Don't be immediately resistant to change. I tended to be superstitious, wearing the same number from Little League through college ball, picking up lucky pennies, or mock spitting upon hearing the prediction of good future outcomes. But there might be something to Aliya's thinking. Judge Black had comedian Don Rickles' personality—attack and belittle. He might pick on a Manhattan attorney wearing the same suit, two appearances in a row. Maybe it would give me extra energy.

"Okay," I said, "I'll give it a try. What are you wearing?"

Aliya snickered. "I'm corseting myself in my navy blue suit, the frilled white blouse, stockings, and heels. Yuk. But my mother's words as I was growing up ring in my ears. 'You never get a second chance to make a first impression.' Over and over, she'd say it to me and my sister. Anyway, I hope it'll be just for my first day." She grinned. "I only have that one suit."

"Hah," I said, "unlike your sartorially splendid husband with his six suits." I jumped up and headed to the shower.

* * * *

We ate a light breakfast of instant oatmeal, banana, and milk. Dressed and about to leave, I said. "I almost forgot. I've got to call Martin. I hope he hasn't left."

Aliya looked at the kitchen clock. "It's only 7:30. I'm going to get dressed. I don't have to leave until 8:30."

"I know," I said, starting to dial. "Come here for a quick kiss. We can wish each other luck today."

Martin answered just as Aliya headed off to the bedroom. "Is there something wrong, Joel?" he asked. "I was about to leave."

"No, no," I said. "I should've mentioned it Thursday, but I'd like us to meet at Jay and Schermerhorn before we enter the courthouse. By 8:30, if possible. I'm not sure any press will be at the hearing, but if anyone is watching, it'll be good to show client and attorney walking in together."

"Yes, of course, if you think it best. I have ordered a car service. It will be here in five minutes. I should arrive by 8:30, traffic willing. Goodbye, Joel."

Martin hung up. He hadn't asked if there was anything else. Luckily, there wasn't.

* * * *

The F train from Union Square got me to the Jay Street Station by 8:15. Five minutes later, walking down Jay, I spotted Martin at the Schermerhorn corner. Quite a change from two weeks earlier. I'd never seen him stooped before. He stood head bowed and arms folded. His suits had fit him perfectly, but now the jacket hung loosely, and trousers bagged over hidden shoes. "Martin!" I called, from 50 feet away.

He looked up and nodded. He said nothing until I caught up and stuck out my hand. He shook it. With jaw tight and crow's feet lining eyes below furrowed brows, he said, "Please excuse how I look. I did not sleep last night."

I shook my head. "You look fine and you'll do fine. Try not to worry, at least too much." I placed a hand on his shoulder. "Shall we?"

He nodded.

As we approached the courthouse's center door, I didn't see any press, except for the tallish figure of Martha Brennan. She wore her signature khaki safari suit with a wide belt and tapered trousers. And like last year, when we met her on the Flaum case, her open-toed sandals showed toenail polish that matched perfectly her pinkish-red lipstick, offsetting her fortyish, angular freckled face. She carried a large, red straw handbag. A Ricoh 35 camera in its case dangled around her neck.

She waved and stepped toward us. "Hello, Mr. Gordon. I take it this is your client, Mr. Ross?" She extended her hand to Martin. "I'm Martha Brennan from *The Daily News*."

Martin fidgeted and looked at me. I gave him a quick nod as I said, "Hello, Ms. Brennan. Yes, this is Martin Ross. At this time, he has no comments to any questions. Are you attending the hearing?"

Brennan withdrew her hand. "I sure am. This case will drive reader interest since the victim was a Nazi hunter."

Martin suddenly turned toward Brennan. I had never seen his eyes so wide. "Excuse me, Miss Brennan, I do not know how much you investigated Henry Casman's life, but he was not much of a Nazi hunter." Martin waved his hand and gritted his teeth. "No, he was more of a…" Martin stopped and turned away. "Miss, you will please excuse my outburst. I find myself living with much anxiety."

Brennan extended her hand again. This time, Martin shook it. "It's okay, Mr. Ross, I can understand what you're going through. And what you said will be off the record." She took the camera out of the case. "Just one request, gentlemen. A picture of the two of you in the front of the courthouse?"

Martin responded before I could say anything. "Yes, certainly Miss Brennan. Please tell us where to stand."

Brennan posed us for a few photos. "That'll be great," she said. "And, oh, Mr. Ross, you're in very good hands with Joel and Mr. Wolf." She smiled at me. "They're the best." Turning, she walked quickly ahead into the courthouse.

What was it that Yogi Berra had said a decade earlier watching Mickey Mantle and Roger Maris repeatedly hit back-to-back homers—"Déjà vu all over again?" That's what it was for me when we walked into the courthouse lobby. Lawyers with briefcases hustling by, the crowd of people speaking various languages—all expressing agony and confusion—and the two lines of attorneys queued up alphabetically to get new client paperwork and location. But this time, I had my client with me, and I knew where to go. The court clerk's office had called PWR—the hearing would be in Courtroom B—same as where the arraignment had taken place. I pointed Martin toward the elevators.

8:40. We entered the courtroom. Except for a bailiff who was puttering around the judge's bench and Brennan who, with an open notebook in her lap and the straw handbag slung over a shoulder—*Ah, she knows cameras are not allowed in a courtroom, at least not visible ones*—had seated herself in a back row, the room was empty. I steered Martin down the center aisle toward the defendant's table on the left.

Martin touched my shoulder and gave a momentary smile. "I know my place, Joel." He seated himself in the same chair as before. I took the seat to his right. We both kept looking to the back of the room.

At 8:45, my grandfather came in.

"Mr. Wolf," Brennan cried and beckoned to him. He waved to us before sidling down the back row toward her. "How nice to see you," she said opening her arms to him. He extended his hand, and she clasped his forearm.

He bowed and took off his hat revealing a kippah. I heard him say, "It is also nice to see you again, Ms. Brennan." They both sat and began to chat in low voices. I no longer could make out what they were saying.

8:48. I did a quick run to the restroom. The state's witnesses I expected, Mira Schnapper, Abraham Schneider, and Solomon Bloch sat on separate benches in the hallway. They didn't seem aware of each other's presence.

8:52. I had just returned to the courtroom. Detective Carlucci and Officer Boykin walked in. Carlucci stopped and saluted toward Grandfather.

"Mr. Wolf, my friend," he said loudly. "Nice to see you again."

"Yes, Detective, it is also nice to see you."

Boykin, dressed in a white, open-collared shirt with a Department of Corrections badge placed a chair between our table and the gallery. A belt with a service revolver circled the waist of his blue trousers.

"Just routine," he said to me. He must have noticed my stare. "There's usually no trouble, but you never know."

Carlucci came over and placed his hands on my shoulders. I could smell his smoker's breath. He didn't look at or address Martin. "How are you, buddy? This is your first criminal case, correct? You'll do just fine." He took his hands off and pointed to his temples.

I stiffened awaiting more from Carlucci.

"Ya know why? Because you've got it up here." He then pointed to his chest. "And in the way you protected your grandpa during the Flaum case interrogation, here, too." He glanced briefly at Martin. "Sorry that I got to do my job and testify for the prosecution." He winked at me. "And in case there's a need for my services, I'm here." He turned and walked back to the gallery.

Martin whispered. "A very odd policeman. What does he mean by 'a need for my services'?"

I shrugged, avoiding looking at Martin. No reason to tell him about our exchange of information.

8:53. By now, about a dozen people whom I didn't recognize had straggled in and taken seats. *Who were they*? Individuals randomly came to court sessions to observe the proceedings as entertainment. None looked like a reporter. Seems Brennan had an exclusive on her hands.

Then Fried, the prosecutor walked in, head high, followed by a young woman laden with folders. He was short, but she even shorter. *An assistant prosecutor*? Fried's finely tailored dark blue silk suit, different from the one he wore at the arraignment, shimmered and made my Mr. Tuesday look like a poor country cousin. *Good thing Aliya suggested the change from Mr. Monday.*

Fried nodded to me, and I nodded back. Then he took the first seat at the prosecution table near the jury box, and motioned to the woman to place the materials on the desk and sit to his right.

8:58. A few more people straggled in—no sign of Payshe Zimmer. I looked at my grandfather. Did I see a slight shrug? Just then, the door opened, and Zimmer took a step in and stood without moving further. The ill-fitting blue denim jacket he wore over heavy dungarees sagged on him. He scanned the courtroom. He looked right toward Grandfather and quickly looked away. Grandfather put a hand to his chin and glanced toward me. Zimmer focused on us, and Martin waved to him. He got no return wave. Martin's jaw tightened as Zimmer walked down the center aisle, turned right at the first row behind the balusters separating the gallery from the prosecutor's table, and sat down.

9:00. A gavel hammered from the judge's bench area. A bailiff called, "All rise." The door behind the judge's bench opened, and Judge Sylvan Black walked out and made his way to his chair. *How big and heavy he looked.* The bailiff announced the case of the State of New York versus Martin Ross in the murder of Henry Casman. Martin cringed when he heard the charge.

The bailiff concluded, "Please be seated and come to order."

Judge Black shuffled some papers and looked up. "Mr. Fried and the pretty young lady next to you—I forget the esteemed assistant prosecutor's name—I don't really need to go over procedural matters on an evidentiary hearing with you, do I?"

Fried sprang up. "No, Your Honor. Both Miss Malzone and I are well versed."

Black looked my way. "And welcome back, Mr. Gordon." The judge lowered his glasses. "I see that my judgment to allow Mr. Ross out on his own recognizance has been well affirmed." Black glanced down toward the prosecution. "There he is, Mr. Fried, in the flesh, sitting next to his attorney."

Fried turned our way. "Yes, Judge," he said. "So I can see."

Black turned back to Martin and me. "But since you're new to my courtroom, a quick word about how things will be done this morning. The judge placed both elbows on his desk and leaned forward. "No grandstanding, no long winded cross-examinations of state witnesses, no niggling points made, save any 'ahas' for trial, and, Mr. Gordon, no endless objections to what I'm sure the prosecution will lay out reasonably as to why your client should be held for trial."

I stood. "I fully understand, Your Honor."

"And one more thing," Black said looking down at a paper. "I see that you intend to call your client as a witness in his own defense—something quite rare in an evidentiary hearing. Mr. Ross, I'm pretty sure your counsel has already informed you, but regardless, I'm going to tell you your rights in plain English." The judge leaned back. "You don't have to testify if you don't want to, and whatever you say on the stand can be held against you. You already have an attorney, so I don't have to say that you're entitled to one. Got it, Mr. Ross?"

I nudged Martin. He rose and said, glancing at me several times, "Yes, sir, I understand."

"Okay, then," Black said. "Mr. Fried, let the prosecution begin."

* * * *

Fried didn't surprise me. He called Carlucci as his first witness who testified as to Martin's fingerprints on the knife and that a witness had identified him as having argued with the victim a few hours before the murder.

I kept my cross-examination short. "Detective Carlucci, good morning, you told us that my client's fingerprints are on the murder weapon?"

"Yes, that's right," Carlucci answered."

"Thank you, Detective. Were any other fingerprints of interest besides that of my client and the victim found at the murder scene?"

Was Carlucci too eager with his answer? "Yes, there was. A partial print not matching your client's or the victim's was found on a bus ticket."

Fried let out, "Objection."

Black waved his hand. "Yes, yes, Mr. Fried, I know and for the record, at this point in the advancement of forensic technology, evidence from a partial fingerprint is meaningless. So noted, and move on. Thank you, Detective, you are excused. Who's next. Mr. Fried?"

The judge hadn't even asked me if I had any further questions. Good thing, I didn't. Still, I was bothered.

In a calm voice, Fried said, "We call Mrs. Mira Schnapper."

A bailiff opened the door to the courtroom, and Mrs. Schnapper walked in followed by a stout, elderly woman in a loose-fitting, ankle-length black, wool dress. White hair peeked out from a kerchief around her head. *Must be the translator.* Fried motioned them toward the witness box.

"If it pleases, Your Honor," Fried announced, "Mrs. Hilda Himmelfarb will serve as a translator since Mrs. Schnapper lacks proficiency in English. She is a Yiddish speaker. We wouldn't want any confusion in her testimony, and it's in agreement with defense counsel."

Black smirked. "No, we don't want any confusion in my courtroom. I see the interpreter is in position near the witness box. Ask away, Mr. Prosecutor."

Fried quickly elicited from Mrs. Schnapper through the translator that she had seen Martin in the apartment hallway arguing with Casman a few hours before the murder and that Martin returned at the time of the murder. Even with my less than perfect Yiddish, I realized that the interpreter had omitted Mrs. Schnapper's having said "*glaipt*," meaning that she *believes* that the man she heard arguing with Casman at the time of the murder was Martin. I couldn't wait to start my cross-examination.

Then it was my turn. I stood and took a deep breath. "Good morning, Mrs. Schnapper, I hope you are well."

I could see Judge Black's impatience as Mrs. Schnapper waved off the interpreter and answered in broken English, "Gut, gut, and you be still a man happy in your wedding?"

Laughter from the gallery. "Yes, I am. Thank you for your testimony, and I will only keep you for a few more minutes."

Mrs. Schnapper smiled. "Nuh, gut, gut. I have no hurry."

I hadn't planned on it, but I asked in Yiddish. "*Vos meinst du ven du host gezogt as du 'glaipst' der man vos hat getent mit Herr Casman in der tzeit fun der mord iz geven Herr Ross. Du 'glaipst' dos oder du hast gezen em mit dein eigeneh aigen?*"

Judge Black shook his head, held out his hand toward Mrs. Schnapper, and motioned to Mrs. Himmelfarb, who blushed. For whatever reason, she'd taken liberties with her translation, and she'd been caught. This time she carefully rendered my Yiddish, "The lawyer who just spoke to Mrs. Schnapper said, 'What do you mean when you said that you believe the man who had argued with Mr. Casman at the time of his murder was Mr. Ross? Do you believe so or did you actually see him with your own eyes?'"

Mrs. Himmelfarb looked to the Judge. "Should I now ask Mrs. Schnapper to answer?

Black exhaled loudly. "Yes, tell her to answer."

Mrs. Schnapper didn't need a translation. She laughed and wagged a finger at me. "A shame you are not a single. I can easy make many good *shidduch*." Then she switched to Yiddish. She said, "I believe it was the same man, but with my own eyes I did not see him clearly. But my neighbor argued with the man both times in Yiddish."

I kept eye contact with Mrs. Schnapper, smiling the whole time. "But it could have been two different men arguing with Mr. Casman, right Mrs. Schnapper?"

Mrs. Schnapper shrugged after translation. "Avadeh," she replied. And then Mrs. Himmelfarb said in a loud voice, "Of course."

I thanked the witness and, before I sat, I cast a quick glance at Payshe. He glared at Mrs. Schnapper as she made her way out of the courtroom.

The next two prosecution witnesses came and went quickly.

After Abe Schneider testified to Casman's having blocked Martin from membership in the Benevolent Society and publicly accused him of being a kapo, Fried asked, "How did it make Mr. Ross feel, accused of being a Nazi?"

Schneider raised his eyebrows. "What a question! How would it make anyone hearing such an accusation in public? He was upset, angry."

Fried nodded. "Mr. Schneider, angry enough to want to kill Mr. Casman?"

The judge saved me from having to jump up. He shook a finger at Fried. "My Lord, Mr. Fried, my first year law students know better than to ask that sort of a question. Do you really think the witness is capable of assessing murderous intent based on the defendant's level of anger? Now cut it out in my courtroom."

Fried went crimson and bowed his head. "Of course, Your Honor. I should have known better."

Did Ms. Malzone snigger?

Fried called Solomon Bloch of the German Reparations Office. Bloch testified that Casman had expressed strong feelings about identifying and punishing Jewish collaborators. "Mr. Bloch," Fried asked, "if Mr. Casman knew that Mr. Ross was a kapo, would that pose a threat to Mr. Ross?"

How stupid. I sprang up to object. Black stopped me.

"Mr. Gordon, yes, yes, you'd be right to object. But Mr. Fried's question is not as out-of-order as the previous. Why don't we have the witness answer? Mr. Bloch, what say you?"

Bloch shrugged. "I guess, maybe, anyone identified as a kapo would probably feel threatened. But I don't know for sure."

The judge opened his hands. "There you go, Mr. Fried, you got your 'maybe' answer. Any other questions?"

"No, Your Honor." Fried sat.

"Do you wish to cross, Mr. Gordon?"

"Yes, Your Honor. Just one question, Mr. Bloch. Did you ever hear Mr. Casman actually say that my client had been a kapo?"

Bloch shook his head.

Judge Black snapped. "The witness will use words to answer, so please Mr. Bloch, what is your answer?"

"No," Bloch said loudly. "I never heard Mr. Casman say anything about Mr. Ross being a kapo."

"Anyone else, Mr. Fried?" the judge asked.

Fried rose slowly. "Your Honor, that is all for the prosecution. Since this is an evidentiary hearing to determine charging the defendant and the question of bail, which I will oppose, I believe I may say that regardless of any other testimony, the fact remains that his fingerprints are present on the murder weapon."

"Yes, they are, Mr. Fried. Thank you for reminding me about something I already know." The judge turned toward me. "Your turn, Mr. Gordon."

I stood. "If it pleases the Court, I'd like to call my client, Martin Ross, to the stand."

Black shook his head but said nothing.

Martin took the stand, looking back at me a few times as he approached.

After his being sworn in, I said, "Mr. Ross, without taking a good deal of time, I'd like the Court to hear about your background to understand your character as to why you certainly are not Mr. Casman's murderer."

I did a theatrical half-rotation so I could get a peek at Payshe. With lips tightly pursed, his dark eyes narrowed and leveled on Martin.

Taking Martin through his background in Europe and his coming to the United States took a few minutes. Judge Black started tapping a pencil. I didn't have much time before he would shut me down. Payshe had come today as Grandfather and I had hoped. I had to get to the central area of questioning to complete our plan.

"Mr. Ross," I continued, "when you and Henry Casman were young men back in the old country, you were rivals for the hand of the same woman, Dora, whom you eventually married after the War. Is that right?"

Martin squirmed. "Yes, that is right."

"And did you or Mr. Casman have any sense as to which of you two she favored when you vied for her hand?"

My client eyed me warily, and the judge leaned forward. *Even if our full plan might not work, now that he was in Brooklyn, Carlucci could still pull Payshe in for questioning—for what it would be worth. Better if Payshe did react.* Could Martin see my eyes silently pleading with him to answer?

He did—wearily. "No, she seemed equally friendly to both of us. But the decision rested as much with her parents as it did with Dora."

"Yes, thank you, Mr. Ross. But did she not lead you on to think that if her parents chose you, she would be quite pleased? I'm asking to establish that by her choosing you after the War, there was more motive for Mr. Casman to want to hurt you than the reverse."

Martin shook his head. His eyes narrowed. But before he could answer, I coughed and added. "And might she have behaved similarly with Mr. Casman? Might it be said that as a vivacious young woman, she flirted with both of you?"

Then, what took place in seconds played out in slow motion. Its memory has stayed with me all my life. I saw the judge lifting his gavel, probably to tell me to shut down my strange and irrelevant questioning. Fried rising to object. The shrill cry of "No!" exploding from where Payshe sat. A woman's shout of "He's got a gun." Before hearing the crack of a gunshot, a white object—later I knew it had been Officer Boykin—hurtling and slamming me onto the wooden floor, hitting my forehead hard. Blood spreading down to my mouth.

I turned, trying as best I could to look up. Above me, Officer Boykin groaned and, through gritted teeth, asked, "Are you okay counselor? Are you okay counselor?" Voices screamed, and the thud of rushing footsteps filled the room. Carlucci shouted, "Drop the gun, do you hear me?"

My shirt stuck to me, wet. I brushed my chest and looked at my fingers—blood. From me? No! My forehead throbbed, and I was sore from hitting the floor, but that was all. It must be from Officer Boykin, who still lay on me.

Through the clamor, I heard my grandfather repeating, "Yoeli, Yoeli. Oy, Yoeli, can you hear me, Yoeli?"

Other voices. "Joe, medics will be here soon. They'll get you to a hospital right away. You took a bullet to your shoulder." Boykin groaned, and the voice continued. "I know it hurts, but Tim and I have to press against the wound to lessen the bleeding until the medics get here. Hang in. You're gonna be okay. Can you hear us, Joe?"

Without hesitation, Boykin answered, "Yeah, I hear you, Marty. It hurts. But best thing you can do is get me off my counselor friend before he suffocates. He needs a medic, too. He slammed his head into the floor."

The medics arrived within the minute. As they gently placed Boykin on a stretcher and wheeled him away, he caught my eye. Through clenched teeth, he joked, "Well counselor, now see what you've done." Two fingers waved goodbye.

A medic sat me up. "Let's clean you up and get you to a hospital. You might be concussed."

I didn't argue as I looked around. The courtroom was empty—no judge, prosecutors, bailiffs, or gallery visitors—except for Martha Brennan who had just snapped a picture of me before leaning down. *Where was Martin?*

"They want me out of here, Joel," Brennan said. "Looks like you took a nasty cut to your forehead. They'll check you out. You may be out of action for a few days. And if you're wondering what happened to your client, some officers hustled him out. I heard they were taking him home."

She put two fingers to her lips and bent them toward me. "I'm sure I'll see you soon."

As soon as she left, the medic motioned toward someone behind me. Grandfather, whom I hadn't seen, came over, knelt beside me, and took my hand. "I am sorry, Joel, I am very sorry. You will go with this gentleman to the hospital, and they will see to your welfare, yes? I will follow. To avert their distress, I also will call your mother at the store and Aliya at her work.

The radio news will surely be filled with the events of what has transpired here."

Grandfather held on to my hand. Before I could ask him why he was 'sorry,' he began to rock back and forth. Throughout, tears streamed down his cheeks. Over and over he lamented in Yiddish, "*Gut in himmel, vos hob ich getton? Vos hob ich getton?*"

While I understood the words, I didn't understand why Grandfather was saying, "God in heaven, what have I done? What have I done?"

* * * *

Good news at the Kings County Hospital emergency room—no concussion. But my aching head had a more important concern—*Officer Boykin*.

The elderly nurse who had been taking care of me and calling me "honey" had no idea how the officer was doing. And she didn't volunteer to find out.

"Yes," I repeated back to her as she was discharging me, "I understand. You just gave me a 500 mg Tylenol tablet, and I'm to take one every six hours until my headache goes away."

"That's it, honey." She pointed to my forehead. "And there's four stitches in that noggin of yours. You'll need to have them taken out in ten days. You can come back here or go to your personal physician. Here's your written instructions. That's it. You've got family waiting for you."

My grandfather, my mother, and Aliya sat on a bench near the entrance of a waiting room. Mom and Aliya jumped up as soon as they saw me. Grandfather rose slowly. Aliya deferred to my mother who rushed over and hugged me tightly. She kissed both of my cheeks and passed a hand close to my bandaged forehead.

I felt her trembling as she blew out a breath. "Oh, my Joel. You are hurt. But from what your Zaida told me, it could have been a great deal worse." She looked up. "Thank you, God. Thank you."

After my mother released me, Aliya came over and carefully kissed me. "Your head must hurt a lot," she said looking above my eyes. "Yes, your mother is right, it could have been a good deal worse without the heroics of Officer Boykin." Aliya put her head on my shoulder.

I patted her hair. "Careful, I've got a lot of blood on my clothes—some mine and some from the officer." I took a breath. "Do you know how Officer Boykin's doing?"

My mother answered. "Yes, we were just in his room here at the hospital. His wife is with him. He has a bullet wound to his shoulder and has lost a good deal of blood. But the doctors say he will make a full recovery. We all thanked him profusely, and do you know what that dear man said? 'No need to thank me, ma'am. Just doing my job.'"

My grandfather came over and placed his hands on my cheeks. What was that look in his eyes? I'd never seen it before. Hie eyes were reddened and swollen from earlier crying, but they were also steely, downcast and narrowed, with eyebrows tightly drawn. He looked at me directly. "And I, in doing my job, caused his injury and might have cost your life."

He took my hand. "You will do me a favor, yes? You will please attend a synagogue service and *bench gomel.*" He was referring to the Jewish ritual where an individual publicly reads a prayer of gratitude for being saved from a dangerous situation.

I nodded.

Grandfather turned, walked back, and sat down on the bench. I glanced at my mother and Aliya before starting after him. I sat beside him.

"Zaida," I said softly. "It wasn't your fault. You didn't know that Payshe would bring a gun, let alone shoot it in a courtroom."

My grandfather shook his head and said firmly, "But it was my fault. And I will never think otherwise. I knew that Mr. Zimmer had an extremely unstable personality capable of violence under various circumstances. How did I fool myself into thinking that he would not erupt violently?"

"But it's okay, Zaida. I'll be okay, and so will Officer Boykin."

Grandfather looked down. "Yes, and I am thankful." And then very slowly, he said, "But I am not okay. I am shaken by my own arrogance, my susceptibility to a darkness that settled over me and blinded me to what was predictable."

He looked up. "Was it because of my success in our previous cases that created a vanity where critical analyses gave way to self-indulgence? Was it because I was personally involved, seeking the quickest path to Martin's vindication despite my insisting that I do not take a case to 'clear' someone's name? Did I fool myself in thinking I was above a personal dislike for Mr. Zimmer, which may have motivated me to play with him? How did I dare become a puppet master thinking my human puppet, easily prone to violence, would follow each pull of my strings?"

My heart ached for my grandfather. *I won't patronize him with empty platitudes.* "What now, Zaida?" I asked. "We'll go back home and relax for the rest of the day?"

Tight-lipped, my mother said, "Joel, your Zaida will not do so, not at least for the rest of the day. He has conferred with Detective Carlucci and arranged to interview that man who shot at you at 4:00 at the 61st Precinct. Please, try to persuade your Zaida not to do so. I fear his being together in the same room with such a dangerous person."

My grandfather shook his head.

No chance he would listen. "Then, I'm going with you," I said. "I don't want to hear no." I'd never spoken to my grandfather this way.

My mother pleaded, her voice shrill. "You will not, Joel. The doctor may be wrong, You may have a concussion. You must rest for a few days."

Aliya only said very quietly, "Joel, are you sure you're up to it?"

"Malkeh," my grandfather said, looking at my mother, "if Joel feels he has the strength to accompany me, then perhaps we can trust to his judgment. As for my safety—and Joel's—I will be in the interview room with Detective Carlucci. Joel will take a place in the observation room. I will not ask that the handcuffs be removed from Mr. Zimmer as I had requested for the suspect in the Flaum case."

His eyes remained steely. "I erred greatly, but I will not fall into depression. Always, we must look for a way out of personal darkness. Now, for me, it is to pursue justice in our case by the means available to me—which is to interrogate Mr. Zimmer. Yes, I believe he killed Henry Casman. But my surety must be brought to light to achieve justice, to free Martin, to free the world, which suffers darkness from anyone's murder until justice prevails." He paused. "And to free me."

Did my grandfather just slightly smile?

He went on. "So to quote from two modern-day philosophers, Mr. Simon and Mr. Garfunkel, I will 'continue to continue' by interviewing Mr. Zimmer. And if we can trust Joel—perhaps I am selfish—but it would be a comfort if he accompanied me to the 61st Precinct."

He looked at his watch. "It is just noon. May I suggest we journey to our house where we may eat a lunch, rest, and reflect?"

My mother shook her head but said, "I'll drive us and prepare something to eat. I brought the car and won't go back to the store. I'll let Rosa know."

Aliya walked over and put a hand on my arm. "Joel, I'm not sure what to do. I have my first client at 2:00 and..."

I looked up and smiled. "Go, you've got to go. Your first day has already been messed up. I'll—we'll all be fine, and I'll leave messages on our machine at home."

Aliya moved a hand from her lips to my cheek. She handed me a large, paper grocery bag she had been holding. "Oh yes, when Zaida called, I rushed home and packed a change of clothes. I said so long to Mr. Tuesday and his shirt and tie partners. A police officer took them as evidence. Maybe soon, we'll go over to the garment district and buy a Mr. Tuesday replacement."

When I returned from changing, Aliya said, "Joel, Zaida, be prepared. There are reporters out front. WINS and other stations have been carrying news of the shooting all morning."

* * * *

A group of reporters from all the major local television stations, newspapers, and WINS Radio roamed the Clarkson Avenue entryway and sidewalk as we exited the hospital. We almost made it past them, but a woman's voice called, "Look, there, that guy with the bandage on his forehead. I think it's the Ross guy's lawyer. Hey, Counselor, hold up a minute."

"Let's keep moving," I muttered, but reporters overtook us and blocked us. Flashes from cameras went off, and voice recorders weaved in front of my face as reporters barked questions.

"Do you know who took a shot at you and why?"

"Did your client kill the Nazi hunter?"

"Do you know the shooter?"

"What happens next with your client?"

I took a deep breath and put up my hand. "I really have nothing to say on behalf of myself or my client besides restating my client's plea of innocence. I'm sure we and the prosecution will hear from Judge Black as to what comes next. The NYPD will probably issue a statement soon. That's all, and please let us pass."

Most reporters moved aside, and we moved down Clarkson toward New York Avenue where my mother was parked and where Aliya would leave us to head back to the City. Footsteps hurried after us. "Joel, Mr. Wolf, please hold up a minute."

We stopped and turned to see Martha Brennan and a man carrying a large camera.

"Ms. Brennan," my grandfather said. "Thank you for trying to shield me when the shooting occurred. I'm sorry if I too violently pushed you aside as I ran to my grandson."

Brennan smiled. "Not at all, Mr. Wolf. Perfectly understandable. I'm glad everyone's okay, including the officer. The hospital just issued a statement saying he is stable and should recover. Anything you can share with me?"

Grandfather shook his head. "Nothing at this moment. I imagine there is much that you have gathered on your own. But if there is news, we will let you know. Thank you. We are now looking forward to some rest."

He opened his hands and herded us forward.

At the car, Aliya hugged me tightly, careful to not brush against my wound. "See you at home. Be sure to call with any news." She stepped away.

I pulled her back and kissed her. "I will."

My mother drove, with Grandfather in the front passenger seat, and I in the back. No one spoke during the twenty minute drive. I kept thinking about my grandfather's feeling that he'd made a terrible mistake by goading Payshe Zimmer. What about my role in what happened? I hadn't been sure about the plan from the beginning. But I didn't push back or even question Grandfather about the wisdom of this approach. Did I take the easy way automatically following my grandfather's lead? Like a small child, did I run to hide in my own little dark corner and rely on my elders because I couldn't think of anything better to do? Was I expecting my first criminal case to be an easy win because of Grandfather's wisdom and insight, not because of my own knowledge and judgement? If Grandfather had erred, wasn't I complicit in the error, since I had my own doubts? I had to face it. *I wasn't a child anymore. I had more growing up to do.*

* * * *

While my mother prepared lunch and my grandfather took to his easy chair, I called Martin.

He responded to my "Hello" with "I have been waiting for you to call. Where is Payshe? What has happened to him?"

I took a deep breath. *After what happened, Payshe's well-being was at the top of Martin's mind?* "Martin," I said, "if you're asking if Payshe is hurt, he's not. He's been taken into custody and being held at the 61st Precinct. He'll be questioned at 4:00 by the police, and my grandfather will sit in during the questioning."

I paused. *Would he be asking about me? Officer Boykin?* I coughed. "You do know that he took a shot at me, and a police officer jumped in the way of the bullet."

Did I hear a sigh? "Of course, I know," he said, his voice brusque. "I was on the stand, and I could clearly see the events unfolding. I saw Payshe's agitation growing as you questioned me on...on, may I say, irrelevancies. I would like to ask, why did you do so? Was it so important to speak of Payshe's mother, may she rest in peace, as being flirtatious? Payshe loved his mother dearly and will take extreme measures to defend her reputation." He paused. "Also, may I ask, how are you and how is the police officer?"

I took a deep breath. *Cool the anger with Martin. At least he asked about us. Given his emotional attachment to his wife and stepson, I guess it makes sense for him to challenge my questioning.* "First, I'm pretty much okay. Officer Boykin took a bullet to his shoulder. He's recovering at King County.

"Second, we thought we had a good reason for my line of questioning. I wanted to show that Casman had more motive to murder you than vice versa."

I cleared my throat. "But there was more to it. Our plan was to provoke Payshe into an outburst that would allow for him to be taken in for questioning. We never thought an outburst would include his trying to kill anyone."

Martin cut in. "But why, Joel? Why did you wish to entrap my stepson?"

Out with it. "Because we believe Payshe murdered Casman. The person who argued with Casman right before he was killed spoke with a *Galitzianer* accent the way Payshe does—unlike your *Litvak* accent. And as I told you, Payshe was seen boarding a bus for New York the day before the murder."

Even though Martin couldn't see me, I held up my hand. "I know, I know," I continued before he could reply." Payshe may have had another reason for travelling to New York a day before the murder. But it establishes proximity to the murder scene. We know from his phone records that Payshe was acquainted with Casman. And finally, Payshe knew that your prints were on the knife before it was publicly revealed. How could he know this? We don't have absolute proof, but we have a strong suspicion that my grandfather will pursue at the 61st."

Martin quickly said, "Does he have a lawyer? Payshe must have a lawyer. And regardless, it is my fingerprints on the knife—not Payshe's or anyone else's. Will that not always be true?"

How strange Martin's wanting to help Payshe when Payshe hated him. "I don't know if he has a lawyer," I answered. "But if he has requested one, the lawyer will sit in at the interrogation."

Why does Martin act like this? I need to ask. "Frankly, I don't get it. Payshe has made it clear how much he despises you. Why are you so eager to defend him?"

Martin's voice rose. "Because he is my stepson, and Dora is no longer with us. He had come under my protection, and now, I still have a duty to look after him. Do you think watching him growing up and despising me was not painful? Do you think that what occurred today does not crush my spirit? But dealing with pain and trying to be a decent human being have been part of my life for a long time. I took on parental responsibility when I married Dora, and I will not turn away from that commitment, regardless of the pain, current circumstances, or how he feels about me."

I heard a long sigh. "You will please let me know the outcome of the interrogation?"

"Of course, Martin."

We exchanged parting words and hung up.

* * * *

I had called Martin from my mother's bedroom, out of her earshot. For now, I'd keep the conversation to myself. It held no bearing on the upcoming interrogation—she didn't need to be further distressed.

When I came out of the bedroom, I walked into the kitchen. My mother sat at the table reading *The Times*. She looked up and smiled. "Of great interest to me in today's news is that the Viking 1 Mars probe has successfully entered its orbit around that planet and is to land in about a month. Oh, what mankind is capable of achieving when it doesn't give in, as your Zaida says, 'to darkness.'"

I took a seat. Her smile slowly disappeared. "You okay, Mom? I was thinking of taking your car and driving with Zaida to the 61st."

She nodded. "Of course. I was about to suggest it myself."

She stood. "If you are done with your calls, I will lie down for a while. The day's events have made me very tired."

"I'm done, Mom. I'll look in on Zaida. We'll leave at 3:30. Don't worry, he'll be fine. As we told you, Detective Carlucci and probably another officer will be in the room during interrogation."

My mother leaned over and kissed me on the cheek. "Thank you. Nevertheless, I will worry until you call to let me know everyone is well."

I followed my mother out of the kitchen and walked over to Grandfather. His feet were up, and in his lap lay the police report, a large book I'd seen in his bookcase called, *Chemical Agents-A-Z*, and a Hebrew copy of *Tehillim*, Psalms in English, open to Psalm 115. Grandfather put out a hand. I grasped it.

"Are you getting any rest," I asked.

He looked up with pursed lips. "I am, Yoeli, to a degree. I am less discombobulated than at the courthouse or hospital. I must now perform my own self-examination, which very much is connected to my preparation for the interrogation just two hours from now."

Hi eyes glazed momentarily before sharpening and looking at me. "There is the practical matter at hand. We will drive to the precinct house, yes?"

I nodded. "Yes, I already spoke to Mom about taking her car. We'll leave at 3:30."

Should I tell him to rest? *He's not a child, and there's no point saying it besides making myself feel virtuous for a minute.* I let go of his hand. "I'll leave you to your, uh, cogitations. I'll be in the kitchen reading *The Times*. Let me know if you need me."

Grandfather smiled. "'Cogitations,' you say? Ah, you are correct to introduce a moment of jest in emulation of how an elderly immigrant speaks the elegant English language. Let us say I will continue to think things over as I prepare for Mr. Zimmer."

I laughed and returned to the kitchen.

* * * *

I found a parking space on Avenue U, about 100 feet down from the station. Grandfather and I walked slowly up the steps to the red, double doors with stained glass above indicating 61st PRECINCT. I opened a door for Grandfather, and we stepped inside. I glanced up at Lady Justice looking down from the frescoed plastered ceiling, illuminated by fluorescent lights, when Carlucci called, "Mr. Wolf, Joel, over here."

The detective stood at the side of an enclosure. A name plate at the front indicated *Desk Sergeant*. The line to the enclosure, behind which stood an officer, was only three-deep—the last time I was here during the Flaum case, it stretched nearly back to the entrance. Nevertheless, in all of the several metallic cubicles at the far end of the room, officers talked with individuals, their voices upset, confused, or disconsolate. Similar to our visits last year, muffled sounds of clanking and a series of curses came from below—the basement area where prisoners were held and through which we would be passing to the interview room.

We waved and walked over to Carlucci.

"Detective," Grandfather said, "thank you for including me in Mr. Zimmer's interrogation. We have a daunting task before us."

Carlucci shook his head. "Not at all, no need to thank me. You taught me that when it comes to your Jewish folks, having someone like you around is really helpful. And this Zimmer character is a piece of work. My forensic guy told me that the pistol he used was a Polish army issue Radom that goes back to the Second War. Zimmer kept asking me why he had to be interrogated when he fully confesses to the courtroom shooting. I told him to wait and see."

Grandfather and I looked at each other. "What you said about the gun does not surprise us, Detective," I said.

My grandfather shook his head. "And without elaboration at this moment, why Mr. Zimmer wonders about his interrogation may also be understandable."

"Detective," I asked, "has he requested an attorney?"

Carlucci threw up his hands. "Nope, he's a strange bird. Said he didn't want an attorney. 'Put me before a judge,' he said, 'and send me away for the shooting.'"

Carlucci pointed toward the basement stairwell. "Shall we, gentlemen? You know the way."

We followed Carlucci down to the basement level. The same chill when I passed by cells, familiar since my days as a law student, came over me. Nothing had changed from last year—same cell formations, but of course, different detainees. On the left, a rectangular cell of around 200 square feet with two toilets partially enclosed by red-ringed curtains held persons arrested on lesser charges such as pickpocketing, shoplifting, and vagrancy. It contained around twenty men, all in street clothes.

On the right, a smaller cell for males arrested on more serious felonies such as murder, robbery, and grand larceny. I saw three men, also in street clothes. Two sat on a bench with their faces in their hands, and the third—my heart raced—was Payshe, standing with balled up fists and glaring in all directions. He was still in the blue denim jacket and the dungarees he had worn to the courthouse. As soon as he spotted us, he flew toward the bars, crashing into them and grabbing on with such force that all chatter stopped. His white knuckles stood out from the black steel bars.

"You," he shouted, pointing at me. "Nobody insults my mother and gets away with it. You sure are lucky. I'm a good shot. Too bad about that police-man who got in the way."

Zimmer slackened his grip on the bars. "But I hear he's going to be okay."

I balled my fists and stepped toward the cell. "You just tried to kill me, and that's all you have to say?" If bars weren't in the way, I would've taken a swing at him.

Grandfather's hand landed on my shoulder, pulling me back. "Joel," he said, "I am equally angry. But let us see what Mr. Zimmer has to say during an official interrogation."

I slowly turned away and continued toward the interview rooms. My grandfather and Carlucci followed. A cement wall on the left separated the men's area from the smaller women's cell. It held about a dozen women, most, from their appearances pulled in for solicitation. *Like it does any good to arrest them. They'll be back on the street in a few hours.*

A woman's voice called. "I guess your lady had enough of you and gave you one with a fry pan. What happened—weren't the eggs she cooked up to your likin'?"

I ignored her, but touched my forehead.

When I came to Interview Room 2, Carlucci said, "Here's where we're gonna be. Just like last time." He pointed to the next door observation room. "Go on in, Joel, and make yourself comfortable. An officer will bring Zim-mer in a few minutes."

I entered the darkened room and stood before the large glass wall that showed the interview room with its rectangular metal table and four chairs. Carlucci flicked on the lights as soon as he and my grandfather came in, il-luminating the room so brightly that I could clearly see everything, including their facial expressions. Carlucci took a seat on the far right side of the table facing the door. Grandfather took the seat to his left.

A few minutes passed before a uniformed officer led—no—pushed Pay-she into the room. He stood in place, his hands cuffed in front, even as the officer poked him to sit opposite Carlucci.

"Sit, Zimmer," Carlucci said, rising. "Do I have to assist Officer Miller in getting you to sit down?"

Payshe moved forward, his eyes narrowing, while the officer pulled the chair out. Zimmer sat, pushed the chair back, and thumped his cuffed hands on the desk. "I don't know why I'm here. There are plenty of witnesses saw me shoot. I admit it, I admit it. So what more do you want from me?"

"Well, I'll tell you what we want from you," Carlucci said, motioning to Officer Miller to remain standing behind Payshe. "You're charged with attempted murder, along with other gun charges. You'll be back at the courthouse tomorrow for an arraignment. Even though you didn't want a lawyer, a public defender will be assigned to you. But that's tomorrow. You're here now to be questioned in connection with the murder of Henry Casman."

Payshe's eyes widened as he pulled his hands against the cuffs. I saw redness and raw skin around his wrists. *He's been doing a lot of pulling.*

"Murder of Henry Casman?" Payshe shouted at Carlucci. "What's that got to do with me? We all know Martin Ross, my stepfather, killed him. I heard it straight from your mouth in court that his fingerprints were on the murder weapon."

Carlucci waved a hand. "Settle down and stop screaming. Couple of things we'd like to ask, startin' with, did you know Casman?"

Payshe's shoulders sagged. "Yeah, I met him once and spoke to him on the phone a few times. So what?"

Carlucci plugged on. "Where were you on the evening of May 29 when Henry Casman was murdered?"

Payshe blinked several times but met Carlucci's gaze. "Probably on my farm. I don't get out much."

Carlucci scoffed. "Really, Zimmer. What if I told you we have a witness who'll testify that you boarded a bus from your town in Jersey to New York the day before the murder?"

With a shrug, Payshe answered, "Oh, yeah, I took a bus to New York and from there to New Brunswick. That's the way I do it. I don't like to drive. I took care of business at the Rutgers Agriculture School Friday morning and returned to Vineland that same day. I guess I forgot about my little excursion."

Carlucci snickered. "And I guess you've got the proof of your trips to and from new Brunswick and back to Vineland that day. So you can give us the names of the folks you met at Rutgers for us to check out your alibi?"

"Alibi," Payshe roared, half rising from his seat. Officer Miller put a hand on his shoulder, and he sank back down "I don't need an alibi. You've got Martin dead to rights. And no, I'm not giving you any names. I don't want people I know dragged into your plot to frame me. You're like the Gestapo *besterds*."

Payshe tried to fold his arms but couldn't. The cuffs stopped him.

Carlucci leaned back and folded his arms. He looked at my grandfather. "Mr. Wolf, your turn."

Throughout Carlucci's questioning, my grandfather sat with hands clasped, looking from Carlucci to Payshe. Slowly, he unclasped his hands, turned toward Payshe, and said in a low voice, "Mr. Zimmer, may I ask, what will become of your chickens now that you are incarcerated for perhaps an extended period of time?"

Payshe tilted his head toward Grandfather. His eyebrows rose. "You're trying to pin a murder on me, and you're wondering about my chickens?" He shook his head. "You're a strange, old man."

Carlucci glared at him.

Payshe pinched his lips and smiled. "But you asked, so I'll answer. You know that one call you get after being arrested? Well, I didn't want a lawyer. Instead I called Luis, my foreman, and told him to open the envelope I left for him on my kitchen table. It's a signed and notarized document drawn up by lawyer Levin in Vineland that says that if I, for any reason, have to be away from the farm for an extended period of time, the farm is his as long as he's willing to run it. A certain percentage of profits to go into an account for me at The Tradesmen's Bank. Luis understands, and I trust him. The chickens will be fine."

Grandfather sat up straight. "Yes, I'm sure they will be. Your care for them and your often generous treatment of your neighbors is commendable, but…" Grandfather pounded the table with his fist before pointing at Zimmer, "you tried to kill my grandson, which is more than 'strange'—it is criminal and at the heart of the evil you perpetrated in killing Henry Casman."

Payshe muttered, "Your grandson had it coming. And I didn't murder Casman. Like I said, "Martin's prints are on the murder weapon."

Grandfather leaned back. "Ah, the fingerprints, Mr. Zimmer, you keep pointing us to the fingerprints. In a few minutes we will discuss how Mr. Ross's fingerprints happen to be on the knife without Mr. Ross having killed Mr. Casman."

Payshe grimaced. "You're not just strange—you're also crazy."

Grandfather's voice softened. "Mr. Zimmer, it strikes me that you place people in two categories. Those, as you said of my grandson, who 'had it coming' and those who are benign to you, even eliciting your solicitude at times. And thus, I surmise strongly, is why you murdered Mr. Casman—due to some reason that 'he had it coming?'" Am I not correct, Mr. Zimmer?"

"Listen, you crazy old man," Payshe snarled, "I'll say it again, they're Martin's prints on the knife, not mine."

It was a fact—Martin's prints on the murder weapon. *What to do with that damning detail?* Martin had asked if the police may have made a mistake, and I had brushed him off. How could there be an error? *What does Grandfather know?*

My grandfather looked directly at Payshe and spoke slowly. "Very well, then, let us address Mr. Ross's fingerprints on the murder weapon. Mr. Zimmer, you are a very intelligent man, and may I also say, clever."

Was that a little smile on Payshe's face?

Grandfather continued. "You were a brilliant student at the university, and now you are an acknowledged researcher and pioneer in poultry management."

Payshe shrugged, but his smile grew. "Yeah, so what about it?"

"About it," Grandfather said, "is that when I entered your house, I took notice in the ante chamber before your kitchen a jar of carbon powder, which you later explained you made use of in producing higher nutrient levels for the corn product you feed to your poultry."

Payshe shifted in his seat. "So, yeah I use the carbon powder that way. What of it?"

I hated being in the dark. *Where was Zaida going?*

Now Grandfather smiled. "Here is the direction of my thought. I had related to you during our visit to Vineland that I took up chemistry for a minor degree when I studied at the university in Vienna. Do you remember?"

Payshe nodded, his brows drawn together.

Grandfather leaned back a little farther. "And during a laboratory session at the university, we explored the nature and use of carbon powder. My professor mentioned that within the forensic sciences, the use of fingerprint detection was emerging and that investigators needed to be cautious in that fingerprints could be—what is the English term?—'planted' on an object to divert guilt to an innocent person. I believe through your brilliance in chemistry, you also knew that one can take an object on which fingerprints exist such as a glass, dust carbon powder where the fingerprint exists, place adhesive tape over the dusted area, peel the tape off the original surface and carefully press the sticky side of the tape onto the new surface where you want to transfer the fingerprint. And I believe you performed this very same action after murdering Mr. Casman. A reliable witness noted that the murderer remained in Mr. Casman's apartment for ten to fifteen minutes after sounds of confrontation ended."

Payshe lurched forward. "You're nuts."

My grandfather waved a hand. "May I continue? We know you lured your stepfather to your house prior to the murder with the excuse of wanting to show him the successes you achieved in running the farm. There had been coldness between the two of you before the invitation and visit, and then a return to alienation soon after."

My heart pounded. *How did I miss this possibility?* Obviously, Grandfather was prompting Payshe to explode in anger. *Zaida's hoping to garner a confession.*

Payshe leaned back and snickered. "Nice theory, but you can't prove anything."

"Ah, Mr. Zimmer, but we can. And I believe Detective Carlucci will bear me out in what I will now convey to you. You are incriminated in the following ways, besides your having been seen traveling to New York the day before the murder. You very well may have traveled back to New York from New Brunswick on the morning of May 29, but the police will find no evidence that you proceeded on your return to Vineland."

Grandfather stopped and exhaled. "But even more incriminating, modern forensics has made great advances in the last few years, and the FBI laboratory in Virginia is, as we speak, assisting the New York Police Department in testing the fingerprints for carbon residue, and if discovered, your stepfather will be immediately released."

"That's right, Mr. Wolf," Carlucci added.

Was my grandfather with Carlucci's help bluffing? I'd seen him stretch the truth in previous investigations to provoke a suspect into revealing what happened. Did Carlucci know what Grandfather would be saying? Was Payshe too savvy for bluffing?

Fists clenched, Payshe roared, "He can't be released. He's a murderer. And even if he is released, that doesn't mean I killed the man."

"Settle down," Carlucci ordered. "Let Mr. Wolf finish."

"Yes, thank you, Detective. Grandfather did not appear at all concerned about Payshe's outburst. "There is one additional matter under investigation at the FBI laboratory. "You know, Mr. Zimmer, that a partial fingerprint was found on a ticket stub for a bus trip between New York and Vineland?"

"Yeah, so," he answered, "but as they said at Martin's hearing, a partial doesn't prove anything."

Grandfather shook his head. "Ah, but the advances I mentioned will be able to establish definitively the owner of a partial fingerprint. Whether admissible at trial or not, it will be contributory to your incrimination, and you will be indicted. Am I not correct, Detective Carlucci?"

"You are very correct, sir," Carlucci answered.

Payshe shrank back, lips tightly pressed, eyes wide. Did I see fear?

"They won't find anything," Payshe muttered.

My grandfather leaned sharply forward. "It won't be long before we know, but now I would like to explore why you killed Mr. Casman and attempted to implicate your stepfather. Is it that you saw a way to address two grievances through one action?"

"I told you, I didn't do anything," Payshe said, his voice weary.

Grandfather barely let him finish his sentence. "Nevertheless Mr. Zimmer, I wish to take you back when we encountered you in the cell block, and even further back to the hearing. Again, what incited such anger in you that you would attempt to take the life of another human being?"

My jaws clenched. *That human being was me! I could be dead! Never know the child Aliya was carrying!* Since the shooting, most of the time I could distance myself from what happened as if it were to another person.

But now, anger coursed through me—this man tried to kill me. And for what, as Grandfather was asking?

Payshe sat up straight. "For what? You were there. You heard Gordon leading him on to say a terrible thing about my mother."

My grandfather drew back and softened his voice. "And the 'terrible thing' that you believe my grandson prompted?"

Wild-eyed and flailing his cuffed hands, Payshe shouted. "He said my mother was a flirt! A flirt! No one can say bad things about her. She was a great woman, a hero, a saint, and a great mother. I was prepared, and I had to act."

Grandfather nodded. "Ay, ay, ay, Mr. Zimmer. In your mind, a man merited death for what you sensed was being said. Ay, ay, ay. And what was it that Mr. Casman told you that prompted you to pronounce a death sentence over him? Was Mr. Casman not an admirer of your mother? Did he not, at one point in his life, love her? Did he not wish to marry her?"

Payshe jumped to his feet, his chair flying back, hitting Miller, who pushed it aside and rushed toward him. Carlucci rose quickly. As Miller grabbed his arm, Payshe bellowed, "He called my mother a *kurveh*. He wasn't going to get away with it."

A '*kurveh*,' I quickly translated from the Yiddish—a whore or, at the least, a promiscuous woman.

"Zimmer," Carlucci barked, "sit down, or the officer will make you sit."

Payshe listened. Carlucci sat, and Officer Miller pulled back.

"Nuh, nuh, Mr. Zimmer. When did Mr. Casman make this statement?"

Payshe leaned forward and rocked slowly. In a calmer voice, he said, "Casman said it on the phone after his trip to Vineland for my mother's *yahrzeit* observance."

His voice hardened. "He asked a bunch of questions about my mother's life after Druya, about what she did in the Partisans, how she came to meet up with Martin and marry him. He became belligerent and said he couldn't understand how my mother could so easily fall in love with my real father, how she could get pregnant while the war was on, how she could even think of marrying Martin. Then he said it—'So she was nothing more than a *kurveh*.'"

My grandfather opened his hands. "And in that moment, you decided you must kill Mr. Casman, yes?"

"Yes," Payshe thumped his bound hands on the table. "Right then and there. He had to die for what he said. So I called him again and played nice to get his address. He said there was nothing more to talk about—didn't want to see me. I called again—same reaction. But I found a way to get to him."

Grandfather closed his eyes for a moment. "I will surmise that you had a weapon prepared when you entered Mr. Casman's apartment, but as soon as you saw the large knife in the kitchen, you calculated that it would be more efficient to use it and plant the fingerprints after slaying Mr. Casman than to attempt first to retrieve a weapon from your backpack."

Did I see glee in Zimmer's eyes? "You may be old," he said looking at my grandfather, "but you're pretty good at figuring things out."

Grandfather's expression didn't change. "But I am not certain of one thing. Why did you wish to implicate your stepfather?"

Payshe snorted. "After I learned that Martin was a kapo, why not? I'd see to it that the *besterd* got what he deserved. Both of them, in different ways, deserved punishment."

Payshe laughed. "And wasn't that serendipity what I heard in the courthouse that Martin had been at Casman's apartment arguing with him earlier in the day? And I was going to make an anonymous call to the police saying that they should look at Martin as a suspect."

He slumped back. Carlucci told him he was being arrested for the murder of Henry Casman and read him his rights. Payshe said nothing. Officer Miller led him out of the interview room. With elbows on the table, my grandfather hid his face in his hands.

I sank into a chair and waited for my pounding heart to settle down.

TUESDAY, JUNE 22, 1976

8:00 A.M., and Aliya hadn't gotten up yet. I gently shook her.

"Hey, sleepyhead," I said, sitting on the side of the bed. "You're going to be late for work."

"I'm not going," she said turning from the pillow. "I'm staying here with you today."

My head ached, but not as much as yesterday. Luckily, still no dizziness—no blurred vision. I said, "I'm better, and it's your first week of work. I'm fine. Seriously, go."

Aliya sat up and shook her head. "A couple of things. One, I'm glad you're better, but one never knows so soon after this kind of injury." She lightly punched my shoulder. "For all I know, it's a stupid macho thing to say you're okay. And two, I'm not fine." She exploded in tears.

She's not fine! The baby? I drew her to me. "What's wrong?"

She rubbed her eyes. "What's wrong? I almost lost you yesterday. How can I be fine? We're pregnant, and our child might have been born without a father. I kept it in yesterday, did what I had to, not letting my emotions make things worse for everyone else. I wasn't fine then and I'm still not fine. Yesterday, before I even mentioned it, my supervisor said, 'You need to stay home tomorrow, both for your husband and yourself.' So Joel, if you're still better tomorrow morning, I'll go to work. Do you understand?"

I did. It wasn't just about my physical condition. The rage I'd felt yesterday at the 61st Precinct when challenging Zimmer returned. The man tried to kill me. He almost killed Officer Boykin. Wasn't I furious? Wasn't I shaken? Hadn't I almost lost—my life, my wife, my unborn child?

"Yes," I said firmly. "I do understand."

I brushed back Aliya's hair and wiped her cheeks. I held back my own tears—*Why? Am I doing a stupid macho thing?* "Thanks, I love you. And you're right—there's no way I'm fine. I'm glad we'll be together today."

She tousled my hair and got up. As she left the bedroom, she called, "I'll make some breakfast. Scrambled eggs and toast, okay?"

Good sign that I was really hungry. "More than okay," I said.

But my shoulders sagged, and I swallowed hard. *I'm so lucky, in so many ways.* A tear rolled down my cheek. When the time came for me at synagogue to *bench gomel,* reading the public prayer of gratitude for being spared, my words would be heartfelt, and I also would be thinking of Officer Boykin.

* * * *

While Aliya prepared breakfast, I walked to the newspaper kiosk and picked up copies of the three New York dailies. *How would they treat yesterday's shooting?*

Aliya and I exchanged papers as we ate. What happened took up the whole tabloid front pages in *The Daily News* and *The New York Post. The New York Times* also featured the story on page one, but at the bottom with just a small picture of the courthouse's exterior.

The Daily News, under a Martha Brennan byline, contained the most comprehensive coverage. The front page banner screamed: "Bedlam in Brooklyn!" and beneath, pictures of Martin and me as we headed into the building, Officer Boykin lying on top of me in the courtroom, Payshe being handcuffed by Detective Carlucci, and another of me outside of the hospital with a bandage on my forehead.

The other papers included no pictures or details of Boykin's heroics nor of Payshe's arrest. *The Times* and *The Post* reported that the unnamed shooter would be arraigned that morning—only Brennan reported that the "shooter," Peter Zimmer of Vineland, New Jersey, had also been arrested for Henry Casman's murder—though no motive was given—and that charges were being dropped against Martin.

Aliya started laughing. "Did Zaida call Brennan to give her the additional information?"

"I'm sure. Let's just say it's part of our 'arrangement.'"

We had just finished eating when it struck me. *Martin!* I hadn't called Martin after the interrogation. *And the news is out that Payshe is being charged with Casman's murder.*

"Aliya," I said, "I really need to call Martin and fill him in. Should have done it last night." *Then again, he hadn't called me.*

Aliya rose and took the dishes to the sink. "Call Martin. We'll wash dishes later. I'll wait in the bedroom until your call is over." As she walked away, she put her hands lightly on her belly. She didn't look any different to me than before. Maybe it was something all pregnant women did.

I dialed, and after a quick greeting, I recounted what happened at the interrogation, ending with, "Martin, you're a free man."

Silence. After a moment, I asked, "Did you hear me? You're a free man."

"I did hear you, Joel." *Was that irritation?* "And I thank you for your efforts. I called the 61st precinct many times. A few minutes ago, they told me that Payshe after his arraignment this morning will be moved to the Detention Center on Atlantic Avenue. I will try to visit him. Given your injury, I didn't want to bother you."

I frowned. *He could have called Zaida—or didn't he want to call the house?*

He continued, "As I explained yesterday, I must see to Payshe's needs. Not only does he face charges for the shooting, but now also for Henoch's murder. Whether he refuses me or not, that is another matter. He must have an attorney—the best we can obtain, regardless of cost. If there is someone you would recommend, please let me know."

I hesitated. Took a deep breath. *Was he serious? Asking the potential victim? It wasn't going to be me.* "I'll check in with PWR's criminal defense team to see if they would take on representation." I couldn't promise more.

"Thank you."

We had nothing more to say.

* * * *

"That was Larry Seidman on the phone," I said as I sat down next to Aliya after getting off the phone in the kitchen. "After talking to Martin, I called Larry to tell him as long as I continue to feel better, I'm planning to be back in the office on Friday morning."

Aliya was watching *The Today Show*. I caught a mention of Reba McEntire marrying some rodeo star.

She sat up. "Friday—that soon? What did he say?"

I took her hand. "He said, 'If you feel up to it. Just don't rush back.' I should be fine on Friday. I want to take back my accounts from Chip and close out Martin's paperwork for his official release from all charges."

At 8:45, my mother called before she left for her store.

"I'm fine. I promise. I'm feeling better and better. Honestly." I said it several times.

"That is very good, Joel. I trust you would tell me if something was wrong. I spoke with Aliya yesterday after we heard about what happened during the interrogation. She's with you, yes?"

"She is, Mom."

"As your Zaida says, Aliya is a wonderful *kallah*. I wanted to take off from the store to be with you since it's her first week at work, but she convinced me that she must do so both for you and for herself. I understand what she means."

After some small talk, my mother said, "I must go. I'm giving you to Zaida."

"Good morning, Zaida," I said. "I'm recovering nicely. Are you off to your office soon?"

"Good morning, Joel. I am most pleased that your health is improving."

After a moment's hesitation, Grandfather said, "No, I will not be at my office this whole week. I will distance myself from where I have always felt most comfortable in my work. And I am glad to hear that you also are refraining from journeying to your workplace for a few days. Perhaps in different ways, both of our heads are aching. I am hopeful that some rest and reflection will reestablish our equilibrium and put us back in kilter."

I laughed as I usually did when he used, "kilter." I waited a moment. *Should I bring up anything about yesterday's interrogation?* Curiosity won out. "Just one thing, Zaida, before I let you go. The stuff you told Payshe about the FBI lab's ability to find carbon powder residue on the knife and to definitively be able to match a partial fingerprint, was that real or just bluff?"

He sighed replying. "Ah, Joel. I just performed a wink. Is not the rapidity by which scientific advancements occur, in this case, forensics, magnificent to behold? All may be possible, if not now, soon, no?"

I've had no trouble admitting through the years that my grandfather had a way of predicting the future.

* * * *

The phone rang all day.

Aliya insisted that she be the first line of answering and passing on the phone selectively. She responded to several calls from colleagues at PWR, our friends, her sister Brenda in Fort Lee, her parents in Florida, and other relatives. Most lasted under a minute, as Aliya assured the callers that I was recovering nicely. The call at 9:15 from Aliya's best friend Shoshi and her husband Ben went on for a while, but Aliya did all the talking.

At 10:00, I called the hospital and spoke with Officer Boykin. Before I could ask him about his condition, he said, "How's your head, Counselor? Sorry about the bang I gave it."

I laughed. "You're sorry? I'm the one who should be sorry about the gunshot you took, saving my life. Thank you again and again, Officer."

"No big deal. They're discharging me tomorrow. I'll be back to work in a couple of weeks. Probably bump into you again at the courthouse."

Amazing man. "Ouch, did you have to say, 'bump'?" I joked. Anyway, I'll always be glad to see you. May I call you at your home, say Thursday, to check in on you."

"Good one, Counselor." He gave me his number.

I immediately dialed Grandfather. When I had spoken to him earlier, he'd asked about Boykin's condition. My grandfather laughed, listening to the exchange, and ended with, "Thank God."

My mother called again, around 7:00, after we had finished dinner. Aliya spoke to her for a few minutes before I got on.

After asking about my health, she said, "Joel, if you feel up to it, and if Aliya is not too tired, please come Friday evening for dinner. If you remember our last Shabbat dinner, it didn't resemble a happy occasion. We walked on eggshells, and Martin left early. Now, it may be different. We have reasons to rejoice."

Aliya and I agreed.

FRIDAY, JUNE 25, 1976

I felt fine as I pushed open the heavy glass door labeled **Prentice, Walters, & Reis** above **Securities Division.**

As I made my way toward my office, briefcase in hand, people waved, and a few clapped. Chip Holden called out, "Welcome back, Gordon. Amazing how you took one for the team."

I grinned and bowed.

Inside my office, I hung up my suit jacket and sat down at my desk. Julie came in, holding a stack of folders. She was tall and wore tailored pantsuits most days, unlike the other women in the office. She eased into the guest chair and took off the glasses that she didn't need. She once told me she wore them, as many young women were doing, to establish a sense of "gravitas" in a "man's world."

She said, "We're so glad you're doing better and took a few days off to recuperate."

Julie placed the folders on my desk. "These," she pointed, "aren't as overwhelming as they look. There are some client sign-offs Chip left for you. I went over them. They look in order. Also, there's paperwork for the Kings County Criminal Court folks to seal Mr. Ross's file and expunge any record of criminal activity on his part. When you're done, let me know, and I'll take it from there."

Julie rose. "By the way, your answering machine ran out of space. I've been taking calls from people over the last couple of days—nothing really important—all from in-house wanting to know how you're doing. I left a list of them for you."

"Thanks, Julie," I said pressing the playback button on my answering machine as she left.

I quickly listened to the 20 recordings. Most were from in-house, inquiring about my health. I jotted down names and numbers to thank them later. Three calls came from the outside.

One began, "Hello Counselor, this is Sylvan Black. Calling to see how you are. I heard that you suffered a head injury, but I am led to believe not too serious. I also understand that the brave officer will recover. Congratulations on the work you did—first criminal defense, and you acquitted yourself quite well. You're always welcome in my courtroom."

He left his home number. *Wow, the judge called.* I wouldn't have expected the gesture.

Rita Malzone, District Attorney Fried's assistant, began with a slight stutter, "Uh, hello, this is Rita Malzone from the Brooklyn DA's office. We sort of met at your client's hearing last Monday. Just wanted to see how you're doing and also say that if you'd like to get together for coffee sometime, I'd like that. Uh, goodbye."

I'd call to thank her and nothing more. *I was quite happy with my kallah.*

The short message from Martha Brennan said, "I spoke to your gramps. He says you're recovering well enough. Glad to hear it. If you have a chance, call me to confirm. We'll probably run into each other again. Hope so."

I'm not sure that I also "hoped so"—not because Brennan was unpleasant—rather the unfortunate circumstances that had been bringing us together.

* * * *

Julie is a real gem. She had all the paperwork in order and ready for my signature. Regardless, I reviewed each document carefully, taking particular satisfaction in signing off on Martin's release from all charges.

But what about Martin? Would Martin really rather that he, himself, be indicted for the murder? *How strange the human psyche! And is that what being a parent entails?* Soon, I'd know. Maybe then, I'd feel differently about Martin's perspective. In the meantime, I phoned Jeff Lewis in criminal defense and left a message to call me about representing Peter Zimmer.

Other thoughts drifted in and out as I worked.

How was Mom? I could never fully tell when talking with her over the phone. Although the family's attention had been on me, she'd suffered a shock at my coming close to being shot, watching her father fall into sadness, and learning of Martin's secret history. This afternoon, she'd be home by 4:00. Aliya would arrive around 5:30. I'd get there early because I wanted time alone with my mother.

And what about Grandfather? After the Stein murder case a few years ago, he'd compared his emotions to those of Sherlock Holmes after Holmes had solved a mystery. Grandfather said, "Yes, a victory over Moriarity was a victory for good over evil. But still, a sadness, though partly from boredom, would envelope Holmes, who would fall into depression and opioid addiction." Grandfather never fell into despair as deeply as Holmes. But this time, he was more disconsolate than ever. I needed to see him in person, too.

With a half hour break for lunch, it took me until 3:00 to finish. I called Julie, who came over and picked up the signed papers. I wished her a good weekend, grabbed my briefcase, and hustled down to Rockefeller Center for the F train to Brooklyn.

As I approached E. 7th Street after walking down Avenue P from the subway, I could see and hear my grandfather bantering with Mike and Dave, the fifteen-year-old Kravitz twins who lived next door. As usual, the banter involved a comparison of the Mets to the Yankees. Too bad for Grandfather—the Yankees were ahead by seven games in their division, while the Mets were fifteen games behind the first place Phillies in theirs.

Thinking back, I laughed. Years ago, after a "neighborly" chat, my father used to come back to our house and say, "How in the world did that Yankees-loving family get into our street?"

I stopped, surprised. *Zaida isn't wearing his suit jacket?* The day's temperature hit 90, but humidity was down, and clouds intermittently shielded the sun. The street was alive with the sounds of stoop ball, hopscotch, and double-Dutch jump rope. Mothers with young children in covered strollers gathered in conversation. A few cars crept along slowly, applying brakes to avoid the children playing street punch ball.

Not only did Grandfather not have on his suit jacket, but he had not put on his fedora—though a kippah covered his head. When he saw me, he handed the Spauldeen he was holding to the Kravitz boys who moved to their stoop. He waved to me.

As soon as I crossed E. 7th, my grandfather walked toward me and opened his arms. First, he looked at my bandaged forehead and winced. But then he smiled as he hugged me and kissed both of my cheeks.

"It is wonderful to see you, and on such a beautiful day. Is it not, Yoeli?"

I nodded. His face, though still drawn, wasn't ashen as it had been on Monday. "Yes, you're feeling better, Zaida?"

Grandfather put a hand to his jaw. "Ay, if you are inquiring if I feel better in the context of the last time you saw me, then, yes, I do feel better. Shall we take advantage of the day given to us? Your mother called to say she would be a little late. Shall we do a perambulation to Avenue O, then to Ocean Parkway, and back on Avenue P? By then, your mother should arrive."

"Take advantage of the day given to us." That's from a Psalm. "Yeah, I'd like that very much. Just let me put my briefcase into the house."

The renewed sparkle in my grandfather's eyes comforted me. I bounded up the steps and returned within a minute. Grandfather looped his arm in mine as we headed toward Avenue O. Neither of us spoke as we made our way along 7th, passing brick duplexes and single-family homes, driveways and alleyways along each side, with aluminum or wood fencing to separate properties. Shrubberies and flowers animated small front lawns, offsetting browning grass suffering from a three-week drought. Fully leafed elms and Norway maples lined the street and further shaded the sun. Air conditioning units hummed from second floor windows. Richie Colavito, my childhood stoop ball partner, called down greetings from high on a ladder leading to the roof of his home.

We turned left on Avenue O. Grandfather released my arm as we continued walking. "Over the last few days, I have thought much about Martin's case, the tragedy we have encountered, my error in judgment, and what I have learned for my betterment."

Before I could reply, Grandfather stopped and held up his hand. "And please, do not try to dismiss my insistence that I had committed an error in misjudging Mr. Zimmer's capacity for destruction."

He cleared his throat. "Ach, was I not listening when Martin spoke of Mr. Zimmer's reverence for his mother? Did I miss the significance of a man, three years after his mother's death, keeping sacrosanct the kitchen chair in which she sat? Did he not meet us with a gun in hand? Should I not have feared that such an unstable personality with a proclivity for violence might perform a harmful act in defense of his mother's memory?"

I coughed. "I wasn't going to say anything, Zaida."

He reclaimed my arm. "You may remember that last Monday afternoon, as I was preparing for the interrogation of Mr. Zimmer, I sat in my chair referencing the police report, a book on chemical agents, and…and, Joel, a volume of *Tehillim*. For me, reading from the Psalms spurs fortitude in the face of confusion and challenges my arrogance when I have thought too highly of myself."

Was Zaida being too hard on himself?

He sighed. "There is one lesson from *Tehillim* I wish to share with you as I reflect on what occurred and what I must take with me into the future. What is my favorite psalm?"

I chuckled. How many times had he talked about his favorite psalm over the years? "It's Psalm 115."

"Yes. And what is my favorite verse within that psalm?"

"Verse 16. And in case you're about to ask me what the verse says, here goes. 'The heavens belong to God—but God gave the Earth to mankind.'"

My grandfather laughed. "Yes, yes, well translated. And I believe I have mentioned on occasions a commentary on this verse that resonates with me."

He paused, but I stayed silent. "It is said that when God informed the heavenly angels that he wished to deliver the Earth to humans, the angels were astounded and angry. They shouted that such frail, confused, and selfish creatures were both not worthy of receiving such a gift and incapable of maintaining and retaining such a treasure."

I interrupted. "And God answered, 'Tough, my decision is made.'"

Grandfather squeezed my arm. "That is one way of phrasing the response. Perhaps more elegantly, God said, 'Let us see what they will make of this gift as I have fashioned them in my image and given them the ability to perform godly acts so that they and the Earth can flourish.'"

I had heard this commentary from both my grandfather and teachers in my religious school.

But look at the history of the world. What have we done with this gift?

"Go on," I said.

Grandfather sighed. "Yet, starting very soon after receiving this gift, we found ourselves east of Eden, with Cain slaying Abel. And ever since, in many ways we have failed, both on the humankind level—as what occurred in the Holocaust—and on the individual level—as with the life and murder of Mr. Casman."

He stopped us again as we were about to turn down Avenue P. "Many have blamed God, but I do not. Many claim that the angels are jeering at us. If they are, so be it."

"So Zaida, what do we do?"

He clenched and released his fist. "Ah, Joel, first it is what we do not do. We do not throw up our hands in self-pity and walk away. We do not attribute blame elsewhere. And we do not cynically accept that 'hell is other people.' As tired as we may be, as beaten down as we may be, it is our duty to strive every day to prove the angels wrong."

I sighed. *Was it possible?*

Grandfather continued. "For myself, I am determined to go on with my work and commit to learning from my errors."

He faced me and squinted as he shaded his eyes from the sun. "My improvements," he said, "may need to be in place fairly soon. A request for my services will be presented to me at my office on Sunday."

Sunday! So soon? Doesn't he need to get more rest, especially if it's going to be a tough case? "What kind of case, Zaida?" I asked excitedly. "Where's it coming from?"

He put a finger to his temple. "You remember Mrs. Wachter from when we did our investigation during the Ori Gold murder case, yes?" He paused and slowly shook his head. "Ach, what a tragedy we uncovered."

How could I forget? During that case, both Grandfather and I almost lost our lives on the roof of The Jewish Academy High School dormitory building in Washington Heights where Mrs. Wachter lived as the dorm mother. My grandfather had been in social contact with her since.

"Of course I remember, Zaida. What about her?"

That glint in his eye. "She is coming to discuss my professional assistance. Of more I am not aware at this time, except that she believes it also may require legal services."

He coughed. "I am not sure if it has been conveyed to you or to Aliya, but Mrs. Wachter is joining us for dinner tonight. She is staying this weekend at her niece's residence on Avenue R."

Zaida had referred to "legal services." I wonder. I may have been intrigued, but I left it alone for now. "No," I said, "I didn't know that she was coming, and if Aliya knew, she would have mentioned it."

My grandfather smiled. "Good, then. But what I just conveyed about the request for my services is for Sunday. Tonight, let us have a joyful Shabbat dinner together. For now, I am content to walk arm-in-arm with my beloved grandson. Let us take advantage of this day. It is a wonderful gift, is it not?"

I hugged Grandfather, perhaps too tightly. A tear trailed down his cheek. "'A wonderful gift,'" I said.

We walked on silently. *Were the angels wrong?* I had my reservations, but at the same time, I was proud of my grandfather. *It doesn't matter, does it? He'll always try to prove the angels wrong.*

* * * *

A few minutes later, Grandfather and I joined my mother in the kitchen. She had returned while we were out walking. Already, ingredients lay on a counter, with dishes and pots and pans at the ready.

After greeting us, she said, "It's good that it's summertime and the days are longer. And as is the custom during these days at the Quentin Street *shul*, the Sabbath will be ushered in earlier than the Sabbath's official starting time, so the two of you will be back from services around 8:15. All should be ready by then." She looked at me. "Aliya will be here soon?"

I laughed. "Yes, Mom, around 5:30. You love her help, but I'm here now. You know, I've been getting high marks from Aliya for my improving culinary skills, especially for dicing and slicing. Where's our Marvelous Mets apron?"

My mother pointed to a cabinet door. "Even if it's just your company, it will be sufficient."

Grandfather looked around the kitchen. "And I sense that any management skills I possess may not be needed. Therefore, I will retire to the living room where I will review this week's Torah portion."

After he left, my mother said, "Please come here and let me look at you."

I walked closer, and she caressed my head with her hand. "Your wound is healing well? Does your head hurt? It's next Friday that your stitches come out? You're returning to the hospital for them to be removed?"

Perhaps a bit too cavalierly, I said, "Yes, no, yes, yes." Dropping her hand, she pursed her lips and shook her head in mock displeasure.

I tied on my apron, studying her for a moment. Had my mother shrunk? Or was it a stoop in her shoulders I now noticed? Was her face more lined, or was I now looking at her more carefully? Unquestionably, the dark under her eyes had deepened.

I leaned over and kissed the top of her head. "You're still not doing so well, are you, even though the case is closed and Martin's free?"

She looked down. "I'm not doing so well. Sleep doesn't come easily at night. My mind wanders constantly to recent events that sadden and frighten me, even if they're now in the past."

She shrugged with a small smile. "But I will be okay. After all, I am your grandfather's daughter."

I returned her smile and nodded. *I might as well ask right off.* "Mom, is Martin joining us tonight?"

She blinked a few times and shook her head. "No, he is not. We've spoken at length over the last few days, and we—let me be honest—I've decided that we should take a break from seeing each other. I did not say this to Martin, but at this moment, I don't believe I will ever reestablish our relationship."

I took her hand. "It's because he was a kapo?" I asked gently. "And, as you told me at the restaurant, he never shared that information with you?"

Was my mother going to cry? No tears came. Instead, her eyes narrowed, and she squeezed my hand tightly. "It's probably as you say—I cannot quiet the distrust of his having not told me something so important. Should I be forgiving? Perhaps, but the fact is, I can't. And if I lie to myself, I'll also be lying to Martin. Quickly, the house of lies will collapse."

She let go of my hand and looked away. "But there's more, Joel. Just think if I married Martin—just think. In a way, you and his stepson would be brothers." Her hand trembled. "The Cain and Abel story enacted within our own family. I…I cannot imagine it."

Payshe? My brother who tried to kill me? I shuddered. "I'm sorry," I said pulling her into a brief hug.

My mother stepped back. "Yes, Joel, thank you. The case brought out much sorrow."

Her hand gestured around the kitchen. "But for now, we have a Shabbat dinner to prepare. By the way, we're having a guest join us."

"Yep, I know, Mrs. Wachter, Zaida's lady friend. He told me earlier."

My mother cleared her throat. "You remember her?"

I nodded as I recalled a short, white haired lady with very European manners who served us tea, coffee, and sandwiches on fine china dishes in her apartment.

My mother tapped two spoons together lightly. "Then, there's much to do. It's now 4:40. You do not wish to be accused of shirking and leaving all your work for Aliya when she arrives, do you?"

"No, I don't," I said firmly.

"Very well, the pot roast and kugel are in the refrigerator, ready to go into the oven a little later. For now, please cut carrots, parsnips, celery, and onion for the chicken soup. If you're not sure how much, ask me. Also, you know what goes into a salad. You know what, we'll do it together."

"I'm with you, Mom."

* * * *

Aliya arrived at 5:30, as expected. After a few minutes, both she and my mother let me know that I was not needed until the after-dinner clean-up.

"Sit with Zaida until it is time for you to leave for services," my mother ordered, directing me toward the door.

I put up token resistance.

Grandfather smiled as I approached and put down the worn, leather-bound copy of his Bible, the one he had brought from Europe. I sat down opposite him.

"The main point in this week's portion of *Shelach*," he began, "on how scouts were sent out to reconnoiter the Promised Land, is that the Earth with all its goodness lays ahead, but what do we make of it? Later in our Torah, this challenge is described as choosing between a blessing and a curse which always looms before us. Even though we are informed of all the good things that come from choosing the blessing, it appears not so easy to do so. We saw that with Mr. Zimmer who chose to live his life in darkness as part of a curse."

I tensed. "He did, and now he'll be punished for the evil acts he chose."

My grandfather held up his hands. "Yes, with that understood, let us depart from that past and view the blessings before us."

He chuckled. "And while the performance of our beloved Mets this season is closer to a curse than a blessing, let us talk about them, nevertheless. They are in St. Louis tonight, yes?"

I nodded, smiling. "Yep, Apodaca is pitching. Let's hope."

We spent the next hour talking baseball, politics, and space exploration. The time went quickly. At 6:45, Grandfather went to his bedroom and changed into his Sabbath suit—which didn't look much different from his two weekday suits. I still wore my suit trousers—so I just had to put on my jacket. At 7:00, we left for the Quentin Street synagogue.

Only nine worshippers were present when services were to start at 7:15. Someone went into the tiny synagogue office to call a nearby member to come quickly to complete the required ten-person prayer quorum. An elderly man arrived at 7:30, and the service proceeded. I looked at the aging faces. *Every time I come, there are fewer and fewer worshippers. Grandfather will be very sad when his synagogue closes down.*

When we arrived home, the Sabbath dishes, wine, and braided challahs lay in their usual places on the dining room table, along with lit candles.

Aliya and my mother, wearing traditional white lace head coverings, stood by the candles at the head of the table. A white-haired woman with a similar head covering stood at the table's side. Even in high heels, she would only come up to Aliya's shoulders. A perfectly fitted, mid-sleeve light wool dress fell just below her knees—the delicate silver-framed glasses that I had seen at her apartment hung around her thin neck from a jeweled chain.

"Gut Shabbos, Velvel," she said, looking at my grandfather and using his Yiddish first name.

"Chanah, gut Shabbos," he answered. "Joel, do you remember Mrs. Anna Wachter, who graciously entertained us in her apartment when we were involved in the Ori Gold case?"

I nodded, "Yes, of course, I do. Good Shabbos, Mrs. Wachter, and welcome." I caught Aliya's gaze. She smiled.

My mother and Aliya came over. We exchanged hugs and made our way to the table where Mrs. Wachter remained. As we were about to sit, she said in a slight accent, "Joel, I wish you also a good Shabbos. And *mazel tov* to you and everyone here tonight. It is wonderful news I heard from your grandfather."

"Thank you," I said. "It's nice to have you with us."

Mrs. Wachter looked straight at me. "Joel, before we begin, I'd like to say that following a brief consultation with your grandfather, I believe it is possible I will be seeing more of you. There is some business I will be bringing to the Frank Wolf Agency. The matter may entail a legal aspect for which a lawyer is needed. And your grandfather indicated that he knows of a good lawyer."

I glanced at Grandfather. He *'knows of a good lawyer.' Oh, does he now?* He closed his lips and smiled.

We all sat, and Mrs. Wachter continued. "We, of course, will not discuss business tonight. It is a time for song and joy. Also, your grandfather strongly maintains that his office is the proper place for such matters. He and I have scheduled an official business meeting Sunday morning at 11:00 at his office." She paused. "I am hopeful you might join us."

My grandfather looked at me, a twinkle in his eye—*He wants me to come.* Aliya gave me a subdued smile—*She's thinking it's up to me.* My mother subtly flicked her head toward Grandfather—*He's your grandfather who may need your help. If you can, please do.*

"Mrs. Wachter," I said, "I'll be there."

ACKNOWLEDGMENTS

After completing my previous book, *Who Killed the Rabbi's Wife?*, I didn't want to put off writing what I had on my mind for a while, this book, *Were the Angels Wrong?*. I set to work right away. Those of you who are familiar with my detective hero, Frank Wolf, know that he believes that we are all created within the illuminated benevolence of God's image, but as life begins, various forms of darkness, rising up from within or descending from without darken that essence of the divine and lead to destructive behavior, such as murder or other terrible criminal acts. Frank maintains that it is the responsibility of the individual to recognize and struggle against the darkness within and society's responsibility to guard against the darkness of others and constrain its spread. Failures, that result in acts of evil, must be rectified through the pursuit of justice which, when achieved even to the smallest degree, illuminates understanding of what transpired and lights going forward.

As a child of survivors, I grew up in the shadow of the Holocaust. The horrors that had engulfed my parents stayed with them, but did not define them. They found rays of light by starting a new family and modeling for my sister and me that while my family suffered extraordinarily and were victims, we were not to behave as victims. Instead, we were to work toward brightening our own lives and contributing to our greater communities.

But early on I knew that the darkness of the individuals who went through the Holocaust was never to be wholly eradicated from their lives. When I started writing my Frank Wolf stories, I felt compelled at some point to explore how Frank and his grandson Joel might solve a crime that emanated from the Holocaust blackness. In *Were the Angels Wrong?,* a survivor is murdered and another is implicated in the death. Frank and Joel investigate. I'd love to hear readers' thoughts on how I portrayed this drama.

Regarding my previous books, readers have asked me if everything I describe of the 1970s milieu is factual. Well, almost. I write fiction in which I try to exert as little literary license as I feel necessary. The streets of New York City—and, in this book, Vineland, New Jersey—reflect a rendering based on my memory and what search engines such as GOOGLE can verify. But there are a few times that for the sake of the plot or convenience of a certain locale, I exploit imagination. For instance, while Kornblatt's Deli in Brooklyn, where much digestion and discussion take place, is of my creation, it is based on many a delicatessen that existed back then. And while the bus route between New York and Vineland that is detailed in this book did not, in 1976, exist exactly as described, it did just a few years earlier, along with the scenery and stops that I remembered when I rode it.

As usual, I owe much thanks for how the book turned out and its publication. I'll always start at my core with appreciation for the first draft reading of everything I write by my wife, Hedy. Your honesty, what I count on, leads me to trust to your feel for tone, character authenticity, and plot consistency. The side of my head often hurts from my slap to it when I read and listen to your comments, and I say to myself, "how'd I not see that?" I've always known that there were many good reasons why I fell in love with you these several decades ago—what you do to improve my writing is just one of many ways that having fallen in love has been good for me.

The writers group into whose fold I was welcomed a few years ago is called "The Doomers," yet except for young, precocious Meg, it might as well be dubbed, "The Boomers." But regardless of name, I have been fortunate to have had on a regular basis the critiquing skills of very talented professional writers who, each on one's own, could teach at the Iowa Writers' Workshop. Barry, Carla, John, Karen, Meg, Sandi, thank you reading every word I wrote in crafting my last two books, for the words disposed and the words added, for the plots enhanced, and for the dialogue sharpened. Your patience and encouragement touch me deeply.

Advance copy readers gave my book final looks prior to publication. Thank you, Rosally Saltsman, for your careful eye to everything from typos, to grammatical correctness, to linguistic integrity, and, most importantly, to monitoring my faithfulness to the ritual and cultural makeup of the Orthodox Jewish communities in 1970s New York for which I want no distortion.

Were the Angels Wrong? marks my first foray in placing Vineland, New Jersey of the 1970s as a central locale for the book›s action. Therefore, having Naomi Ingraldi, a Trustee of the Vineland Historical Society, and Seth Stern, author of *Speaking Yiddish to Chickens—Holocaust Survivors on South Jersey Poultry Farms*, an encyclopedic and groundbreaking history—as pre-publication readers provided me with suggestions and corrections that reinforced the accuracy of my depiction. Thank you.

Since Frank Wolf's knowledge of Yiddish is integral to the plot and Frank's figuring out *whodunit*, I wasn't comfortable releasing the book without a pre-publication review by a Yiddish *maven*. So I am grateful to Sebastian Schulman—Director, Special Projects and Partnerships, at the National Yiddish Book Center—for his willingness to *Yiddish-check* my book. Sebastian, *a greisen dank*.

Once again, my heartfelt thanks to my editor and publisher, John Betancourt of Wildside Press. John, you have supported my writing from the first Frank Wolf short story to now—our third book together. "Show, don't tell," you constantly remind me, helping the soul and inner thoughts of my characters come alive to the reader. The same maxim can apply to you, John. Though you are a person of many fine words, at the heart of your personality you *show*—through your actions—a deep devotion to the English language, the writing craft, and to the advancement of fellow writers. May you and your press live long and prosper.